Findin

Suzanne writes contemporary and uplifting fiction with a vibrant sense of setting and community connecting the lives of her characters. A horticulturist who lives with her family in Lancashire, her books are inspired by a love of landscape, romance and rural life.

Her first novel in the Thorndale series, *The Cottage of New Beginnings*, was a contender for the 2021 RNA Joan Hessayon Award and she is currently writing the Love in the Lakes series for Canelo. Suzanne is a member of the Romantic Novelists Association and the Society of Authors.

Also by Suzanne Snow

Welcome to Thorndale

The Cottage of New Beginnings
The Garden of Little Rose
A Summer of Second Chances
A Country Village Christmas

Love in the Lakes

Snowfall Over Halesmere House
Wedding Days at Halesmere House
Starting Over at Halesmere House

Hartfell Village

Finding Home in Hartfell

Finding Home in Hartfell

SUZANNE SNOW

CANELO

First published in the United Kingdom in 2025 by

Canelo
Unit 9, 5th Floor
Cargo Works, 1-2 Hatfields
London SE1 9PG
United Kingdom

A CIP catalogue record for this book is available from the British Library.

Print ISBN 978 1 83598 113 9
Ebook ISBN 978 1 83598 111 5

Look for more great books at www.canelo.co

Printed and bound in Great Britain by Clays Ltd, Elcograf S.p.A.

I

To Lisa, with love.

A fabulous friend, to me and all animals.

Chapter One

Pippa Douglas turned off the car's engine and the brief view she'd had of golden stone walls and mullioned windows framing a farmhouse vanished in the darkness. She glanced at her daughter in the passenger seat, letting a long, weary breath escape. Finally, they were here; she couldn't remember when she'd last driven so far. London to the Yorkshire Dales was a journey she'd not made in many years, and she didn't want to think of the last time, not now.

Harriet's eyes were closed, her pale, oval face shadowed by darkness. Pippa reached across, tucking a long strand of sun-kissed brown hair behind Harriet's ear, a maternal gesture often denied her now that her daughter was a teenager. How had that happened so fast? It seemed only moments since she'd been tiny, toddling from nursery into primary school and beyond.

'Harriet? We're here, sweetheart.' Pippa was gentle, not wanting to jolt her from sleep too suddenly. 'Time to wake up.'

'Huh?' Harriet grimaced as she rearranged herself on the seat and rubbed her neck. Her eyes automatically fell to the phone in her hand, the light from the screen brightening her confused expression. 'Already?'

'You've been out for the past two hours, since we set off after the services. You obviously needed the rest.' Pippa held back a sigh as Harriet's fingers darted over the screen, brightening it some more. 'Come on, we may as well get on with it.'

'Aren't you even a little bit curious about the house?'

'Are you?'

'Stop trying to deflect.'

Pippa's hand was on the door, and she pushed it open, deciding to ignore the suggestion of sharpness in Harriet's reply. 'You know me too well.'

'So that's a no, then. Come on, Mum, it'll be an adventure.'

'I'm not looking for an adventure, and the last thing I needed was your grandad dumping another of his problems in my lap right at the beginning of the summer holidays.'

Pippa had long been the unofficial head of her dad's blended family, a role he was perfectly happy to let her occupy. Everyone automatically gravitated to her when a decision needed making or a problem solved. As the eldest of his five children, she was the one who remembered birthdays, arranged meet-ups, sent flowers, checked in. Somehow, she held them all together.

She didn't resent the role she'd taken upon herself twenty-five years ago after her mum had died, but there were occasions when she wished the family didn't ping everything they wanted sorting out straight to her inbox. It wasn't that their dad didn't love them, but he led a relatively unconventional life, and family was something he fitted in alongside his career.

Jonny Jones was almost as famous for his northern roots as he was for being the lead singer of legendary rock band Blue at Midnight. For Pippa, it was a given that he wouldn't slide quietly into old age and stop attracting

2

headlines for his love life as well as the band's long-awaited, supposedly final album. Currently on the Australian leg of a seemingly never-ending world retirement tour – the dates of which only Pippa in the family had marked on her calendar – Jonny had flown to Bali for a break away from the mayhem of his own life.

But then last week, just when Harriet's summer term had ended – which immediately made Pippa suspicious because generally her dad knew nothing about such things – he'd got in touch by email to say that a property he owned needed sorting out and she was the only one he trusted to take care of it. And seeing as she'd need to visit and have a proper look at the house, why didn't she take Harriet along as well? Pippa, at the beginning of her own summer break from her job as a Fine Arts lecturer at a London college, had tried to put Jonny off and suggest his business manager or the family solicitor step in, but he'd been absolutely insistent on Pippa being the one to deal with the house.

She said no very firmly at first, firing off a couple of frustrated emails and pointing out she was busy with her own plans in reply to his increasingly pleading ones. But then he'd deployed his secret weapon and swerved right around her to Harriet, who, to Pippa's utter astonishment, had been all for Jonny's scheme, and so here they were: parked in the dark outside a house she had never seen and couldn't remember her dad ever visiting or mentioning.

'So far as I'm concerned, the sooner we're in and out of here, the better. We still have plans for the summer and none of them include spending time in this backwater, wherever it actually is. I've forgotten.'

Pippa shoved the car door open, and Harriet followed her onto the drive with a degree of enthusiasm she'd almost forgotten her daughter possessed. Usually it was only the threat of her phone running out of charge that would send Harriet moving rapidly in search of the nearest source of power. Or playing wing attack in netball, at which she excelled.

'Hartfell, Mum. The jewel in this unspoiled Yorkshire dale, to be precise.' Harriet slammed her door, the noise reverberating through the night, and Pippa shuddered when an owl screeched somewhere in the trees leaning towards the house. Where was all the traffic and the ever-present background noise she was used to? The artificial lights blotting out the stars? Gravel was crisp under their feet, the late evening air warm and still.

'Who told you it was a jewel?'

'Google.'

'Ah. Right. Not your grandad, then?' Pippa was surprised that Harriet had bothered to look up the location of their base for the next week or so. She knew her dad had grown up somewhere around here, but he rarely talked about those days, and she hadn't thought to question the location of this property.

'No, haven't spoken to him since he went to Bali with whatshername.'

'Dana, Harriet. Your grandad's partner is called Dana.'

'She is this month.'

Pippa was rooting through her bag, feeling for the unfamiliar set of keys her dad's solicitor had couriered round yesterday. 'That's not entirely fair, they've only broken up and got back together twice as far as I know.'

'Three times, Mum. Freddie told me. He doesn't like her, he thinks they'll be over by Christmas, for good this time.'

'And what else has your uncle said to you about…?' Pippa hesitated. She didn't generally discuss her dad's love life with her daughter, but these things did tend to crop up when you were the eldest child of a rock legend, and online gossip was sometimes hard to ignore. Harriet was way savvier and more clued up about life than Pippa had been at that age, and she still thought it a very good thing that the internet had barely been invented when Jonny's band had been in its heyday back in the Eighties.

As his much adored and only grandchild, despite the three daughters and two sons he had fathered, Harriet had access to Jonny that even Pippa couldn't attain. He always picked up Harriet's calls and he checked in with her online every week, no matter where in the world he was.

'About Grandad?' Harriet hitched her tote bag over a shoulder. 'Not much, Freddie was more interested in hearing about what we think of this place. Asked me to send him some photos.'

Freddie, the youngest of Jonny's children and at eighteen, only four years older than Harriet; the two of them had always got on well and were more like cousins than uncle and niece.

'He did?' Pippa halted on the drive, squinting at Harriet beneath the flicker of a security light which couldn't seem to make up its mind if it should be on or off. 'Why?'

'Dunno. Didn't say.' Harriet's eyes were glued to her phone and Pippa didn't expect to get much more from her. 'Why?'

'No reason,' Pippa replied casually. She'd have to find out what her brother might be up to later. Property was something her dad had accumulated over the years and his offspring had been promised one each eventually. Maybe that was where Freddie's interest in Hartfell lay.

They crunched along the drive and reached the studded, heavy wooden door of the farmhouse, set between more mullioned stone windows, *Home Farm* lettering pale against a dark slate sign on the right. Pippa stuck the largest key from the set into the lock and turned it. The wooden door creaked alarmingly, and she gave it a hefty shove, sending it flying open into the dark recesses of what she assumed was a hall. The air was cool after the summer evening outdoors and her hand, still grasping the key in the lock, seemed to have vanished.

'Harriet, can you put your phone torch on please?'

'Why are you whispering?'

'Was I?' Pippa tried to laugh away her nerves, imagining unseen eyes staring. The solicitor had mentioned getting someone to meet them on arrival and she'd refused the offer, unwilling to face a welcome committee. She fumbled for Harriet nearby, thrusting a protective arm in front of her.

'What are you doing? Get off!'

'Just keeping you close.'

'What, are there like, ghosts or something?'

'Don't be silly.' Pippa aimed for brisk this time as Harriet shoved her arm away. 'Torch?'

'Can't you? I'm nearly out of battery. There'd better be electricity in this place.'

'Of course there is.' Pippa hadn't dared tell Harriet yet that there wasn't actually Wi-Fi in the house; she'd never have got within fifty miles if her daughter had known that before they'd set out on their reluctant road trip. The solicitor had dropped that into the email as well, and she hadn't found the right moment to mention it to Harriet.

Harriet's exaggerated sigh was followed by a narrow beam of light, and they both let out a scream. Sitting beneath a dark panelled staircase was a dulled suit of armour staring straight at them, one arm clutching a lance with a sharpened point. Pippa's heart rate settled a smidge as she realised it wasn't actually clunking towards them.

'Looks lovely, Mum, the house. Very welcoming.'

'There's no need to be quite so sarcastic. The state of it is nothing to do with me, and anyway, it doesn't matter how rough it is, we're not staying long.'

'Is there any furniture?' Harriet pointed her phone at the suit of armour and there was a flash as she took a photo.

'I'd certainly like to think so. Someone apparently looks after the house, and they are expecting us.'

'Yeah, right. Looks like it. It's warmer outside than in.' Harriet stomped off and thrust open a door to her left, leaving Pippa in a pool of darkness and trying to remember from her brief glance if there were any trip hazards between the stairs and where she stood. 'There's a sofa in here, Mum. It's orange, like someone threw up on it and left it to dry.'

Ugh, that sounded revolting, and Pippa resisted another shudder. 'At least there's somewhere to sit. It doesn't matter about the colour,' she replied brightly.

'Wait until you see it.' Harriet emerged, light from her torch flashing off the walls as she raised her phone to look around. 'There's probably still bits of carrot stuck to the cushions.' She stuck her head through another door. 'Dining room. Grim.'

The front door was still open, and Pippa turned in the direction of warmer air and other thoughts. 'Let's just get our luggage and go to bed. We can sort everything out tomorrow, right now we need sleep.'

Harriet's torchlight disappeared and she seemed to vanish in the gloom as well. 'My phone's dead. Thanks for that.'

'It's hardly my fault, the amount of time you spend on it. Charge it in your room.' Pippa was on her way back to the car and she returned moments later, lugging a case in each hand. 'I'll go up first. Take my phone and use the torch so I can see where I'm putting my feet.'

'Or we could just use the lights, like normal people.'

Harriet hit a switch and Pippa let out a relieved breath as the rest of the hall was revealed. The woodwork was yellowed; the only other door Harriet hadn't yet opened stood straight in front of them, past the stairs. Pippa couldn't decide if the orange-and-brown pattern of the carpet was even more repulsive than the oversized green flowers on the wallpaper. The stairs turned up and out of sight, that same pattern on the walls inviting them up to the first floor. Her heart sank as she thought longingly of their lovely London home with all its familiar comforts.

'Bed,' she said firmly. 'I'm absolutely beat. That journey was brutal.'

'Okay.' Even Harriet's usual confidence seemed dented by the view, and she trailed after Pippa, giving the suit of armour a wary glance. Upstairs the landing was square too, similar to the hall, with the same wallpaper and a bulb without a shade hanging in the centre of the ceiling. A large, square blue rug in place of carpet felt thin and didn't quite reach any of the five plain doors, exposing ancient and uneven wooden floorboards.

Pippa noticed a couple of average farming landscapes on the walls opposite a small, ugly grandfather clock and some black-and-white photographs. She had no idea which room was which, and the first two doors she tried revealed double beds neatly made in each.

'They'll do,' she said tiredly. Really this whole escapade was bonkers, and she'd be having a serious word with her dad. He always did this, set her some ridiculous task he wanted her to sort and then took himself off-grid where she couldn't reach him to give him a piece of her mind. Well, she would track him down this time for sure, he'd gone too far, and she wasn't going to be…

'Mum? Are you even listening?'

'What?' Pippa whirled around, still mentally giving her dad the sharp end of her tongue, and enjoying it.

'I *said*, will you check on me in the morning when you get up?'

'Of course I will.' Pippa's irritation with her dad dissipated as she looked at Harriet standing in the doorway of the first room. She didn't often seek comfort from her mum these days and seemed to be aiming for nonchalance as she fidgeted with the phone in her hand, but Pippa had caught the flash of uncertainty in her gaze.

'And if I'm still asleep, don't wake me up, okay?'

'That's fine.' She didn't mind in the least how long Harriet slept in tomorrow; it might delay the row about the Wi-Fi that was on the way. 'And I won't go out until you're up. We'll have to go shopping, though heaven knows where. It's probably miles to the nearest town but those few bits we brought won't last long.'

'Didn't you even google Hartfell before we came, find out what's here?'

'No. What did you discover?'

'Well, there's a shop and a pub so we won't starve.'

'Okay, I'll take a look tomorrow. And the house will be up for sale just as soon as I find a local estate agent.' Pippa knew her lack of online curiosity would be astonishing to Harriet, who barely made a move without checking it on her phone first. But she wasn't about to confess to her clever and intuitive daughter that she'd half hoped if she ignored the plan her dad had set in motion, then it might have simply gone away. But now here she was, knowing barely anything about the house and even less about its surroundings. Harriet dragged her case into the room and Pippa followed, watching her dump it on the floor.

'Night sweetheart, sleep well.'

'Night.' Harriet came over to give Pippa a quick squeeze and she held her daughter for those few, brief seconds until Harriet wriggled away. 'You too. Close the door on your way out.'

Pippa obliged, pressing her lips together. Once they would have snuggled on Harriet's bed to read a story before she tucked her daughter beneath the covers, but those days were long gone. She trailed into her own room and shut the door. This one was slightly larger, with floral green wallpaper and similarly coloured curtains that reminded her of wet moss. Cushions on an armchair in one corner were edged in lace, matching those on the bed, and she tossed them to the chair. A wooden dressing table and wardrobe were looming and dark, and the only thing she liked about the room was the size and the bed framed in brass.

She heard Harriet trying doors on the landing until she found one that was presumably the bathroom, and when she'd finished, Pippa followed to freshen up. Blue tiles didn't suit a turquoise suite and the only mirror was the door of a small, wall-mounted cupboard. It had been a long drive up from London, with all the traffic problems that holiday getaways usually brought, and she found all this clashing colour adding to her exhaustion. It probably wouldn't help get the house sold in a hurry, but if the price was right, it would surely sell soon enough, and then she and Harriet would be back in their little corner of Maida Vale in no time.

Her short silk pyjamas were perfectly adequate at home, but Pippa was shivering as she got into the brass bed, plain cotton sheets cool against her skin. She'd stayed in plenty of hotels when she and her siblings had travelled with their dad, and was used to falling asleep in strange places, but this one seemed different. There was a stillness to the silence that felt empty, eerie even, and not even the owl hooting outside could drive away the sense of isolation creeping over her.

She knew the village was nearby, but they'd barely passed any lights along those last twenty miles since leaving the motorway, and she had no idea how far away proper civilisation might lie. She tossed and turned uneasily for a good hour, trying to stay warm and ignore the clock on the landing chiming every fifteen minutes.

Several hours later, the green curtains were no match for the glare of the morning sun and Pippa jerked awake from an unsettling dream in which she was being followed by a clanking suit of armour. She breathed deeply, waiting for the vision to fade from her mind, and reluctantly emerged from the duvet and bright patchwork quilt thrown across it. An old-fashioned triple mirror on the dressing table helpfully revealed three tired versions of her own self, dark circles beneath her eyes. She found a socket and plugged in her phone, which she'd forgotten to do last night, half expecting crackling, and was relieved when none came.

The house seemed to be holding its breath too and she opened her door quietly so as not to disturb Harriet, even though a marching band might not manage it when her daughter was asleep. She stepped onto the landing and her feet nearly left the floor when the grandfather clock cheerfully chimed six a.m. She shot it a filthy look as she released her grip of the banister, mentally adding 'get rid' to the list of jobs in her mind.

Now would be a good time to check on Harriet as promised, making sure she was warm and comfortable. For all that Pippa did everything she could to create a normal life for her daughter, their family wasn't exactly the most ordinary one, and Harriet had declared an unwelcome degree of independence when she'd set her heart on attending a secondary school outside of London. Pippa had been vehement in her opposition to parting with her during the week and, as usual, Jonny had stepped in to support his granddaughter until Pippa had eventually relented. The compromise had been found in the school's exceptional reputation for sport as well as other subjects, and she still had to cling onto unshed tears every time she drove Harriet back to Kent.

Harriet had settled well and soon flourished as a flex-ible boarder, one of her friends from primary joining her at the co-educational school. But since she'd returned after the Easter break, Pippa had known that all wasn't quite right. Harriet was spending more time in her room and Pippa definitely felt at times that her daughter was avoiding conversations and their usual closeness seemed to be disintegrating.

Though she'd obviously not wanted another of her dad's problems to sort out, the main reason she'd agreed to represent Jonny in Hartfell was because it would be a rare chance to spend time with Harriet and somehow try to reconnect. Life in London didn't stand still for anyone, and if she didn't act soon then Harriet would be gone, on to A levels before university and studying for a career in physiotherapy. In quiet moments at home when it was just the two of them, Harriet would still allow the occasional sofa snuggle and Pippa felt acutely the threads holding her daughter to her stretching, becoming thinner with every month that passed.

She was more than ready for her first coffee of the day and just as soon as she'd checked on Harriet, then she'd go in search of the kitchen and supplies. Whoever had prepared their rooms was supposed to have left some shopping essentials to get them started, and she hoped there might be fresh fruit or even yoghurt in the fridge. Her stomach rumbled at the thought; dinner had been twelve hours ago in a service station on the way up.

'Harriet?' Pippa whispered as she tapped gently on the bedroom door. She was certain Harriet was still asleep, otherwise the lack of Wi-Fi would definitely have got her out of bed in search of a network and a password. She'd have a quick look and then leave her to rest.

She knocked a second time and carefully opened the door to peep around it. On the opposite side of the house to her own room, the sun wouldn't filter into this one until much later and dark curtains were helping to hold back the morning light. It took her vision a moment to adjust, and she blinked as her gaze landed on the bed. A large dog was flat out on the duvet and someone beneath it, presumably Harriet, was snoring in a manner she'd never heard emanate from her daughter before. Pippa's jaw dropped as she loosened her grip on the door, and it swung back to clatter against the wall.

'Harriet,' she yelled, forgetting how slowly Harriet liked to come to in the mornings. 'Where did that dog come from and why is it sleeping on your bed?'

The results of her shout were twofold, and Pippa wasn't expecting either of them. The dog leapt to the floor and set up a cacophony of barking that she thought might actually wake the dead and certainly bring to life whoever had inhabited that suit of armour downstairs. The top half of the figure beneath the duvet sprang up, revealing messy blond hair and a bare chest that quite possibly would have taken her breath away if she hadn't been so busy trying to fend off the dog, which had decided it didn't mind the look of her now and was trying to lick her to death instead.

'What the…' The man ran a bewildered hand through his hair, squinting at the sight greeting him in the doorway. A scowl spread across his face, shadowed by rough, golden stubble. 'Ah. You're here.'

Chapter Two

'Could you possibly, if it's not too much trouble, call off your wretched dog?' Pippa was practically hopping from foot to foot in her short pyjamas to avoid it and this wasn't generally how she liked to present herself to strangers. This one, despite the lingering scowl, seemed faintly amused by her predicament as she flashed him a glance. She didn't mind animals, and lovely though the dog was, she really didn't want those sharp claws making contact with her bare skin.

'Lola, come here,' he said sharply. The dog hesitated, giving him a look as she pondered which of the two options she preferred. With a final lick on Pippa's bare thigh, making her squirm again, Lola ambled back to the bed and jumped on it. 'And for the record, she's not wretched, she's delightful.'

'Debatable,' Pippa muttered. And on the bed too. Urgh.

She hated being caught unawares, and barefoot in pyjamas with bed hair was far from ideal for having this conversation. But she couldn't return to her room and change, that would make it seem like she minded her appearance. Because she didn't, even if she was wondering whether translucent orange blended with yellow, red and a touch of phthalo blue would create exactly the right shade of watercolours to capture the darker lights in his hair.

'What are you doing in my room?' The words were delivered in a lazy Yorkshire drawl as he rested a gentle hand on the dog's head.

'Your room?' Pippa's eyes were racing around it, taking in the view of a brass-framed bed matching hers, more dark furniture, and blue-and-white striped wallpaper. Harriet! Where was she? Pippa took what she hoped was a menacing step forward, jamming hands on her hips. Right now she wouldn't have minded borrowing that lance downstairs as well. 'Who the hell are you? And where exactly is my daughter?'

'Let's deal with the second question first. Your daughter isn't in here, obviously. And who the hell am I?' He glared back from red-rimmed and shadowed eyes. It was scant consolation that he looked as drained as she did, if the sight of her face in the triple mirror before was anything to go by. A phone beside the bed was flashing and he leaned over to pick it up, peering at the screen. 'I'm Gil. Or at least I think I am after two hours' sleep, thanks to you barging into my room. I was hoping for a minimum of four.'

'Barging in! I came to check on my daughter! How was I supposed to know there was a strange man…' Pippa was glad she'd managed strange, because she was thinking gorgeous, if rather dishevelled and bad tempered. The dark blond streaks were shot through with lighter ones and a suntan let her know he lived a life outdoors. His eyes – a blue that was dazzlingly bright against his skin – were still crinkled into a scowl, deepening the lines carved beside them.

'I've been called a few names in my time but never strange.' He put the phone down and sank back against the pillows, a faint curl lifting the corners of his lips.

'But who are you?' She closed her mouth lest he thought she was gaping.

'I thought we'd established that. I'm Gil. Haworth, if you want the rest. My middle name's Pilkington. Don't ask.'

'I heard you the first time,' she replied shortly. 'But I'm afraid none of your names explain why you're in my house.'

'Your house?' Even his brows managed to be sardonic. 'Doesn't it belong to your father, Pippa Douglas?'

'How do you know who I am and what are you doing here? And how the *hell* do you know my father?' Pippa took a deep breath, trying to disguise her shock and quell her rising anger with both Gil and her dad. If it took her all day, she was going to track Jonny down and…

'Again, let's start with the second question; I live here. Now, back to your first. I know your name because it was in an email I received from your father's solicitor. And how the hell do I know Jonny? He's my landlord, unfortunately. Although we've never actually met. No plans to change that, incidentally. If you were wondering.'

'I wasn't and he's told me nothing about you,' she shot back, forcing herself to stand still and ignore the goose-bumps quivering on her skin. She put that firmly down to the chill and not the sight of this man half naked in bed.

And what was her dad up to? He was as sharp as a tack, except when it came to women, and as he hadn't told her about this man, then the only reason Jonny had avoided passing on the information was because he knew it would make her unhappy. Because it did. She was. She couldn't be bumping into Gil on the landing every morning and sharing a bathroom for however long she and Harriet were marooned in this blasted house on one of her dad's bloody whims.

'Well, we can't both stay here. At the same time.' She glared at Gil, determined not to look down. Although every time his hand moved on the dog's head, she caught another unplanned glimpse of that chest. Suntanned as well, but not quite as much as his face. Damn.

'Technically, we can because I'm allowed to live here and you're an invited guest. Just not by me.' Gil's phone was flashing again, and he checked it, typed a quick response, lips quirking when the dog nudged his hand, and he returned it to her head. 'But you're right, we can't stay here together. I was planning to move out the moment you arrived, and I would've already done it if I'd known exactly when you were going to turn up. The solicitor wasn't very clear about that.'

'So you'll move out today, then? Because I wasn't aware of… you.' Pippa tailed off. She hadn't been expecting him to agree so easily and her shoulders loosened a fraction. She wasn't too sure how complicated selling the house with a tenant in place would be, but if Gil was planning to go of his own accord, then that would help enormously.

'This minute, if you prefer. But perhaps you'd like to give me some privacy.' He raised the duvet enough to reveal a lower leg just as distracting as the rest of him. Her glance raced to the heap of clothes on the floor. Faded jeans, socks, a grey T-shirt. And a pair of shorts, green, sitting on top of everything else. Her pulse skipped a beat, and she took a hurried step backwards.

'Urgh Mum, watch it! You nearly knocked me over.'

Pippa whirled around to find Harriet right behind her, staring blearily and clutching her ever-present phone. Long hair was fastened in a careless ponytail and her gold-flecked hazel eyes still had the power to stop Pippa in her tracks to marvel at her daughter's emerging beauty.

'Harriet! Sorry, did I wake you?'

'Well, you weren't exactly being quiet. Do you actually know how early it is?' She peered around Pippa and gave Gil a grin, which he quickly returned as he pulled the duvet up. 'Hi, I'm Harriet. I love your dog.'

'Hey Harriet, I'm Gil. Nice to meet you. And thanks, I'm sure Lola will love you too.' His cool gaze returned to Pippa, and she glowered back, noting she hadn't received as warm an introduction. *Nice to meet him* wasn't a phrase she'd use either and she really wasn't sure about the dog yet.

'Mum didn't tell me you were here.'

'That's because I didn't know.' Pippa backed onto the landing with as much dignity as she could muster covered in dried dog slobber and golden fur scattered around her feet. 'Gil is moving out as soon as he gets up.'

'Oh? That's a shame. Are you taking Lola with you?' Harriet was looking longingly at the dog and Gil's smile was polite.

'I'm afraid I'll have to, sorry. She goes pretty much everywhere with me. Besides, I don't think your mum would want me to leave Lola behind. I'm not sure they're going to be good friends.'

Harriet shot Pippa a look she really didn't think she deserved. When had Harriet seriously been interested in pets, other than that time she'd wanted a hamster and Pippa had refused, imagining it escaping behind the skirting boards and dying a horrible death trapped in some dark corner? Of course Harriet had pleaded for a puppy on occasion, like most children, but Pippa had successfully fended off those demands as well.

'We'll leave you to collect your things, then.' Pippa leaned forward to grab the handle and closed the door none too gently, causing the landing window to rattle alarmingly.

'What's going on, Mum? Who is he?' Harriet was staring at her phone again, having long ago perfected the art of conversing without making eye contact. 'And why do you look all hot but not in a good way?'

'Coffee,' Pippa replied casually. 'You know I'm hopeless until I've had the first. Let's talk at breakfast and make a proper plan.'

'Wi-Fi? You find the network yet?'

'No, Harriet.' Pippa resisted a groan. 'There really are more important things to deal with first.' Like Gil Haworth, who was probably getting dressed right now behind that door.

'Yeah? Like what?' Harriet flashed her a rare smile as she backed into her own room and Pippa knew she wouldn't get another the minute her daughter found out the unwelcome news about the Wi-Fi.

'Something to eat, for a start. I'm hungry and I'm sure you must be too.' Pippa retreated to her own room and yanked her phone off the dressing table. This time, that ugly mirror revealed three flushed versions of herself, with darkened pupils and wild blonde hair falling to her shoulders. Another glance failed to conceal two undone buttons on her grey silk pyjamas. The rest were thankfully fastened but not quite in the right order. She really had been tired last night, and she was going to have to work hard to regain some dignity in front of Gil after that introduction. She fired off a furious message to her dad, who would probably chuckle and ignore it.

Pippa threw her case on the bed in search of clothes, musing over her dad's reasons for wanting her in Hartfell. Both her parents had grown up in Yorkshire, meeting when Jonny was twenty-two and her mum just eighteen. Her mum's family had owned a furniture-making business in town and one day Jonny had turned up in search of a job. He'd got it and come away with a girlfriend too, and Pippa had been born when her mum was twenty. Her brother Raf arrived eleven months later, and his birth was followed by a wedding.

Jonny had founded the band, Blue at Midnight, with three mates, and he always said they'd been in the right place at the right time when they were noticed by a scout and then signed by a label. Back in the Eighties, that was how things were done. There were no social channels, no opportunities to release music online to find a following. It was down to hard graft, night after night on the road, playing clubs no one had heard of, and sometimes luck as well. And after that first runaway hit, even more work to keep at it; to keep producing, performing, selling.

Life on the road was a given for Jonny when Pippa and Raf were little, and time spent with the family at home grounded him back in the real world. The band was soon onto their second album with a US tour booked, and the family followed Jonny south, settling in a house in north London.

Pippa had never forgotten those days and it still hurt to think too far back. Life had been normal for them then; she and Raf didn't know any different, and without the internet they were mostly untroubled by their dad's growing fame. Their mum, Stella, was content to raise her family and remain in the background while Jonny performed around the world. But he always came home, and a baby sister, Tilly, joined them five years after Raf.

But those days ended, as all days do, and it was her mum's illness when Pippa turned thirteen and then her death a year later, that totally transformed their lives. Not fame, number one albums, or sold-out stadiums. Lost, stricken with grief, Jonny took time away from the band and the whole family struggled to find a way forward. Fun and loving though he was, he didn't have any real idea of what it meant to be an ordinary parent day by day. Homework was missed, schooldays skipped, and routine flew out of the window and took their contentment with it.

Pippa couldn't get used to the house without her mum; no longer was it a proper home. Raf showed up for school but that was pretty much all he did when it came to education. Tilly had seemed to cope best, too little to remember everything or even fully understand the magnitude of what she'd lost with their mum's passing.

Jonny bought a holiday house in Majorca where they could hide away and avoid school, family, news – anything he thought might upset them. He carted them off to Disneyland and hired a yacht to sail around the Caribbean. Finally he admitted defeat at home and employed a housekeeper to bring order to the chaos, escaping onto a long-planned tour and leaving his younger sister in charge. The children were left behind, trying to lead the lives they'd had before but without the anchor that had held them steady.

Pippa liked the housekeeper who came in daily because she was kind, and it meant that chores were done, lunches made, and uniforms ironed. She craved order after all the turmoil and hated that her mum wasn't there to cheer them on or track down their dad when they wanted to share something with him, though Jonny tried his best, even from a distance. Whenever Pippa caught sight of his face on a newspaper or on the television, it seemed like a stranger was staring right back at her. Her dad, far away; her mum, gone. And with it the life she'd known.

The only way she could find comfort and strength for herself was to reach out to her brother and sister, and try somehow to make their world better. Art had always been her go-to, her passion and now it became her therapy. She drew and painted in every spare moment, tucking away beautiful sketches and watercolours that filled page after page. She encouraged Raf to study before it was too late and she read with Tilly at night before bed, both sisters escaping the real world to process their grief in another.

It was to Pippa that Raf turned when a first girlfriend dumped him, to Pippa her siblings gravitated when they wanted support or merely a hug. She made herself available for them always, tried her best to step into her mum's shoes and become what they needed, watching, loving, mothering, from the sidelines of her own life.

When Jonny came home, he never quite fitted back in. Somehow, they'd made a way to manage without him, and as money became more plentiful, he filled the emotional void with stuff. Walkmans, albums, clothes, trips, even another holiday cottage in Scotland. But he wasn't always there, and their mum never would be again. Stuff didn't hold them when they were sad, or wipe away tears after a breakup. Stuff didn't sit by the phone and comfort a bereft sister when the boy she wanted to call never did.

Once, Jonny brought up the possibility of returning to live in Yorkshire and Pippa was aghast. She made him promise that he would never sell their home and drag them back north to distant relatives that had fallen away over time. Fame did that, she'd found. Only those people who'd stuck close knew who this fractured family really were. Their lives were rooted in London, and she couldn't bear the thought of leaving behind all she knew.

Pippa pushed away thoughts of the past and went to freshen up in the bathroom. She decided to leave a shower for later, when Gil was safely out of the way. Downstairs, she glanced in at the sitting and dining rooms, decorated in the same style as the first floor of the house. The final door in the hall led into a kitchen, a pantry off that with grimy yellow walls lined with empty, dusty shelves. The fuse box looked as though it had been installed when the house had been built and she resolved that she and Harriet would go nowhere near it. The state of the electrics would probably knock another few thousand pounds off the price of this place when she got it on the market.

Given everything she'd seen of the house so far, Pippa's expectations of the kitchen were suitably low, and she wasn't disappointed. Smaller than contemporary living now required, three walls were covered in plain beige cupboards with metal handles, the space between the wall-mounted units and the lower ones filled with pale yellow tiles, a dark blue range jammed between them.

She was ready to weep as she thought of the clean and bright kitchen back in her beloved London home. A mullioned window framed in stone let in some light, but it was up against it with all these clashing colours. She noticed another door and window to her left; a glance through the glass revealed a terrace and large garden with a path leading towards a farmyard.

Two dog bowls were near the back door and a Formica table with pale, spindly legs had one flap raised, the other hanging down, with four cheap plastic chairs set haphazardly around it. If Gil really did live here, then he hadn't made the place much of a home and she wondered why not. And it certainly didn't look as though he shared the house with anyone else. Who would put up with such a state?

She checked inside the old white fridge. A small door at the top revealed an empty, iced up freezer tray and the shelves beneath it held cheese, bacon, mushrooms, milk and butter. Not the yoghurt she had hoped for, or even a scrap of fruit, and she jabbed the door shut again. *A few provisions left ready*, the solicitor had mentioned in the email. At least there was milk for coffee. Pippa was desperate for that caffeine hit now and one cupboard revealed coffee, a box of cornflakes, a few tins, packets of dried pasta, quite a bit of chocolate, chopped tomatoes, a jar of crushed chillies and a half-empty bottle of olive oil.

Whatever she'd been expecting, it wasn't this, and now she had yet another decision to make. Did she spend time trying to make the house look like a home before inviting an estate agent in to value it? Or did she laugh away the state of the place and declare it the perfect project and price it accordingly? It was going to take a lot more than fresh bread rising in the oven and the aroma of coffee in the kitchen to make this house a home.

But right now they were questions too complicated to answer and she was grateful for small mercies when she ran the tap and the bowl in the sink began to fill with hot water. Not for anything was she going to make even a single cup of coffee without washing the mugs first.

Once everything was dripping dry on the draining board, Pippa switched on the kettle, staring through the window as she waited for it to boil. It really was the most glorious view and Harriet had been right, she should have googled the house and Hartfell before they'd arrived. She'd employed her usual tactic of avoiding anything she didn't want to think about. It had always been her default since her mum had died; focus on the good and deal with the bad only when necessary.

The sun was climbing higher in a blue sky, patches of dappled light falling between trees and overgrown shrubs in the garden. The grass was too long to be a lawn and there was an abundant and natural beauty to the deep borders blazing with summer colours, delphiniums and verbena tall and stately amongst clumps of lavender geraniums and pink achillea.

Wooden furniture sat on the stone terrace, green with moss and tatty from neglect. Over the hawthorn hedge bordering the garden on the right, Pippa saw the farm-yard, a converted stone barn between two more outbuild-ings, windows set below the eaves. The driveway where she had left her car last night continued on to the yard, an area next to a small paddock set aside for more parking.

Beyond the barns, fields bordered by mature trees sloped up to a fell, shaded by moorland and dotted with grazing sheep. Her long-ago visits to Yorkshire had been to the small town where her mum had grown up. That last time, staying with family after Stella's death, Pippa had been too blurred by grief to notice anything other than the people around her. But this view was exceptional, and her artist's eye was noting details she was surprised to realise she'd love to capture later if time allowed.

Behind her, the kettle was making a very strange noise, and she hastily switched it off before it exploded; she didn't want to knock out what power they had. No Wi-Fi for Harriet was one thing, no phone at all quite another. Pippa made herself a cup of coffee from the jar of instant and returned to the window to ponder some more, cradling the warm mug between her hands.

'I see you've found my coffee.'

Chapter Three

Pippa spun around to face Gil, dressed now in the clothes she'd seen on his bedroom floor. Lola wandered over to the bowls by the back door and sat down, staring up at him expectantly.

His coffee? 'Whoever was preparing the house for us was meant to be leaving some basics as well,' she said stiffly. She was so far on the back foot with him now she might as well be in the yard.

'Preparing the house?' He laughed as he shook out some dog food from a biscuit barrel on the worktop and Lola had inhaled it before Pippa had barely even blinked. 'I made the beds, I'm afraid I don't have time to run around with a duster or go shopping for a couple of vegetarians as well. Sorry, Lola, that's your lot.' He patted the dog gently before replacing the lid on the barrel. Lola sighed as he opened the backdoor and she trotted through it. Gil leaned outside, bending to pick something up and when he turned back, Pippa saw that it was milk. 'You're not bloody vegans as well, are you?'

'I don't see that it would matter to you either way seeing as you haven't been shopping for us. The solicitor said…'

'I'm not interested in what the solicitor said.' He was in her space now, reaching past her to stand the two bottles on the worktop. He refilled the kettle and set it back down with a clatter.

'You should be,' Pippa told him coolly. She'd taken a step out of his way but that was all. She wasn't going to be cowed by his antagonism; until an hour ago she hadn't even known he existed, much less lived in this house. But not for much longer, thankfully. She wouldn't be pushing the point about the solicitor though, seeing as she'd only skimmed the email she'd received about the house. 'I'll replace your coffee when I go shopping.'

'I'm not that mean. I can run to a cup of coffee.' Gil flashed her a glance and her pulse caught at that same awareness from before. 'But yeah, if you don't mind. I'm not great without coffee first thing so I'd appreciate not running out. Not that you look like the kind of person who drinks instant.'

'And what's that supposed to mean?' Pippa banged her empty mug onto the worktop. 'You don't seem like the kind of person who'd be any nicer when they've had coffee.'

'I guess I deserved that. Sorry.'

This time she couldn't read anything more than indifference in his look. She straightened up and he yawned as he turned away. She'd have thought he'd done it on purpose if he didn't look so wiped out. She must have been more exhausted than she'd realised seeing as she'd missed his arrival in the early hours.

'So you've noticed the kettle doesn't turn off by itself. You need to listen for it boiling and then do it.'

'Is there anything else dangerous you ought to warn me about before you leave?' She wanted to make certain he knew she hadn't forgotten.

'I think that's it.' Lola returned, helping herself to a noisy drink and sloshing water onto the worn lino before flopping into a cosy bed. Pippa pulled a face. Another good reason why she'd never wanted pets. Mess everywhere.

Gil's phone was ringing again, and he propped himself against the blue range with his coffee, listening to what she presumed was a voicemail when he didn't pick up in time. He swiped the message away and looked up. 'I've got to go to work. Would it inconvenience you terribly if I moved out when I get back?'

He raised that brow again and the politeness he was pretending made her decide to retaliate in kind. She just needed him gone and quickly, suspecting that the more impatient she appeared, the longer he'd draw out the process. She was quite certain he didn't want to share the house with her either and it was likely to be that which got him through the door. 'Not at all. I have to find an estate agent and go shopping so I won't be here all day anyway.'

He scowled again and a glimmer of triumph followed. She'd meant that comment to hit home. So, he wasn't happy about her plans to sell the house. Why? How long had he been living here and how was he connected to her dad? Or was he? These were questions Pippa wasn't prepared to ask him directly, imagining his scorn if she tried, so she'd have to find answers another way.

'Where do you work?' She could at least ask that; praying it wasn't from home and he was planning to perch at that rickety kitchen table all day. Surely not, not without Wi-Fi?

'There.' He jerked his head towards the yard and her startled gaze followed his to the window.

'You're a farmer?' That would at least take him outside and away from her.

'No. I'm a vet.'

'A vet? Oh, that's so cool.' Harriet had wandered barefoot into the kitchen, still in her pyjamas, and Lola jumped up to greet her. She bent down, giving the dog the kind of smile that made Pippa wish her daughter was still a toddler. She used to get those cuddles, too, and a wave of sadness rushed through her. 'Is Lola a Labrador? I love her colour.'

'She is a Labrador, a very hungry one, so I wouldn't leave anything around that you don't want her to eat. Making food disappear without me noticing is her superpower, one I'm still trying to train her out of.'

'How old is she?' Harriet was still cuddling, and Lola's tail was thumping happily against her thigh in response to all this attention.

'She's eighteen months, still a baby, really.'

'So you've had her since she was a puppy then?' Harriet shot Pippa another glare; the lack of their own dog something else that was Pippa's fault. She opened her mouth to repeat her objections to pets and why they couldn't have a puppy at home, but Gil was quicker.

'Not quite, she was five months old when I got her, so still very young.'

'You rescued her? Wow, that's amazing. Could I take her for a walk sometime?'

'I don't think so, Harriet, seeing as Lola will be moving out with Gil later today.' Pippa wanted to make sure that was clear. There was absolutely no point in letting Harriet get attached. Pippa had experienced that once in her life with a pet and she certainly wasn't going there again, nor would she allow Harriet to be exposed to those

31

same feelings. 'Mind where you're putting your feet, she's spilled water all over the floor.'

'So? I'm not bothered.' Harriet scowled before returning her curiosity to Gil. 'So, you like, save sick animals and stuff?'

'When I can.' His smile for her was weary, tinged with something Pippa thought might be sadness. He was slightly less guarded, not as resentful, when he was speaking with her daughter. He yawned again, covering his mouth with a hand. 'Sorry, very late night. I was called out. Sadly not every animal I treat gets a happy ending, it goes with the job.'

'But still, you make a difference, right?'

'I guess I do. It's worth trying, anyway.'

'Where are you going to live?' Harriet had left Lola snuggling down again and opened the fridge door. She shut it again and shot Pippa another look, one which Pippa understood all too well. A look that implied she could magic up whatever food it was that Harriet wanted right now. In London, where there was every kind of shop, she usually could. She made sure to keep all Harriet's favourites well stocked at home; her daughter played a lot of sport and was always hungry. Harriet came and went as she pleased between Pippa's house and her dad's, but there was no doubt who was the better cook, and it wasn't her father. Pippa often wondered if that was the real reason why Harriet still lived with her; she always seemed to be angry with her these days.

'Well, I—'

'That's none of our business, Harriet,' Pippa said coolly. Partly because it wasn't and partly because she didn't care, as long as Gil was out of her sight. Her mind was still tugging her back to that first glimpse she'd had of him in bed earlier; that bare chest, the tousled blond hair…

'Mum, stop it! I can hear you grinding your teeth again, it's disgusting. You always do that when you're stressed.'

Oh, she was stressed all right! Faced with an angry vet who couldn't stand the sight of her and a grumpy daughter who'd already made friends with a dog who wasn't staying. And that was before she'd even got to the bottom of her dad's connection to this house and what exactly Gil was doing in it.

'Mum hates Hartfell,' Harriet offered Gil helpfully, folding her arms. 'She didn't want to come here.'

'She didn't?' Gil had apparently honed the ability to ask a question whilst conveying absolutely no interest in the answer.

'Harriet, that's not fair. I know nothing about the place, and we've only been here ten hours.' Pippa was doing her best to unclench the tension in her jaw and decided a change of subject was needed. 'So, what are your plans for today?' She'd learned a while ago to let Harriet come to her, not to make her own suggestions anymore.

'Eat, obviously, when you've done the shopping. And if you want me to do some homework then I'm going to need the Wi-Fi network and a password.'

'Wi-Fi network? Sorry, Harriet, we don't have one of those in the house.' Gil laughed and Pippa really didn't like how he directed his amusement at her as she braced herself for battle. He raised a disdainful hand to the kitchen. 'You can see the state of the place, it's barely even habitable. I'm afraid Wi-Fi isn't going to find its way in here anytime soon.'

'*NO WI-FI!*' Harriet screeched, her face turning pink with fury. 'Did you know about this, Mum?'

'I didn't have time to do much research before we arrived and now we're here, I've realised the house is even more outdated than I'd expected.' Pippa settled on a version of the truth, wondering why Harriet thought doing homework was more for Pippa's benefit rather than her own.

'*Outdated?*' Harriet jabbed her phone furiously in Pippa's direction. 'Do you even actually understand what this means? Just because you don't care about Wi-Fi and need it like I do doesn't mean it's not important! How am I supposed to stay in touch with Isla and my own life now you've dragged me up here and dumped us in the middle of nowhere?'

Pippa was feeling guilty that Harriet wouldn't easily be able to reach her best friend. And neither would she, seeing as Isla's mum Cassie was Pippa's closest friend. 'That's not what you said last night. You said it would be an adventure. It'll be fun, Harriet, like living off-grid for a bit. A digital detox.' She took a calming breath, reminding herself who was actually the parent in this relationship and trying to quell the knots that had erupted in her stomach. Harriet's face was red now and she flounced from the kitchen, offering a parting stab over one shoulder.

'*Off-grid?* Without Wi-Fi you can forget me doing homework, Mum. I'm going to look up trains back to London. Oh that's right, I can't. Because we're now living in the dark ages and trains probably don't even run up here.'

Pippa's fingers were trembling, and she took another breath as the door shook in its frame after the slam. She'd need to talk to Harriet, but she knew from experience it

34

would be best done when her daughter had eaten and for that she'd have to go shopping first, delaying the conversation required after that outburst. A wave of misery washed through her and she wished with all her heart they were still in London. At least there Harriet was familiar with home and all they both loved about the city. Gil was staring through the window, and he slowly turned around.

'Thanks for that! You obviously enjoyed letting Harriet know about the Wi-Fi, probably because you knew she'd be angry and would blame me.'

'Well, she's right.'

'It's not my fault!'

'Not having Wi-Fi in the house isn't your fault but maybe you should have told her because then she would have known the facts before she came and made an informed decision, not one based on assumptions.' He raised that brow again and Pippa wanted to swipe it from his face. 'Or were you afraid that she wouldn't come, and the lack of Wi-Fi would've sealed the deal?'

Pippa thought wildly her teeth were grinding so hard now it was a wonder she wasn't spitting dust, and she could feel her face heating up, her hands clenched into fists. 'How dare you,' she roared, tempted to grab her empty mug, and hurl it at him. 'We've barely met and you think to mansplain to me about how I parent my daughter. You clearly know nothing about teenagers!'

'Funny, considering I've raised two of my own.'

'Sorry, is this a bad moment?' A head appeared around the back door and Pippa spun around in shock at the disturbance. 'I did knock but I don't think you heard me.' The woman offered her an apologetic smile before her look went to Gil, standing impassively at the sink. 'It's an emergency, Gil. That heifer up at Roland's place has taken a turn for the worse and he wants you to come as soon as possible.'

'On my way, I've just picked up his voicemail. How's the rest of the list looking?'

'Full. Wendy will be in soon.'

'Right. Come on, Lola, time to go.' He stuffed his phone in a pocket and strode past Pippa, who was still trembling. Lola jumped up, sensing an adventure.

'You must be Pippa.' The woman was hovering just inside the room, as though she didn't quite dare come any further. 'I'm Elaine, Gil's receptionist. Welcome to Hartfell.'

'Thank you.' Pippa let out a shaky breath, offering a smile of her own. Elaine stepped aside to let Gil through the door, and he disappeared, Lola at his heels. 'I don't think I've got off to the best start.'

'Don't mind Gil, he can be a bit sharp when he's upset. Doesn't happen often.'

'Upset?' Pippa was just about holding onto furious tears, and she wondered if he hadn't washed up his mug just to annoy her. She was fighting the desire to do it herself and looked away; she'd leave it for him to deal with when he returned for his things. 'I don't understand why he's so angry with me.'

'You're a threat to him, that's why.' Elaine shook her head. 'He loves this place and he's convinced you've come here just to sell it from under him.'

Pippa firmly quashed the flare of guilt. That was her plan, and she wasn't about to share it with his receptionist. Best to say no more about estate agents for now and find out how the land lay first, as it were. Maybe she'd look further afield for an agent as well. In the next county, maybe, not someone who knew all the locals and would make her plan public before she was ready. Then she'd have them stick up a *For Sale* board and hotfoot it back home at the same time, hopefully within the week.

'He'll calm down, don't worry. Why don't you pop over to the practice for a coffee when you have a minute? I'll fill you in on some of the history.'

'Where is that, the practice?' Not far enough, probably. Through the kitchen window Pippa caught sight of a Land Rover racing down the drive, a stony-faced Gil behind the wheel.

'The main branch is in town, but the original surgery is just across the yard. I'd better run, we've got a locum doing consultations this morning and clients will be arriving soon. See you later, Pippa.'

'Bye. And thank you.' Pippa walked over to the table and sank onto one of the plastic chairs, head in her hands. This adventure, as Harriet had optimistically called it last night, had rapidly become a nightmare. Gil Haworth didn't even know her and already he hated her. And now Harriet was sulking in her room and probably scheming to get her grandad to stage a rescue, which would put her beyond Pippa's reach whilst she was marooned in Hartfell.

She'd left her phone upstairs so she couldn't check if her own message to her dad had sent out. And even if it had, she didn't expect a reply anytime soon. Given the situation, he must've known all about Gil and had landed her in it on purpose. Yet again, she was battling her inability to say no to her family and worse, she knew deep down that some of what Gil had said about Harriet was true. She *had* been worried about the Wi-Fi, because if Harriet knew it was non-existent or even unreliable, why else would she have come? Not for Pippa's sake and a bit of mother and daughter bonding, of that, she was sure.

From experience she knew that Harriet was best left to cool down for a while. She would go in search of shopping, so she could at least feed her daughter. Perhaps when Harriet had had an hour or so to think about her predicament with the Wi-Fi, she might – and Pippa knew it was a long shot – just might come around to the idea of being on an adventure again. She desperately needed to uncover what was bothering Harriet, if her moodiness was due to more than teenage hormones.

She was hungry too and not for anything was she going to touch a single scrap of food that belonged to Gil, especially as none of it was the promised provisions he was supposed to have bought. She had no idea how the hot water system in this house worked and when she went upstairs and saw the rough contraption attached to the wall above the turquoise bath, she decided to leave having a shower for later. She sent Harriet a text to let her know she was going out in search of the shop.

She locked the back door and set off at her usual brisk pace, braced for avoiding strangers in her path. In daylight, the house wasn't as ugly as she'd expected given the state of the inside. It was rather gorgeous, built of a stone that appeared golden, dozing in the early morning sun.

The driveway was separated from the yard by a row of overgrown hedging, curving around to the barns she'd seen from the kitchen earlier, bordered by trees, a paddock one side and a front garden on the other, wide grassy verges laden with wildflowers. The whole effect was very pretty, and her eye caught on a clump of cow parsley. She thought of sketching it, capturing those faded, flat flower heads before they fell. She shook the idea firmly away; she didn't have time for that.

The small paddock was almost devoid of grass, a stubby little brown-and-white pony grazing between thin lines of white tape fencing off one corner, a thick tail almost reaching the ground shaking away flies. It raised a head to stare as Pippa marched past, and she smiled. Its face was half hidden by long white hair, and the pony soon returned to the more important business of snatching at grass through a muzzle attached to the headcollar.

The scent of freshly mown grass was on the air, and she breathed it in, trying to think back to the last time she'd noticed it. Not in her own garden, certainly, which was a courtyard filled with pots and plants she wasn't always diligent about taking care of. She paused where the drive met the lane, checking for traffic, of which there was none, unless she counted a group of five middle-aged people all striding purposefully past with rucksacks and walking poles. Every one of them offered a greeting along with curious looks and she muttered a distracted hello back.

A glance to her right revealed the high square tower of a sturdy, solid church and she turned towards it, glimpsing more rooftops through the trees. The lane sloped gently down as she headed towards the village, realising that Home Farm wasn't as far away from it as she'd imagined. She passed a primary school next to the church, the play-ground silent on a Saturday, unlike her phone, which had picked up some signal and was busy pinging notifications. She glanced at it, too distracted by the view right now to open the messages from the family, who probably all wanted to know about the house and why their dad had never told them about it.

Pippa slowed her pace as she crossed a neat bridge in the same golden stone as the house, matching some of the cottages she saw up ahead. Others were painted white with black windows, doors opening directly onto the cobbled lane. One or two houses were larger, smart front doors tucked behind railings and rows of low hedging. Beneath her feet, the shallow and burbling river spilled busily over rocks and she took a moment to enjoy it, feeling a little more of her tension slip away as she tilted her face to the sun. Her stomach rumbled, reminding her to continue in search of shopping, and she paused again when she reached a T-junction.

To her right sat the village green, the far side bordering the river and edged with bright planting, her eye picking out pleasing shades of lemon, cream and apricot. In the centre, a stone cross stood at the top of three wide and crumbling steps, the remains of a wooden stocks fastened between posts smudged with moss perched nearby.

On her left she spotted a pub; creamy stone walls smothered in ivy clambering above huge wooden planters on the cobbles. Each was filled with plants, and evergreen topiary had been pruned into upright columns between softer pastel hues. Opposite was a disused youth hostel, its dull rendered walls and tatty white windows making the building plain. A couple carrying cases were leaving the pub, heading for a car parked beneath the dappled shade of a horse chestnut tree.

It was all so much prettier than Pippa had expected, imagining the village to be some windswept moorland wilderness. Her visits to Yorkshire were long in the past and from what she remembered, her memories were of towns and busy streets, not this glorious cluster of build-ings perched amongst a rolling green landscape dotted with farms. She took a few pictures for the family and swiftly decided not to send them yet; love them all though she did and very much, she didn't want any of them descending on Hartfell for a nosy.

There had been just the three of them when her mum had died, not the five siblings they became after her dad eventually met someone else. Phoebe and Freddie, her youngest sister and brother, had arrived during Jonny's most meaningful relationship after becoming a widower, with his publicist Vanessa. Even now he would still say fondly that she was very good at her job, and he'd never had publicity like it. Pippa wasn't sure that he'd ever grasped the irony of the headlines he'd garnered by fathering two children with Vanessa, who was still very much a part of their lives and also excellent at the job she continued to do for Jonny and the band.

Another growl in her stomach reminded Pippa of Harriet, sulking back at the house. They both needed a good meal, and soon. Thinking about her daughter and lulled from her usual city senses as she went to cross the lane, she very nearly stepped straight into the path of a quad bike.

It jerked out of her way with an angry blast of the horn, and she caught the irate glare of the elderly woman driving it. A terrier was perched on her lap, a lurcher clinging on behind. A trailer was attached to the bike and Pippa did a double take, heart still fluttering, wondering if she really had just seen a sheep riding shotgun with a pair of alpacas.

Chapter Four

Outside the village shop, cunningly disguised as another white-painted cottage that Pippa missed the first time she walked past it, her phone rang. She pulled it from her bag, half hoping it might be her dad and she could vent some of her frustration. Of course it wasn't Jonny, and she swiped to answer the call anyway, anticipation replacing some of her anxiety.

'Hey, Cass.'

'Darling! You said off-grid, but I was about to send a search party. I've called three times and sent countless messages, I even tried Raf to see if he knew you were okay. What about Harriet, how is she? Are you both surviving? Is it hell? When are you coming home?'

Pippa laughed, her shoulders loosening some more at the sound of Cassie's familiar voice. They'd grown up on the same leafy street in north London and had notorious dads in common, their friendship thriving and adapting down the intervening years. Pippa had Jonny to contend with and Cassie's father was an ex-MP following a scandal some years ago. With her mother now firmly ensconced on the Amalfi Coast and living with a gorgeous Italian DJ half her age, Cassie understood perfectly what life was like for the offspring of infamous men.

'We're fine, really. I had planned to call you earlier but the signal's not great. I've just seen the missed calls.'

'Wi-Fi?'

'As expected. Non-existent.'

'And Harriet's still there?' Cassie's quick laugh was astonished.

'For now. And if your goddaughter asks or even begs you to rescue her, please don't.' Pippa moved aside to let an elderly man enter the shop, a bell jangling as the door opened. 'We really need this time together while I sort out the house.'

'I won't, I promise. Guide's honour.'

'We were never in the Girl Guides.' Pippa tried to imagine her bubbly and brilliant friend collecting badges and wearing the uniform, and couldn't.

'That's because there were no boys, darling.' Cassie's voice faded from Pippa's ear as she spoke to someone else. 'Sorry, back now.'

'Work?' Pippa knew how much her career meant, especially now.

'Of course.' Cassie sighed. 'Manic as ever. But I didn't call you to whine about that, I wanted to make sure you're not stranded in a bog or facing down some gloomy Mr Rochester type.'

Pippa laughed again and Gil flashed into her mind. For all his grumpiness, she wouldn't refer to him as gloomy. His eyes were too bright, too blue, for that. She resolved to mention nothing of him to Cassie, at least not yet. Her friend might be head of public relations for a small group of luxury and intimate London hotels and busy with her two children, the eldest of which was also Harriet's best friend, but even the whiff of a new and attractive man in Pippa's vicinity might have Cassie hitting the pause button on her own life and hurrying north to intervene.

'No, we're good,' Pippa said firmly. 'No bogs or women in the attic, at least not yet. It's actually very pretty. Not quite what I remembered Yorkshire looking like.'

'So have you crossed your dad off the naughty list then? All is forgiven?'

'Absolutely not.' Pippa wondered if Jonny had even read her message yet. 'He's not getting away with it that easily. I'll still be having words when I see him.'

'And when will that be? Christmas?'

'Probably.' Pippa pressed a hand to her temple. Hosting Christmas was something she'd taken upon herself years ago, and no matter where in the world her family was, they always came home, laden with presents and tales of far-off places. By New Year, her dad would be itching to escape back to work, and Raf and Tilly would be chafing too. Pippa would watch them all leave and gather up their own lives whilst she retreated back into hers.

'So, netball camp. Are you driving Harriet to Warwick on the Sunday?'

'I am. She wanted to get the train but it's not that far and heaven knows how many times she'd have to change.' Pippa still found it hard to get used to Harriet's newfound freedom since becoming a teenager and her ability to travel around London with her friends. London transport Pippa understood; the rest of the country not so much, and driving Harriet to netball camp had been a fight she'd refused to concede. 'But as it's three weeks away, we'll be travelling from home, not here.'

'Sure about being back in town by then?'

'I certainly hope so.' Pippa frowned. Three weeks in Hartfell sounded like an unimaginable eternity, and she wondered what people actually did here. 'It's ages off. Why?'

'I just thought that, seeing as we're heading to Galloway after camp, I could pick the girls up and we could have a night with you in Hartfell en route.'

'That does sound lovely.' Pippa was cheered by the thought of seeing Cassie. Their summers did sometimes overlap, usually when Harriet's dad Nick had let them down when he was meant to be having his daughter. That was the problem with falling in love with unpredictable people, Pippa reminded herself, shuddering at the thought. They tended to like doing things that were totally unplanned, or took themselves off to places where planning should be of the utmost importance.

'I really hope we'll be long gone by then, but just supposing we aren't, are you sure it wouldn't interfere with your plans?'

'Not in the least. Everyone comes and goes, my in-laws are the best. You know them, open house, they won't mind if we're a day or two late. Room for another if you fancy it when Harriet goes away with Nick.'

As a wildlife cameraman, Nick was constantly on the move and Pippa had attributed their break-up when Harriet was six to a case of opposites attracting and eventually failing to get along. She still loved him in a way, but she'd never been able to live life quite as casually as he did, and her inability to say no to her own family hadn't helped their relationship.

He'd want to take off at a moment's notice, while Pippa had planted her feet and stayed in London in case her family needed her. She still felt guilty every time she thought of it, for putting them and not her marriage first. They'd let each other down. And, as a father, Nick had never grasped why he couldn't take Harriet out of school for weeks on end. In that, Jonny had supported him, and

Pippa was sometimes at odds with both men, who lived as they chose whilst the women around them saw to it that life in all its ordinariness carried on.

Thankfully, Harriet loved London as much as Pippa did and Nick had eventually learned that his daughter no longer appreciated tents, paddling in streams, or being stranded in a hide on some windswept cliff. This summer, they were spending their time together on a Greek island and Harriet had already informed him she would book her own return ticket if he so much as looked at a pair of binoculars.

'Thank you, that's so kind but I'll be glad to get back to London and have some time on my own after this place.' Pippa realised that her casual dismissal of the village didn't match her current view. Two people on horseback were chatting as they rode towards her, and she smiled back when they caught her eye. The horses, one grey, one bay, looked gorgeous ambling past in the morning sun, and she nearly laughed at the name of the road painted on a sign. There was nothing main about this street; it was delightful.

'That bad, huh?' Cassie's voice brightened with her next words. 'So no hot blacksmiths hammering over anvils or hunky farmers tossing bales around, then?'

'It's been twelve hours, Cassie.' Pippa was picturing the mischievous expression on her friend's face without needing to see it. She knew precisely what Cassie would say if she happened to mention a hot vet instead. 'I've been asleep for most of them.'

'You're permanently asleep where men are concerned, Pippa. You're so gorgeous, you could have anyone you wanted.'

'Well if I can't have Dave, is there even any point?' Pippa and Cassie had adored the Foo Fighters since the earliest days of the band and Pippa had loved Dave Grohl forever. They'd met him once at a festival with her dad, and she'd been so overcome she'd burst into tears. Not remotely cool for a thirty-year-old and she preferred to nurture her love from afar these days. He'd scrawled a message on her Foo Fighters T-shirt that memorable day and she'd still never washed it in case his words wore out.

'How was Raf?' Pippa remembered Cassie saying she'd recently contacted her brother. 'I haven't seen him for a while, he cancelled our last lunch.'

'Actually we didn't speak, couldn't find the right moment in between everything else. He replied though, to say he thought you were fine and not to worry. Why?'

'Just wondered. I know he's back from Sweden and Freddie mentioned they were supposed to be going to a gig in Islington, and then Raf pulled out at the last minute.' Pippa bit her lip; her brother might be only a year younger than her, but she'd never stopped worrying about him. Raf had dealt with his grief over their mum differently and the occasions when he let Pippa in were rarer since he'd begun drumming with their dad's band ten years ago.

'Last time we spoke I got the impression that all is not well with Lina since he got back from Australia, and this is what he does when he's unhappy. Takes himself out of reach somewhere. Just like Dad.'

There was a pause and Pippa heard Cassie drag in a breath before she huffed out something not quite a laugh.

'I very nearly said I'd get Ewan to check in with him,' Cassie said quietly. 'It's what we always did, when Raf took off. Ewan could usually track him down. They were always close.'

'Cass, I'm so sorry, I didn't think…'

'Please don't worry. It's been eighteen months, Pippa. I'm getting used to it.' Cassie hesitated. 'It's just sometimes there are still days when I wake up, Ewan's not there and then I remember about the accident and it's like starting again, with the grief. I'm fine, we're fine. You're not to worry.'

'I can't help it,' Pippa said softly. Cassie's husband Ewan had been Raf's best friend; it was how he and Cassie had met back in the day, and they all kept an eye on Raf in their own way. 'I wish I didn't have to for your sake, that you're not all going through this.'

'I know. Thank you. It helps, having you there for us.' Losing Ewan in a cycling accident on his way to work had left his family distraught, and Cassie and Raf bereft.

'Is there anything I can do?'

'Just keep doing what you do. Being there, supporting us. It means everything. I love you for that and many other things.'

'Me too,' Pippa said softly. It was easy to get caught up in her own life and that of her family's, and Cassie deserved more of her time, especially after what she and her children had lost. 'I'm hoping the house won't take long to sort out, but if we are still here when the girls finish camp, then definitely come and stay. The girls would love it and we could have some time together before you go to Galloway.'

'That sounds perfect,' Cassie said wistfully. 'I'm sorry, I have to go. Urgent meeting about that effing chef who wants to hold a book launch at The Bennington. You know the one, charm personified in public. Another catch-up soon?'

'Definitely. I ought to head off anyway. I'm hungry and Harriet's hangry, which is even worse. I'm outside the village shop in search of breakfast.'

'I love a village shop,' Cassie replied, and Pippa knew she was determined to focus on now and not before; it was how her friend coped with the new life that had been forced upon her. 'All those freshly baked carbs and cakes. Can't beat it, it's how I always know I'm on holiday. Ambling down first thing and coming back with all the goodies I never eat at home. Lunch on me when I see you, then?'

'Perfect, thank you. Loads of love and big hugs to Isla and Rory.' They said goodbye and Pippa put her phone away, looking forward to hopefully seeing Cassie properly when the girls' netball camp was over.

Inside the shop, Pippa only needed a few moments to realise it far exceeded the few expectations she'd had. Crammed into what must once have been the front room of the cottage, every single shelf was laden. One wall was completely given over to groceries, another to books, greeting cards and maps, a huge fridge between them. Old fashioned jars of sweets lined the shelves behind the till, a set of scales and a pile of paper bags beneath them. One corner held practicalities like batteries, bicycle pumps, bulbs and even some basic tools, from hammers to screw-drivers.

Her gaze caught on the noticeboard, and she read that a wine tasting evening was coming up at the pub. She scanned details of the village hall and saw classes for Pilates and yoga, an adult and toddler group, creative writing and a Women's Institute meet-up. Hartfell's country show was taking place soon and much was expected of the day, judging by the entertainments outlined on the poster. All this and the unmistakable aroma of baking too, and her mouth watered as she helped herself to a fresh sourdough loaf. She took a quick picture of it to share with Cassie when she could, smiling wryly at the reminder of carbs.

A woman behind the counter was chatting with the elderly man who'd entered earlier, and they offered cheery greetings. Pippa smiled back as she picked up a basket and began to fill it, trying not to listen to their continued conversation. The chap gathered up his shopping and with a final nod at Pippa, who took his place at the counter, disappeared, the bell tinkling merrily behind him.

'Good morning, you must be Pippa. I'm Daphne. How do you do?'

'I am, yes.' Pippa dredged up a smile for Daphne, impressed by the speed at which news of her arrival had already spread, and began unloading her shopping; wholemeal pasta, granola, milk from a local dairy, actual butter, and homemade marmalade alongside the sourdough, two tubs of freshly made soup from the fridge and some vegetables. A trip to town for more provisions was still on the cards but this was a good start. 'Lovely to meet you.'

Daphne was immaculate and attractive, with short grey hair tucked behind her ears, a pair of red-and-black glasses framing wise hazel eyes, an apron over a cream blouse navy and neat. 'Welcome to Hartfell. How are you settling in?'

'Oh, well, I'm not sure we have yet, but thank you.' Thoughts of Gil darted through Pippa's mind, and she pushed away the reminder of his antagonism. From what she'd seen so far, she fully expected that Hartfell was the sort of village where everyone knew everyone, what was going on and who had fallen out with whom. She hadn't got off to the best start, at least where Gil and her own daughter were concerned, and didn't want that getting around. 'The house is a little basic but that's all part of the fun, right?'

Daphne nodded doubtfully. 'And how long are you planning to stay?'

'I'm not sure. A week, maybe two.' Pippa wasn't here to make friends, simply to get the house on the market and be on her way. She was used to strangers attempting to draw her into conversation. It had often been like that, growing up. Children who'd wanted to be friends because she had a rock-star dad; single women who'd taken a shine to them and had a long-range eye on Jonny as well. She'd learned long ago to be careful with whom she shared her confidences.

'You must be tired after that long drive, we heard you live in London.' Daphne's look was kind. 'We were only saying how lovely it is having the house occupied again after standing empty.'

'Empty?' Pippa's hand stilled over the basket, a carton of soup hovering. 'But I thought Gil lived in it?'

'Oh, he does now. He moved back in February but he hadn't lived in the village for years. We'd see him sometimes, between the practice and visits to see his gran at the farm before she passed.'

Pippa smiled, hoping to learn more about Gil Haworth and precisely why he was now living in her dad's house. 'I'm sorry, I didn't think to bring any bags. Could I have one, please.'

'Of course.' Daphne bent down and produced a cotton tote bag in green, emblazoned with a cream alpaca logo. 'Could I persuade you to buy one of these? We sell them to raise funds for the local animal sanctuary.'

'Absolutely. Better make it two, please.' Pippa began loading her shopping. 'You were saying? About the house and Gil being back in it?'

'Oh yes. Well, sadly he's on his own now his boys are grown up. It's a big house for just the one but then it was only him and his gran all those years. It must seem so different without her, but of course he never lets it show.'

'Mmm.' Pippa removed a purse from her handbag, looking up to see a second woman approaching along a corridor behind Daphne. That they were related was obvious; both had the same hazel eyes and round faces, although this woman looked older and her voice when she spoke was tremulous.

'Daphne, can you switch on the oven for me please?' She looked at Pippa curiously, her own navy apron dusted with flour. 'I can't quite remember what the temperature should be for the scones. You know, don't you?'

'I do.' Daphne nodded and Pippa saw the quick sadness in her face. 'Pippa, this is my sister Violet, who does all the baking. I'm sorry, she's not familiar with the card machine so she won't be able to help you. Would you excuse me for a moment please, I won't be long.'

'Of course.' Pippa closed her purse.

Daphne disappeared along the corridor and Pippa helped herself to a couple of postcards, surprised to see that Violet was watching intently, and she held them up.

'They're lovely, aren't they, the village looks so pretty. Do you make the bread as well? It smells amazing, I can't wait to try it.'

'I do. I hope you like it. It's an old recipe I've been using for years. I have to look it up now.' Violet tilted her head and the seconds eased by, making Pippa fidget under the scrutiny. 'I've got it now. I knew I'd seen you before.'

'Oh, probably,' Pippa replied casually, doubting it. Violet didn't seem like the kind of person who'd listened to a rock band in her life, never mind read a tabloid or scrolled social media for gossip. 'And I'm sure I'll love the bread.'

'You have a look of her.'

Pippa's laugh was startled, and she wondered if she'd misheard. Violet couldn't possibly be referring to Harriet, who was still presumably barricaded in her bedroom. 'Do you mean my dad? Jonny?'

Violet shook her head, a frown creasing her brow. 'Ivy. I remember she had hazel eyes, just like yours. Her hair was dark though and she always wore it up.'

'Sorry about that, Pippa.' Daphne emerged from the corridor and gently touched Violet's arm. 'All done, love. The scones are in the oven, and I've set the timer. Do you want to make us a cup of tea?'

'I'll do that. Thank you, Daphne.' Violet gave Pippa a final look before she turned and disappeared from view.

'I'm sorry for keeping you waiting.' Daphne pushed a card machine across the counter. Pippa was fumbling for her purse again, her thoughts still with Violet and what she'd said. 'Violet gets confused quite easily these days and I've learned it's better to help with tasks there and then if I can. Saves her fretting.'

'I understand. Have you been running the shop a long time?' Pippa hoped a more ordinary conversation would be easier to deal with than the disease afflicting Daphne's sister's mind.

'Violet's lived here all her life, she never married.' Daphne tore off the receipt from the card machine and handed it to Pippa. 'The shop was our parents' and she's never really left the village, except for the occasional holiday and of course hospital appointments now. I lived in Harrogate until my husband left three years ago.' Daphne's lips pursed together and her hand on the counter trembled. 'Afterwards I came to stay with Violet, and that's when I realised she wasn't quite as well as I thought. She's eight years older than me and it seemed sensible to make the move back here. We both like the company and I can keep an eye on her.'

'I'm sorry,' Pippa said quietly, wanting to offer more, but Daphne waved her concern away.

'That's very kind. You get used to it, of course. Now, can I tempt you into a banana loaf as a welcome gift? Even though I say it myself, Violet's really are the best. Perfect with a generous dollop of butter.'

'How can I resist,' Pippa murmured, tucking the proffered loaf wrapped in greaseproof paper into her bag along with everything else. Carbs and cakes, indeed. She picked up the bags, ready to eat and certain Harriet would be equally hungry.

'Thank you. Daphne, when we were chatting before, Violet mentioned someone called Ivy. Do you know who that is? She said I had a look of her.'

'I'm sorry, I'm afraid I don't.' Daphne turned a shoulder to the corridor. 'I can ask her, if you like. Her memories are like that, sometimes they all get muddled together and then she remembers other things as though they happened only yesterday.'

'No, don't disturb her, it was probably nothing.'

'Do you think he might visit, your dad?' Daphne's voice lowered as she leaned over the counter. 'It would be lovely to see him again, it's been such a long time.'

'I doubt it, I'm sorry. He's on holiday and then he's touring again in Australia. I don't expect to see him for months.' Or dust, Pippa thought grimly, given the situation he'd got her into. When she returned to London, she was going to practise saying no to the family every single day, and mean it. One of the messages she'd scanned earlier was from her sister Tilly, who ran a B&B on a Greek island and wanted to know whether Pippa thought Vanessa would manage her PR, and would Pippa mind finding out.

'Of course, Jonny was a few years younger than me, but I remember him and Bryan running wild. All the girls were in love with them, and they were always getting into scrapes. Then when he brought your mum here, he only had eyes for her.'

'Bryan?' Another name Pippa didn't recognise, and her thoughts caught on Jonny; of him as a boy and growing up in Hartfell. How strange it was, to be meeting those who'd known him back then, before he became a rock star and everyone had heard of him. People here had memories of Jonny, and maybe even her mum, that she didn't. Their life together had begun in this place and suddenly Pippa felt ambushed by the past coming at her without warning, dragging long-buried thoughts of family to the surface.

'Bryan Haworth, Gil's dad. The boys were best friends all their lives, until Bryan died, anyway. Far too young, it was such a tragedy. I don't think his gran ever got over it.'

Chapter Five

Back at Home Farm, Pippa was relieved that Gil's Land Rover hadn't returned so she wouldn't have to face him again just yet. After the conversation with Daphne and Violet in the shop, she was wondering about doing a little research on the house and her family's history here. It might help her understand more of her own story and where it fitted in this place. And then there was Gil. Who was his gran and where had he been until now? And even more importantly, why was he back?

Pippa found antibacterial spray under the kitchen sink and wiped down the worktops and cupboards before unloading her bags. She ought to learn more about the vet practice on the property too, and for that she needed to speak with Elaine. She realised, as she put the shopping away, that she'd forgotten to buy coffee. She'd have to and soon; she couldn't be without it, and she was not going to be beholden to Gil for anything.

But first, Harriet needed breakfast. She filled a bowl with granola and made toast with marmalade, carrying it upstairs. At home she'd usually text Harriet when meals were ready, but her daughter might ignore it in her current mood. And however angry she was with Pippa right now, food could only improve things.

'Harriet?' Pippa knocked gently on her bedroom door. 'I've brought you some breakfast.'

A few seconds stretched by before she heard a muffled 'Come in.' Opening the door awkwardly with one hand, she pushed it aside to enter, just in time to see Harriet swipe at her face.

'Are you all right?' Pippa put the tray down beside the bed. Her question probably hadn't been the right one. Too direct, because Harriet nodded fiercely as she lunged at the toast. This room was chilly, and Pippa tried not to feel oppressed by the gloom. It was no more attractive than her own, but the furniture was at least a nice set of antique oak.

'When did I ever eat granola, Mum?' She scowled and Pippa took in a slow, silent breath as she perched on the end of the bed, ignoring the sting in her heart at such a greeting.

'On occasions, in an emergency.' She pasted on a smile, working hard at her patience. 'And I thought this might qualify as one, given the state of the house and barely any food in it.'

'Gil's right,' Harriet said resentfully. One slice of toast was half gone, and her stare was accusing. 'You should have told me about the Wi-Fi.'

'But then you wouldn't have come. And I didn't know for sure until we got here.'

'I might,' Harriet replied eventually, and Pippa felt a glimmer of hope. Maybe there was still time to salvage something of their adventure. 'But I want to go home. I've got loads of homework to do and I can't FaceTime Isla or message anyone online.'

'You can't stay at home on your own, Harriet, not yet,' Pippa replied carefully, preparing herself for a fight as the hope faded. 'And your dad's away again, he'll only be back in time for your holiday at the end of the summer.'

'So? Brooke will be there. She can keep an eye on me. It's not like I need looking after anymore. Plus, Isla's around until netball camp and then we'll be together anyway.'

Pippa's quiet optimism was swiftly replaced by alarm. She needed to knock that notion on the head right now.

'I'm sorry but that's not a feasible option.' Nick's current girlfriend, Brooke, was a thirty-three-year-old model who occasionally had to be reminded of Harriet's own name. Nurturing she was not and right now Pippa felt her daughter needed loving care more than she needed Wi-Fi, whatever Harriet thought. 'You know Brooke is at home even less than your dad. Besides, I might have a plan about the Wi-Fi. I'm going to have a chat with Elaine, who's the receptionist at the vets.' Pippa hoped Harriet was feigning her disinterest as she picked up the second piece of toast. 'Maybe she can find you a quiet corner where you can hang out, do your homework and keep in touch with Isla and everyone else.'

'Mmm.'

'Mmm good or mmm bad?'

'What if Gil says no?' Harriet took a bite and swallowed it. 'It's his decision, he's the boss. And you haven't exactly made a good impression.'

Pippa didn't enjoy knowing that Harriet must have overheard more of the row with Gil in the kitchen than she'd realised. 'Well, neither has he,' she replied briskly. 'So let's just see what Elaine says and take it from there.'

Harriet did have a point though, and Pippa really hoped her own standing with Gil wouldn't count against her when it came to getting Harriet access to the Wi-Fi. He had children of his own, surely he wouldn't deny her to spite Pippa.

'So how did you sleep? I didn't get a chance to ask you earlier.'

'When you were arguing with Gil, you mean.' Harriet ceased twisting bedclothes between her fingers and leaned across to slide her empty plate onto the bedside table. 'Who is he, Mum? Grandad never said a word about a lodger.'

So Jonny and Harriet *had* discussed Hartfell, which was more than he'd done with Pippa. 'I really don't know. I had no idea there was someone else in the house either, but he's moving out later.' When he had time in between all the life-saving heroics, presumably. 'At least not having a tenant in the house will make a sale easier.'

'Where will he go?'

'I don't know that either and it's none of our business anyway. What do you think of your room?' Pippa decided a swift change of subject away from Gil was opportune.

'S'all right.' Harriet's gaze skimmed over the bedroom. 'And before you ask again, I slept fine. What about you?'

'Me?' It took Pippa a moment to reply; she couldn't remember the last time Harriet had enquired after her well-being, unless it was related to a temporary inability to cook or drive. 'Not bad thanks, once I dropped off. Not keen on the mattress though. Yours doesn't feel much better.'

'It's not going to matter, is it, seeing as we'll be gone in a week.' Harriet had a way of looking at her sometimes, as though she could read Pippa's mind like a map, and now it was her fingers winding the bedclothes under the scrutiny.

Even mentioning Gil brought back the memory of him introducing himself in bed this morning, those scowling and sardonic blue eyes, the glorious bare chest and untidy blond hair. Pippa really hoped she didn't look flushed again; Harriet would definitely not approve of such thoughts.

It probably was a good thing he wasn't very amenable to Pippa. It was so long since she'd been on a date, much less had a relationship, that she might've been tempted to shove Lola out of the way and join him in bed if he'd shown any encouragement. She offered Harriet a hasty and over-bright smile to disguise her wild imaginings. 'So, have you any plans for today?'

'Dunno.' Harriet picked up her phone and stared pointedly at it. 'What is there to do here?'

'I'm afraid you've got me there.' Pippa's laugh was light, thankful she hadn't said 'nothing' out loud. 'But that's the fun of our adventure, isn't it? That we can explore Hartfell together.'

'Make up your mind, Mum. Are you having an adventure or leaving as soon as possible?'

'Can't we do both? A bit of adventuring together and be home in a week? And, in the unlikely event that we are still here after netball camp...' Pippa hadn't been planning to play her trump card yet, but needs must. 'Cassie will pick you and Isla up, and they'll stay with us for a couple of days en route to Isla's grandparents.'

'Really?' Harriet's face lit up and Pippa felt a rush of joy at making her happy again. 'That'd be brilliant, Mum.'

'You do know, don't you, that if there's something wrong you can tell me.' Pippa wasn't expecting the wobble in her voice and had to gulp back the worry. She hadn't intended to bring this up either but the chance to press home her advantage was irresistible. 'Anything, whatever it is, I promise I'll help and support you. I'm on your side, Harriet, always.'

'Why would there be something wrong?'

Even if Harriet's words were meant to appease, her flattened tone was enough to set Pippa's alarm bells ringing.

'I just wondered, that's all,' Pippa replied casually. 'We haven't had much time together recently.'

'I'm fine.' Harriet shot her a look as she slid earbuds in, and Pippa knew the conversation was over. 'Let me know about the Wi-Fi, yeah?'

Pippa nodded as she got up, squeezing Harriet's free hand anyway, trying to impart her love and concern without saying the unwelcome words out loud. She'd just have to keep trying and she'd message Cassie too, see if Isla had let anything about Harriet slip.

She needed another coffee after trying and failing to get Harriet to open up, and right now she couldn't care less whose it was. She made a mug of instant to drink with her own toast and wolfed both down, her stomach growling gratefully. Then she picked up her phone to go on Amazon and order a basic coffee machine, until she remembered the lack of Wi-Fi, and clunked her phone back down again. Now she understood more of how Harriet felt, and it wasn't nice.

If they'd been in London, they'd have plans for the weekend. Probably separate ones, but plans nonetheless. For Pippa it would likely be a gallery, one she hadn't yet discovered or visited for a while. She was often invited to openings, and she loved meeting others who understood her passion, however relieved she felt not to be the artist having their work on display. Harriet would be playing netball or off somewhere with Isla, catching a movie, hanging out in town or at friends' houses. She and Pippa both adored musical theatre and down the years they'd seen everything.

Pippa's gaze was drawn back to the view from the kitchen window, certainly a much prettier one than hers at home, which looked out onto the courtyard garden with tall buildings on every side. She collected her plate and mug and washed them up, defiantly leaving Gil's dirty mug for him to deal with, even though her fingers itched to wash it. She opened the back door, ready to explore.

The terrace stretched across the back of the house, a cloudless blue sky uncluttered by buildings, cranes and planes helping to lift her mood. She followed a rough stone path through the garden, listening to the unfamiliar sound of sheep bleating somewhere beyond it. Hand brushing her thigh, she trailed her fingers through the long grass as she strolled, ancient trees around the edge of the garden tall and lush with vivid green leaves. Birdsong and buzzing insects were gentle in the warm air and when her eyes landed on a clump of bright blue cornflowers, her mind leapt ahead to painting it, capturing those fragile petals in shades of violet, blue and lavender.

The untamed garden seemed part of the wild landscape rising to a heather-topped fell beyond a spiky hawthorn hedge. At the end she leaned on a gate leading to a field, smiling at merry white lambs plump from summer grass, bounding in the sun as their mothers dozed, shorn of their thick woollen coats and strangely thin beside their babies. She turned away and followed the path back towards the house, swinging left when she reached the terrace. She opened another gate onto the farmyard, deciding that now might be the right moment to take Elaine up on her earlier invitation for coffee.

The yard wasn't quite as unkempt and unloved as the house, with three stone buildings forming a courtyard with two more open-sided barns behind. One building was almost empty when Pippa stuck her head inside, wooden beams soaring to the exposed roof timbers. A channel leading to a drain ran along the floor and the barn was divided by concrete panels into stalls. Pipework and metal drinking troughs were rusting, in places hanging loose. Years of muck had left yellowed stains on the walls, and dust and spiders' webs were thick in every window.

She opened a door onto the far end of the barn, finding a huge workshop crammed with tools, old furniture, slates propped against a wall, rolled up lengths of carpet, a rough mangle and even a tatty upright piano. She doubted new owners would fancy keeping any of that tat and a massive skip was another thing she needed to sort.

Outside, double doors led into the second barn, half of the roof hidden by a loft full of sweet-smelling bales that she presumed were hay. This building had been split into four stables divided by wooden partitions, and a glance over the first door was enough to reveal evidence of occupation. A haynet was suspended from a ring in the wall, and a bucket of clean water and neat bedding made from what looked like wood shavings covered the concrete floor.

She pulled a face, guessing this stable belonged to the chunky little pony in the paddock along the drive, but what about the rest? Were there more residents she hadn't yet discovered? She sincerely hoped not. A fifth stable was a makeshift storeroom, with metal bins for feed and more buckets and ropes hanging neatly from hooks on the wall.

Was all this what her dad had meant when he'd said the house needed sorting out? Was she expected to evict an array of four-legged sitting tenants along with the irascible human one? She wished she'd paid more attention to the email from her dad's solicitor. After looking in at the vets, she'd go back to the house, risk having a shower in that bathroom and see if she could persuade Harriet to join her in doing something nice. What that might be, Pippa had no idea.

A discreet sign on the wall of the final building was white with blue lettering and read *Haworth & Fuller Veterinary Practice*. Right. So Gil's name was on the door, as it were, and she suspected it made things a whole lot more complicated. She pushed it open and stepped into a practical and neat waiting room, white again with pale green lino on the floor. Half a dozen chairs were set against two walls, a mop and bucket leaning nearby. Animal and pet products were stacked on shelves and in cabinets on the third wall, collars and leads hanging from hooks a bright splash against the white.

Two doors, plus another with a WC for clients, led off the room. A portly middle-aged man in a shabby blue jacket with a cat carrier perched on his knee was waiting, and he gave Pippa a curious look as she hovered uncertainly. At the far end Elaine was sitting behind a reception counter, more rows of shelving offering a selection of medication above her head.

'Pippa, hi, you found us.' She stood up with a bright smile. Her olive green gilet and striped shirt were practical and stylish above jeans, and auburn hair was drawn back from her face, revealing excellent cheekbones and lip gloss. 'Would you like that coffee now?'

'I'd love one, thanks.' Pippa thought of Elaine discovering her and Gil in the middle of a slanging match only a couple of hours ago as she approached the counter, wondering uncomfortably how much of it Elaine had heard. She was usually so careful with first impressions, especially if people were likely to know to whom she was related. She'd had her share of social media misfortunes and was wary of more. 'If you're sure you have time?'

'Absolutely I do. Why don't you sit here, then we don't have to try and talk over the counter.' Elaine pointed to a second chair beside hers and Pippa sidled around to join her. Elaine went to a kitchen next to reception, a kettle, microwave and fridge on a worktop opposite a table and four chairs. She pressed a button on a compact coffee machine, waking it up.

'Morning consultations are almost over anyway; we've only got one more patient to see.' She glanced towards the chap and his cat, which was mewling quietly. 'Then Gil's on call for the rest of the weekend, but hopefully it'll be a quiet one.'

'You mentioned something about a locum earlier. How many vets do you have here?'

'Nine in total, plus the nursing team and admin staff, but that's across the two branches.' Elaine raised an empty mug, covered in sheep. 'How do you like your coffee?'

'Espresso would be perfect, thanks.' Pippa had noticed a box of capsules next to the machine. 'I could do with the caffeine.'

'I imagine you could,' Elaine said sympathetically, removing a capsule from the box. 'I'm sorry that you and Gil haven't got off to the best start.'

'That's one way of putting it.' Pippa wished she could laugh but humour simply wouldn't come. 'I hadn't even heard of him before I—'

She'd been about to blurt out 'barged into his bedroom' and abruptly changed her mind. She already liked Elaine and didn't imagine her gossiping about her boss, but she couldn't vouch for the chap still casting sidelong glances Pippa's way. One of the doors opened and a middle-aged woman in dark jeans and a navy polo shirt appeared. She smiled at the chap as she called a name and he ambled into the consulting room, clutching the carrier and still-mewling cat, and the door closed.

'That was Wendy, our locum.' Elaine passed Pippa the mug, which she accepted with thanks. 'She's covering for someone who's off sick. Gil would like to hang on to her as she's got plenty of farm experience, but of course he can't offer a full-time job right now, not with things the way they are.'

'I see.' Pippa didn't, not really. She noticed two black-and-white photographs pinned to the only wall without shelves; two men in each, standing beside a cow and a calf in one and amongst a flock of sheep in the second.

'Biscuit, Pippa? We keep some for clients, along with the tissues. I promise they're not dog treats.'

'Yes please.' Pippa wouldn't normally resort to sugar before lunch but today was not turning out well, and she was half tempted to ask for a tissue as well. She wasn't generally given to weeping either, but her dad and his scheming might reduce her to tears soon. She thanked Elaine again, this time for the tin of wrapped chocolate biscuits she was offering. Pippa took one, along with a deep breath.

'So how are things, at the practice? I hope you don't mind me asking but my dad didn't give me much inform-ation before we arrived here.'

'Of course not, I should think you need to know what you're dealing with.' Elaine settled back in the chair with her own coffee. 'The practice was originally set up by Mr Fuller and Eddie Haworth, who farmed here when it was still part of the old estate. Gil's grandad,' she clarified, raising a hand to the photographs. 'That's him there, on the left in both pictures.'

Pippa was searching for a family resemblance to Gil in the stern-faced man staring back. But the images were too old, too faded, to distinguish anything other than perhaps a similarity in height and build.

'When Mr Fuller died,' Elaine continued, 'another partner joined and eventually as modern medicine, treatment and surgery improved, the practice merged with a larger one in town. They kept this branch open, mostly for the local farmers, although we do have regular consultations for clients with companion animals who prefer not to go into town. But of course we can't offer everything here. The building is outdated, and our kennels and X-ray facilities desperately need an upgrade, as well as the operating theatre and the lab. We have two consulting rooms, a treatment room and dispense drugs, but if it's anything more serious then clients have to go into town. Occasionally vets on call will see patients out of hours here but it depends on the type of emergency they present.'

'I see.' Pippa was savouring a final mouthful of espresso after the two mugs of average coffee earlier. Gil had been right about that at least; she didn't enjoy instant. 'So when the house is sold, this branch will close, and all the clients will have to go into town.'

'Sold?' Elaine's manicured eyebrows jumped upwards. 'So that's Jonny's plan, is it? Gil suspected as much, he thought Jonny had sent you to do his dirty work for him and persuade him to quit.'

'Er, well, it's not decided yet,' Pippa said hastily, trying to backtrack. 'There's a lot to think about before any decisions are made. Obviously, having a tenant in situ complicates things a bit, and then there's the vets.'

She had been the one to translate her dad's instruction of 'sort' into 'sell'. But what else was there to do with Home Farm but sell it, and put Hartfell behind them once and for all? This place was nothing to do with Pippa and her life in London, even if Violet from the shop did think she resembled someone local.

'So I take it you don't know the practice is up for sale and that Gil wants to split it, take on the farm work and expand here, then?' Elaine's eye contact was unwavering. 'Or about the time limit Jonny gave him to raise the money?'

'I'm afraid I don't.' Pippa made a conscious effort to relax her jaw, wondering if steam escaping from ears was an actual thing. If it was, hers would be hissing by now as she began to realise the full extent of what Jonny had landed her in the middle of. 'Could you please enlighten me, Elaine?'

Chapter Six

'Gil's had plans drawn up to convert the other barns into treatment rooms and a lab, plus new facilities for X-rays, scans and surgery. His dream is expanding with a full staff and a dedicated farm building for overnight monitoring and more intensive care. Of course, his family history with the practice goes back a long way. He's desperate not to see it swallowed up by a chain and lose the long-standing relationships and goodwill with farm clients who rely on us.' Elaine glanced at the monitor and touched the keyboard, sending it to sleep again.

'Farm practice is his beating heart and there are less independent rural ones left now. It's hard to find vets who are prepared to put up with the work–life imbalance, being called out at all hours to a difficult calving or lambing in an isolated barn in the middle of winter, when the wind and the cold could knock you right off your feet.' Elaine raised a shoulder. 'Factor in a place like Hartfell, for all that it's pretty and there's lots going on… Well. It's not for everyone. It won't be easy for him, whatever happens. I'm sure you get the picture, Pippa.'

Pippa did, all too clearly, and she nodded slowly as Elaine continued.

'There's a new vets opened up in town, part of another group, and they've got their eye on us and consolidating both businesses. Of course they've already taken some of our clients, there's only so many to go around. But by anyone's standards, expanding here and investing in the kind of technology it would need is a huge financial risk. There's no guarantee of more patients even if Gil can pull it off. It's a wonderful way of life, farming, but it's very hard and it needs more young people.'

Elaine took a sip of her coffee and put the mug down. The door to the consulting room opened and the man appeared with his cat carrier, looking more cheerful as he headed towards them.

'Elaine, do you have any idea why my dad sent me up here now?' Pippa lowered her voice lest the client overhear, desperate for the reply.

'I think I do, yes. Your dad gave Gil six months to come up with the finance to buy him out and there's only a few weeks left before the deadline expires. Gil's trying hard to raise the money but we're all aware he's running out of time.'

'And when the six months is up?' Pippa felt the beginnings of a headache. No wonder Gil disliked her so much and assumed she'd been sent here to sell the place from under him, believing her as devious as her dad. A glimmer of sympathy followed before she reminded herself that none of this was her fault.

'We just don't know, it's all up in the air.' Elaine stood to deal with the client, brightening the monitor into life. 'And no matter what Gil says, Pippa, I'm very glad you're here. He's just as stubborn as your dad, and I'm hoping you can get the pair of them to see sense and work something out.'

Time seemed to slow as the chap paid for his cat's treatment, a course of antibiotics and a follow-up consultation was booked for the following Saturday. Elaine sorted him out with quiet and friendly efficiency, and then he was gone, the cat still mewling as the door closed behind him. Wendy emerged from the consulting room and said her goodbyes too, disappearing out into the yard.

'So has Gil always worked here, then?' Pippa asked casually.

'Yes, for his entire career. He's a Yorkshireman through and through.' Elaine collected their empty mugs and took them through to the kitchen, washing them in the sink. Pippa followed and found a tea towel to help. 'Thanks, Pippa. He was born here, but moved to Dorset when his mum wanted to go home. His dad left the farm and went down with them.'

Pippa's mind was running over the brief conversation with Daphne in the shop earlier, the mention of Jonny and Gil's dad Bryan being best friends. A growing sense of unease niggled, that whatever Elaine said next might very well impact the future of Home Farm and the practice.

'It was so dreadful, what happened to Gil's mum and dad.' Elaine sighed as the water in the sink burbled away. 'I'm afraid he lost them when he was seven, they drowned in a sailing accident. Afterwards, he moved back here to live with Ruth and Eddie, his grandparents. His mother's family wasn't in a position to look after him and they weren't keen on his dad anyway.'

'Drowned?' The word was a whisper and Pippa felt the adrenaline rush of shock and sympathy. Despite her own loss, she couldn't equate her secure and comfortable life to Gil losing both parents at such an early age. She was twisting the tea towel between her fingers, trying to force down all the questions she longed to ask and that weren't her business.

'I'm afraid so.' Elaine's nod was resigned. 'There was no question that Ruth and Eddie would take him. Bryan was her only child and she never really got over the loss. I think she and Gil saved each other, in a way. She had a young boy who desperately needed a secure and loving home, and he gave her a reason to go on after Bryan and then Eddie.

'They were very close, adored one another. Hard to imagine, isn't it, what life must have been like for him then. The estate let Ruth keep the lease after Eddie died so she and Gil could farm it together, and she lived here for the rest of her life. Then when she passed last year, the farm went up for sale and unbeknownst to Gil, who was trying to find a way to keep it, someone else stepped in and bought it. We found out later it was your dad.'

Pippa was almost sorry she'd asked now. Emotions were leaping through her mind and she was trying to cling on to them, to process them before another one barged in. Frustration with her dad, worry for how she was going to proceed here, and sympathy; another rush of it for Gil and the tragic childhood forced upon him. She knew so well what devastating loss felt like.

'Your dad and Bryan were a bit older than me, but I remember them well.' Elaine smiled. 'Your mum, too, when she came here with your dad. She was beautiful and Jonny adored her. I'm sorry you lost her so young.'

'Thank you.' Pippa's smile was a reflective one as she put the tea towel back, wondering what else she might learn from strangers who seemed to know as much, if not more, about her own family history than she did.

Her dad used to talk about the first house he and her mum had bought from the proceeds of playing clubs to top up the earnings he made in the furniture factory. He liked to remind his children that he'd saved every penny he could to buy that house and he was glad that they didn't have to scrimp and save liked he'd done to get a good start in life.

There was so much Pippa didn't know and she'd learned not to push him about life before her mum had died. His eyes would fill with tears, and he'd swiftly change the subject. Somewhere deep down she'd realised that didn't help her, Raf or Tilly, but as a teenager stumbling through the new life thrust upon them, she hadn't known what else to do. He'd loved their mum and Pippa had clung to that as a comfort to them all.

And now here she was, in this tiny Dales village she'd barely ever heard Jonny speak of. It wasn't difficult to imagine him and Gil clashing over the future of the farm, metaphorically banging heads and making no progress. Her dad was pretty easy-going, but when he refused to back down, he rarely gave way. Another flare of frustration with him followed; no wonder he hadn't wanted to sort out Home Farm himself and instead had launched her into his fight.

What she couldn't understand was why he'd bought the farm in the first place, especially when he'd barely ever mentioned it to the family and seemed intent on moving Gil out. And why sell it again now, when Gil so desperately wanted to keep it? Although Jonny hadn't actually said it was to be *sold*. He'd asked her to sort it out, and right now she felt as though she'd uncovered something that could turn out to be a complete nightmare.

'Thank you for sharing that, about my mum,' she said quietly, trying to gather her senses and not let them overwhelm her. 'That's so sad, about Gil's family.'

'It is, not that you'd ever hear him complaining or letting you think he'd been hard done by.' Elaine sighed as she put the two mugs into a cupboard. 'Even I'm not really meant to be here. I'm retired, I only came back part-time to help him out. I lost my husband a year ago, to motor neurone disease, and we'd always planned to travel. I'd still like to, but I can't leave Gil, not until I know everything's settled. It's the least I can do for him.'

'I'm so sorry for your loss,' Pippa whispered, a wave of nausea churning in her stomach. That had been the disease which had taken her mum too; she might need that tissue after all.

'Thank you, Pippa, that's very kind.' Elaine sniffed, offering a bright smile. 'However much you think you're prepared for it and you don't want to see them suffer anymore, nothing's quite like the reality of being left on your own. Learning to get used to the silence, cooking for one, trying not to mourn the things you thought you'd do together.' Her hand was gentle, brief, on Pippa's arm. 'Gil's desperate for more time to raise the money. He approached your dad to ask for another three months and Jonny said no, that he was sending someone to sort everything out.'

'I see.' Pippa flushed, she'd better keep her search for an estate agent quiet for now, it really wouldn't do to let that get about. 'Elaine, could I ask a favour please?' She didn't dare ask Gil, not after what she'd just learned, and hoped his receptionist would be amenable to her plight. 'I'm assuming you have Wi-Fi here and I wondered if you'd mind my daughter Harriet popping in to use it, please? She's missing her friends without it and of course she has some homework to do.'

'Absolutely, she's very welcome.' Elaine pointed to a door off the kitchen. 'We have an office through there and I'm in the surgery four mornings a week. We've got high-speed fibre broadband in the village now and it's made such a difference, especially for families and opportunities to work from home. We need young people here, to keep the school open and the community evolving. I suppose you have a key so you can come and go, and we do have very strict drug protocols in place.'

'Actually I don't, I just have keys to the house. It's probably better if we don't have a key to the surgery. I'm sure Harriet will be very grateful, as am I, and of course she'll only be here under supervision.'

Pippa didn't quite cross her fingers about Harriet being grateful, but the thought was there. Monday was a very long time away from Saturday in a teenager's world, especially where Wi-Fi was concerned. But some Wi-Fi was a significant improvement on none.

'Thanks, Elaine, I really appreciate it. And for letting me know about the history here.'

'You're welcome.' Elaine stepped past Pippa to return to her seat in reception. 'I hope it's helped, given you a picture of the place, as it were.'

'Absolutely.' Pippa's mind was still spinning after all she'd learned. She flashed Elaine a smile as the older woman shut down the computer and tidied her desk. Her attention jumped to the main entrance as the door opened and a woman she swiftly recognised as the one driving the quad bike earlier strode towards them.

In complete mockery of the sunshine outside, she was wearing a full length waxed green coat so creased that Pippa almost expected it to creak. Unfastened, it revealed what appeared to be a quilted gilet underneath, gathered at her waist with orange twine. The coat hung stiffly around dark trousers that might once have been the bottom half of a man's suit, tucked into green wellies. Without the hat, a lined and suntanned face was revealed, intelligent and bright blue eyes sharp beneath grey hair spilling from a loose bun perched on the top of her head. Tall, upright and lean, she shot Pippa a look that made it clear what she thought of people who were foolish enough to step into her path.

'Gil back yet?' she bellowed at Elaine, and Pippa wondered quite how far away she thought the receptionist was; that voice could have woken Harriet in the house. 'No sign of the Landy.'

'Not yet, he shouldn't be too long. He had a heifer to see and then he was going to check on a ewe before examining a lame horse at the Edwards' place.'

'Righto.' The woman halted and planted a hand on the counter, making Pippa quite glad there was something solid between them. Beautifully spoken, she wouldn't have sounded out of place as a 1940s television announcer. 'Tell him I've injected that nanny again and she's still not right. I don't want to lose another one to tetanus and I'd like him to have a look when he can. She'd been disbudded before she came to me, but I strongly suspect they failed to vaccinate and infection set in.'

Lost in all this vet language, Pippa really hoped that was an animal and not some random child minder. And where were the dogs, the alpacas and the sheep who'd nearly mown her down outside the shop? Were they in the yard, still parked in the trailer attached to the quad bike?

'Pippa, this is Dorothy.' Elaine was unfazed, clearly used to such talk. 'She farms just outside the village and runs the local animal sanctuary. Pippa is Jonny's daughter, Dorothy.'

'I know exactly who you are.' Dorothy turned that sharp gaze on Pippa, who did her best to stare back, refusing to be daunted. Another one who'd already decided they didn't like the look of her, despite Pippa never having set foot in Hartfell before last night. And Dorothy's expression made it perfectly clear that she was firmly on Gil's side of the fence when it came to landlords and local vets. Oh dear. Pippa supposed that an animal sanctuary must require the services of a vet occasionally and when – not if – she sold up, Dorothy would have to find another one like everyone else. She firmly quashed a flare of guilt and squared her shoulders nervously.

'I remember your father. Scrawny sort of a chap. And your mother. You look just like her.'

Pippa's knees trembled and she clutched the counter. 'I do?' As a teenager she used to pore over old photographs, searching for resemblances between her, Tilly and her mum. Sometimes now she saw tiny details of her mum emerging in Harriet, every glimpse enough to drag her straight back to the past.

Voices outside snagged at her concentration, and she glanced at the open door as another woman entered, followed by Gil. They were chatting as Lola made a beeline for Dorothy, who bent stiffly to make a fuss of the dog sniffing in happy anticipation of treats in her pockets.

That T-shirt Pippa had seen on his bedroom floor was clinging to his chest and the battered jeans sat snugly on his hips and thighs, and she swallowed. She realised his eyes were more sapphire than cerulean, and her pulse fluttered again. Was it only four hours since they'd met? It felt more like four days. His smile, as he listened to the younger woman who'd arrived with him, faltered the moment he saw Pippa.

'What are you doing here?' he said coolly. 'Checking out my practice?'

'Actually, Pippa popped in to ask if her daughter can use the Wi-Fi, Gil.' Even Elaine's calm couldn't dissipate the tension thrumming between them. Dorothy appeared ready to pounce and Pippa really didn't fancy taking on the pair of them, wishing she could channel a bit of the older woman's natural confidence.

'That's all right, isn't it? I said it was.' Elaine swung a handbag over her shoulder. 'You know how it is with teenagers and their phones.'

'I suppose it'll have to be.'

'Thank you very much,' Pippa said with all the politeness she could muster. Gil seemed to be finding it difficult to meet her eyes too and he nodded. 'I'll make sure Harriet's not in anyone's way.'

'Unlike you,' he muttered as he strode around the counter, bringing a trace of fresh air and farms with him. He bent to switch the monitor back on and quickly logged in. 'No doubt you'll be happy to hear I'll be moving my stuff out of the house later.'

Dorothy snorted, leaving Pippa in no doubt of her own view of such proceedings.

'Hi, it's Pippa, right?' The younger woman who'd entered with Gil crossed the room, a wide smile brightening an already lovely face. Dark eyes resembled milk chocolate and rich brown hair, tucked behind one ear, tumbled beyond her shoulders. She made ripped jeans, muddy boots, and a striped shirt over a green top look effortlessly elegant. She held out a hand and Pippa was so grateful for a warm welcome after Gil's chilly resolve and Dorothy's disdain that she could've hugged her instead.

'I'm Rose, it's so great to meet you. Big fan of your dad's.' Rose laughed awkwardly. 'Sorry, blame an older brother who loves rock music, it's all I ever heard.'

'Thank you, that's very kind.' Pippa had said these words to strangers countless times, and it felt good to appreciate the pleasure they brought Rose. 'I'll tell him, he'll be thrilled.'

'Would you? My brother will be so jealous.' Rose glanced to her left. 'Morning, Dorothy. I was just talking about you and the fundraiser. I've got some cards for you to hand out.'

'Jolly good.' Dorothy looked Rose over and didn't appear to find her wanting. Pippa wondered how long one had to be a resident in Hartfell before Dorothy might bestow that level of approval. 'Hand 'em over, then. Not really my thing, skincare. Not unless I can use it on m'terrier's eczema.'

'You can if you want to,' Rose assured her, delving into a tote and handing over postcards held together with an elastic band. 'There's calendula oil in the dry skin balm and it's really good for sensitive skin. Worth a try, at least. I'll drop one in or ask Alfie to when he's next at yours.'

'Righto.'

Elaine was on her way to lunch with a friend and she said goodbye, leaving Pippa stuck behind the counter with Gil. She couldn't escape without asking him to move and really didn't want to brush up against him if she tried.

'My son had eczema when he was little,' Rose explained to Pippa. 'We tried loads of different treatments and eventually I began making my own skincare products. It's become a bit of a thing now, and I sell them online and at shows. That's what this is about.' She passed Pippa a postcard. 'I'm hosting an event and any money we make is going to the animal shelter. I'd love it if you could come.'

'Oh, that's very nice, thank you.' Pippa hadn't been expecting any invitations and when she scanned the postcard, she was relieved to have an excuse to avoid this one. Social interaction in Hartfell was not on her list of things to do. 'I'm sorry, we'll be back at home by then, but thank you for thinking of me. My daughter and I have a busy summer planned.'

'Busy evicting people from their homes,' Dorothy said and there was no chance of Pippa pretending she hadn't heard that. It wasn't nice to be cast in the role of evil landlord, especially given what she'd learned of Gil's past this morning. 'Perhaps you'd like to make a donation to m'shelter instead?'

Was Dorothy serious? One glance and Pippa knew that she was. 'Er, I'll think about it,' she replied stiffly, caught unawares. Normally she wouldn't think twice, and it would probably have been easier to have agreed immediately.

'How's that nanny, Dorothy?' Gil glanced up from the monitor. Lola had scoffed her treats and settled in a bed behind Elaine's chair.

'Not too well, which is why I need you.' Dorothy abandoned her scrutiny of Pippa to regard him instead. 'When are you free?'

He pulled a phone from his jeans pocket and checked it, sending unwelcome sparks dancing across Pippa's arm when he brushed it with his hand. 'About an hour? There's something I need to borrow as well whilst I'm there.'

'I thought you might. It's all ready for you. Cheerio,' she barked and nodded at Rose. She turned and left without offering Pippa a goodbye. Something was definitely creaking as she marched off and Pippa wondered grumpily if it was Dorothy's joints or the coat.

'I'd better run too, I've got to drop Alfie at a Young Farmers' thing.' Rose's smile for Pippa lit up her face. 'Teenagers. I swear I do way more running round after him now than when he was tiny.'

'I've got one of those too,' Pippa said wryly. 'I know exactly what you mean.'

'Would you like to have a coffee sometime?' Rose laughed awkwardly. 'I promise I won't ask you about your dad, I just thought you might welcome a friendly face.'

'I'd love that, thank you.' Pippa was ready to clamber over the counter to embrace Rose now, hyper aware of Gil and certain he was blocking her on purpose. After meeting Dorothy, Pippa decided she needed all the friends in Hartfell she could get, and coffee sounded simple enough. 'And ask whatever you like about my dad and the band, I don't mind, and neither will he.'

'That's so kind. I work from home on Tuesdays and Thursdays, so pop round whenever you can, Pippa.' Rose left another pile of postcards on the counter for clients to pick up. 'Alfie and I live with my brother and his family on Abbeywell Farm, it's about a mile outside the village.'

'Thank you, I will.'

Rose left and Pippa really didn't want to be alone with Gil and his grumpiness. She held her breath and everything in as she squeezed past him, still bent over the monitor.

'So, when can I expect Harriet to turn up?'

'Er, Monday, I suppose.' Pippa was braced for some cutting comment, refusing to allow any lingering sympathy to soften her defences. 'Thank you for allowing it.'

'Not sure I had much say in the matter.' He straightened up and she took the opportunity to make for the door. 'I suppose you'll be coming with her?'

'Is that a problem?'

'Maybe more than you realise.' His eyes found hers and she felt the air between them vibrate with something different, something altogether more dangerous than displeasure. Her breath stuttered as his gaze held hers before he dropped it and turned back to the monitor.

Chapter Seven

Pippa returned to the house, her mind caught on Elaine's story of Gil's past and her own connection to Hartfell. Two families entwined, reaching back to a pair of young boys who'd been best mates until one of them had died, and Gil had lost his parents. And Ivy, whoever she was, whom Violet believed was connected to Pippa in some way. She'd never delved into her family's past before; their present had kept her occupied enough until now.

She couldn't unravel the reason Jonny had stepped in and bought the farm when Gil had wanted it for himself. Her dad already owned a London apartment, the holiday home in Majorca they all still used, and a rambling cottage on the Norfolk coast where he escaped alone to write music. That was his place, one where he didn't like to be interrupted and he shared it with her brother Raf, whom Pippa knew also required solitude to write songs he refused to reveal to the world.

She knew Jonny was toying with buying a place in Australia as he was coming to love it there so much, but surely things weren't so uncertain that he'd have to sell Home Farm to fund it. As she opened the back door into the kitchen, she decided she'd better find out. Raf would know. Of all of them, he spent the most time with their dad.

Whilst the band were on a break from the tour, Raf was supposed to be summering on a Scandinavian island with his girlfriend Lina, a stunning Swedish journalist. He and Lina had been very loved up in the beginning, but Pippa knew from experience that it might not last. Raf loathed the idea of permanent commitment and she longed for him to find a true home for his sensitive soul, one he was careful to keep hidden. Of all her siblings, she was closest to him, but even their lives had become more distant and their catch-ups rarer.

Her phone was on the kitchen worktop, and she picked it up, opening the email application. It failed to refresh, and she felt another glimmer of sympathy for Harriet, wishing she'd thought to take the phone with her when she'd gone to see Elaine. The kitchen felt different now Pippa knew exactly whose home it had once been, and judging by the state of the cupboards and the ancient range, she didn't imagine it had changed since Gil's grandmother's days.

Was she really going to insist that he move out now she knew something of his history here? Was she even legally entitled to, if he changed his mind and decided to stay? Unlikely, if he had a formal agreement in place with Jonny. Pippa was hazy on the rights of sitting tenants, but she was pretty sure they couldn't be evicted without notice. She was still trying to decide whether he'd be more inclined to leave if she was really nice or utterly foul to him when Harriet appeared, phone in hand.

'What's for lunch?' She glanced up momentarily from the screen. 'Can I borrow your hairdryer please? Mine's still at Isla's, I forgot to bring it back with me.'

'Of course, it's in my case. Lunch will be soup and fresh bread I bought in the village. The shop is lovely,

Harriet, you should pop down and have a look.' Pippa was clutching at straws with that one. Used to London markets and the odd boutique when she wanted something special, Harriet wouldn't be impressed with Violet's old-fashioned treasure trove.

'Mmm. Where's Gil?'

'I presume still at work, somebody called to ask him to have a look at a nanny. I think that's a goat.' Pippa considered her next words carefully, hoping to find an opportunity to talk on neutral ground. 'What would you like to do this afternoon?' Probably best to see if Harriet had any suggestions rather than making her own right now.

'Dunno.'

'Right.' All that money on a nice school and Harriet still didn't speak in sentences. Jonny had paid for it and that was another bone of contention between them. Pippa didn't think she'd ever stop missing her; the house always felt so much less of a home without Harriet's presence in it.

'I thought I'd go for a walk and explore. It is very pretty, from what I've seen so far. Would you like to come with me?'

'Since when did you come over all rural?' Considering the lack of Wi-Fi, Harriet seemed to spend just as much time staring at her phone.

'I don't think I have come over "all rural".' Pippa decided that Harriet could probably teach Dorothy a thing or two about disdain. And she'd speak to her daughter another time about her attitude; there were only so many battles she could have on the go. 'You know I enjoy my running and I'd like to find a nice route while we're here.'

'S'bad for you,' Harriet muttered. 'You'll knacker your joints and by the time you're fifty you'll barely be able to walk. It's not that long off, either. You're closer to sixty than you are to twenty now.'

'Thank you for that, Harriet. I'm hardly a geriatric just because I'm about to turn forty. And technically I'm still closer to twenty, at least until my birthday.' Pippa wasn't used to the idea of her fifth decade yet, but it was a huge relief, whatever Harriet thought of the state of her joints. Her mum had died at thirty-four and it still took Pippa's breath away to remember how young her three children had been too.

She hoped Harriet hadn't noticed the occasional creak in her knees. Unlikely, seeing as her daughter was usually plugged into earbuds. Occasionally, Harriet would remove one and stare at Pippa when she spoke as though she'd never clapped eyes on her own mother before.

'I'm going for a shower.'

'Okay. Lunch won't be long.'

A bit later Pippa poured the soup into a pan and only realised that the two plates on the range were either for boiling or simmering when she picked the wrong one and left it to warm up. The soup nearly exploded shortly after, splattering some on the tiles. She cleaned up the mess and divided what was left into two bowls and buttered some bread. She picked up her phone to text Harriet and changed her mind, instead going into the hall and shouting up the stairs that lunch was ready. That suit of armour was going too, and soon. She would need an awfully large skip to make this house look even halfway appealing to buyers, and shook away guilty thoughts of Gil's grandmother.

Harriet returned, looking fresh and lovely after her shower, and Pippa just wanted to slide her arms around her daughter and hold her close. But any such attempt was bound to be rebuffed, so whilst they ate she settled for making general conversation, and at least the meal put Harriet in a better mood.

Pippa excused her the washing up and carried the dishes to the sink. Gil's mug from this morning was still there and she decided that two could play the 'what's mine is mine' game, conveniently forgetting that everything here probably was his. A few minutes later the door behind Harriet at the table flew open and Gil marched in with Lola.

Pippa flushed. How should she greet someone she was evicting from their own home? No, not his home, not any longer, she reminded herself. The farm belonged to Jonny and had done for a while. She was doing nothing wrong, and hopefully nothing illegal either, seeing as Gil was leaving of his own accord.

'Hi Gil.' Harriet had already perked up as Lola settled at her feet for a pat, and Pippa disliked him just a little bit more at Harriet's easy warmth. 'Mum said you've been treating a sick animal. Did it make it?'

'Gil was just doing his job, Harriet,' Pippa said coolly. She'd only mentioned it because Harriet had asked, not to make him out to be some kind of hero in her daughter's mind. 'Nothing out of the ordinary.'

'I think it will.' He smiled at Harriet before picking up Lola's water bowl, carrying it to the sink and making Pippa wonder if he was trying to get in her way on purpose yet again. She'd been drying the dishes and made herself continue as he rinsed and refilled the bowl. She breathed out when he replaced it on the floor, but he was back at the tap again a moment later.

'What was wrong with it?'

'Acute pneumonia, which can become fatal in young cows and calves pretty quickly.' Gil turned around, his back to the sink. 'We caught this one in time, thanks to the farmer knowing his stock and recognising the symptoms. I'm pretty sure the heifer will make it, with continued treatment.'

'So, like meds and stuff?'

'Yeah. Antibiotics and anti–inflammatories. Infection can spread quickly if the sick animal isn't separated from the herd, and it's vital to reduce their temperature and keep it within normal limits.'

'Wow, that's so cool.' Harriet rarely looked impressed these days and Pippa offered a faint smile in response. She didn't want to dampen Harriet's rare show of enthusiasm, even if it was for Gil and his life-saving heroics. Harriet had even put her phone down and Pippa longed for the days when her daughter had wished to converse with her. 'What's a heifer?'

'It's a young female cow, one who hasn't had a calf yet, usually under three years of age.'

He picked up the mug he'd left on the worktop earlier, raising a brow as his gaze caught Pippa's. Warmth stained her cheeks, knowing he'd realised she'd refused to wash his single item on purpose. He refilled it and downed the water in one long gulp.

'Right, I'll get my things.' He banged the mug down onto the worktop.

'Where are you going to stay?'

'Harriet, that's none of our business.' Pippa was folding the tea towel neatly. 'Let's go to our rooms and leave Gil to pack in peace.'

Harriet flashed her a defiant glare before addressing Gil. 'Are you married? Do you have a family?'

'That is—'

'Divorced.' He interrupted Pippa and bent to pat Lola, who'd wandered over and was giving him an adoring look she felt he didn't deserve. 'Two boys, Joel and Luca. Joel works on a vineyard in Adelaide now he's graduated, and Luca is travelling with friends on summer break from university.'

'So they don't live with you?' Harriet gave Pippa a look which implied she'd also quite like to be grown up and beyond her parents' reach, thank you very much.

'They come when they can, but Luca's studying in Portsmouth and Joel's a long way off, so...' Gil shrugged, and Pippa wondered if she'd imagined the suggestion of sadness in his eyes. 'Luca will be up for a visit over the summer.'

'So where will he stay, if you've had to leave your home?'

'Harriet, enough!' Pippa wasn't often sharp, and Harriet's lips pressed together. 'Gil's family circumstances are private.'

'Is that right?' He turned those blue eyes on Pippa, and she breathed in slowly, trying to calm the leap in her pulse. 'They don't feel too private right now.'

'And it is our business, if we're chucking Gil and his family out of their own home,' Harriet said coolly. 'That's not very you, Mum. You've always been all about home.'

Pippa *was* all about keeping the family together despite their differences and lives that ranged around the world.

She'd always found solace in the loss of her mum by being the one left behind, trying somehow to cling to them all, let them know she loved them and was there for them.

'You can't just make Gil leave! He's a tenant, he has rights. This is not his fault. Grandad should never have bought the house and cheated him out of his home!'

Pippa gaped at her, still trying to unravel the previous accusation, her mind stuck on Harriet's antagonism and what was causing it.

'I appreciate the thought, Harriet, but we can't all live here together.' Gil was impassive in the face of all this emotion and Pippa just wanted to crawl away. 'And I have a place lined up. I don't know what your mum's plans are, but I expect I'd have to move out eventually anyway.'

'She wants to get back to London as soon as possible.' Harriet aimed another accusatory glare at Pippa. 'Back to telling me what to do and how I should live my life.'

Harriet flounced from the kitchen and tried to slam the door, which refused to cooperate and bounced back again, rattling through the tension. Pippa was shocked, ashamed that Gil had witnessed another outburst and seen firsthand Harriet's horrible new hatred towards her.

She straightened up, clutching her hands together to stop them trembling. 'I'll leave you to get your things,' she told Gil, unable to look him in the eye and face yet more disdain and possibly even amusement at how that scene had played out.

'Pippa, I…' He hesitated. 'Maybe we should…'

Refusing to be drawn by the uncertainty in those few low words or what he might have gone on to say, she left the kitchen, calmly closing the door behind her. The moment she was out of sight the tears began to fall and she ran up to her room and collapsed on the bed. She heard him come upstairs soon after, saying something to Lola she couldn't quite make out. His bedroom door opened and then closed again. There was nothing she could do whilst he was still in the house, no one who needed or even wanted her right now. She crawled into bed and huddled up, waiting for him to go as she worried about Harriet and how she was going to handle their situation. Some adventure this was turning out to be.

Pippa woke later, groggy from the nap, something she'd never normally succumb to during the day. She sat up, her mind hazily replaying the row with Harriet and another uncomfortable encounter with Gil. The house was silent, and she really hoped he had gone and taken his belongings with him, even though Harriet would blame her for the loss of Lola too. A glance at her phone revealed it was almost four p.m. and she'd been asleep for two hours. She got off the bed and headed for the bathroom.

Fifteen minutes later she was back in her room and shivering from a cool shower. Hair dried, she stared into the triple mirror. Barely twenty-four hours since they'd left London and she already felt like a shadow of her own self; tired, even more worried about Harriet, and unsettled by the situation with the house and Gil. And curiosity about Ivy and a past connection to Hartfell seemed to have lodged in her mind as well.

But those were thoughts for another day. For now she needed to think about dinner. She left her room and tapped on Harriet's door. 'Hey. Can I come in?'

'If you must.' An exaggerated sigh had Pippa holding in her own as she stepped inside and perched on the edge of Harriet's bed. Close but not too near; Harriet didn't seem to want her within touching distance these days.

'I was thinking of making pasta for dinner. I bought some lovely veg at the shop this morning. They even had aubergines, and you love them roasted.'

'I'm not five, Mum. I don't need to be reminded about what food I do and don't like. And I'm not hungry.'

'Oh?' Pippa's heart jolted and her reply was deliberately calm. 'Usually I can never fill you up. You're always hungry.'

'Yeah, well, I'm not likely to be playing netball up here, am I? At least I've got summer camp with Isla, and I can get away.'

Pippa waited a beat, twirling a loose thread on the duvet cover. 'From what?' she asked lightly, half afraid of the reply.

Harriet raised an arm, flicking a dismissive hand. 'This place. Homework. No Wi-Fi. And...'

Her voice fell away, and Pippa was braced, waiting for Harriet to add 'you' to that sentence. The word didn't come, and her arm slid down as Pippa slowly expelled the air in her lungs.

'Harriet, have you been crying?'

'No!' Harriet was staring at her phone and flung it away.

'Are you sure?' Pippa gulped. 'Because checking you're all right is what mums are for. And dads, obviously.' Harriet's was a good one, just a bit scatterbrained. The only things predictable about Nick were his love for his daughter and his tendency to take off.

'Nothing to tell.' Harriet let long hair fall over her face.

'Okay. But if you change your mind...' Pippa paused, letting a few seconds slide by. 'So tomorrow, we do need to go shopping. And then afterwards, I was thinking about our adventure and what we might like to do. It's a Sunday, but I'm sure we can find something.'

'The adventure was a stupid idea, Mum, and I just want to go home.'

'It won't be long,' Pippa assured her. 'But until we do, I've asked Elaine, who's the receptionist at the vets, if you can use their Wi-Fi in the office.' Pippa was cheered by the sudden hope on Harriet's face and readied herself to deliver the less good news. 'They're not open every day, just four mornings a week, but it's better than nothing, isn't it?'

'S'pose.'

Pippa wished she had more idea of what it was Harriet did so much of online. Homework, daily video calls with Isla, messaging friends, but it was impossible to keep up. Thank heavens for good old-fashioned family messaging groups. Harriet still responded to those, and it was the easiest way to keep in touch with everyone, scattered as they were. Pippa thought longingly of her home in London and all she loved about the city. She wasn't going to be distracted by a picture-perfect main street dotted with pretty cottages and rolling meadows outside the windows, or thoughts of a moody vet. *Hot* was the other word spilling unbidden into her mind.

'You do know that Gil's moved into a crappy old caravan?' Harriet was staring at her phone again.

'He's what?' Pippa laughed, shoving away that thought about Gil. It was an awfully good thing Harriet couldn't read her mind, although sometimes Pippa wondered. 'A caravan? Where?'

'Like, duh! In the yard.'

'He hasn't?' He wouldn't dare. But Pippa knew he would. He very much would.

Harriet pointed to the window triumphantly. 'See for yourself if you don't believe me.'

'Of course I believe you, it's just… A caravan?' Pippa got up and went to the window, and her mouth fell open.

She had little experience of caravans, having never stayed in one, but didn't doubt that this one, sitting slap bang in the centre of the yard and no doubt visible from every window at the back of the house, was the most miserable and ancient caravan she'd ever seen. It had probably been white, once, but had now faded to a muddy sort of grey with a broad and dulled burgundy strip running around the middle.

The two windows she could see were more rust than metal, one covered by a patterned net curtain, the other a metallic-looking blind, half raised at an angle. One tyre was squashed flat, and the door lay open, revealing a glimpse of dark carpet. Lola was curled in a comfy bed on the cobbles, soaking up the sun. If Gil was trying to invoke yet more sympathy from Harriet, then he was no doubt succeeding, and Pippa took a hurried step back when he appeared at the window behind the blind in case he spotted her staring.

'This is all your fault, Mum! You made him move out of his own home.'

'Harriet, I did not.' Pippa turned away, bright spots of colour rising in her cheeks. 'Gil offered to go. And the house does actually belong to your grandfather, whether you, me or Gil likes it or not.'

She wondered if squatters in caravans had more rights than sitting tenants. Surely not? Could she legally make him shift the caravan out of the yard? And if so, would he simply move back into the house, if only to irritate her? Perhaps she could have the caravan towed away but she really didn't have the heart for such underhand tactics. If they hadn't got off to such a rocky start, she would have been perfectly amenable to him staying on in the house for now. She needed to track down the solicitor and it would be Monday before she could do that.

'I'm not sure why you feel so strongly about his situation when we know little about it. Or why his living arrangements are our fault, or our problem. We are here to sell the house and go home as quickly as possible.'

'Sell?' Harriet looked up sharply from her phone. 'That's what you're going to do? You said we were coming here to sort it out.'

'And we will. I'm sorry for whatever difficulty Gil is in right now, but it's not our problem. He offered to move out and now he's gone.' But not far enough, sadly. Pippa decided she needed to keep her plans about selling entirely to herself, seeing as Harriet was now firmly on Gil's side and until she'd established what rights he actually had. 'I would very much appreciate you not laying the blame at my door. It may surprise you to learn that not everything is my fault.'

She saw hurt flaring in Harriet's face and immediately regretted it; this was not the way to reach her and breach the distance between them.

'Let's have a think about tomorrow, yes?' Pippa made for the door. 'I think our first adventure might be cooking dinner in that kitchen. Coming?'

'I'll be down in a bit.' Harriet's fingers were trembling around her phone. 'Sorry.'

Chapter Eight

Back in the kitchen, Pippa set about cooking dinner. She went to the cupboard where she'd found the pans this morning, only to discover that they'd disappeared, and only one bowl, side plate and dinner plate remained. She hurriedly checked the others in case she'd put them back somewhere else after washing them. The draining board was also empty, and she yanked open the cutlery drawer to be greeted by the sight of a single knife, fork, spoon and teaspoon.

She slammed the drawer shut, stormed through the back door into the yard and across the cobbles. Lola jumped up to greet her and Pippa offered her a single cursory pat as she thumped on the caravan door, trying to ignore Lola's wagging tail and urgent attentions. A few seconds slid by, and her right foot began to tap as she stared at mouldering green and orange curtains. Lola gave up and settled back in her bed as Pippa applied her fist to the door a second time.

'I'm not deaf and Lola's not the only one trying to sleep. What is it with you and waking people up?' Gil appeared, rubbing a hand over rough stubble. 'What do you want now?'

'You know what!' Pippa's neck was uncomfortable from having to tip it back so far and she jabbed a hand to a mug and plate sitting on the draining board. 'You've taken all the pans and the crockery from the house!'

'No, I haven't.' That mocking smile was playing on his lips, and she wanted to swipe it from his face. 'If you look properly, you'll see that I only took one of everything. I brought Lola's bowls as well, I wasn't sure you'd find a use for them.' At the mention of her name Lola looked up and thumped her tail.

'But there's two of us! Me and Harriet, and you knew we were coming. You're being ridiculous! And selfish and mean and…'

'And what?' Gil leaned against the door frame and folded his arms. 'That stuff is mine and I need it.'

'So do I! How am I supposed to cook tonight, now you've done this?'

'I'm afraid that's really not my problem. The contents of the house do belong to me, and I would've brought more if I could fit them in here.'

There was no folding step to split the distance between the caravan and the cobbles, and she loathed the advantage this extra height afforded him. 'But the shop is shut, and they don't sell plates and pans anyway. I have no idea where the nearest town is and…'

Pippa was ready to weep, and her jaw felt like it had been set in concrete as she took a step back. Right now if she'd had a tow bar on her car, she would've hitched up the damn caravan and him in it, and dragged them both out into the middle of nowhere. She fumbled for her phone in a pocket, realising too late that there was no signal. And she certainly wasn't going to ask him for the Wi-Fi network so she could google alternative plans for dinner.

He yawned, sliding a large hand over his mouth. 'Now, if you don't mind, I'd like to go back to bed.'

'You're insufferable!'

'Well, we can talk about that some other time.' His phone was ringing, and he glanced at it. 'You'll have to excuse me, I'm busy.'

She took another hasty step back as he grabbed the door and shut it. Shocked by her uncharacteristic outburst and Gil's response, Pippa stared at the caravan. Without pans or enough plates, cooking dinner was off the menu, and she made a snap decision to try the pub instead. They would probably even have Wi-Fi. She returned to the house more slowly than she'd run out of it to find Harriet, and let her know she was going out in search of dinner and would be back soon. Though she suggested they go together, Harriet firmly shut that idea down. She left through the front door, dreading the idea of another glimpse of Gil or that caravan right now.

The Pilkington Arms seemed to be dozing peacefully in the late afternoon sun, looking as golden and gorgeous as the rest of the lane it sat upon. Pippa pushed open the front door and stepped into a stone-flagged reception, a staircase set at the back of the panelled hall. A glance at the rooms on either side revealed the bar on her left and a restaurant to the right. She chose the bar, aware of curious eyes watching as she pulled out one of only two free stools, every table occupied.

Comfortable and contemporary tables and chairs sat well with dark blue walls covered in what she saw was excellent artwork; some modern paintings, others more traditional, and she resolved to have a closer look when she was in a better mood. A fire was laid but unlit and felt welcoming all the same, and the chatter was a pleasant hum, a distraction from the miserable thoughts chasing through her mind.

'You look parched, darling.' A handsome middle-aged man with cropped grey hair stood behind the bar and she dredged up a smile. Pale blue eyes were as friendly as his greeting, a beard barely more than stubble framing his jaw. 'And I'm guessing it's not a tonic water you're after, not unless it comes with a hefty shot of gin.'

'That bad, huh?' Pippa huffed out a laugh, aware she sounded like Harriet. Her shoulders began to relax at his warmth, the tension gripping the back of her neck easing.

'You're Pippa, right? Up from London?'

'Right.' Here we go, she thought wearily. 'Does everyone in the village know who I am and hate me already?'

'Pretty much, in answer to your first question, and definitely not, for the second.' He offered an arm across the bar. 'Hi, I'm delighted to meet you. I'm Kenny, my partner Vince and I bought this place two years ago, he's the head chef. We moved up from Brighton and it took a while to find our feet away from the city, so I know how you're feeling. Hartfell's a wonderful place when you get to know it.'

'I'm afraid I'll have to take your word for that, I won't be here long enough to find out. Hi Kenny.' Pippa shook his hand, her smile wry. 'Thank you for your welcome, it's very kind.'

'My pleasure. And please just let me get this out there, I'm a huge fan of your dad's and the band.' Kenny laughed as Pippa pulled a face. 'Saw them play that headline set at Glastonbury back in the day and I've never forgotten it. I know, sorry. You probably get that from everyone you meet.'

'Not always.' It was why Pippa had kept her married name, helping her to live a life away from the limelight Jonny loved. 'And it's very sweet of you to say so, he has a lot of fans, and he loves them all.'

It was true. Jonny always said the band would be nowhere without their following and they'd managed to attract new fans down the years. Including, it seemed, Kenny, who must be a good fifteen years younger than her dad.

'So what can I get you?' Kenny turned a shoulder to the bar, a young woman to his right busy serving another customer. Pippa's gaze landed on a bottle.

'Actually, I think I'll take your advice and have a gin and tonic, the dry one please.' She'd had no intention of lingering in the pub, a stab of guilt for Harriet lurking in the house swiftly following. But Kenny had been so nice, and she needed a bit of that right now.

'Excellent choice, it's a local distillery and our customers love it. I'd recommend it with Indian tonic or the rhubarb and raspberry if you fancy a sweeter twist.'

'The Indian please. I'll try the sweet one another time.'

'Coming up.' Kenny set to work, and Pippa was trying to remember when she'd last drunk before six p.m., even on a Saturday. Although Harriet generally used public transport to get around the city with her friends, Pippa still liked to be available for run arounds if required. Kenny placed a glass on the bar, and she picked it up, savouring a long, slow mouthful.

'Gorgeous, thank you. Just what I needed.'

'That bad, huh?' They both laughed as Kenny repeated her words from a few moments ago. 'Let me guess. You're sharing Home Farm with Gil Haworth and he's not happy?'

'Wow, you're good at this game.' Pippa took another slug of gin. 'Better than that. We're not sharing the house because he's moved out, taken all the pans and plates with him, and he's still not happy. Neither is my teenage daughter. As far as she's concerned, I might as well have been trying to rehome a puppy.'

'Well, he does have rather puppyish eyes.' Kenny, busy serving another customer, threw her a mischievous glance and she pulled a face.

'Not you as well?'

'He could charm the birds out of the trees, that one.'

'We are still talking about the same person?' She inadvertently swallowed a chunk of ice and coughed. 'Gil Haworth?'

'The very one.' Kenny thanked his customer and returned to stand opposite her. 'Just don't tell him I said so, he has quite enough fans around here as it is. So why does your daughter feel so sorry for him?'

'Oh, you know.' Pippa tried to quash the sadness that Harriet hadn't wanted to come with her to the pub. 'She's at the age when everything wrong with her life is apparently my fault. Not her dad's, you understand, because she doesn't live with him. He's the fun one who lets her do what she likes and doesn't nag her about homework or staying up late on school nights.'

'How old?' Kenny's gaze was sympathetic, and Pippa liked him all the more. She wondered if the pub had any rooms free; maybe she could move in here instead and give Gil the house back. She bet Kenny would look after them.

'Fourteen.'

'Bless you. You'll get through it – both of you – I'm sure.'

Pippa smiled gratefully. 'You have a beautiful pub here. So, what made you choose Hartfell?'

'We were looking for a project and a change of pace. Vince worked in Paris, I was in marketing in Brighton, and this place came up. I have the best job, because I get to choose the wine. And drink it, of course. Alongside the marketing.'

'Well, you've certainly done a brilliant job. I love it.' She tended to avoid noisy city pubs, packed full of people. This one was comfortable, stylish and welcoming.

'Thanks, Pippa, that's kind of you. We wanted to keep the country house feel but make it contemporary, you know, a home from home. We worked with a fabulous designer who took care of everything, and the brand-new Pilkington Arms is the result.'

'Pilkington?' Something caught in Pippa's mind, and she was trying to land on the memory. 'I've heard that name before.'

'Landed gentry back in the day around here.' Kenny was busy serving another couple and a waiter was adding drinks to a tray. 'Although I think most of them have scattered now. There's still a family up at the Hall called Pilkington, though. Lovely place, if a bit rundown. Rolling acres and a tennis court, that sort of thing. We don't see much of them, it's empty half the year.'

'Right.' She couldn't place the name and gave up trying. She took another mouthful of gin and suddenly remembered why she'd come here in the first place, reaching for a menu along the bar. 'I have a favour to ask, Kenny. Seeing as that bloody Gil Haworth has made off with the contents of the kitchen, is there any chance of me ordering something and taking it back to the house please? My daughter's still there, waiting for me to provide a solution for dinner.'

'Bloody Gil Haworth, did you say?' Kenny's smile widened.

'Yes.' Pippa felt a happy warmth stealing through her. Somehow her glass was already empty, and she really shouldn't stay for another. 'Very bloody and very grumpy. Quite good looking though, if you like that kind of thing. All rough edges and no sense of humour. Not that I've noticed, you understand.'

'Can't say as I've noticed you either, Pippa Douglas.' Gil slid onto the free stool to her left, Lola settling at his feet. 'Can't see past all the shrieking.'

Pippa shot him a glare before trying to concentrate on the menu. Ordinarily she'd have taken issue with Gil referring to her shrieking, but the pub was too busy and pleasant for another row, and maybe she had yelled a little. Once or twice. Space was at a premium and she felt a tremor on her skin as his arm brushed hers when Kenny offered him a menu as well.

'Beer?' Kenny held up a glass questioningly.

'Please. The Copper, a half.' Gil nodded at a pump and Kenny tilted the glass beneath it. 'Been a rough day. I'm ready for it, even if it is non-alcoholic.'

Of course he drank nothing but beer, Pippa fumed irrationally. She bet he'd never been near a good glass of wine in his life.

'Can I have the wild mushroom risotto for two, please, Kenny.' She replaced the menu on the bar. 'It sounds wonderful and I'm sure we'll both love it.'

'Mate, you do know she's a vegetarian?' Gil added what he apparently considered another of Pippa's faults to his list of grievances. 'So you won't be needing any of your outstanding grass-fed Shorthorn steak or shrimps caught fresh in the bay for her. Cheers.' He held up his glass in mock salute and she stared straight ahead.

'Don't be so naughty, Gil. You take no notice, darling.' Kenny patted her hand, and she could've kissed him.

'I thought you liked saving animals, not eating them,' she told Gil coolly and he laughed, wiping his mouth with the back of his hand.

'I don't generally eat my patients, at least not knowingly.' He took another long drink and set the half empty glass on the bar.

'Seeing as you've had a rough day too, Pippa, why don't you take a bottle of wine to go with the risotto?' Kenny had an iPad in his right hand. 'Then you can drink it at your leisure.'

'You'd better send the glasses as well,' she said glumly. 'I don't suppose there are any of those left in the house.' But necking the wine straight from the bottle did seem rather tempting. 'Oh, go on, then, thank you. Whatever you'd recommend.'

'Why don't you suggest something, Gil?' Kenny arched a brow. 'You two should be playing nicely, not falling out.'

'You're the expert, Kenny,' Pippa said quickly. 'I'd rather have your suggestions.'

'The New Zealand Pinot Noir?' Gil glanced at her. 'Or if you don't like red, try a French Pinot Gris instead.'

'Perfect, Gil.' Kenny beamed. 'Think dark plum, rose petal and violet for the red, Pippa, with a deliciously silky palate. But the white is gorgeous too, creamy and fresh, not too rich on the finish. Perfect with a risotto.'

She pursed her lips, not sure she was up to such complicated decision-making. 'The red please. Thanks.'

Right now it was the wine that mattered, not the colour of the grape skins, or even that Gil had suggested it.

'Here you go. Uncork it at home and give it a few minutes, won't do it any harm.' Kenny set down a bottle and a glass in front of her. 'On the house.'

'Kenny, please.' Pippa was reaching for her bag, and he held up a hand.

'I insist. Call it a welcome present. You can thank me by coming back for another meal and bringing your daughter next time.'

'Done. That would be lovely. And thank you, that's so generous. I think you and me might become great friends.' She shot Gil another filthy look, which he ignored.

'I certainly hope so.' Kenny smiled as Gil put his menu down. 'What would you like, Gil?'

'Steak and chips please, with everything. Béarnaise sauce too.'

Pippa let out a silent breath, certain Gil was ordering the most carnivorous choice on the menu just to spite her. Well, he could eat whatever he liked, she wouldn't be hanging around to watch him. The minute her risottos were ready, she'd be straight back to the house and Harriet.

'So what's this about you moving out of the farm-house?' Kenny was busy with Gil's order on the iPad. 'I thought you were joking, when you said you would.'

'I was not.'

Pippa couldn't care less. She'd hooked up to the pub's Wi-Fi and was staring at the email and message notifications winking back at her. Sunday lunch here tomorrow might be nice, then Harriet could catch up too. She resolved to ask her over dinner.

'You might see me a bit more often now, the new digs are a little primitive. No oven.'

'You haven't gone and borrowed that rickety old caravan off Dorothy, have you?' Kenny unscrewed the top from a bottle of tonic water, ready to add to a glass for another customer. 'I saw it when we went to the farm for eggs, it barely looked fit for scrap.'

'Doesn't matter. I prefer my own company to the alternative.'

For once Pippa agreed with Gil, wondering if she'd ever be able to go a day in this village without running into him.

'It seems to me that there's an obvious solution to both your problems.' Kenny was in between customers, one hand on the bar as he regarded them in amusement.

'And what's that?' Gil placed his empty glass down and shook his head when Kenny asked if he'd like another. 'No thanks. On call all weekend. I'll have a lime and soda please.'

Pippa was scanning messages, including the one from Cassie with more details on the girls' netball camp. Her breath rushed out in relief as she saw Raf's name pop up and she read his message. He had no plans to return to Sweden and was in London, holed up in Jonny's apartment until he rejoined the band. She'd call him another time, find out how things were. The email from the solicitor wasn't very enlightening, other than to confirm she had Jonny's permission to act on the house and farm as she saw fit. There was also a scan copy of boundaries, showing a few acres surrounding the house after most of the land had been sold to another farmer.

'Why don't you two share the cooking at least, if living together is a bit of a stretch right now?' Kenny raised a hand to wave at a couple making their exit. 'Pippa's got the stove, you've got the pans, Gil. Both of your problems solved.'

Pippa put her phone down and a splutter of laughter escaped. 'I don't think so, Kenny, thanks. I'd rather share the house with Lola.'

'And I'd rather share it with one of my patients. No offence, mate, but that's really not going to work.'

'Well, the thought's there.' Kenny seemed highly amused and not in the least daunted that his suggestion had been so swiftly dismissed.

Pippa was staring at the bottle of wine. Dark plum, Kenny had said, with rose petals and hints of violet. Delicious. She was so tempted to open the bottle now and knock it back. But she really didn't think it would enhance her reputation around the village if she were spotted staggering back drunk from her first visit to the pub. And Harriet, she was quite certain, would not approve. Gil was addressing her, and she turned her head, offering a contemptuous gaze.

'You don't even like dogs. Lola prefers to share with people who enjoy her company.'

'I never said that,' she replied carefully, hurt clutching her heart at the reminder. She couldn't read that cool blue gaze, couldn't decipher what might be running through his mind.

'You didn't have to, it's perfectly clear. But it's obvious Harriet's crying out for something to love. A pet would be good for her.'

'Don't say another word about my daughter,' she hissed, every motherly hackle rising. 'I don't care how many teenagers you've raised or whether your vet skills are heroic, in demand or not. I'm not interested in whatever you think of me, Harriet, or my parenting. And we're not getting a pet. That's final. We live in London and she's far too busy to take care of something else and I certainly haven't got the time.' Pippa's voice had risen with every word, and she caught sight of a couple gaping at a table behind Gil. She shut up abruptly; she really didn't want that on someone's social media.

'Pippa, sorry.' Kenny cleared his throat, a waitress hovering beside him. 'Your risottos are ready.'

'Thank you, Kenny.' Pippa got down from the stool and collected her bag, if not quite her wits. 'I really appreciate it and we'll definitely be back for another meal.' She glanced at Gil as she took the paper bag Kenny was offering. 'When the company is more amenable.'

Halfway back up the lane, the enticing aroma of the risotto making her hurry, a thought struck her, and she stopped dead. The pub was called The Pilkington Arms. Gil's middle name, so he had informed her this morning, was Pilkington.

Chapter Nine

On Sunday morning, Pippa was jolted from an uncomfortable dream about being chased by a herd of cows. It probably had some significant meaning, but she was too distracted by thoughts of the shopping she needed to do to worry about it now. She dressed in her running gear and left a note for Harriet to let her know she was going out. The risotto from the pub last night had been amazing and they'd both fallen on it. Pippa had also seen off some of the wine and had let Harriet have a bit, too.

The sun was lurking behind clouds when she let herself out of the house, and she glared at the ugly caravan in the yard. The curtains were still drawn, and Lola was nowhere in sight. Living in there, Gil had probably got fleas by now, and she allowed herself a little daydream of him irritable and itching from the bites. She increased her pace and headed towards the field beyond the garden. After her run, she'd set her mind to shopping and replacing all the stuff he'd swiped. Then the house might feel slightly more like a home, and she wondered if she could fit the suit of armour in her car for a trip to the nearest recycling centre.

She ran through the field, avoiding the sheep, who eyed her warily. At the border she climbed a stile over a wall onto the fell, following a footpath sign and keeping her eye out for wandering cows in case her dream came true. So very different from London, and Pippa loved the complete calm and solitude, the occasional bird of prey wheeling above her head, sun breaking through clouds to glint on thick clumps of heather. Running was harder as the path climbed and she paused for a breather she wouldn't normally need beside a winding river slipping over uneven rocks.

She stared across the huge expanse of land soaring to the sky, dotted with farmhouses and barns, and marked by high stone walls. In winter the weather must be brutal, but on a summer's day like this, the view was glorious. Back in London the city, beautiful though it was, didn't make her long to sketch quite like this and she'd return when she had more time to enjoy it. She was the only one in the family who painted; her dad and Raf wrote songs, and Tilly had trained as a chef and created exquisite dishes almost too good to eat. As she turned around, Pippa was musing again from where her longing to express herself in colour, form and texture had come from. She needed to download a proper map to explore out here; it would be easy to get lost and she didn't want to leave Harriet for too long.

Back at the farm Pippa spotted Lola ambling across the yard as she snuck into the garden, hoping to avoid Gil. But two voices were drifting on the breeze, and she clamped her lips together. Had he brought someone back to the caravan last night and in full view of Harriet's room?

Pippa forgot all about remaining out of sight and stormed into the yard to confront him. She halted the moment she saw Elaine talking with Gil outside the caravan, and heard him say that it was totally fine, and he'd manage. The older woman looked upset, and Pippa smiled uncertainly as Elaine looked across. 'Hi Elaine.'

'Oh, Pippa, hi.' There was an anxiety in Elaine's expression that hadn't been present yesterday. 'How are you?'

'I'm fine, thanks.' She hesitated, not wanting to intrude but concerned about Elaine. 'Is everything okay?' She glanced at Gil, who gave her a nod and folded his arms.

'Not really.' Elaine bit her lip. 'I'm sorry to call so early. My father's in hospital after a nasty fall, and he lives on his own. I don't really know how he's going to manage, or even if he'll be able to go back home at all.'

'Oh Elaine, I'm so sorry.' Pippa's irritation with Gil for assuming he'd had an overnight guest was gone. 'I hope he's going to be okay. Is there anything I can do to help?'

'I don't think so, but thank you. It's very kind of you to offer.' Elaine's eyes were darting between Pippa, Gil, and the phone in her hand. 'I don't know how long I'll be away, and I'm worried about leaving Gil on his own. I know it's only four mornings a week, but there's lots to do.'

'Elaine, it's fine, really. Please don't worry about me. Your dad needs you and that comes first. Take as long as you want, there's no rush.'

Pippa blinked, unused to the sincere tone and warm words from Gil, and steeled herself against liking it too much. There was no point in suddenly wishing that things between them were different and she could avoid all confrontations. She had some decisions to make about Home Farm and soon, and it was a shock to remember quite how much they would impact his life.

'Maybe there is something you could do, please?' Elaine laid a trembling hand on Pippa's arm. 'I know you're busy with things here, but perhaps you could help Gil, in the practice? Look after reception when he's consulting so he doesn't have to do it all on his own? The system is quite straightforward and I'm sure you'd pick it up very quickly. Clients can book appointments online, but the farmers still prefer to ring and speak to someone.'

'Me?' Pippa spluttered, her gaze jumping to Gil in time to see the kindness fall from his face, swiftly replaced by a look of dismay. 'I'm sorry, Elaine, I really don't think I could.'

'No, of course not, it was only a thought.' Elaine offered a weak smile, the glimpse of hope gone. 'It's just that he's working so hard to keep the practice going and I wouldn't want to be the reason why it would have to close. Perhaps you can get a temp in, Gil.'

Pippa felt another flicker of guilt. She'd literally just offered to help and had refused Elaine's only request because it involved Gil. She *was* on her summer break, and she supposed there would be hours to fill whilst she was here. And Elaine had been kind, had supported her request to use the Wi-Fi when Gil would have likely refused her. She took a deep breath, silently praying that it wouldn't mean she'd have to extend her stay.

'You really mustn't be worrying whilst you're away, you have enough to think about with your dad,' she said firmly, trying not to look at Gil to gauge his reaction. 'Of course I'll do it.'

–

After a lovely lunch at the pub, where Harriet had got on brilliantly with Kenny, and Vince had been summoned from the kitchen to meet them, she'd returned to her room for the evening and Pippa was perched on the lumpy orange sofa in the sitting room. None of her plumping could improve the cushions and she was finding it difficult to settle in what she now knew had been Gil's childhood home, after the one with his parents in Dorset.

She'd gone shopping earlier and Harriet had decided to go with her. They'd driven to a lovely market town about fifteen miles away and stocked up on food, cutlery, pans, and a basic white dinner service for four. Harriet had thawed as she'd soaked up Wi–Fi in the pub afterwards and they'd even laughed together, which to Pippa felt like a huge win.

Another unexpected consequence of Elaine going away, Pippa had learned earlier, was that she also looked after Posy the Shetland pony, popping down each day to take care of her. She'd showed Pippa how to muck out Posy's stable, refill the haynet and how much feed the pony was allowed to keep her weight at a reasonable level. Over lunch at the pub Pippa had been thrilled when Harriet agreed to help.

So tomorrow, she had Posy to deal with before her first morning in the surgery. Gil had made himself scarce during the induction with Elaine and Pippa had known from his glittering blue eyes that he wasn't comfortable with the new arrangement. But having her in situ was apparently preferable to managing alone and he'd wished Elaine all the best with her dad.

Pippa picked up her phone, frustrated at the lack of signal as she attempted to message Cassie. She couldn't be bothered to stroll down to the village now, it would keep until tomorrow when she'd be at the vets. Just the thought of being around Gil made her stomach clench with nerves. Her sister Tilly had sent another request, which Pippa had read at the pub, asking if she could put her in touch with an influencer Pippa knew vaguely who might be interested in Tilly's Greek B&B.

Her youngest sister Phoebe, who was twenty, effortlessly stunning and dabbling with modelling whilst she decided what kind of career she might like, also wanted to know if she might borrow Pippa's house for a shoot, could she recommend a caterer and if so, would she mind contacting them on Phoebe's behalf? Pippa sighed and shoved her phone away; they were all requests she'd deal with tomorrow.

She couldn't escape thoughts of Gil in this room with his grandmother, imagining them cleaving together through their shared loss. The house seemed trapped by the past and she doubted the decor had altered in decades. Beige walls were plain above a dark green carpet and every scrap of wooden furniture was dark. Her gaze went to a cabinet on the left of the mantelpiece, its four shelves filled with clutter. Curiosity getting the better of guilt, Pippa got up to have a closer look.

She turned a tiny key in its lock and carefully opened the doors. Everything was layered in thick grey dust and some fluttered to the floor at the disturbance. A porcelain tea service was dirty but still pretty, bright with delicate yellow flowers. She saw a blue trinket box with a jewelled lid and a small silver bell, dulled from neglect. She ran a finger over a miniature bible in a box, the clasp broken, and her breath faltered when she noticed a group of medals held together by frayed ribbon and realised they were awards for swimming.

The bottom shelf was full of photograph albums, and she removed one, settling on the window seat overlooking the back garden for better light. She flicked through black-and-white images of farming life down the years, searching for anyone who might be familiar. She didn't recognise the faces of men, women and children lined up outside the chapel in their Sunday best, or gathering the harvest in the fields alongside horses and carts. Was Ivy, whom Violet had mentioned, in these photographs, and would Pippa even know her if she was?

She got up and replaced the album with another, retaking her seat in the window. This one was more recent, the photographs moving gradually from black and white to colour. Her fingers on the page froze when her eyes landed on an image of her dad as a teenager, probably not much older than Harriet was now. His arm was slung around the shoulders of a taller boy, blond and unmistakably familiar, both laughing.

'What are you doing?'

Pippa yelped, startled from thoughts of the past and the photograph album slid to the floor. She shrank back as Gil marched across and snatched it from the carpet. A muscle was pounding in his cheek, and she scrambled up, trying to gather her thoughts.

'I'm so sorry, I—'

'Your father might own this house but that doesn't give you the right to rifle through anything you find. All this belonged to my grandparents and I haven't got anywhere else to put it.'

'Gil, I'm sorry. I didn't mean to pry, truly.' She made herself hold his gaze, chilled by that cool stare. 'In the album, is that...?' She had to know, and she swallowed. 'Your dad, with mine?'

He wasn't quick enough to disguise despair and it flared in his face before he resolutely blinked it away. 'Yes.' His reply was a hollow one and Pippa's hand darted out to rest lightly on his arm, her attempt to delay him pure instinct.

'It's just…' She took a deep breath, trying to hold back the tears pricking at her eyes. 'I had no idea, that our families were connected.' Her gaze dropped to the album he held between taut fingers, thinking of the two young boys. 'That they were friends.'

'It's not going to change anything, Pippa,' he said, his voice low, rough. 'And I really don't need any more complications in my life.'

'I'm not trying to make it complicated for you,' she whispered, utterly aware of the warmth of his arm beneath her fingers, the soft golden hairs brushing her skin.

'You already are, even if you don't know it yet.' His gaze was unflinching, and she read the awareness in it, her heart bumping in shock and something else: recognition that he felt it too, this pull between them. Gil was staring at her hand as though it was burning him. She snatched it away, horrified that she'd touched him, had tried to make him understand why she needed to know what more of her parents' lives he held.

The moment crawled into another and he slowly raised a hand, as though he was going to touch her face, smooth away the hair brushing her cheek. Her breath caught and then he hurriedly stepped back and let it fall away. Still holding the photograph album, he spun around and left the room, rattling the door shut behind him.

Pippa couldn't settle after that, couldn't shake off what she'd done and had discovered. She made drinks in the kitchen and took a mug of hot chocolate up to Harriet. Her daughter submitted to a surprising and brief good night hug and Pippa forced away the longing to hold her close, to find some comfort in being held too, her thoughts caught on that earlier and unexpected moment with Gil. She crossed the landing to her own room and placed a cup of camomile tea on the bedside table. Without Wi-Fi she couldn't learn anything else about their families now but there was so much she wanted to understand.

–

'Hello, Posy.' Pippa wondered if the Shetland pony would detect the nervous note in her voice as she approached the stable door, and Posy whinnied. 'Sorry, I don't speak pony. But maybe that means you'd like your breakfast?'

She hadn't been expecting the knot in her stomach as she'd crossed the yard, dreading having to face Gil after last night. A whack on the stable door suggested that Posy did speak human though, and Pippa went to fetch the bucket of feed that Elaine had measured out yesterday. She opened the door warily and Posy almost knocked Pippa backwards in her haste to shove her nose into the bucket.

'I thought you were going to wake me up.' Harriet was still drowsy, a coat pulled on over her pyjamas.

'Oh, hi! I wasn't sure you'd appreciate it.' Pippa backed up and shut the door. Her daughter didn't usually appear out of bed this early for anything less than a summons to school, sport or a shopping trip. 'But I'm glad you're here.'

'I said I'd help, didn't I?' Harriet's eyes were smudged with sleep, and she yawned. Her long hair was gathered into a rough ponytail, phone sticking out of a pocket.

'You did.' Pippa flashed her a grateful smile. 'Thank you for coming. Posy needs to go in the paddock but first we have to get this on.'

She pointed to a contraption hanging from a nearby hook. Part headcollar, part muzzle, Elaine had explained yesterday that it was vital Posy wasn't allowed to graze without it, as allowing her to guzzle as much grass as she liked was apparently very bad for her.

Posy knew the routine much better than they did, and both Pippa and Harriet were laughing as they tried a fourth time to buckle the headcollar in place and fit the muzzle comfortably over her nose. Tiny though the pony was, she managed to evade them at every turn. Despite the mayhem, Pippa decided it was lovely to laugh with Harriet, as though the sun had come out to shine on her. Bits of shavings were stuck to her jeans and Posy had upended the water bucket, soaking Harriet's pumps.

'I never saw two people so useless at trying to get a headcollar on one small pony.'

At Gil's words Pippa froze, instantly forgetting she was meant to be helping Harriet have another go at fastening the headcollar. Tension made her fingers clumsy, and she looked at him warily, remembering him snatching the photograph album and running from her last night. She wasn't expecting a quick smile as he propped his arms over the door, and she inadvertently let go of Posy, who took the opportunity to back herself into the far corner of the stable with a triumphant and very loud fart.

'Mum! I nearly had it right this time. Eww, that stinks!' Harriet approached Posy again, talking quietly, and Pippa watched in admiration as Posy stood meekly and let Harriet slip the headcollar back on, and carefully fasten the muzzle in place. Apparently even the pony knew when games were over.

Gil opened the stable door and Harriet's grin was wide as she led Posy into the yard, Lola following. Pippa sidled past him; she hadn't factored in the extra time spent chasing Posy and needed to get over to the vets if she was going to be ready for the first clients arriving. She'd never felt less equal to a task in her life, regretting that her offer to help Elaine meant she was forced to spend time with someone who rattled her so much.

'Pippa?'

'What?' She wasn't going to stop, not for him, and the keys Elaine had given her yesterday were in her hand.

'About last night.' He caught her up and she busied herself unlocking the door to reception. 'I'm sorry I reacted so badly.'

She took a deep breath. 'It's okay, I'm sorry too. You were right, I shouldn't have gone looking.'

'I understand why you did it. Your dad lived in Hartfell too.'

'Yes.' She turned, surprised by the glimpse of something softer in his eyes. Her fingers were on the door handle, delaying the moment when she'd have to open it and their conversation would be over. 'I wasn't expecting a family connection here, one that maybe goes even further back than my dad. I was hoping to learn more.'

'I know Elaine told you about my parents.' Gil swallowed. 'It's not something I'm good at talking about. It was a long time ago and I've moved on.'

'I understand.' Pippa did, perfectly, for similar and yet quite different reasons. 'I lost my mum at an early age too. I know it's not the same.' She wasn't expecting another rush of sorrow at the reminder. So long ago and still it could knock the air from her lungs.

'I'm sorry.' His gaze was tangled with hers until the shutters came back down, and she wondered if he'd ever let her back in. 'So are you ready for the onslaught? Mondays are always busy.'

'I hope so.' She finally pushed open the door and walked inside, Gil right behind her.

'You know you don't have to do this?' He glanced at the empty chairs, waiting to be filled with clients and their pets. 'Help me, I mean.'

'I promised Elaine I would. It's one less worry for her.' Pippa's pulse was still hurrying from that long look they'd shared. The unexpected and brief glance into his past, their mutual connection to this place. She settled behind the counter, recalling her induction with Elaine yesterday.

Lola flopped in her bed as Gil disappeared into his consulting room. Pippa switched on the computer and scanned the online booking system, glad of something practical to distract her. Through the open door she spotted Harriet and hopefully her daughter's grin meant that Posy was safely in the paddock and not thundering loose down the lane.

'Thanks for that. How do you fancy tackling the mucking out? I can help but it will have to be when I'm finished here.'

'Sure.' Harriet slid around the counter and crouched down to cuddle Lola, whose tail was wagging madly. 'I just need to get rid of the shit and neaten the shavings, yeah? And fill the water bucket?'

'Please don't swear, Harriet.' A forlorn hope, Pippa knew, and that was hardly the most unpleasant thing her daughter could have come out with. She'd said far worse inside her own mind since they'd arrived in Hartfell.

'"Shit" is hardly swearing, Mum. Everyone at school…'

'Well, we're not at school, are we.' Pippa was aware she sounded like a geriatric aunt; Raf was always telling her to loosen up, especially where Harriet was concerned. 'Just, you know, keep it clean.'

'Apart from the shit?' Harriet was on her way out again and Pippa rolled her eyes.

'Yes, apart from that.'

Chapter Ten

'You can't cancel the village show! Have you lost your bloody mind?'

The back door flew open and Pippa flinched as Gil burst into the kitchen, the plate in her hand wobbling. Harriet, sitting at the table, silently picked up her phone and slid out of the room, and Pippa was very tempted to follow. So, their temporary truce was at an end, and she wished she was clutching something more substantial than a tea towel.

Harriet had washed the dishes after dinner and Pippa had been drying them, lost in thoughts of the history of the house and Hartfell, and her own connection to this place and its people. Without her bed in its usual spot near the table, Lola didn't seem to know quite what to do with herself and wandered up for a pat.

'I think you'll find that I can,' she replied, ignoring Lola, and trying to even out the uncertain note in her voice as the Labrador's tail continued to wag hopefully. 'It was apparently being held on my land.' She paused, that didn't sound right, and it wasn't exactly true. 'My dad's land, and no one thought to check with me if it's okay to hold the show here. I haven't got time to oversee the arrangements and I have other things to worry about right now.'

Like finding an estate agent, which she still hadn't had time to do in the past two days in between dealing with the practice's clients, handling calls and queries, and clearing up accidents from the floor. Harriet had been a very welcome help; she'd caught on to the management system in a flash and accepted payments, saving Pippa a job, while messaging friends and updating her social media.

After each patient, Gil accompanied the client to the desk, leading Pippa to wonder if he didn't trust her, as he dispensed medication and arranged follow-up appointments. Elaine had kindly taken the time to send good wishes, and Pippa had thanked her, glad to hear in return that Elaine's dad was stable as they awaited news of scan results.

After consultations had ended this morning, Pippa had been taken aback to see people tramping around the field behind the garden, setting up gazebos, a flapping marquee and marking out rings with rope. The sheep had disappeared, and she'd found out from a helpful chap in a high-vis jacket, when she'd gone over to enquire what was going on, that it was all in preparation for the village show being held on Saturday.

'Besides, I haven't actually cancelled it.' She put the tea towel down and finally gave Lola a pat, wondering why bestowing attention on Gil's dog felt akin to being nice to him too. But ignoring Lola wasn't fair, and Pippa felt some of her tension ease as she stroked the friendly dog.

'I simply said I was very sorry, but they'd have to find somewhere else to hold it.' Hopefully by Saturday she'd have an estate agent round and she didn't want them thinking the village had free rein to trample across the farm as they pleased.

'Is that right?' Gil's bark of laughter was scornful. 'So you're quite certain, then, that the committee don't have rolling permission from your father to hold the show on this weekend every summer? And that should either party wish to cancel, the notice period is actually twelve months, not three days. The village is alive with panic and indignation, not that you care.'

Rolling permission? Twelve months? Pippa's hair was doing a fair job of hiding her face as she stroked Lola, and she took a moment to compose herself before her own panic took hold. She'd assumed that her dad knew nothing about the show, and she didn't want the field all dug up before the farm went on the market. After she'd informed the chap they'd have to leave, the workers had gathered in a huddle and finally disappeared, abandoning everything they'd brought.

'And the only reason you've told them to shove it, as far as I can see, is because you can't be bothered with the minor inconvenience of a few locals enjoying themselves for a day on your dad's land.' Gil folded his arms. 'I don't even know why I'm surprised. It's exactly what I'd have expected from a townie like you.'

'Clearly it's not just the one day, is it?' Pippa hoped countering his sarcasm with politeness was a more effective weapon than resorting to a slanging match. A townie, indeed. She supposed that was true. 'People would've been turning up all week and then been here half of the next one as well, clearing up.'

'This show goes back generations, Pippa.' He was forcing the words out slowly and she choked back a wild giggle as she wondered if he ground his teeth too. This was definitely not the right moment to laugh, though – he'd think she'd totally lost the plot. But her dread was still mounting as he carried on. 'To the old days when people travelled to the village in search of work, and you think to cancel all that tradition and the effort it takes at a moment's notice?'

'Isn't it just a few stalls and a burger van?' This time she did laugh, and it bordered on the slightly hysterical. From the look of the activity in the field earlier, she thought it might be a bit more, but surely all village shows were just that. A few stalls in the garden of the nearest vicarage served up with tea and cake, not the rows of metal seating she'd seen lined up on a lorry in the lane. That, thankfully, had been turned away before they'd started unloading.

'I guess you would think that.'

Gil ran a hand through his hair but Pippa wasn't going to be drawn in by the tiredness on his face. All his own fault, working the hours he did and trying to cling on to a crazy dream of taking over the practice instead of letting go and moving on.

'But seeing as you are apparently serious about ruining one of the best local days of the year, I've made a quick list of the people you need to contact.' He slapped a piece of paper onto the flimsy table, making it wobble. 'Why don't you start with the school, have a chat with the headteacher? See what she makes of telling the kids all the artwork they've made to sell at the fete to raise funds for their new trim trail is a waste of time. Then pop into the WI and tell them not to bother arranging flowers or baking, and while you're at it maybe you could make a donation to cover all the ones they'll lose from the cakes they won't sell on the day. Drop a line to the Young Farmers' group and let them know the sponsored fell run and tug of war is off too; I'm sure they'd appreciate a few quid slung their way to make up for it. Then there's the Morris Dancers, they were booked months ago so I don't suppose they'd mind a Saturday off, given how much practice they do.'

The table bounced again as Gil's hand thudded down a second time. 'Make sure you let the car parking people know, so they can contact the students after extra cash and tell them the show's off, seeing as the committee won't find another suitable venue that's large enough with two days' notice. And the food stalls. Off the top of my head I thought of the cocktail bar in a bus, the vintage caravan serving afternoon tea and the local caterer who makes a month's turnover in one day at the show. Then there's the expenses already incurred, like printing the catalogues and arranging prizes for competitions.'

Anxiety had knotted so tightly in her stomach she could feel cramps clutching at it and panic was rising, along with an acid feeling in her chest as Gil stared at her.

'You haven't thought this through, have you? It's all over social media and you're public enemy number one in Hartfell right now.' His anger had abated to a weary disbelief and somehow that felt even worse as he huffed out a long, harassed breath. 'You just don't give a toss.'

'I'm so sorry. I had no idea,' she whispered, wondering how – if – she could even put her colossal mistake to rights.

Gil straightened up and at the door he turned, Lola at his heels. 'And that's just it, isn't it? Because you can't wait to swan off back to your London life and leave all this behind. People live here, Pippa. They love living here. And you're a part of this place, even if you don't realise quite how much.'

After he'd left, she pulled out a chair and flopped onto it, head in her hands. She had been guilty of assuming the show didn't much matter, and that the few locals who bothered with it would find another venue easily enough – there was a whole village green, after all. She went outside and walked through the garden to the field, staring at the chaos left behind when she'd halted proceedings. There was only one thing she could do, so she used the key Elaine had given her and let herself into the vets.

Logging into the Wi-Fi, she brought up Facebook, the colour draining from her face when she found the show's page. Alongside the previously jolly posts about all there was to look forward to on Saturday, a new one had gone up this afternoon, suggesting the day was in doubt due to an issue with the landowner, and some of the comments made Pippa cringe. She took a deep breath and messaged Cassie, hoping her friend would put her considerable PR skills to use and post Pippa's apology for her.

Cassie came straight back with a promise to help, and after fifteen long minutes of mindful breathing, Pippa picked up her phone again and returned to the show's page. Comments were pouring in on the new post and amongst the relief, there were still a few angry for the confusion, which she supposed was only to be expected. She really needed something to make up for her mistake, an apology and offering to help in some way wasn't going to be enough. She called a familiar name in her phone, holding in tears when her brother finally picked up.

Afterwards, she placed a call to the haulage company, promising compensation if they could return first thing and deliver the seating they were meant to drop off earlier. They agreed, bemused by the about-turn, and in the morning, she was there to greet them. The team who'd been setting up yesterday had also returned, and she nipped down to the village shop to bring everyone freshly made bacon butties. It seemed she would be playing good-will catch-up for some time yet, and they were decent enough to accept her apology and get on with their work.

'I see you didn't bring one back for me.'

Pippa looked up to see Gil returning from a walk with Lola, who was snuffling in a patch of long grass beneath a hedge. He glanced at the huddle enjoying their impromptu breakfast and she checked her phone for the latest from Raf. Signal sometimes popped into range out here and she was hoping to hear from him.

'I didn't bring one for me either,' she told him as he halted nearby, Lola's unattached lead in one hand now that the sheep had been temporarily removed.

'That's different. You're a vegetarian. Or a vegan. We never did establish which.'

'Does it matter?' She read the new message from Raf, and it produced a dazzling smile she inadvertently turned on Gil. He blinked, and she wondered if the sun was in his eyes. Sunglasses were pushed into his blond hair, and he pulled them down. 'It's not as though you and I are ever likely to share a meal.'

'I guess not.' Lola ambled over and he bent to make a fuss of her. She wagged her tail and transferred her attention to Pippa, who enjoyed the quiet pleasure she found in making Lola happy.

'Look, Pippa, I was pretty angry about the show yesterday and I'm sorry I came down so hard on you.' He lifted a hand to their surroundings, the resumed activity and people working to get the show back on track. 'What you're doing, this, it's very decent of you.'

'Not really, you made that clear last night. But I hope everyone will still have a good day and I haven't ruined things completely.' She bit her lip. Maybe this would be the very last Hartfell village show held here. Next year, Home Farm would be in the hands of new owners, and she wondered if Gil was thinking of that too, as his eyes narrowed on hers.

'Are you coming to the show?'

'Why? Are you planning to ban me?' She'd prefer to be miles away given the chaos she'd caused, but she couldn't avoid it, not now with Raf on board as well.

'Don't think there's any point, I reckon you'd turn up anyway.'

She stared at him, unable to read his expression behind the polarised glasses, and she'd had enough of fighting. It was exhausting and she wasn't used to it, much preferring diplomacy and treading carefully to keep the peace in her world. Instead, she laughed, and Gil's lips twitched before widening into a grin.

'I was going to ask if you'd be helping on our stall, seeing as Elaine can't make it.'

'Your stall?' Pippa squinted at him, wondering if the sun had gone to his head. 'Doing what?'

'Greeting clients, maybe charming a few new ones as I'll likely be busy with the farmers. Somehow I think you'd be much better at that than me.'

'You'd trust me to do that?' She was searching his face for signs of sarcasm or an imminent put-down. 'Aren't you worried I'd try and sabotage your reputation or your business?' She hadn't yet called either of the two land agents she'd found yesterday; she was planning to do that later on.

'I think my reputation as a vet is secure and the business is doing okay. So is that a yes or no?'

'It's an "I'll think about it."' She wasn't about to commit to anything else involving Gil. It was quite enough, seeing him at the practice or around the yard every day, with both of them trying to avoid catching one another's eye. 'I have other things to do.'

'Yeah? Like what?'

Like getting Raf settled and sorted for one, but Pippa wasn't going to reveal that. She wasn't used to Gil smiling in her direction, never mind prepared to share her plans with him. Someone was beckoning her over his shoulder. 'You'll have to excuse me, I think I'm needed elsewhere.'

–

'Mum? MUM?'

'What?' Pippa was in her bedroom, debating whether to unpack her clothes and hang them in the ancient and musty wardrobe or carry on living out of her case until they went home again. 'What's the matter?'

'Can you come downstairs?' A tap on her door was followed by it bursting open and Harriet charging in. 'Gil wants a word with you.'

Oh, no. What had gone wrong now? Pippa carefully laid the one dress she'd brought on the bed and forced a casual note into her voice. 'What about?'

'Posy. He needs some help and when I offered, he said I had to ask you first.'

'What kind of help?' Pippa wasn't sure she liked the sound of this, but she did love the new excitement and colour in Harriet's face and didn't want to be the cause of it dissolving in a second if she refused. 'Is it dangerous?'

'Like, duh! Course not.' Harriet rattled the door, pointing to the stairs with her other hand. 'Can you come now, he's waiting.'

'Okay.' Pippa didn't have any choice if she didn't want to upset Harriet, and she followed her downstairs and into the kitchen.

Gil was staring through the window towards the yard, and he turned slowly, that impassive blue gaze landing on her. She hadn't seen him since yesterday morning in the field and was coming to expect the tremor on her skin whenever he was near.

'Harriet mentioned you need some help with Posy?' She sensed the shutters had come down once again and her voice was level lest he thought she was a pushover after a couple of grins and a glimpse of warmth.

'Please.' He glanced at Harriet, and she beamed, irrationally making Pippa want to kick him. Why didn't Harriet smile like that at her anymore? 'Posy needs an injection, and I wondered if Harriet would hold her for me. She did offer, but I thought it best to run it past you first. Posy and I aren't the best of friends and I quite like my teeth attached to my gums.'

'So you're suggesting that my daughter, who has very little experience of animals, should hold on to a dangerous pony whilst you stick a needle in it?' Pippa laughed. The idea was ridiculous, even if said daughter was currently making a fuss of Lola, and the big, friendly dog was lapping up the attention. 'That pony is barely taller than this table. Can't you tie her up?'

'Tried that last time. Haven't got round to fastening the metal ring back to the wall yet. And it's only me she doesn't like, she's fine with everyone else.' He fixed Pippa with that stare again and she had to remind herself not to fidget as she folded her arms.

'Perhaps she's a very good judge of character.' If she needed another reason to get rid of Gil and his part-time practice in her yard, then Harriet was it. No one was getting attached to anything or anyone around here, she told herself firmly. Least of all her impressionable teenage daughter.

'Oh, Mum, come on! How bad can Posy be? She's been fine while I've been taking her in and out of the paddock.' Harriet was already inching towards the door with Lola. 'Like you said, she's tiny.'

'But Harriet…'

'Mum, seriously! I'm doing it.'

'Fine,' Pippa muttered. Maybe it would be best to let Harriet find out for herself that this wouldn't be the jolly jape she was expecting if someone built like Gil couldn't even manage the pony without help. 'But I'm coming too, just in case.'

She was expecting Harriet to object to that but instead she was disarmed by the grin Harriet flashed her before she and Lola took off. Pippa and Gil got caught performing an awkward sort of a dance when they both tried to insist that the other went first and she won, closing the kitchen door behind them to follow him across the yard.

Posy looked very sweet in her stable, having her fluffy neck scratched by Harriet, making a hairy top lip curl in pleasure. Pippa nearly laughed; clearly, he was talking nonsense, and the pony was perfectly safe. She looked as though butter wouldn't dream of melting in her mouth, one neat little hind hoof tilted in relaxation.

Posy submitted to the headcollar, minus the muzzle, that Harriet slipped over her head, one eye half closed. Pippa was already thinking ahead to a lovely dinner with Harriet in the pub so she could use the Wi-Fi to reply to the email from the land agent she'd received. She'd popped into the pub on her way to the shop earlier and Kenny had promised to save a nice quiet table for them.

Gil followed Harriet into the stable and Pippa spotted the needle in his right hand. Posy's ears twitched as he slowly approached, her eyes fully open now, and Pippa sensed a sudden change in atmosphere. With a swift jerk of her head, startling Harriet, Posy shot through the open door and tore off across the yard, lead rope trailing like pink string behind her. Pippa and Harriet were left staring open mouthed at Posy's plump and retreating bottom, tail swishing in the sun. The whole episode had lasted about three seconds and Posy freewheeled out of sight towards the front garden.

'Why didn't you shut the bloody door?' He rounded on Pippa, and she clenched her fists, filled with an unfamiliar longing to let them do the talking for her.

'It's not my fault.' Pippa jumped sideways to let Harriet scoot past when she and Lola set off after Posy, Lola leaping excitedly. 'You never said to close the door.'

'Well, it's not exactly rocket science, is it?' He treated Pippa to a scowl over his shoulder as he marched after Harriet and his dog, and presumably the pony. 'Anyone with even a degree of common sense would have known she'd try to escape.'

'And anyone with a degree of decency would have explained what was required to two people who are unused to dealing with stroppy—' Pippa's lips tightened, the toes on her right foot were throbbing after Posy had stood on them on her way to freedom. '—ponies.' She wished she'd said vets instead.

'What's the matter?' Gil paused, watching as she took a hobbling step.

'Nothing,' Pippa muttered. Posy really was heavy, that tiny hoof had hurt but she was damned if she'd let him see how much. 'Now what are you going to do?'

'Spend the next thirty minutes chasing Posy around the garden probably,' he said sourly. 'She's a little demon. One of these days I might be tempted to give her an injection she won't wake up from.'

'You can't do that!' Pippa stared at him, aghast. 'Don't you have to take some sort of oath to swear you'll always save lives, not end them?'

'I think you're confusing me with a doctor. And I'm excusing myself from all promises made when I qualified where Posy's concerned. Get some ice on that foot or you'll still be limping tomorrow. Anyway, it's just me she has a problem with. If I really thought she was dangerous I would have asked you to help instead.'

'Thanks for that,' Pippa retorted, stung by the realisation of just how much Gil actually disliked her. She disliked him too but that wasn't the point; she wasn't trying to kill him. 'Death by demon pony.'

She was expecting him to agree but instead he laughed, and quite without meaning to let it, her breath caught. The grin softened his blue eyes into something she absolutely refused to admit might be close to irresistible and revealed a whole other side to him, one she was horrified to notice was devastatingly attractive.

'Coming?' The grin was still lingering, and he glanced at her foot. 'Can you walk on it?'

'Of course I can.' Pippa took a faltering step, then another, still thinking about that smile.

'Right. Round two.' Gil grabbed a bucket, and waited for Pippa to cross the yard. Maybe espadrilles weren't the best thing for her feet out here. She probably ought to buy her and Harriet some wellies, steel-toe capped ones preferably.

Chapter Eleven

Posy was grazing on the lawn at the front of the house and to Pippa's surprise, she stuffed her nose inside the bucket Harriet had taken from Gil. The pony let Harriet grab the rope too and lead her back to him, having evidently decided to submit this time, and he wedged her firmly against the post and rail fence on the drive. Although she flattened her ears and gave him what even Pippa recognised from ten feet away was a filthy look, she offered no further objection to the needle he jabbed efficiently into her neck.

'Done. Same again next month.' He straightened up and gave her a pat. 'Well done, Posy, you were very brave,' he said loudly, and Pippa caught his amused glance on her as Harriet giggled. 'Thanks, Harriet. I literally couldn't have done it without you. She barely lets me near her.'

'You're welcome. She's sweet.' Harriet was stroking Posy whilst the pony tried to stick her nose in the now-empty bucket. 'How old is she?'

'Don't know exactly but at least twenty. That's why she needs a close eye kept on her, she's not quite as fit as she thinks she is.'

Pippa seriously doubted that. Geriatric or not, Posy clearly still had a decent turn of foot. Those stubby little legs had shot across the yard pretty smartly from what she'd just seen.

'Can you tell their age by their teeth? I read that some-where.' Harriet looked away shyly and Gil nodded.

'Well done, you do. I'll show you some other time, when Posy's not expecting it, okay? There's only so much attention from me she'll submit to at any one time. Her teeth are quite brown, which is a sign of age, as well as the way they're sloping. She's also prone to laminitis brought on by a hormonal condition called Cushing's Disease.' He paused and Harriet was waiting for more, listening intently. 'It's incurable but it can be managed by medication and good care. Laminitis causes severe pain in the worst cases as a bone inside her hoof can rotate or sink. If she eats too much lush grass the extra sugars and starch ferment in the gastrointestinal tract and create a bacterial imbalance that can also cause attacks of laminitis. It's very serious.'

'Wow. I had no idea. It's so cool that you know all this stuff.'

'I'm a vet, I'm supposed to.' He was still smiling at Harriet and Pippa was finding it hard to cling to her anim-osity in the face of his kindness and patience towards her daughter. 'So that's why she's turned out in the morning and comes back in around lunchtime. Are you taking her back to the stable? Just make sure you close the door.'

He shot Pippa another look and she caught his amuse-ment. At times he was so hard to read, it was like trying to decipher a book in a language she'd never learned. She watched as Posy walked quietly alongside Harriet towards the barn, something clenching in her heart at the sight.

'You'd better get that foot up and some ice on it, Pippa.'

'I'm fine.' She wasn't expecting his concern. 'Posy really doesn't like you, does she?'

'It's because I'm the voice of reason in her life and won't let her stuff her face on summer grass until she drops dead.'

'Who does she actually belong to?' The thought had only just occurred to Pippa. 'You?'

'Don't be ridiculous. What would I want with a small, angry pony who can't stand the sight of me?' He shrugged. 'She was here when I moved back into the house. Legend has it she was left behind by a client who didn't want her, and I've been supervising her diet ever since, much to her disgust.'

'But you'll take her with you when you go?'

'I will not. Where do you think she's going to live when I'm in a rented flat somewhere?' Gil set off towards the yard and Pippa hurried to catch him up, ignoring the discomfort in her foot. 'She's like a bloody homing pigeon. I reckon if I let her loose on the fells, she'd just find her way back again.'

'Well, she can't stay here! The last thing I need is another tenant, and a four-legged one at that. You'll have to sell her or something.'

'I won't. Your house, your pony, your problem. You sell her. She must be worth fifty quid to someone. Oh and by the way.' He paused to stare at Pippa and her heart sank. She recognised that expression and knew she wouldn't like whatever was coming next. 'Dorothy's looking for a bit of help with her animals. I had a word with Harriet earlier and she's up for it, seeing as she doesn't have much else to do right now. Be good for her and I'm glad to get Posy off my hands as well.'

It took Pippa a few seconds to process his words and her own were a furious splutter when she eventually found her voice. 'You what? How dare you talk to Harriet without speaking to me first? And the answer's no, by the way. She has hardly any experience of animals and I'm not sure she should go within twenty feet of Posy again, not from what I've just seen. Nor any of Dorothy's animals, whatever they might be!'

'Fine.' His lips curled. 'Then be sure to let Harriet know your decision, because Dorothy's expecting her at the farm in an hour to show her around. I said I'd go with her.'

—

'You should've asked me first!' Back in the kitchen, Pippa was trying with everything she possessed not to let her temper get the better of her. 'He had no right talking to you without involving me. You're still a child, and one who knows almost nothing about animals.'

'Yes, but I'm not stupid, am I? And I'm not a child, Mum. Not any longer.' Harriet dipped her head but not before Pippa had seen the glimmer of tears. 'You're the only one that thinks I'm not up to it.'

'I don't think that at all, Harriet. Of course you're not stupid, or not up to the challenge.' Pippa dragged out one of the rickety chairs and sank onto it. 'It's just, well, I'm worried about you, that's all. How much help can you be to Dorothy if you've never really looked after animals before?'

'I can learn.' For once Harriet wasn't holding her phone and Pippa caught the hopeful note in her voice. From everything she'd seen of Harriet and Lola together so far, she had no idea how she was going to separate her daughter from yet more animals when it was time to leave for home. Harriet might get attached to them all and then

Pippa would be the one dragging her back to the London life she'd yearned for right up until Gil had interfered.

'And what if you get bitten or kicked, or something.' Pippa hadn't forgotten all the unpleasant odours she'd been subjected to in the practice this week and she pulled a face. 'It'll be filthy, smelly work.' She hoped that might do the trick and put Harriet off.

'Mum, I don't care! I want to do it and as usual you're the only one standing in my way.'

Pippa's shoulders slumped. The only one, it felt sometimes, standing between Harriet and actual harm. Bad cop again. When had she stopped being the good cop, or had she never been one? 'I just want to keep you safe, that's all.'

'Keep me stuck in this place with nothing to do and barely any Wi-Fi, you mean. I thought you'd want me to be outside and getting some exercise in the fresh air and away from my phone. Isn't that what all parents want for their kids?'

There was no way Pippa could refute that and they both knew it. She'd lost the argument before she'd even known one was coming. Gil had seen to that by getting Harriet onside first. Bloody, bloody man, Pippa fumed. The sooner she got this place sold and them far away from it, the better.

'Can we at least go and see the farm, Mum, please?' Harriet had injected a sweeter note into her voice and Pippa sighed.

'Fine. But if it's dangerous in any way, then you're not doing it, okay? And do not forget that it's temporary.'

'Okay.' Harriet leapt up and Pippa melted the moment her daughter's arms flew around her neck, submitting to the hug and squeezing Harriet back tightly. It wasn't for long, and Harriet might hate the farm. Pippa could but hope.

–

'Safeguarding?' Dorothy had a way of snorting that expressed several emotions at once and all of them were scornful. She peered at Pippa over a pair of glasses perched halfway down her nose and held together with tape. 'Is that one of those meaningless words you ruddy millennials have invented?'

Pippa attempted to unclench her teeth before Harriet – or worse, Gil – caught her grinding them again. They'd only arrived at Dorothy's farm five minutes ago after he'd offered them a lift and they'd piled into his Land Rover, Lola sprawled across Harriet's lap in the back. And now Harriet was already shooting *Seriously?* vibes at Pippa and clearly wishing her mother would just shut up and back off.

'It's a widely accepted and reasonable term for making sure young or vulnerable people are properly taken care of and kept safe, Dorothy,' Pippa replied as evenly as she could. Gil was looking at sheep in a pen, but she was certain he was enjoying himself very much, if the shaking in his shoulders was anything to go by. She decided that Dorothy could give Lady Catherine de Bourgh a run for her money when it came to withering stares, and tried not to quail under the scrutiny.

'If—' and Pippa emphasised the word very firmly '—Harriet is going to be helping you for a few hours each week, then I'm sure you understand that I need to know her safety is paramount and she won't come to any harm.'

'Can't guarantee it,' Dorothy said cheerfully, giving Harriet a wink and Harriet grinned. 'Child's clearly been safeguarded all her life. What she needs is a few risks and a good run around in the fresh air. Pale as a peony, that one. Get her off that phone whilst she's at it and I could do with the help.'

'Harriet is fourteen, Dorothy. And as you quite rightly pointed out, she is still a child.'

'So? I was driving by the time I was her age and could lamb a sheep in my sleep.' Dorothy fixed Pippa with another look and Pippa made herself hold it. This was one battle she wasn't going to lose. 'Are you going to keep her cooped up forever, staring at a screen and tracking her phone so you know where she is every minute of the day?'

Pippa quashed a flare of guilt. Didn't everyone track their children on their own phones, counting the minutes until they walked back through the front door? But such a thing wasn't quite so easy in Hartfell, where signal was patchy at best.

'Anyway, it's only the bull she needs to watch out for but he's a sweetie really.'

'Bull?' Pippa's eyes widened in alarm as she glanced around the yard. 'As in, an actual bull?'

'Yes, an actual bull.' Dorothy slowly shook her head, giving Pippa the clear impression she didn't like dealing with people she thought were dimwits. 'The kind of bull that likes to impregnate cows and make calves. Mine fired blanks though, so he lives a quiet life now he's been castrated. That's the official term for having his—'

'I get the picture, thank you very much.' Pippa was checking out the yard, mostly so she didn't have to keep facing Dorothy. 'Could we at least have a look around?'

'If you like. Come on, Harriet, I'll introduce you to Rufus and Rupert. They're the alpacas.' Dorothy was already striding off and Harriet rushed to catch her up.

Three dogs were at Dorothy's heels; a small terrier that looked as though it might have your leg off if it took against you – much like Dorothy, Pippa thought warily – as well as a beautiful red setter, sleek and glossy, and a three-legged lurcher who was prancing through patches of dried mud alongside a gambolling Lola.

The farm sat at the end of a short track, a square house facing a front garden that had mostly been given over to orchard, grazed by three pale brown sheep, one of which was impressively horned. A nice height for stabbing someone in the thigh, Pippa mused uncomfortably. The plain white farmhouse was attached on either side by a stone barn and Dorothy disappeared around the side of the largest one, Harriet close by.

Inside the beautifully neat barn, almost all of it divided into pens, two alpacas were staring as their little group approached and Pippa heard a low humming as one of the pair, its woolly coat the exact shade of caramelised sugar, backed away. The second alpaca, chocolate brown, watched curiously.

'This is Rufus,' Dorothy said fondly, unfastening the gate to enter the pen. She rubbed a gentle hand on the first alpaca's back.

'May I?' Harriet held out an arm, throwing Pippa an excited grin which made her gulp, and Dorothy nodded.

'But quietly and slowly, please. The boys aren't used to strangers and although they're generally calm, they can be wary. Stroke his shoulder, just here. He likes that.' Dorothy held open the gate and Harriet slipped inside as Pippa watched, Gil nearby. Harriet crept nearer, hand slowly reaching out. Rufus had a cautious eye on her, but he submitted to her touch as Dorothy murmured to him.

'They're so soft!' The second alpaca was approaching, ears down. 'Mum, you try.' Harriet was stroking Rufus gently, and Dorothy stepped away.

'Not in the pen,' Dorothy warned. 'One stranger is quite enough.'

'I can see them from here, Harriet,' Pippa said, silently agreeing with Dorothy. She'd be ordering wellies the minute she was next connected to Wi-Fi; she didn't fancy getting any of that poo on her trainers, or Harriet's either.

'Have you had them a long time?' Harriet asked, her attention on the alpacas. Pippa knew, with a sinking heart, that this was a done deal – her daughter was entranced.

'About six years.' Dorothy's hand went to a pocket, and she held out some food. The chocolate brown alpaca nibbled at it greedily and Harriet laughed when Rufus tried to grab some too, pushing past her. 'They came to me when their previous owner died and nobody else wanted them.'

'Mum, aren't they lovely?'

'They are.' The two boys did look very sweet, and Pippa took a step nearer as the brown alpaca eyed her right back, making a noise a bit like expelling air. She held out a hand, unable to see his eyes properly underneath a fluffy topknot. Dorothy was saying something, and Pippa glanced at her.

'Don't touch his face, he—'

Pippa's hand was hovering and with lightning reflexes, the alpaca launched an evil-smelling blob right onto her chest. 'Oh!' She stared at the green stain spreading across her top.

'Spits,' Dorothy finished. 'Naughty boy, Rupert. Remember that, Harriet, if you don't want him to spit on you. Shoulders and back only, not his face.'

Harriet was choking back laughter, clearly trying not to startle the animals. Pippa shot backwards in case the naughty boy fancied another go, taking the stink with her. Straight into Gil, whose hands landed on her shoulders.

'Steady,' he said quickly, and she heard the grin in his voice. No doubt he'd enjoyed that too. The hot sting of tears rushed into her eyes; even the wretched alpacas hated her. All she wanted was to go back to her lovely life in London and prevent Harriet getting hurt in any physical or emotional sense, not stand around here being attacked by unruly animals and laughed at by Dorothy and an irascible vet.

'It's only the contents of his stomach, I daresay it'll wash out eventually.' Dorothy said briskly, treating Rupert to a back rub that Pippa felt he didn't deserve.

'You okay?' Gil's voice was low in her left ear, and she wasn't expecting his hands tightening on her shoulders as she stumbled again, the heat of his body startling and sudden against hers. She nodded hurriedly, freeing herself from his fingers warm and gentle, sure on her skin. Was that a deliberate touch or just a means of soothing her after the shock?

'Mum, we're going to see the sheep.' Harriet barely glanced at Pippa as she left the pen and Dorothy fastened the catch. 'Dorothy said they're Soays, descended from the feral sheep that used to live on St Kilda. There are lambs too, born in spring. They're a rare breed.' Harriet looked over her shoulder, already following Dorothy, the four dogs skipping ahead.

'Pity alpacas aren't,' Pippa said shakily. Her smile for Harriet was a tremulous one, her thoughts caught on Gil and those last few moments; his chest firm against her back, arms brushing hers. She forced one foot in front of the other, giving Rupert a wide berth and a wary look. 'Let's go, then.'

'Can I stay for a bit, Mum, please?' Harriet hung back to walk alongside her. Pippa saw the light in her daughter's eyes and knew there was no refusing. 'I'll be back in plenty of time for dinner, I want to help Dorothy feed the animals.'

'You can stay this afternoon and then let's talk properly tonight, Harriet.' It wasn't a question and Harriet nodded grumpily. 'There are a few things we need to consider.'

'Like what?'

'Like how long we're staying in Hartfell, for one.'

'Well, you're helping Gil at the vets now and we have to stay until Elaine gets back.' Harriet shrugged. How simple she made everything sound, but Pippa had a sinking feeling that their being in Hartfell had suddenly got a whole lot more complicated.

Gil gave Pippa a single, unreadable stare and excused himself, pleading work. He jumped into the Land Rover with Lola, and Pippa was relieved to follow Dorothy along another track towards more fields.

'Don't worry.' Dorothy halted and placed a hand on Pippa's arm. She stared at it, nonplussed by the older woman's brusque tone and kinder words, and realised she was talking about Harriet. 'I'll keep an eye on her.'

The roar of an engine had everyone turning to see a tractor pulling into the yard, a huge trailer loaded with plastic-wrapped bales attached to it. The cab door opened, and a teenage boy jumped down, followed more slowly by a man, maybe late thirties. If Vikings did farmers, then Pippa strongly suspected that this strapping pair would fit the bill.

Tall and probably blue-eyed to boot, the teenager's hair was white blond, and he had the kind of looks that made girls – and probably some boys – behave very much as Harriet was doing now. Usually so confident and assured, Pippa saw her pulling her phone from a pocket with one hand and flicking her long hair over a shoulder with the other, trying to look more nonchalant than she clearly felt. Pippa's heart plummeted even further when the boy grinned at her and Harriet smiled shyly back, warmth tinting her face pink.

'This is James and his nephew Alfie.' Dorothy tilted her head before resuming her stride. 'Farmers,' she added, quite unnecessarily in Pippa's opinion. 'Thanks chaps, you know where to go, the Dutch barn around the back. I won't be long, I'm just showing Harriet around the place. She's helping me out.'

'Well, it's not exactly decided yet, Dorothy.' Pippa hadn't even merited an introduction and the last thing she needed was another reason for Harriet to want to hang around here. Now, one had just jumped down from a tractor and probably stolen Harriet's heart as well, if the look on her face was anything to go by. She'd had a boyfriend at Easter, but he'd been more of a mate with whom she'd had a few dates before they'd decided to revert their relationship back to the friend zone. Alfie was an altogether different prospect.

With another smile for Alfie, one that he returned before dropping his gaze to examine his boots, Harriet managed to drag herself away and caught Dorothy up. Pippa lagged behind, alternately marvelling at Dorothy's energy, and cursing the number of animals she had tucked in every corner of the farm. She must be eighty if she was a day and reluctant though Pippa was to let Harriet come here regularly, it was obvious why Dorothy needed the help. Chickens and ducks were free range, scratching through the muck heap, and a grey cat eyed them warily from the top of an open bale of haylage, a couple of adorable kittens leaping around her.

Heading out of the last barn after the grand tour, they came across Alfie in the tractor, unloading the bales with some kind of pronged attachment into an open-sided barn, lifting and storing them with easy efficiency. Harriet dug out her phone from a pocket and was soon videoing him, no doubt to share with friends. Dorothy left them to talk with James, still swaddled in her hat and gilet, despite the mild air.

'So, what do you think, Mum?' Harriet's eyes were shining when she dragged them from Alfie long enough to glance at Pippa, who hadn't missed him grinning every time he caught Harriet watching. 'Can I come and help Dorothy, please? I'll be careful, I promise, and I'm sure she'll give me lots of training.'

Pippa seriously doubted that, and she tried not to sigh. 'Just please don't forget that we're going home soon, and you mustn't get attached to any of the animals.' Or boys, she added mentally, determined to take her own advice. At least Harriet would agree that her mum was too old for all that nonsense now.

The bales were off the trailer now, safely stored in the barn, so Alfie cut the engine and got out. He and Harriet were sidling towards each other, drawn like magnets, and Pippa felt another clench in her heart at yet more evidence of Harriet growing up. Her daughter definitely needed an outlet for her energy but if she formed an attachment to Alfie, then Pippa had absolutely no idea how she would get her back to London without a battle.

Chapter Twelve

Pippa was glad to finish at the practice on Friday the moment the last patient had left, and she offered Gil a hasty goodbye and made her escape. She still hadn't gone public with her plans for a surprise at the show tomorrow, and she wouldn't, not until Raf was actually here in person. Commitment, except to his music, was something her mercurial brother was not prone to. There was still time for him to change his mind, or for the lift he'd been promised in a helicopter from a mate of a mate to fail to materialise. At the far end of the next-door field was a flattish area marked out for car parking tomorrow, and she was crossing everything in the hope that the helicopter would be able to land without any difficulty, or anyone really noticing.

Harriet had finally returned at eight p.m. last night, after having messaged to say that Dorothy had invited her and Alfie to stay on for supper, and did Pippa mind? Pippa did rather, but had more sense than to say no. She'd toyed with still going to the pub but had decided not to; she wasn't sure she could face the village alone until the show was safely over and the day done.

The fields around the farm were packed with trailers, stands and pens for livestock, and she checked Raf's latest message as she hurried back to the house to sort out a bedroom for him. The room Gil had been sleeping in was the obvious choice, with the only spare double bed. She found clean sheets in an airing cupboard and changed them, feeling as though she was invading his privacy just that little bit more.

He'd left nothing personal in here, nothing to suggest he planned on returning. The room was empty of all but the old-fashioned furniture and huge brass bed. She'd been careful not to open more cupboards or investigate drawers since their row on Sunday, when he'd caught her with the photo album. Daphne from the shop had mentioned that a local historian was compiling an archive of the village, and that Pippa might like to ask him if he knew of anyone in her family named Ivy.

Four hours later, she was hurrying through the garden again when she heard the buzz of the helicopter, adrenaline surging at the thought of seeing her brother. Moments later it came into sight, lowering slowly, flattening grass and flapping tents in the field as it settled on the ground. A door opened and Raf jumped out, ducking to avoid the blades as he jogged towards her, hand raised in thanks to the pilot.

'Raf!' Pippa almost fell into his arms, raising her voice above the noise as the helicopter rose into the sky, ecstatic to see a beloved face. Like their dad, Raf poured his emotions into the lyrics he wrote, and she understood from his embrace how deeply he cared about their family. 'It's so good to see you! It's been way too long.'

'I know.' He squeezed her back just as tightly, dropping his bag to hold her close. 'Missed you, sis.'

He'd got his height from their mum, who'd been five ten, but his looks were pure Jonny. Nut brown hair was streaked with blond, short and swept up at the front. He was deeply tanned from his travels and the surfing she'd seen him doing via his Instagram.

She'd always thought Raf seemed to carry the weight of the world in his eyes. To his public they were full of mischief, alive and ready for fun; in private, he often seemed sad and with each year that passed it became harder to reach him. Losing Ewan, his best friend and Cassie's husband, had hit him hard and Pippa was certain his wanderings were a way to try and forget the pain they all lived with.

'How was the island?' she asked casually. She knew he'd been back in London for a bit, but wanted to get his take on his relationship and whether it really was over.

'Yeah, good.' Raf pulled back and tilted his head to look at her. 'But eventually not quite as much fun as I thought it would be.'

'Ah. So it's over then, with Lina?'

'Yep. Somehow we went from a summer road trip to conversations about sharing her apartment in Malmö and, well, you know.' Raf let Pippa go, reaching for the leather holdall he'd dropped.

She did know, and a glimmer of sympathy followed for his ex-girlfriend. She'd liked Lina and thought she might finally persuade him to settle.

'I'm sorry. Are you both okay?' She linked arms with him as they set off across the field, watching the helicopter disappear into the distance.

'Sure. Lina knew the score from day one. Not for me, all that playing house stuff.'

'But you do it with Cassie – take Rory and Isla out, look after them. I know how much they love seeing you and she really appreciates the time you give them.'

'That's different,' he said quickly, dragging Pippa around a cow pat to avoid it. 'They're family, good as.'

'You know, eventually you will find what you're looking for, probably without even trying.'

'Like you, you mean?' He was an expert at changing the subject and she gave him a sisterly shove as they reached a gate.

'You don't need to worry about me.' Gil flashed into her mind. They'd been extra polite to one another in between consultations this morning. And she was still thinking about his hands on her shoulders the other day, shocked that his brief touch had left her wanting more. 'I'm divorced and not interested in going there again. And I can't thank you enough for stepping in here to save me, I'd probably have been in the village stocks by now. I'm sorry to crash in the middle of your summer.'

'No problem, anything for you.' They resumed walking. Pippa always relished these first, rare moments alone with her brother. 'I'm actually quite looking forward to it. Something new for the 'gram.'

'Do me a favour though?' She led him through the garden, hoping to keep him under wraps until Cassie posted his presence on the event's Facebook page later. 'Please don't take your shirt off. It's a village show full of families, Raf, not Glastonbury.'

He'd quickly gained a huge online following when he'd posted an image of himself drumming topless, rehearsing a tour a few years ago. It had gone viral, sending his fame soaring. He played up to it when he wanted to, dropped in a few mischievous shots on his social media, and most Blue at Midnight gigs weren't complete until the band had seen out their encore with a classic track and Raf drumming minus his shirt.

'Can't promise, Pippa. Gotta give the public what they want.' He winked as she shot him an exasperated look and they laughed. Time together was too precious to worry about such antics for now. 'You gonna show me the house, then? Tell me why you still haven't got it on the market.'

'I haven't met the agent yet,' she said casually. 'I'm on it. We can start the tour in the kitchen and then hopefully your expectations for the rest of it will be low enough.'

Raf liked the house, pointing out the beautiful aspect from almost every window and the excellent proportions of each room. Pippa, who hadn't properly seen past the situation with Harriet and then Gil, plus the uncertain plumbing and primitive kitchen, had to appreciate her brother was right. Raf had still not bought a home of his own, preferring to travel and lay his head wherever he laid his hat.

Harriet was ecstatic to see him, and Pippa watched their hugs and conversation wistfully as he caught her up on the band's tour and all the gossip. Harriet in turn was enthusiastic about Dorothy's farm and casually dropped in that she was off to a Young Farmers' meeting with Alfie later. Pippa nipped down to the pub for another takeaway, not ready to face the circus that might accompany Raf if they sat down to eat there instead. Kenny was not only amused by her attempt to cancel the show, but shocked into temporary speechlessness by her hushed whisper of her rock-star brother's surprise appearance.

–

Early showers on Saturday gave way to sunshine as the morning wore on. Pippa had been up since first light, worrying about the show and if it would be a success given the chaos she'd caused. She'd been round to see the headteacher at the primary school; not, as Gil had suggested, to make an excuse for trying to cancel, but to introduce herself and to offer a few hours of her time to help with an art project before the school broke up for the summer. The headteacher had been delighted to accept, and Pippa planned to return soon to make good on her promise.

She'd barely dared open Facebook since Cassie had posted on the show's page, introducing Raf as a special guest, but she knew from her friend that the news had blown up as excitement and comments mounted. Crossing the yard after sneaking into the vets to use the Wi-Fi, she'd bumped into Gil, who'd heard about Raf's arrival from Harriet while she was mucking out Posy's stable. Gil had made his displeasure perfectly clear, pointing out that the show had managed without the appearance of a rock star for over a hundred years, and where did she think all the extra visitors Raf might generate were going to park?

Thankfully, Pippa had already thought of that and coolly informed Gil the logistics were taken care of. In reality she'd sent a panicked email to the head at the school, who'd got the governors to agree to open up the playground if necessary, plus there was some parking at the vets. According to Harriet over breakfast, tickets were selling like hot cakes since Raf, who loved a crowd, had dropped a couple of hints about his whereabouts on Instagram.

The village was buzzing with anticipation when Pippa ran down early to the shop for fresh bread, with even Daphne having come over all peculiar as she enquired after Raf and how long he might be staying. Pippa was just relieved that her mistake appeared to have been forgiven. Visitors began arriving before the planned ten a.m. start and Harriet had already disappeared, taking care of Posy straight after breakfast and then haring off to help at Dorothy's before the show. Pippa was bemused by this sudden new commitment to caring for animals, but relieved that the smile was back on Harriet's face. She even seemed to mind less about the Wi-Fi.

When Pippa made her way to the show, she set off to explore, passing farmers across every generation gathered around the various holding pens, chatting as the animals nibbled at feed before the serious business of showing began. Further on, rows of stalls were lined up, offering mental health support to those working in rural locations, charities raising funds with a tombola and coconut shy on others. Dorothy had brought the alpacas, Pippa spotting Rufus and Rupert penned just along from the sheep, staring warily at the crowds descending. She prayed Rupert wouldn't spit on Raf; she didn't imagine that her brother would appreciate such animal antics.

The food courts were doing a roaring trade, and children were already slithering down a bouncy slide and leaping on trampolines, parents waiting nearby glad of momentary respite. The double-decker bus repurposed as a bar had seats, already full, on the top deck and the list of cocktails looked tempting. Pippa promised herself one later if the day went to plan. A band was tuning up on a shallow stage beneath an open-sided marquee, their first set due to begin in an hour.

Native ponies were being shown in hand in the main arena and vintage tractors were proving popular as visitors inspected them and posed for selfies. The local fell rescue service was well represented, as was an artisan gin distillery, handmade soap, candles and locally produced chocolates, and she bought some of each, saving her goodies for later. She was welcomed wherever she went, and realised she was actually starting to enjoy herself. The show was clearly a success, and she breathed a sigh of relief.

'Pippa, hi!'

She turned, thinking about collecting Raf from the house for his appearance. Rose was standing behind a table at another stall offering advice and support to those farming in protected landscapes, alongside a second displaying a beautifully presented range of skincare. Each box was white, with the brand name, Remedy & Rose, pretty inside a soft pink rose.

'Can I tempt you into reading our latest newsletter?' Rose held out a few A4 pages stapled together. 'Or you can scan this QR code and download it later, I'm afraid the 4G isn't brilliant out here.'

'I'll scan.' Pippa reached for her phone and scanned the code; something to read later perhaps. 'Thanks, Rose. Good day so far?'

'For sure, it's very busy. The weather helps of course, but then we don't usually get a rock star and a rock star's daughter as special guests.'

'Not sure about special,' Pippa said wryly, putting her phone away. 'Notorious might be more like it.' She admired the beautifully presented range of skincare, everything from bars of soap and handwash, to shower gels, moisturiser and muscle rub.

'I think it's brilliant, I hope I get to meet Raf.' Rose's striking brown eyes were merry, and she thanked a couple who picked up a leaflet before wandering off. 'Do you think he'll have time to say hello?'

'I'll make sure he does.' Pippa also made a mental note to tell Raf to behave himself. Rose was different to his usual girlfriends, but that didn't mean he wouldn't do his best to charm her. Lay off the locals, would be Pippa's firm message. The last thing she needed was her brother breaking someone's heart here and taking off on tour again.

'Are you a volunteer?' She was scanning the information laid out on the table, details of an upcoming farm visit, a talk on farm diversification and a social evening next month.

'No, I work part-time for the Yorkshire Dales Park Authority, I'm one of the FPL officers.' Seeing Pippa looking blank, Rose smiled before carrying on. 'Farming in a Protected Landscape. We're a link between the park authority and the farmers, offering information and support, and helping the two to work together. I farm with my brother, although he does most of the day-to-day. I help out but I'm more on the diversification side of things, hence the skincare.'

'It's gorgeous.' Pippa picked up a muscle rub and two lip balms. 'I'll take these please. Harriet will love the vanilla one and I'm definitely feeling the difference when I run on those fells.'

'Thanks, Pippa, that's lovely.' Rose reached for her phone. After Pippa tapped her own phone and the internet thought about it, the transaction went through. 'I hope it helps. There's ginger in the muscle rub because it's anti-inflammatory and the chamomile is very calming.'

Pippa thanked her and slipped her goodies into a bag which was becoming heavy; she'd leave it at the house when she returned for Raf.

'Actually, I think you and I have another connection.' Rose leaned forward. 'My son Alfie has very recently met Harriet. He was delivering haylage to Dorothy with my brother the other day, and James said Alfie came home with stars in his eyes.'

'Alfie's your son! Right.' Pippa liked him even more now. Not that she hadn't to begin with, but there was a warmth and an openness to Rose that was very inviting. 'I've barely seen Harriet since.'

'Same. Although Alfie helps James as much as he can anyway. He can't wait for school to finish next week so he can farm all summer.' Rose raised a hand to point. 'If you're looking for Harriet, I think she's over at the Young Farmers' with him. They've got a few things planned for fundraising and he's taking his turn on the dunking stool. Not a bad thing to do on a lovely day like this.'

'No.' Pippa agreed, turning to have a look. Harriet was laughing with a bunch of teenagers, Alfie at her side, as another boy picked up a hammer and whacked it down on a high striker, trying to make the bell at the top ring. Pippa and Rose shared a smile at the cheers that followed his success.

'How would you fancy joining me for a walk sometime, Pippa?' Rose was tidying the flyers on the table after a little boy had muddled them up. 'It's not a formal thing. A few of us local women got together for coffee and decided we'd rather meet outdoors and do something active. Early morning works best before we're swallowed up by other commitments, so we meet outside the pub every Wednesday at six. Kenny's a sweetheart and he has takeaway coffee and muffins ready for when we get back. Usually it's a walk but if it's nice we might strip off and have a dip in the river. Not skinny dip,' Rose added hastily as she caught the look on Pippa's face. 'Not unless that's your thing. No pressure either way, you do you.'

'It does sound lovely. I'm not sure how long we'll be here but I appreciate the invitation, thank you.'

'You're very welcome,' Rose replied. 'We'd love to see you, even if it's only just the once. You can message me if you like, my details are in the newsletter.'

'Thank you. I'll let you know if I change my mind.'

'So what do you think of Alfie and Harriet? She's a wonderful young lady, Pippa. So polite and respectful.'

Pippa was very thankful that Harriet's good manners extended beyond their home. But that had never been in doubt, it was just her mum with whom she was so tetchy. 'It's very sweet,' she said carefully. 'But I really hope neither of them find it hard to separate once we leave, probably in a week or so.'

'So soon?' Rose's hand stilled on a sheaf of flyers. 'Harriet said she thought you might be here for the summer.'

Pippa coughed, wondering where that idea had come from. 'I'm not sure. I have some decisions to make on the house and we'll be going home once Elaine returns. Harriet has netball camp coming up and she'll be going away with her dad in August.'

'So you're selling it, then, the house? That's what everyone's expecting.' Rose nodded sadly. 'It does make sense seeing as you don't have a connection to the village now, but it'll be devastating to lose the practice. All the local farmers rely on it.'

'It's not certain. There are some things to decide first.' Pippa loathed fabricating the truth and felt that was a compromise she could hang on to for now.

'Of course you have to do what's best for your family.' Rose found a smile. 'I'll have a word with Alfie, make sure he knows Harriet's not likely to be here all summer.'

It wouldn't be fair to let Harriet and Alfie think otherwise. However much they liked each other now, feelings would change once their lives reverted back to normal and they were hundreds of miles and worlds apart.

'Thank you for inviting Harriet over to eat with you. It was very kind, and she loved it.'

'Oh, she was most welcome. With my brother and his family, plus Alfie, getting taller by the minute and constantly hungry, there's always plenty.'

Under normal circumstances, Pippa wouldn't think twice about reciprocating. She felt incredibly mean, not inviting Alfie round just because Harriet wouldn't be staying in Hartfell. And would that really make a difference, as though the lack of a meal at Home Farm would be the deciding factor in their budding romance? She decided on another suggestion instead.

'I thought I'd take Raf to the pub tonight. He's heading back to London tomorrow and Kenny's desperate to meet him. Would you and Alfie like to join us?'

'Oh, we'd love that! Thank you.' Rose's pleasure made Pippa feel she'd done the right thing, but still, she couldn't shake off the doubt clutching at her heart at having to take Harriet away. She prayed she wasn't making things worse, inviting Rose and Alfie along too, and she knew from Harriet that Rose was a single mum like her. 'Are you sure?'

'Of course. Kenny's booked us a table for seven p.m., does that work for you?'

'Totally. I'll let Alfie know the minute I see him. Thanks so much, Pippa.'

'You're very welcome, it'll be lovely to see you both again.'

Rose smiled at someone over Pippa's shoulder and, from the goosebumps springing up on the back of her neck, Pippa knew exactly who it was without having to look.

'Hi, Gil.'

'Hey, Rose. How's that heifer doing? Alfie said her foot was much better.' Gil paused beside Pippa, Lola's lead looped over one hand, and smiled at Rose.

'It is, she's back with the herd, not lame anymore. Thanks for sorting her out.'

'My pleasure, it's what I'm here for.' He narrowed his eyes as he looked at Pippa, sending a quiver darting down her back. 'I thought you were avoiding me on purpose. So, are you ready to find out how important the practice is to the farming community here?'

'And why would I be avoiding you?' She forced every degree of casualness she could muster into her reply, hoping it sounded more offhand than she felt. 'Maybe later. I've got Raf to find first.'

Chapter Thirteen

Raf was a person possessed of a gift that made him beloved wherever he went. Whether it was the barely hinted at sensitivity beneath the rock-star image, his effortless dress sense or his natural charm – making women want to mother him (amongst other things) and men want to be like him – Pippa had never quite been able to fathom. To her, he was still the little brother she adored, and they were fiercely protective of one another. She very rarely asked him to present his public self on her behalf, but she'd known he would do it for precisely the same reasons she would. Because he loved her and knew she was in need.

He was mobbed by the crowd the moment he arrived at the show, and he posed patiently for endless selfies, friendly chats, and autographs. He visited every stall, high-fived children, and charmed elderly farmers, who were bemused by a handsome and tattooed stranger in their midst as he presented what she knew to be an entirely fabricated interest in the various breeds of sheep on display.

Raf took his turn on the high striker and rang the bell three times, hit the target on the dunking stool and sent Alfie sprawling into a tank of dubious-looking water, making Harriet roar with laughter, and caused a kerfuffle in the craft marquee when he learned the WI chair loved *Strictly* and spun her into a quick waltz. She'd had to sit down after that and was overheard denying that a stiff gin had been required to bring her round.

Pippa had promised that an hour of his presence would be enough, but he seemed in no hurry to leave and sent her an apologetic grin when he was invited onto the small stage. The band were only too keen to make way for him, and he settled behind the drums, drawing a large crowd as he warmed up. He played a brilliant, improvised set, with the band joining him for half of it, and she was grateful that he kept his shirt on, to the obvious disappointment of a very vocal group of women who looked as though they'd stumbled into the show straight from a hen party.

He played three encores, finishing with a Blue at Midnight classic track before leaving the stage to huge cheers and another queue for selfies, signing programmes and a few T-shirts. She was just relieved there were no breasts; she couldn't imagine that was an image the show committee would choose to go viral. Pippa decided he'd be fine on his own for a while, she couldn't get near him anyway. She'd been invited to the WI tent by the chair-woman to present some prizes and headed over, intending to walk right past the vet's stall until Gil called out.

'When are you taking a turn?' he taunted. 'I thought you'd be first in line after the week you've had.'

'At what?' She turned a shoulder, eyeing him with suspicion.

'That.' He pointed to wooden stocks set up between the two rows of stalls. Someone she recognised as a client who'd brought in a poorly rabbit this week was inside and making the best of being pelted with wet sponges. A week ago she'd have run a mile rather than stick her arms and head in there and she laughed, overcome by a sudden madness.

'I will if you will.'

'You're on. You first.'

Pippa watched as Gil excused himself from colleagues and left Lola fastened to a handy table leg to stride over. She was remembering his hands on her shoulders the other day, the rapid beating of his heart against her back and how she'd instinctively known he hadn't wanted to let her go.

'Oh no,' she said nervously, wondering what she'd let herself in for. 'I'm not falling for that one. You'll soak me and then disappear before I get to return the favour.'

'Are you suggesting I'm not a man of my word?' He halted in front of her, their gazes tangled, daring her to deny it.

'Prove it.' Anticipation was dancing across her skin, butterflies snaking through her stomach.

'I will.'

They had to wait until the client had been released before he swapped places with Gil, who by the grin on his face was clearly expecting an easy ride. Pippa hovered whilst a few children took aim, mostly missing until a sponge hit him on the side of the head. Then it was her turn and she lined up the first of her three attempts, frowning when it missed, and he smirked at her.

This was ridiculous, she couldn't even make him suffer when he was trapped between two planks of wood. She refused to be distracted by him laughing, daring her to do her worst. Instead she thought of all the times he'd been rude, had deemed her incapable of anything much, even being a good mum, and her temper twitched satisfyingly.

She dunked her second sponge well, drips catching on her jeans and wellies when she lifted it. She took a deep breath, steadied her hand, and launched the sponge with every scrap of strength she could muster. It smacked him full on the face and she leaped in the air, squealing with glee as he shook his head, drops flying.

Her third clouted him on the nose, which felt even better, and if it hadn't been for the children queuing, she'd have paid again and had another crack at him. Water was running down his face onto his navy polo shirt and when he was freed from the stocks, she wasn't too sure she liked the look on his face now and sidled away, heading for the relative safety of the craft marquee.

'Don't you dare. That's not the game we're playing.' Gil caught up and took her hand, gently tugging her back to the stocks. 'Your turn. I want my revenge.'

'If you were a gentleman you'd let me go,' Pippa muttered, eyes catching on his fingers threaded through hers.

'Then it's a pity for you I'm no gentleman.' Patches of water had darkened the polo shirt and her pulse skipped as he slicked back wet hair. He only let her go when he presented her at the stocks, and she reluctantly slid her hands and face between the planks. Given the debacle over the show, she was expecting a long queue but after a few children had tried to soak her and mostly missed, he was surprisingly the only adult. A small crowd had gathered, and she wondered if they thought he was going to do their dirty work for them.

She gasped when the first sponge hit her square in the face, the water cold and already running down her neck. His second belted her on the forehead before the third sponge caught her right cheek. She shook some drops away, tensed and prepared for him to have another three shots. Instead she was very relieved to be freed and gratefully accepted the towel she was offered.

'Happy now,' she retorted as Gil joined her, and she ran the towel over her face. 'I'm drenched.'

'So I see.' His laughter fell away when his eyes dropped to take in her wet, clinging top. She hadn't been expecting a soaking when she'd dressed and her fitted white T-shirt had been a nice combination with a jacket and skinny jeans. Her white bra wasn't the only thing visible through her top and she tugged at the T-shirt, trying to separate it from her skin. The crowd hadn't entirely dispersed, and she noticed a couple of phones out, making her fold her arms in panic.

'Where's your jacket?' He stepped forward and she almost leaped back until she realised he was shielding her from sight, planting his body in front of hers.

'I left it at the house when I went back for Raf,' she muttered, trying not to make her gratitude for his presence too obvious. 'I was warm.'

'Here.' The gilet he'd been wearing before the stocks was hanging on the back of a post and his hands brushed her arms as he slid it around her shoulders.

'I don't need…' It wasn't the cold she thought to avoid with his gesture, but the warmth, the distraction of having him so close, his chest almost skimming hers.

'Your choice, Pippa,' he said softly. 'But maybe right now you do need it. Those phones pointing your way probably aren't the only ones.'

'Thanks.' She zipped the gilet up, trying to look at anything other than him. 'I suppose it'll be on someone's social media somewhere.'

'I guess.'

Feeling safer, hidden inside his too-large gilet, she took a step backwards. 'I'd better go. The WI have roped me into presenting prizes, which was a surprise. I was half expecting to be run out of town, not seated at the chair-woman's table and fed cake.'

'Make sure you don't eat the exhibits. At least you don't have to judge the novelty dog show.' Gil rolled his eyes. 'I'll probably upset half my clients.'

'I'd offer to swap but I don't think I'd be any good at deciding which dog looks most like its owner.' Pippa was very aware of her warm face, breath catching as he laughed.

'How are you on the dog the judge would most like to take home?' He quirked a playful brow and she swallowed.

'Easy. I wouldn't be able to pick a winner because I wouldn't want to take any of them home.'

'Shameful.'

They parted and Pippa was still smiling as she resumed her progress to the WI tent.

–

By the time she emerged – surprising herself with how much she'd enjoyed the prizegiving – the tug of war was underway in the main arena and Harriet had taken a place on Alfie's team and was pulling the rope with all her might, encouraged by the commentator clearly on the side of the local Young Farmers', and the crowd. Alfie's team won and Pippa was torn between happiness at Harriet's face when he swung her off her feet in triumph, and sadness at the parting to come. All this excitement and adventure must not lead to a broken heart, and she mentally added it to her list of things to talk to Harriet about when the right moment arrived.

'So can I have my gilet back please?' Gil had joined Pippa at the ringside, distracting her from thoughts of Harriet. 'Are you decent now?'

'What?' Warmth darted into her face at the reminder of her wet T-shirt, and she laughed, covering her embarrassment. Of all the people to catch her like that... 'Oh yeah, thanks. Think so.'

'Want me to check?'

Her fingers stilled on the zip she was undoing, her cheeks positively scarlet now, as her gaze raced back to his. His own eyes were amused but there was more there now, another confirmation that he felt it too: this attraction blazing between them, as though their bodies were replying to questions their minds had never voiced.

'I'm fine.' The scratched note in her voice was a surprise and she cleared her throat. Even grinding her teeth would be preferable to the fizz bubbling in her stomach, and she slipped the gilet off. 'Here you go.'

'Thanks.' His eyes never left hers as he settled it around his shoulders.

Pippa bent to pat Lola and the dog responded enthusiastically, tail wagging, checking her pockets with an inquisitive nose for treats.

'Lola's so pretty, she could never have won the "dog most like its owner" class if you'd entered with her.'

'I suppose you're trying to insult me.' Gil offered her a lazy grin as he lengthened Lola's lead, and she felt that kick in her pulse again.

'If you're not feeling insulted, then sure, I need to do better.'

'By the way, well done.'

'For what?' She snapped her attention back to him, Lola's tail thumping against her leg. Praise from Gil was totally unexpected.

'This. Today.' He tipped his head to the crowd accompanying Raf as he walked towards them, other people trickling away. 'You did good.'

'That's not what you said the other night. And it wasn't down to me.'

'The extra visitors were. He's pretty talented, your brother.'

'Pretty talented?' She huffed out a laugh. 'Have you seen his Instagram?'

'Okay, it was a great set. I try to keep away from all that online stuff. So how are you planning to top it next year?'

'Next year?' Pippa drew in a long, slow breath. 'I could come back and present a few prizes, I suppose.'

How much will have changed by then? Where would they all be in twelve months time? The house would belong to a new owner, the farm practice closed and the one in town in the hands of new partners.

'So you won't be here?'

'It's a year from now, Gil, what do you think? This isn't my life.'

'No, I guess it's not,' he replied quietly. 'Is London really home for you, Pippa? Or maybe it's meant to be somewhere else?' He walked away and she was left watching, trying to work out what his question and that last, long look had really meant.

The show was all but over when she and Raf finally returned to the house. Harriet tore in soon after to charge her phone, delighted that Alfie and his mum were invited to the pub, and took off again to settle Posy for the night. Pippa and Raf wandered down in time for their table booking, a few locals greeting him like old friends, which he took good-naturedly.

Only she would see how tired he'd be later, with the effort of keeping a merry face in place and making those around him feel welcomed. Kenny was thrilled with his celebrity guest and gave them a table tucked away in a quiet corner. Rose arrived soon after with Harriet and Alfie, and Raf was charming, learning about her job and the skincare range she was developing.

After a superb dinner, Harriet and Alfie didn't linger, instead leaving the adults to their coffee and disappearing to a Young Farmers' social at someone's farm. Alfie promised to see her safely home and Pippa nodded, concern lodged in her heart. When they left, Rose insisted she was fine walking home on her own and Raf hugged her, saying something that to Pippa sounded as though he would see her again. Rose waved, and Pippa set off up the main street with Raf at her side.

'You're not planning to start up something with Rose, are you?' That would be another worry. She didn't want her brother forming his own Hartfell attachment alongside Harriet's. 'She's a single mum, Raf, her life is here.'

'I'm not a freakin' idiot,' Raf said, shoving into her on purpose. 'Sure, she's gorgeous but there's nothing doing there, not for either of us.'

'You're certain?' Pippa wasn't convinced. 'Because you were very friendly towards her.'

'Come on, Pippa, that's why you got me up here! To get you out of a hole and be nice to people. But Rose is sweet, as is Alfie. Harriet's picked a good one there.'

'It's only been a few days,' Pippa retorted. 'I don't think anyone's doing any picking. I've barely seen her since she started at Dorothy's. She's down there every spare minute, mucking out.' Coming back each night with colour in her cheeks, happy smile lighting up her face.

'So? Back off, let her have some fun. From what I saw, Alfie's not the one who'll be doing the breaking up. Besotted is the old-fashioned word for it. And if she gets her heart broken, so what? You can't protect her forever, sis. It comes to everyone, eventually.'

'That's typical of you.' She really didn't want to fight with Raf but thoughts of a broken-hearted Harriet being hauled back to London were too much right now. 'I don't think you've ever really had your heart broken in your life. You never let anyone near enough.'

'I guess that's what you would think.'

They'd only gone a few strides when Pippa halted and threw her arms around him to mutter into his chest. 'Raf, I'm so sorry. I didn't mean it, I'm just worried about Harriet. I'm sorry.'

'I know, it's okay.' He sighed. 'How are things between you? You talked yet?'

'Not really, I haven't found the right moment. But we will. I hope you know you're lovely. Don't ever change.'

'Funny, that's not what Lina said when I told her it was over.' Raf offered a wry smile. 'She said I'm terrified of making a commitment in case it won't last and that she deserved better.'

'Oh I'm sorry, for both of you.'

'Don't be sorry for me, she was right on both counts. That's why I left, no point in hanging around when we wanted different things.'

'So what about you, when this never-ending retirement tour is over?' Pippa worried about this. Her dad, whatever he decided to do, would be fine. He always managed to find the joy in life, latched onto something that suited him, whether it was touring, recording, songwriting or festivals. She didn't really believe that he'd ever give it up, not fully. But Raf, her adored eldest brother, was different.

'What will you do, after the band? You know, if music doesn't make you happy, you can just stop doing it.'

Since Ewan's death, there was a deeper sadness in him now, a level of disconnect from his feelings that Pippa had never seen before. She knew he loved them all and showed it, in his own way, but he seemed even more rootless, pouring his heart into notes and lyrics he wouldn't even let family hear.

'I have absolutely no idea. I'll take some time out, write a bit, see Cassie and the kids. I'd like to be there for them more than I have been.' He paused. 'Ewan would want that, he'd want to know we were taking care of his family.'

'He would. And he'd want us all to be happy, too. You included.' Pippa threaded her arm through Raf's. 'And you'll always have a home with us, if that's what you want. Come and stay, when you take that time out.'

'What, here?' They'd reached the house and Raf glanced up at it; the golden stone warming and welcoming, sunlight glinting off mullioned windows. 'It's nice, or it could be. Someone could do a job on it.'

'Of course not here,' she said firmly. Confirming the appointment with the land agent was first on her list for Monday, just as soon as Gil was too busy with clients to notice what she was up to. 'None of us will be here when the summer is over.'

She opened the front door and Raf followed her through to the kitchen. 'Beer, glass of wine or coffee?'

'Let's have a beer and sit outside. It's a nice evening.'

In the garden Raf pulled out a chair and faced her, but Pippa wasn't fooled by his easy relaxation. There was something on his mind. 'So what's the story with you and the hot vet?'

'Who said he was hot?' She jolted, but righted her glass before she sloshed any more beer on the terrace. She still couldn't get that last look from Gil at the show and his question about her future out of her mind.

'Just an impression I got from Harriet. Apparently you can't stop grinding your teeth whenever he's around and come over all flustered. She said either you think he's hot or you're starting the perimenopause.'

'She what!' Pippa had put her flushes firmly down to Gil and their differences but maybe her daughter had a point. Surely forty was too early for perimenopause... Wasn't it? She didn't fancy either of those reasons and resolved on the spot to be a lot more careful whenever he was nearby. 'Is there anyone in this family to whom my behaviour isn't being reported on by my daughter? Between you, Dad and Freddie, it seems she's got tabs on me every minute of the day.'

'Makes two of you, then.' Raf's eyes were closed, and he opened one to regard her thoughtfully. 'So you do think Gil is hot.'

'What I think about him is utterly irrelevant to my present situation, when Dad decided I could park my own life and sent me up here.'

'You're staying on?'

'For another few days, I suppose.' To Pippa that didn't sound as awful as it once had. She was getting used to dealing with clients at the vets and managing the system, but there was no denying she'd be ready to throw Elaine a welcome party when Gil's receptionist was able to return home. 'Anyway, I wanted to ask if you knew anyone in our family called Ivy? Like from the past, who might have lived here?'

'No. Should I? Who is she?'

'No idea, I just wondered if you might, that's all. Someone in the shop said they thought I looked like her, but there's no one in the family I can think of called Ivy.' Pippa pulled a face. 'Never mind. How's things with Dad and the tour? All going to plan?'

Raf shrugged. 'Yeah, fine, I'm heading back in three weeks, we pick it up again in Perth. I still can't see him giving up and retiring, though. Can you? It's his life.'

'Maybe. But you know what he's like. He'll make his own decisions. Is he serious, about buying a place in Australia?'

'Very. He's still looking after an offer fell through.'

'What about Dana?'

'Oh, she'll stick around as long as she can. Freddie and Phoebe aren't keen.'

'Neither's Harriet. She thinks it'll be over by Christmas.'

'I'm not sure your daughter hasn't got more sense when it comes to relationships than the rest of us put together. Even if she is only fourteen.'

'Hmm.' Pippa took another mouthful of beer, wondering why everything seemed to be running out of her control. Even Gil was being a bit nicer to her, although she had pretty much flashed her breasts at him in the wet T-shirt, which had probably helped. She wouldn't be doing that again, even if he did go back to treating her as an enemy out to ruin his business and probably his life.

'Hey, are you even listening? You were miles away.' Raf stretched out a leg and shoved hers with his foot.

'Sorry,' she replied hastily, hoping he couldn't read her mind as well as he once had.

'Thinking about the hot vet?' he enquired, and she huffed out a laugh.

'No. Maybe. What were you saying?'

'I was asking when you last saw Cassie.'

'A few days before we came up here. Why?'

'No reason.' Raf leaned forward to place his empty glass on the table. 'Just wondered how she is, that's all.'

'When did you last see her?'

'After I got back from Melbourne, before I went to the island with Lina. Cassie invited me for lunch. I wanted to see Rory and Isla, check in with them. And Cassie, of course.'

'I know, she told me. She said how lovely it was of you to make the time and Isla and Rory were so excited you made it.'

'Do you think she's all right? I mean, I know she can't be, not after losing Ewan, but I worry about them.'

'I think she's as okay as she can be right now.' Pippa got up to give Raf a hug, suddenly needing to hold him close. 'Everyone who loves and understands her and the children is priceless right now.'

Chapter Fourteen

Sunday morning was a lazy one, with Raf sleeping in and Pippa cooking breakfast before a car arrived to collect him for the return trip back to London. Harriet had already said her goodbyes after introducing him to Posy, and it seemed the pony was as keen on Raf as he was on her. Posy had flattened her ears and backed away, and Harriet hadn't been able to contain her laughter as she assured her uncle that Posy probably thought he was another vet and about to inject her.

He held Pippa close as they hugged goodbye, promising to look after himself and come and stay just as soon as the tour was over in November. Harriet and Alfie were meeting some of his friends on a farm to practise calf-handling skills, and she rolled her eyes at Pippa's instruction to be very careful and wash her hands afterwards.

Pippa couldn't settle to sketching in the garden, not with Gil power washing his Land Rover in the yard. The noise and the sight of him without a T-shirt was too distracting, so she shut herself indoors with a book instead. The house felt heavy with the weight of history all around, but she wouldn't go searching, not after last time, when he'd discovered her with the photograph album and had taken it away.

The afternoon sidled into evening and she ate alone, leaving a pasta dish ready for Harriet to heat up when she returned. She'd read Rose's newsletter, learning that her brother James bred highly prized pedigree Shorthorn cattle and ran a large flock of Rough Fell sheep. He and Rose were third-generation farmers and from what she'd seen of Alfie so far, it looked highly likely he would be the fourth. He had the look of a farmer about him, a sense that the landscape was bred into him every bit as much as the city was a part of Harriet.

Pippa was finding new pleasure in being up early to run most mornings and then she'd settle in the garden with a coffee and her sketchpad before she went to the vets, hand flying over the page as she captured the views around her. A dahlia just coming into flower, a robin perched on a branch and a sheep staring and wary, poised for signs of danger.

Out there, she didn't have to think about decisions concerning the house and she was loving working so freely, with no pressure or expectation on the results. She didn't do it often enough at home, where there always seemed some task she must accomplish, either for work or Harriet. Even her career and teaching students didn't provide quite the thrill it once had. When she'd spotted a job in a gallery a couple of months ago, she'd talked herself out of having a go in favour of sticking with what she knew.

Tilly was still pressing her for contact with the social media influencer and Pippa had given in, sending a cheery DM, and putting the two women in touch. She'd also agreed to Phoebe using the house for a shoot and had booked the caterer as requested.

On Tuesday evening she decided on impulse to accept Rose's invitation for an early walk. She was enjoying getting to know her and it would make a change from measuring the miles on her Fitbit. The next morning Pippa headed into the village in her running gear; she hadn't got anything better for walking the fells. Dorothy shot past on the quad bike, a couple of sheep in the trailer and the terrier on her lap. She raised a hand, which Pippa took to be an improvement in their relationship as Dorothy had actually acknowledged her presence. Despite the gathering clouds threatening rain, she felt her mind easing, a sense of problems unravelling and slowing her feet.

'Pippa, hi, so glad you could make it.' Outside the pub Rose stepped forward to greet her. 'Everyone, this is Pippa, who's staying at Home Farm. Pippa, this is my neighbour Audrey, who was a GP in town until she retired and is now a volunteer ranger with the National Park Authority. Maryam farms down the road from us and in her spare time creates the most gorgeous handmade chocolates. Hazel here has a cottage in the village and works up at the Hall for the family. Occasionally we have one or two more, but this is the core, we're usually the ones out in all weathers. And don't worry about remembering names, you must meet loads of people.'

'Not as many as you might think. Thank you for welcoming me to your group, it's very kind.' Pippa was smiling at each woman in turn, trying to lock in those details and attribute them to the right person. Audrey looked to be the oldest, with Hazel and Maryam somewhere in the middle.

'Mostly I'm the mum of a teenage daughter, and an art teacher.' Pippa pushed away thoughts of the sketches she'd done and the pleasure they'd brought since she'd arrived; they were only for her, and no one would ever see them.

'It's my dad who loves to travel and meet people. My life is pretty quiet compared to his.'

'Harriet's delightful, she's been spending time with Alfie. Haven't they made plans for tonight, Pippa? I think they're going bowling with Young Farmers'. There's a minibus taking them into town.'

'I think so.' Pippa smiled brightly, hoping it wasn't obvious that Harriet hadn't mentioned it yet, or asked if it was okay for her to go out with a group of people Pippa had never met. She would have to catch her before Harriet disappeared to Dorothy's, probably for the rest of the day.

'So this morning we're going to a waterfall, it's about a mile and a half each way and a decent climb. We usually gather there for a swim or a chat, or even just to sit in silence.' Rain was beginning to drizzle, and Rose zipped up her coat. 'Feel free to take part or sit as quietly as you like. No expectation.'

'Thank you.' Pippa hadn't even thought of buying a waterproof before arriving in Hartfell and hoped her lightweight running jacket would be enough to protect her from the worst of the weather.

The riverside path from the village was one she hadn't explored yet and it was lovely, treelined and rocky as it rose above the houses. Even low clouds skimming the fell couldn't dent the glorious view of misty meadows dotted with cows further down. It was a more expansive scene than she'd usually draw but the desire to capture something of it came again, freeing her mind from her real mission here. Maryam and Audrey were at the front, chatting with Hazel as they set off at a good pace. Despite her running, the gradient had Pippa puffing before too long and Rose was keeping her company.

'Okay?'

'Yes, thanks,' Pippa said wryly as she unzipped her coat, hands briefly on her knees. 'I thought I was fitter than this but it's level at home. That's my excuse, anyway.'

'I was going to say you'll get used to it, but of course you might not if you're going home soon.' Rose flashed her a glance. 'Sorry, that wasn't me prying, by the way. Just an observation.'

'So how long have you been doing this?' Pippa took the opportunity of a pause for a quick drink as well.

'About a year. At first I went out on my own, once Alfie had got on the school bus. But he's always up early now because he has his own animals to feed so he doesn't need me to check on him. I mentioned it to Maryam when we were having coffee, she told Audrey and then we were a group. We all love it, and we always go out, rain or shine. There's just something about being outdoors that I find necessary.' Rose threw Pippa a smile as they resumed walking. 'Sorry, blathering on as usual. James says I'm like a dog with a bone once I get going, but I'm so lucky to live and work here.'

'I can totally see the appeal. I run at home but it's nothing like this. Mostly I'm dodging vehicles, other people and litter, half the time I don't even notice what's around me. But these views are incredible.'

'So it's all about the run?'

'I suppose it is.' Pippa had given up wearing her Fitbit for now as she couldn't access the app as often as she usually would. She ran for exercise and some time alone, a need to pound problems into the pavement, not for connection or a sense of space widening her mind. She imagined running back in London again, the return to cool drizzly autumn mornings; the lunchtime dash at work when it was too dark to run first thing.

'Harriet mentioned you're an artist. She said that you're brilliant but don't show your work.'

'She did?' Pippa hadn't imagined Harriet discussing her in anything other than dismissive terms. A rush of gratitude for the compliment was swiftly followed by the familiar squeeze of anxiety at the thought of anyone seeing the sketches and watercolours she produced. 'I teach art but drawing and painting is something I do just for me, a hobby.' That was usually enough to dissuade any further interest.

'Harriet told us that you painted a mural in her bedroom, and she's never redecorated because she loves it so much.'

'Oh.' Pippa gulped, tilting her head to flip her own hood up, hoping Rose hadn't noticed her face.

As a little girl Harriet had adored fairies and Pippa had created an enchanted woodland on the wall behind her bed; tall trees topped with blushing blossom and butter-flies, fairies prancing over a carpet of colourful flowers. Pinks, purples and mauves swaying through the grass, a secret fairy house hidden in a corner. It had been a labour of love and a joy to create, and Harriet used to say it was like falling asleep in a secret glade watched over by a fairy kingdom. It made Pippa's heart happy to hear that Harriet still loved it, even though she was way too old for fairies. But then, she mused, maybe you should never be too old for enchantment.

Hazel fell into step with her, chatting about the village and London. They soon discovered a mutual love of musical theatre and Hazel was enthusiastic about an upcoming visit to family in the south and seeing three shows. She had to make the best of her time away, she explained, with her husband having Parkinson's disease and her youngest daughter coming up to take care of him.

Pippa learned that Hazel had lived in the village for fifty years and she enquired about Ivy. She was thrilled to learn that Edmund, the local historian Daphne had mentioned, was Hazel's next-door neighbour. She suggested that Pippa call round so she could introduce them, and in the meantime would look through her own family photos to see if anything popped up. Pippa thanked her, delighted to be making progress with her tentative search into the past.

They reached the spot where the river tumbled down rocks from the high fell and widened into a pool, clear and inviting. She'd never swum in the wild before, except in the sea on holiday, and watched Audrey and Hazel shrugging off layers until they were left in their swimming costumes before wading in. Maryam was taking photos of a plant with her phone and Rose settled on the bank with Pippa, who was wishing she'd brought a swimsuit and joined in; the two women were floating in the water, and it looked blissful.

It was enlightening to walk without expectation or set a pace to measure on an app, to feel the rain on her face, make conversation or stay silent, the village specks of stone beneath them. She could see Home Farm from here too, and somewhere down there Harriet would be waking up and rushing off to take care of the animals she was coming to love.

And Gil. He was there too, squashed into that caravan in the yard and maybe making plans for his own future, plans that would take him away from Hartfell and home when the practice closed. The feeling of guilt, every time she thought of it, was becoming all too familiar.

The walk down was easier, and Kenny was ready with coffee and muffins, which they enjoyed on a table outside. Pippa thanked everyone, feeling lighter as she returned to the house, not yet ready to commence battle with Gil or Harriet – she was too relaxed and at ease for that.

She had a quick breakfast and an equally fast shower, and when she let herself into the vets, discovered that Harriet had texted to say Dorothy had invited her for lunch and not to expect her back until later. Oh, and did Pippa mind if she went bowling with Alfie tonight? It was all arranged, and she'd be back by ten. Pippa replied to say it was fine. If Rose was okay with it then Pippa was too, and there was no sense in spoiling Harriet's fun just yet.

Pippa and Gil had eased into coffee-making terms when they were in the practice, polite with each other now. She'd made his one morning, simply unable to make herself coffee and exclude him. Since then, whoever was in first would switch on the machine and make coffee for the other. He still hadn't appeared by the time she settled in reception and was looking over his list of consultations. Someone had already called wanting their vomiting dog to be seen as soon as possible, and she'd slotted them in the only appointment available.

When he arrived just before his first patient, he was shivering and with a hacking cough. He caught her look of alarm and shook his head, searching for a tissue to blow his nose. Pippa stood up and kept her distance as she proffered the box kept for clients.

'Thanks. It's not Covid, by the way. I've taken two tests over the past twenty-four hours and they're all negative. I'm fine.'

'Right.' Clearly he wasn't. 'But even if it's not Covid, you look dreadful, and I can't imagine clients wanting you anywhere near them.'

'What else am I supposed to do?' Any further protest was lost in another bout of coughing and Pippa was on her feet.

'Go back to bed,' she told him firmly. 'You can't possibly see patients like that, and no one will thank you for passing it on, whatever it is. I'll call Angie.'

Angie was the head receptionist at the practice in town and she'd helped Pippa out more than once with queries. She was capable and calm, and Pippa was certain she'd help if she could.

'And say what?' Gil sneezed and even Lola looked worried, barking in alarm.

'To ask if they can spare anyone to take the consultations here. Wendy might be able to do it.' Pippa was already dialling, holding up a hand when he opened his mouth. 'Bed. I mean it.'

'Not until I know you've got cover,' he wheezed crossly, dropping onto one of the waiting room chairs. The first two clients had arrived and backed out hurriedly when they spotted Gil clutching his chest. Pippa went over, phone to her ear, and opened the door, letting in all the fresh air she could and hoping she hadn't already caught whatever it was he had.

'Right, we're sorted,' she said briskly, ending the call as she gave him a wide berth and resumed her place behind the counter. 'Wendy's on her way. Angie texted her whilst I was holding, and she can do it. She'll be here in twenty minutes, so I'll just apologise when clients arrive and hopefully they won't mind waiting a bit longer.'

'I could do it.' He gave Pippa a look from red-rimmed and watery eyes, and blew his nose so loudly that Lola barked again.

'Get out of here,' she said firmly, pointing to the door. He obeyed, clambering to his feet, and grumbling under his breath. He called Lola, scowling when she refused to join him and settled in the bed beside Pippa instead. Thankfully, it was a pleasant morning, and she left the door open, trying to clear the room of any lingering bugs.

Wendy arrived soon after and dealt with the patients, including the vomiting dog, and Pippa was glad to finish when lunchtime arrived. She had a free afternoon without Harriet at home to clean the house and hopefully make it a little more welcoming. She locked up, Lola beside her as they crossed the yard to the caravan. She knocked tentatively in case Gil was asleep, not certain that she'd heard him call 'Come in' until she tried a second time, and he fairly bawled it. She pushed open the door and Lola leaped inside.

'Just returning Lola,' she called cheerfully. 'Hope you're feeling better.'

His reply was another bout of coughing followed by swearing and she hesitated. 'Can I get you anything?' Enemies they might be, but she couldn't leave him without checking. 'A drink, or some medication?' She paused, trying to make him out between the coughs and stepped inside the dark and gloomy caravan. 'Sorry, what?'

'I *said*, don't come in.'

'Oh, right.' She laughed awkwardly, horrified by the cold in here when the air outside was warm. Lola's bed was on one narrow sofa, and through the gloom Pippa made out Gil hunched on the other, a fold-up table between the two. A duvet was pulled up to his ears and he had a cushion for a pillow.

'Gil, I can see from here you're shivering. You've obviously got a temperature,' she said worriedly. 'When did you last have some meds?'

'Dunno. Ran out.'

She glanced at the sink full of dishes, the tiny two-ring hob, marvelling that it hadn't blown up the caravan yet. 'Right, get up,' she said firmly. 'You can't stay in here, it's foul and damp, and that's being polite.'

'Not getting up.'

'You are, even if I have to drag you out myself.' She'd never be able to do that in a million years, not with those shoulders, but she hoped the threat might make him move. 'Get up.'

'Not got anywhere else to go.'

The words sliced through Pippa's heart, and she held back a gasp, startled by their truth and how much of it was her fault. He shouldn't be living in this caravan, even if he'd chosen to. He had a tenancy agreement for the house, and he ought to be in it.

'Yeah, you do. That's your house right over there and you're moving back in.'

'Am not,' he muttered in between coughs. 'Not while you're in it. Don't need any more complications.'

Pippa had had enough, and she nearly flew the three steps it took to grab the duvet and yank it off him. 'Get up, you stubborn and stupid man,' she roared. 'Or do I have to get half the village in here to help me?'

He shot her a furious glare as he hunched into a sitting position. His T-shirt was soaked in sweat and boxers were the only other thing he had on, apart from socks. She threw a pair of jeans and another T-shirt at him, and grabbed Lola's bed. Two for the price of one, she thought wryly, as she escaped into the sunshine to let him change.

He trailed after her into the house, still shivering as she moved to the kettle. She hadn't replaced it and kept forgetting to order a better one, telling herself there wasn't any point as she wouldn't be here much longer. She switched it on and found a mug. 'When did you last have meds?'

'Think about four a.m. Couldn't sleep after that.'

'Right, then it's definitely time for more. Sit down.' She pointed at the table, and he pulled out a chair, Lola already settled in her bed in the usual spot nearby. Pippa brought over a mug of ginger tea and a packet of paracetamol. He accepted both with quiet thanks, so unlike his usual self around her.

'Give me ten minutes to change the bed, then come up.'

'Hardly seems worth it when I'm feverish.'

'Clean sheets feel so much nicer,' she said, thankful she'd found extra bedding in an airing cupboard on the landing when Raf had stayed over. 'And these aren't damp, which is a major improvement on your previous arrangement.'

She'd just finished pulling the duvet in place and plumping the pillows, wondering why she was doing this for Gil of all people, when he appeared in the door, Lola behind him.

'No, Lola,' she said firmly, giving the Labrador a hard stare. 'Gil doesn't need to be getting up and letting you out.'

'Not your job to look after her,' he muttered, still clutching the mug as he walked to the bed.

'It's not my job to look after you either, but I seem to be doing it. I think I can cope with one dog for one day.' She slid the duvet back and saw the relief and blissful anticipation racing into his face at the sight of a proper mattress and actual pillows.

'I don't need looking after,' he said grumpily. 'I can do it myself.'

'Is that right? You didn't look very capable thirty minutes ago.'

'You planning to undress me as well?' His hands were on the belt around his jeans, and she tore her gaze away, hoping her hair would hide her face. Although his eyes were so red, she doubted he could even see her properly.

'If you don't think you can manage?' She swallowed, hoping that calling his bluff might do the trick.

'Think I can.' He undid the belt and Pippa fixed her eyes on his, flashing now with amusement. 'But it's good to know I can call on you for help if I need it.'

'You do that,' she told him briskly, heading for the door. 'I'll be back later to see if there's anything you need.'

Lola followed her downstairs and seemed happy enough to return to the kitchen, even though she kept looking to the hall and whining softly.

'I know,' Pippa told her gently, bending down to give her a cuddle. 'It's just for a bit so he can sleep. Let's leave him to it.'

She was quite certain that the minute he'd shrugged off the virus, Gil would get up and take himself straight back into the caravan. He would need another change of clothes so, refusing to think of his rage at what she was doing, she left Lola in the house to investigate the caravan. It was even more hideous than she'd imagined; dark, dull and damp, and she hated to think of him staying in there any longer. There wasn't even enough headroom for him to stand up straight. She opened the single wardrobe and pulled out the remainder of his clothes.

There was one way she could make certain he wasn't able to return, and she fetched the wheelbarrow from Posy's stable. She tugged and heaved the long cushions from the sofas, hoping she wasn't inhaling germs, realising they formed a double bed if the table was dropped to sit between them. She marched them one by one on the wheelbarrow to the muckheap, undaunted by thoughts of Dorothy's ire and accusations of criminal damage, never mind what Gil might have to say.

Harriet had mucked out Posy earlier and there was plenty of fresh supplies piled up. Pippa found a pitchfork and liberally scattered manure over both mattresses and stomped it in, an occupation she thoroughly enjoyed. She'd have set fire to them if she didn't think they might burn out of control and cause serious havoc. He definitely couldn't have them back, only a madman would sleep on those now. She doubted even Lola would fancy it.

Chapter Fifteen

Pippa practically lived on soup for lunch, and she'd made some yesterday from the glut of plump local tomatoes Violet had in abundance in the village shop. A couple of hours after eating her own, she warmed up a generous portion and carried it upstairs for Gil. She knocked quietly and heard him mutter, 'Come in.' Taking a deep breath, she pushed the door open.

His hair was dishevelled, and he blinked blearily as he ran a hand through it and eased himself up on the pillows. 'How long have I been asleep?'

'About three hours, it's almost five p.m. I thought you might be hungry.'

'Is it vegetarian?'

She toyed with launching the tray onto his lap from where she stood until she saw his smile. 'Tomato and Wensleydale soup and Violet's finest sourdough. But you know, if you can't eat a meal without meat, I can always take it away.'

'Why are you cooking for me?' He avoided her gaze as he rearranged the pillows again.

'Technically I'm not, it was ready, and I just heated it up.' She placed the tray on his lap, thinking he looked a little better. He turned away to cough, clutching the tray with one hand to keep it steady.

'You'd be better keeping your distance.' Gil straightened up and glanced at her, voice cracking. 'This doesn't feel very nice. I haven't been ill for years.'

'Lucky you. There's ibuprofen too, to keep you topped up. And it's probably too late to worry about that now, seeing as I've been in the caravan.' She paused. 'Where do you shower in that thing?'

'I don't, Dorothy lets me use hers. Does my washing too.'

'Dorothy does?' Pippa couldn't have been more amazed if he'd said Lola did it. Dorothy seemed like the kind of woman who'd never met a household chore in all her life, much less took care of Gil's.

'She is my aunt,' he said, eyeing the sourdough hungrily. 'Well, great-aunt. Pretty much the only family I've got, apart from my boys.'

'Oh! Your aunt? Right.' Pippa backed away. That explained a few things. 'Lola's fine, if you were wondering. I thought I'd take her for a walk, I've brought her food over from the caravan.'

'No point, I'll be going back later.'

'Actually, you won't.' She was at the door, ready to sprint down the stairs just in case. 'I've staged a little intervention.' Might as well get it over with.

'What are you talking about?' He put down the spoon to stare at her.

'It's for your own good,' she babbled. 'Sometimes you're too stubborn to do what's best.'

'What have you done?' Each word was delivered more slowly than the last.

'I might have removed the mattresses, that's all. Put them somewhere else.' She was on the landing now, wondering if he'd catch her before she could reach her car.

'Where have you put them, precisely?'

Oh well, she thought wildly. In for a penny, and all that. 'The muck heap,' she told Gil triumphantly, enjoying the disbelief filling his face.

'You what?' he roared, shoving the tray aside and slopping some of the soup. 'The bloody muck heap?'

'Yes,' she shouted back, finding it very cathartic. 'The bloody muck heap, where they belong! You're staying in this house even if I have to chain you to the bed.'

Oh, that sounded a bit exotic and was way out of her remit here. Maybe another time. She shot down the stairs, grabbed Lola and her lead, and raced out of the door. Hopefully by the time she returned he would have calmed down.

During the walk this morning, Hazel had pointed out where she lived, next door to Edmund, the local historian, and Pippa was soon outside his picture-perfect cottage on a narrow lane just off the main street. A red front door was cheerful between white rendered walls and sash windows, a pair of matching pots stuffed with summer bedding plants either side. Her knock was answered a moment later by an elderly man with a thin but very upright frame, whose sharp eyes belied the tremble in his hands.

'Ah, Pippa, my dear. Come in, I've been expecting you.' He moved back to allow her to pass him.

'Hello, it's lovely to meet you. Thank you for seeing me.' She glanced down at Lola, sitting patiently at her side. 'I hadn't planned to bring Lola with me. Is it okay if she comes in as well, please? I can drop her back if not.'

'No need, the more the merrier. She's very welcome.'

'Thanks so much.' Pippa stepped straight into a sitting room, and blinked. Every surface was laden with books, box files and teetering piles of paperwork. Cluttered didn't do it justice and she wondered how he ever found anything in here.

'I'm Edmund Osborne, and of course I know who you are. Hazel told me.' Edmund nodded. 'She sends her apologies, by the way. George is rather poorly this evening, and she didn't feel she ought to leave him.'

'I'm sorry to miss her. I hope he's okay.' Pippa thought she might pop some tomato soup round to Hazel; she had plenty left and it would be a way to thank her for the introduction to Edmund.

'Well, he's not too good, but they cope. Marvellous neighbours, we've been friends for nearly forty years.'

'Wow. How lovely.' She hovered with Lola as Edmund swept a heap of magazines from a wingback chair beside the fireplace and pointed to it. She thanked him and sat down, Lola at her feet, excitement tightening in her stomach. Might she find out Ivy's story here, learn how it connected to her own life? The fire was lit and the room warm, so she slipped off her gilet, leaving it on the arm of her chair.

'May I offer you some refreshment, Pippa? Earl Grey I'm afraid, it's all I drink.' Edmund chuckled. 'That and the whisky to help me sleep.'

'Earl Grey would be perfect, thank you. Can I help?' She made to move out of her chair, trying not to be too impatient.

'No, thank you. Why don't you have a look at this whilst I make the tea?' Edmund removed an A4 book, pale green and thick, resting on top of a box file on a coffee table. 'I think you might find it helpful for the period you're interested in. Hazel mentioned Nineteen Twenties.'

'Thank you.' Pippa accepted the book and opened it, realising it was a history of the village, beginning in 1918 after the end of the Great War and continuing to 1938, right before the Second World War. Pulse pattering a little faster, she carefully turned the pages, eventually pausing when she saw a wedding notice from May 1931, when a twenty-three-year-old Ivy Dixon had married twenty-five-year-old Albert Walker.

Pippa was transfixed by the accompanying black-and-white photograph, gulping at the sight of the young couple staring solemnly back. Who were these people and how might they be related? She hoped very much that Edmund would have the answer.

'Ah, I see you've found who you are looking for. Ivy Walker, née Dixon.' Edmund had returned with a tray and he set it down, with some difficulty, at one end of a square dining table. 'She and Albert were well known and liked around these parts from what I've discovered. Lived here all their lives. Hatched, matched and dispatched, as the saying goes.'

'I wondered if she and Albert may be my great-grandparents.' Pippa was stroking Lola's head resting on her knee, taken by surprise at the sudden catch in her voice. She'd been thinking about the possible connection, and this was the most obvious one.

'They were indeed. Their daughter, Janet, was your grandmother, your mother's mother. Milk or lemon?'

'Oh!' Pippa's hand flew to her mouth. She'd been half expecting this news but still it startled, to have her suspicions confirmed. 'Oh er, lemon please.'

Edmund poured two cups of tea and added lemon to both. He passed one across and she thanked him, itching to continue the conversation. But she sensed he would not hurry, that he was methodical and would find the details in his own time and in his own way.

'I expect you'd like to learn more about them, Pippa? I take it you haven't researched your family tree?'

'I haven't, but I'd love to know more. Thank you.' Staring into the past meant confronting her family's loss and until now she'd always preferred to look forward.

'There are more photographs in the book. Why don't I let you know what I've found so far, and you can ask questions as we go along.'

'Perfect.'

'Well, like many folks around here, Ivy and Albert both came from farming families. The estate in the village was considerable back then, although much of it has been sold now, and the farms are in private hands. They both went to church at the old Methodist chapel and attended Sunday School, and I expect they would have helped on their respective farms from an early age. Later in life, Ivy was known as an excellent cook and she baked for occasions like weddings and funerals, church events. Each farm would have had their own dairy and produced butter and cheese. All traditional skills which are almost lost today, sadly.'

'And school?' Pippa was slowly turning pages, finding Ivy and Albert's names popping up in church notices and faded farming photographs. One depicted Albert leaning on a rake beside a trailer piled high with hay, the women in headscarves sitting with baskets, children at their feet. Ivy was at the back, and Pippa gasped as she stared, recognising something of Harriet in Ivy's determined stance and dark hair.

'She went to school in the village and would have left at fourteen. There was no high school then and she likely went straight to work on the farm. Her own family one, in those days. Perhaps she still helped out there after her marriage.'

'Fourteen?' Pippa couldn't keep the surprise from her voice. Exactly the same age as Harriet now, and she couldn't imagine launching her daughter into the world of such toil so young.

'Yes. Ivy was a countrywoman, she would have known and understood that life. I can see how that might look regrettable to us now, but it was just how things were then.' Edmund drew his cardigan more tightly around his narrow shoulders. 'Ivy and Albert had three children but only Janet survived into adulthood.'

'Survived?' Her mind caught on that word, almost dreading the reply she expected to follow. Her family had eased further from their Yorkshire beginnings as her dad's fame grew, and she remembered her grandparents, but only just. There was so much she didn't know, so much she'd never thought to question.

'I'm afraid so. Sadly, I found a record of two more births, both of which infants only lived for a few weeks, I'm sorry to say. I imagine your grandmother was especially precious to Ivy and Albert.'

'I had no idea. How terribly sad,' Pippa whispered, startled by the hurt she felt for family she'd never known, the immense pain Ivy and Albert would have carried for the loss of those tiny babies. They'd lived so long ago and yet they were connected to her, related by blood. Edmund was speaking again, and she refocused.

'Have you visited the churchyard yet, my dear?'

'I haven't.' It hadn't occurred to her, though of course the church was a place where she might learn more.

'You'll find Ivy and Albert's graves on the right-hand side, about halfway along the path. I believe your grandmother is buried somewhere else, with your grandfather.'

'Yes, my grandparents lived in town, it's where they had their furniture business.' Pippa remembered the last time she'd seen them, after the loss of her mum. They'd been shocked and distraught, hollowed out by grief for their daughter and her family. Within two years they'd gone too.

'Thank you, Edmund, I really appreciate everything you've shared with me. I knew my parents were born in Yorkshire but until I came here, I didn't realise my dad was from Hartfell and my mum had a connection to it as well. Now I understand who Violet meant, when she said I had a look of Ivy. I think I can see Ivy in my daughter too.'

'Yes, Violet would have been a very small girl, but she remembers some of those days, more clearly than recent ones, I fear. And of course your dad lived in the cottage next door to the shop.'

'Next door? Wow.' Pippa had barely touched her tea and she drank it quickly, impatient to visit the churchyard and check out the cottage. One day she'd ask if the owners would let her have a look inside – this was where having a famous dad would come in handy. And she'd thank Violet too, when she saw her. Hands reaching down through history, a person who'd met both Pippa and her great-grandmother. It was staggering.

'Would you like to take that with you?' Edmund nodded at the book on her lap. 'It's my only copy, though, it's been out of print for some time.'

'I'd love that, thank you so much. And of course I'll look after it.'

Edmund seemed a little tired and she didn't want to keep him. She stood up, placing the precious book on her chair as she slipped the gilet back on, and he handed her a card with his telephone number and email address. Lola looked expectant, so Pippa gave her a cuddle for being so patient and good.

'There is one more thing about Ivy I think you might find interesting, Pippa.' Edmund reached past her to open the door. 'I understand that she was a very gifted artist. Watercolours, I believe. Apparently she loved the landscape around Hartfell and painted it extensively.' He patted Pippa's arm kindly. 'I see I have shocked you again, my dear.'

'Do you know what happened to her paintings?' Pippa's palms were clammy, and her heart was racing.

'I'm afraid I don't. I doubt that she ever showed her work and there's no trace of what happened to them. They may never have been sold as they probably had little commercial value. Perhaps she kept them, or gifted them to friends and family, and they've been lost down the years. There would have been no thought of her pursuing art in a professional or educational sense. We'll never know if Ivy ever questioned her life on the farm or whether she wanted a different one. We can only hope that she found fulfilment in the life she led, with her husband and family, and the paintings she created.'

Pippa thanked Edmund again as she left, the book tucked carefully under one arm, Lola's lead in her other hand. She wandered on through the village, unseeing of anything other than a woman from the past, painting the landscape Ivy loved, and which must have been such a part of her soul. Eventually, she returned to the shop and stared at the narrow and neat cottage next door, trying to picture her dad living in there and running these lanes with Gil's dad. She'd come back another time and knock on the door.

She walked on to the church, running up the steps to open the gate, knowing she wouldn't be able to settle until she'd found where Ivy lay and could acknowledge her in some way. Neat pots of brightly flowering plants lined the uneven stone path and some of the headstones were faded and leaning, names and details of lives blanked from all but the memory of those who'd come after them. Pippa checked each in turn until she found the right one.

A plain and simple headstone marked the resting place of the Walker family. Albert, who'd died nine years before Ivy, passed away at seventy-nine; both parents lying with their two tiny babies, gone before their time. Standing in this place, staring at the past, Pippa felt connected to the village and these people in a way she'd never imagined. This couple had spent their lives in Hartfell and all she wanted was to escape and return to the city. Who, other than a few friends and perhaps a couple of colleagues, she was shocked to realise, would really notice if she never went back?

She took a photo of the headstone with her phone and walked slowly back to the house, thinking about Ivy's life and her art. Had it sustained her through troubled times, the loss of her babies, in the same way painting had lifted Pippa from the depths of grief for her mum and the worry over her brother and sister? She drew because it was necessary to her, because she simply couldn't not. Had it been that way for Ivy, too?

She fed Lola, who devoured her dinner and settled in her bed after a quick trip into the garden. Thankfully being parted from Gil for a few hours hadn't put the dog off her food, and it was an unpleasant reminder for Pippa to realise that as far as Lola was concerned, this house was home. She was ready to eat too, and decided she'd better check on Gil and see if he was hungry. Upstairs his door was partly open, so she tapped and peeped around it, letting out a shriek when he spoke behind her.

'I am decent, you can turn around.'

Decent wasn't the word she'd have chosen. Magnificent, with just a towel wrapped around his waist, was more like it, and her voice was a croak. 'I'm not sure you should've showered with a temperature.'

'Too late to worry about that now. I felt like my skin was crawling off me. Were you looking for me, seeing as you were in my bedroom? Again.' Amusement was glinting in his gaze. 'Are you after stealing another mattress? And what have you done with my grandfather clock?'

'I wondered if you'd like something to eat. I've made chilli, I'm going to heat some up for me. And the clock is quite safe, it's in the workshop. I have no idea how anyone slept with it in the house.'

'Right. So, is this when you tell me you've taken the hob from the caravan as well, so I can't cook?' He walked past her to the bedroom, leaving the door open.

'Not yet. But, you know, if you have any crazy ideas about going back in that thing… So do you want me to bring you some up or not?'

'Is this chilli vegetarian as well?' He caught sight of her face and his laughter turned into a bout of coughing. 'Sorry, I was kidding. Right now, I'd eat anything and would appreciate it. Thanks.'

'You're welcome.' She couldn't get used to having a conversation with Gil that was polite and him mostly naked. 'You should get dressed before you catch a chill.'

'Well, I would if I was alone.' He raised a brow, and she backed out hastily before he did anything silly, like dropping that towel. 'Unless…'

'No thank you,' she squeaked, catching her heel on that blasted rug, and nearly going over backwards.

'Pippa, what did you think I meant?' His eyes were dancing with laughter as he approached the door. 'But, hey…'

'Still a no.' She charged down the stairs and into the kitchen before *she* did anything silly, like shoving him onto the bed. A startled Lola leaped up and barked when Pippa burst in, apparently believing that she must be in mortal and immediate danger. Pippa patted her, trying to reassure both of them that she really wasn't. At least not the kind that could easily be fought off by a sturdy dog.

Chapter Sixteen

By the time Pippa had heated up enough chilli for two and added it to a bowl with tacos and sour cream, Lola had leaped up in delight, letting her know that Gil had joined them. She turned, about to slide one bowl onto a tray.

'Didn't want to put you to any more trouble,' he said, making a fuss of his dog, who was ecstatic to see him. 'Thought I'd eat down here.'

'With me?' She threw an alarmed glance at the flimsy table; it was so small, it would be akin to eating on his lap. 'Where?'

'What about the sitting room, on our knees?' He tilted his head to the door on his right. 'But if you'd rather not…'

'No, that's okay.' She'd have the space to avoid him in there and it wasn't as though she could insist he eat in his bedroom. She pointed to the bowls. 'Why don't you take these through and I'll bring drinks.'

She poured water for both of them and left his on a side table near the armchair he'd chosen beside the fireplace. She settled on the orange sofa; it was where she curled up most evenings. She was getting used to the house, surrounded by silence now that Harriet was out more often.

Her insistence on Gil moving back in had been an instinctive offer when she'd felt sorry for him. But it had changed her situation too, especially since she'd trashed the mattresses from the caravan to make sure he couldn't return. They'd have to contend with sharing that bathroom and who was going to cook for whom. And then there was the matter of an estate agent and having a sitting tenant in place.

'This is really good, thank you.' Gil was tucking into the food with relish, and she wondered how he managed to produce a decent meal in the caravan when the facilities were so poor.

'For a vegetarian dish?'

'I wasn't going to say that.'

'Again.' She held back her smile until he grinned. 'How are you feeling?'

'Better. Thanks to you.'

'That's not what you said when you found out about the mattresses.'

'I was pretty mad, but I can't fault your execution of the plan.' Lola was stretched out on a threadbare rug patchy with burn marks in front of the unlit fire. 'Are you serious, about letting me stay in the house?'

'Gil, it's your home and you have an agreement,' she said helplessly. 'Legally I doubt I could make you move out even if I wanted you to.'

'I'm not really used to someone looking out for me.' His voice was very low, and her pulse jumped. As they ate she was thinking of the touch of his hands on her shoulders that day, wanting more. How she'd longed to lean into him and allow her senses to take over, to loosen some of the control she usually relied on.

'Are you saying now you don't want me to leave?'

'I'm saying that I don't want you to live in the caravan. Lola deserves better.'

'Ouch.' He clutched his heart. 'All this is for Lola's benefit?'

'Absolutely.' They shared a smile, Pippa the first to look away as she put her empty bowl on the floor. Gil was overtaken by a bout of sneezing which turned into a cough, and he leaned back, closing his eyes with a yawn.

'Sorry.'

'It's fine. I hope you're not on call this evening.'

'Nope. Glad it's not me, to be honest. I really don't feel like it.'

'Tell me about the practice.' Twenty-four hours ago she wouldn't have asked; sitting here with him as dusk eased into evening, all was different.

'Why do you want to know?' He opened his eyes, turning his head to find hers.

'I'm interested, I suppose,' she said, half relieved, half surprised he hadn't refused. 'I found out tonight that my great-grandparents were farmers here and I know your grandfather was a farmer too and set up the practice with someone else. Maybe mine were clients of yours.'

'Maybe they were. And maybe it's a crazy dream, trying to keep it going because it means something to me.' Gil ran a hand over his jaw, roughened by a couple of days' stubble. 'I did my student work experience here and always knew I'd stay so I could support my gran on the farm. I met Clare, my ex-wife, when we were at Bristol, and she was pregnant before I graduated. Then Joel was a month premature and spent three weeks in hospital.' His eyes darkened at what was obviously a painful memory.

'Clare's parents were in Australia and once Joel came home, she moved in here and I came back straight after graduation. Living with my gran wasn't exactly the life we'd planned but money was tight, then we had Luca and when we eventually bought a house it was twenty miles away in town. I was commuting, on call, Clare was working, and...' He shrugged. 'You know how it is. Life goes on. It wasn't until my gran passed away and the estate wanted to sell the farm that I seriously thought about moving back in and taking on the practice myself. Clare and I, we were going in different directions by then.'

'I'm sorry. You must miss her, your gran?' Pippa didn't mean to make it a question, just a statement of fact.

'Yeah. Especially here, the house hasn't changed much since I first lived in it.' Gil's smile was a wry one, tinged with regret. 'She was a proud housekeeper and a great cook, but I'm not sure anyone would say she had a flair for design. But it didn't matter what the place looked like. It was home.'

Pippa felt the guilt twisting inside her, clouding her mind with sorrow for his situation and that she'd dismissed his home and everything in it as ugly and irrelevant. She'd viewed the house as a problem to solve for her dad, a thorn in her side keeping her from her own plans, when it was clear that love had lived here too. 'I'm so sorry. I didn't know, not until it was too late.'

'Too late for what?'

She couldn't admit it was too late not to care, both about the house and the future of the practice. And Gil, filling her heart and her mind in ways she would have found absurd just a few days ago. Perhaps it was easier when they fought, because then she could hide behind her frustration.

'Too late not to come.' She settled on a truth, one which didn't reveal everything. How could she even be

205

thinking she'd miss him when she returned home? Her life in London had seemed full of energy and noise but from here it felt flat, colourless, as though she was viewing her future in black and white. The moments lengthened, the air between them laden with unspoken meaning.

'Why do you always do everything your dad asks?'

'What makes you think I do?' Pippa heard the defensiveness creep back in. It was exhausting sometimes, always being the one in control, making decisions and providing support. Raf's role was to roam around the world without really standing still, and Tilly had eventually found her place. Phoebe and Freddie led different lives and Pippa occasionally wondered if they saw her more as their personal assistant who could put things right than their sister.

'Harriet might have mentioned that you're always available to your family. That your dad expects you to step in if he needs you.'

'It's a two-way thing.'

'How? It's looks pretty one way from where I'm sitting.'

'My dad provides for us, he loves us. He always has.' Pippa was twisting her fingers together, trying to defend Jonny, the lives they both led. 'I chose to look after my family a long time ago. They needed me.' She'd never doubted it or regretted it. But maybe sometimes she should step back, let them work things out for themselves.

'So who do you turn to, when you need someone to lean on?' Gil's voice was low, but his words seemed to be shouting, rattling through her mind like crossfire. Her shoulders slumped as she remembered leaning against him, the solidity, the relief of having someone there to catch her, even for just those few brief moments.

'I don't…'

'Yeah, you do. We all do sometimes.'

'Even you?' She tried to smile.

'It has been known.' He smiled too, but Pippa was utterly aware their eyes were holding a very different conversation. 'It's good to see Harriet enjoying herself at Dorothy's and my aunt really appreciates the help.'

'Not that she'd admit it.'

'Never.' Gil hesitated. 'Look, I know it's an impossible task, but try not to worry about Harriet. She's having a blast.'

'That's maybe easy for you to say, when you won't be the one having to drag her back to London.' This reality was beginning to trouble Pippa almost as much as the house. 'No doubt you've seen that we're not getting on too well right now and going home will be my fault. As was fetching her here in the first place. I thought it might be a chance to reconnect, but instead she's spending every spare minute at Dorothy's or with Alfie, so I'm seeing even less of her.'

'And you think those are bad things?' Lola wandered over to Gil, nudging his hand until he was gently stroking her head. Pippa wasn't expecting the rush of longing at the sight; the desire to touch and be touched, to lean into his strength, feel herself supported.

'Only because it's going to make it harder for her to leave,' she said quietly, only too aware she wouldn't be able to hurry home without a backwards glance either, not now after all she'd learned about her family, and even Gil. 'It's so different to her life in London and she's never met anyone like Alfie before. Someone who could maybe break her heart.'

'Nothing you say or do will change her feelings, Pippa,' Gil said gently. 'No amount of caution, trying to keep them apart or telling her to wise up, will stop her falling in love if that's what's going to happen.'

'You're saying it's inevitable? That we can't stop these things?'

'Yeah. I think it's true. The heart wants what the heart wants.'

Pippa couldn't afford to learn what was in his eyes now. The gruff gentleness in his voice, the words she sensed he believed were enough to reveal a glimmer of the feelings she was certain he preferred to keep hidden. She needed to bring this conversation back from the brink and not imagine he felt it too, the pull of their attraction intensifying with every moment they spent together. The sketch she'd done yesterday, of Posy grazing in the field, lay on the coffee table and she realised he'd noticed it when he spoke again.

'Why do you teach art and not show it?' Gil nodded at the sketch. 'And don't say it's complicated. You're amazing, I'd recognise that demon pony anywhere.'

Amazing? 'You're just being kind,' she replied stiffly.

'Kind? You know me better than that, Pippa.' His smile was a quick one. 'It's brilliant.'

'Thanks.' The familiar squeeze came again in her stomach, the memory of presenting her heart and soul to the world, laying herself bare to scorn. Her palms were damp, and she took a deep and calming breath the way she'd been taught. She'd been careless, leaving her work in here, not imagining that anyone other than Harriet and least of all Gil, would ever see it.

'So tell me.'

'I don't have the time. I'm always busy with my job, Harriet and the family.' Most people bought it if they ever questioned her, and friends and family had stopped asking, but Cassie knew the truth and understood it.

'That sounds like an excuse.'

'How would you know?' Pippa made herself hold his stare, daring him to push her, make her confess.

'Because I know one when I hear it. I can see it in your eyes, what it means to you. And I can't explain it, why I already know that about you.' His voice had lowered yet further, and she was completely tuned into it through the fading light. 'Why do you pretend it's a hobby when you clearly love it so much?'

'How do I know you won't mock me?'

'I guess you don't,' he said softly. 'You'll have to trust me.'

It would be madness to trust him and confess, to return to those far away days she'd tried to put behind her. But she took a deep breath, wanting it out there suddenly, wondering why she'd always hidden behind it and allowed herself to believe that one single evening should define her passion for ever.

'I did have a show, just once, right after I left university. It was my dad's idea, he was so proud, thrilled about my achievement and that I had something of my own to love. He found a gallery and someone to organise it, leaned on a few contacts and all I had to do was paint. Get myself ready.'

She was staring at the empty fireplace, Lola lying before it again. She became aware of movement on her left, Gil getting up, crossing the room until he settled beside her, shoulders, arms, thighs touching.

'Only the opening night wasn't the success my dad had envisaged and some of the reviews were scathing, suggesting that it was pure nepotism and I wouldn't be anywhere without his influence. That I wasn't good enough and would never have a name of my own, on my own merit.' She could feel herself drawn to Gil's strength, his warmth a pillar beside her.

'It absolutely flattened me, and my dad was livid, threatening all kinds of consequences which thankfully came to nothing. I stopped painting for two years and half the work I produced for the show went in the bin. My dad salvaged the rest, apart from the couple I did sell. Looking back, I know I was far from ready, and I let myself get swept up by his enthusiasm to help me. It wasn't his fault, and he was devastated too. I disappeared to Majorca for a month and worked in a bar, trying to get past it.'

'I'm sorry that happened to you.'

'Thank you.' She was barely breathing, having Gil this close, wanting him near and afraid to like it too much. He was a mirage really; he'd disappear from her life as quickly as he'd entered it. 'A career in art was a dream and I'm not big on those. Not for me.'

'I disagree. Sometimes a dream can keep you going when everything seems against you.'

'You really don't strike me as a dreamer, Gil.' Pippa's laugh was light, helping her past the confession she'd never imagined voicing to him. 'You're way too pragmatic.'

'Maybe I'll surprise you again.' There was a smile in his voice too. 'I'm not big on quitting.'

'And you're saying that I am?' She felt hollowed out by shock, letting him glimpse a piece of her soul only to have him think her weak. 'Because I don't want to put myself out there again?'

'I'm saying that you have an incredible gift, Pippa.' He stood up and a tiny part of her was relieved; it was easier to think more clearly when he wasn't quite so close. 'And

I don't want you to let that experience define how you view it. You're amazing, and one day I hope you'll see it too.'

Chapter Seventeen

'Mum, look!' Harriet emerged through the back door, her arms full of something that Pippa saw, with a mixture of horror and awe, was a squirming and utterly perfect puppy, white with liver splodges and the cutest button nose she'd ever seen. 'I hope you're not going to be mad at me.'

She stood up hastily, rocking the kitchen chair. She'd been making some notes and was expecting someone soon but certainly not her daughter with a bundle of trouble. 'I thought you were going to Alfie's. And being mad at you might depend on exactly what's going on here.'

'Alfie's gone out with his uncle, they're going to see a bull. Look, Mum, isn't she just gorgeous?'

Harriet carefully extended her arms and Pippa almost didn't dare take another peek at the puppy for fear of falling instantly in love. Harriet's heart had apparently melted faster than a snowball in the sun and Pippa's was halfway there. She knew exactly where this conversation was going and gripped the back of the chair to put a barrier between her and the puppy, feeling a tremor of panic at what Harriet clearly wanted.

'She's a springer spaniel and she's only eighteen weeks old.'

'Is that right? Are they the bouncy ones?' The puppy whimpered and Pippa's heart clenched at the sound, a tiny tail thumping gently against Harriet's arm.

Two deep, knowing pools for eyes were staring right back at Pippa, set between brown ears on a perfect face with neat little whiskers divided by a white stripe running through the middle. Harriet snuggled the puppy close, murmuring to her, and Pippa seriously doubted she'd ever get the dog out of her daughter's embrace.

'She's a stray, dumped on Dorothy's doorstep with a broken leg!' Harriet kissed the puppy as it whimpered again. 'Dorothy thinks she was the runt of the litter, and nobody wanted her. She's not even microchipped. She's better now, Gil treated her.'

Of course he had. They'd reverted back to a version of their previous relationship since the intimacy of that evening in the sitting room a few days ago. One where they were polite but cool, moving carefully and awkwardly through the house and around one another.

'She must belong to someone,' Pippa said helplessly.

'Not so far as I can tell. Mind if I come in?' Dorothy appeared through the kitchen door and Pippa wondered if Harriet had called for reinforcements on purpose. 'My guess is she's from working stock and they decided dumping her was kinder than drowning once her leg got broken. Stood on, probably.'

'Drowning?' Harriet's eyes were swimming with tears, and she clutched the puppy fiercely. 'That's despicable. But what's going to happen to her, Dorothy? Will she have to be rehomed, or—'

'Definitely rehomed,' Dorothy confirmed, giving Pippa a sideways look. 'She's got plenty to offer the right family and years ahead of her. No good reason for her to see out her days with me, she'd make a lovely pet. Pop her down, Harriet, let her have a sniff.'

'I thought you said working stock?' Pippa was trying to be rational, but it was nearly impossible with those eyes imploring her, and that was just Harriet's. Pippa didn't really want to look at the puppy again but couldn't help it, as Harriet lowered her to the ground and she looked around cautiously, tail curling up adorably.

'Doesn't that mean she isn't suited to a family home, Dorothy? Wouldn't she be better on a farm, running around?' Not in a city house with a courtyard garden. Pippa had to make a stand somehow. Try, at least.

'In theory, but beggars can't be choosers.' Dorothy bent down with a grunt, and the puppy smiled up at her as she gave it a gentle push, encouraging her forward. 'Give her plenty of exercise and the right food, and she'd be absolutely fine. Do a job for someone.'

'Mum, please, can we, pleeeeeeease?' Harriet looked ready to get on bended knee and Pippa was grasping for resolve coupled with sense, trying to ignore her fears. 'I'll help, I promise. I'll walk her every day and do all the dirty stuff.'

'For about a week,' she muttered. 'Then it'll be me tramping the streets and scooping poo off pavements.' As if to prove her point, the puppy squatted down and left a puddle on the floor.

'But you'll at least think about it?' Harriet gently lifted her up, beaming as a little pink tongue licked her cheek before tiny teeth tried to nibble her nose. 'Promise?'

'I promise to at least think about it. Watch where you're putting your feet, Harriet,' Pippa said weakly, grateful for the huge grin Harriet threw her, obviously believing that the puppy moving in was a done deal and Pippa had the sinking feeling that it was. Harriet would have her jumping in the car and rushing to the nearest pet shop for a cosy bed and a cute collar if she didn't watch out. 'Does she have a name, Dorothy?'

'Maud,' Dorothy replied. 'Seemed to suit her. Name of m'favourite aunt, too. Nice sort, knew her way around a tup as well as anyone.'

Pippa was so distracted it took her a second to realise Dorothy was still talking about her aunt and not the puppy as she gathered some kitchen roll to wipe up the mess. She jumped nervously as the door opened.

'Ah, Gil, excellent.' Dorothy nodded at him. 'Puppy needs another wormer, did you bring it?'

'Yep.' He glanced at Pippa, who'd backed away at his appearance while Lola set about investigating the new arrival. Harriet lowered her arms, laughing as Maud let out a tiny bark and Lola jumped back. Gil drew liquid into a syringe and approached Maud, talking to her as he gently opened her mouth and slid the syringe into a corner. He gave her a pat and she licked his nose, not appearing at all affronted by his treatment.

'Well done, little one. Same again in four weeks, until she's six months old. I'll microchip her in the surgery once we know who the new owner's going to be.'

'Harriet, Maud can't stay with us,' Pippa said as gently as she could, ignoring Harriet's glare. 'We don't have anything we'd need to take care of her, and it wouldn't be fair if she's not going to be permanent. I will think about it, but I'm not making any decisions right now.'

She'd already made a decision today and if she couldn't get Gil and Dorothy out of here and quick, then that one could very well blow up in her face any minute.

'Mum, seriously! Look at her.' Harriet stomped over and thrust the puppy under Pippa's nose. Maud smelled divine, all babyish and desperate for a cuddle as she squirmed. 'Why can't she stay with us? Can't we foster her or something, until we go home?'

'Foster? Are you kidding me? Once that puppy gets its paws under the table what do you think will happen then, Harriet? And how are you planning to look after her when you're away at school all week? What about when I'm at work? You can't just take in a dog without thinking it through, it's not fair on anyone. This is years and years of commitment, not something you do on a sudden whim.'

'Your mum's right.' Gil's voice was level and Pippa hadn't been expecting the show of support. Of course he had the puppy's best interests at heart, but still, it was something to be on the same side. 'Let Dorothy take her, have a proper talk with your mum and sleep on it. The puppy isn't going anywhere for now.'

'Fine.' Harriet shot Pippa another look and reluctantly handed Maud over to Dorothy, who tucked her cheerfully under one arm.

A knock at the back door had Pippa rushing to answer it but Gil was nearer. The room fell silent at the sight of the man who'd entered and even the dogs seemed riveted. Harriet's sulky expression dissolved, and Dorothy shot the chap a filthy look as she stomped past. He might have stepped straight from the pages of *GQ* with his immaculate dark hair and trimmed beard, and Pippa couldn't fault indigo jeans with a tweed blazer and open-necked white shirt.

'Sorry, I did try the front but there was no answer.' He offered her a dazzling smile and she hoped her cheeks weren't quite as pink as they felt as he stepped forward, hand outstretched. 'I'm Miles Gray, the land agent. I believe you're expecting me?'

'Mind where you walk, the puppy's peed on the floor,' Pippa shrieked just as Miles stuck a smart brogue straight in the puddle and Gil laughed.

Miles was very gracious about the mishap, and he accepted the anti-bac wipe she offered. She was expecting Gil to march out but instead he and Harriet sat down at the kitchen table and started discussing what sounded like back ailments in horses. Whenever Harriet was home, she would pump Gil for information about his work and he was very patient, answering her questions and encouraging her interest, something Pippa was uncomfortably aware she was not doing very well.

She introduced herself to Miles, wondering if she was imagining the glint in his eye as they shook hands. That look was one of the reasons she'd never signed up for online dating after her divorce; never certain if a potential match might see her or Jonny Jones's daughter, and she found it easier not to bother trying. No wonder Cassie thought she was a lost cause where relationships were concerned.

'It's quite a place, I can see the appeal.' Miles let go of Pippa's hand to glance around the kitchen. 'Great project for someone, as you said.'

Pippa certainly did not want to be reminded of what she'd said on the telephone when she'd made this appointment. She'd been counting on Harriet and Gil not being home and was aware she was now going to have to lead Miles around what would be a very tricky tour of the house. 'Mmm. Shall we start in the hall?'

'Pippa, when would be a good time to talk about my tenancy agreement?' Gil leaned back to catch her eye, looking way too comfortable at the table for her liking. 'Over dinner, tonight?' He ignored her gape as he stood up and offered a hand to Miles, shaking firmly as Harriet watched on gleefully. 'I'm Gil Haworth, Pippa's tenant, and this is her daughter Harriet.'

'You didn't mention a tenant.' Miles looked at Pippa, the smile just a smidge less dazzling. 'What kind of agreement is in place and for how long?'

'We can talk about that whilst I show you around.' She was sorely tempted to grab Miles's hand and haul him away from further trouble. She edged into the hall and stood in front of the suit of armour, hoping it wouldn't put him off. That was another thing she'd have liked out of the way for today. In a skip, preferably. 'Would you like to see the sitting room first? It's beautifully proportioned, if a little dated.'

'I think that's my line,' Miles said with a wink and this time she knew she wasn't imagining the glint.

Good glint or bad glint, she wondered? Did he think she was attractive or raving bonkers?

'Four bedrooms, you said?'

'Yes. Just the one bathroom though.' Pippa resisted a shudder. She had no idea what was wrong with the plumbing and didn't intend to find out. 'And there's no downstairs loo.'

'That won't matter. Buyers will want to put their own stamp on it and probably extend. There's plenty of space and the kitchen could use a reconfigure.' Miles paused. 'And obviously a sitting tenant is something you need to work out before the house can be sold, with or without him. It would definitely lessen the appeal to someone looking for a family home and narrow the market.'

'Of course. Here we are.' Pippa opened the door with a flourish. In the early evening sun, dust flickered through the air, landing on the layers that had come before. The vomit sofa, as she always thought of it, looked particularly bright and the purple cushions really didn't help.

Miles made all the right noises as they continued the tour, and downstairs in the kitchen again, she was dismayed to find Gil and Harriet still talking. Lola was in her bed and Pippa had a sudden vision of Maud safely snuggled up beside her.

'The house certainly has masses of potential and would sell in no time for the right price, once the situation with your, er, tenant is clear.' Miles glanced at Gil, who ignored him. 'Interest in the village is rocketing now the new broadband is in place. The house could appeal to lots of buyers, from someone looking to go self sufficient, work remotely, or most likely, a holiday home.'

'A holiday home?' Pippa hadn't given that one much thought and wasn't sure she really liked the idea, not that it was her choice. The house had been a home for so long and she felt it deserved to have full-time occupants again, a family who'd understand its quirks and its past.

Harriet got up, grabbed an apple from the bowl on the table and ran out of the back door. Pippa glanced at Miles, grateful for the one person in the room who actually didn't seem to mind her company. She was getting used to all this angst, sharing a house with her daughter and Gil. When this adventure was over, she decided she was going to take herself off to a deserted island and speak to absolutely no one.

Miles was saying something as he consulted his phone. Goodness, he really was attractive, and she focused again, trying to make up for her distraction.

'So shall we say Thursday at one? We could make it lunch at the pub, if you fancy it?'

'Lovely.' Pippa's smile became a beam. Live a little, she told herself firmly. She was due a little fun and if that meant getting her kicks, such as they were, with a handsome young land agent then she was willing to give it a go. She'd better be careful all the same, she didn't want to make a fool of herself. 'I'll look forward to it.'

'Excellent.' Miles nodded at Gil who glared back, and edged towards the door. 'You've got my number, Pippa, if there's anything you need before then.'

'Thank you, I'll bear that in mind.'

Pippa closed the door behind Miles and tried to think back to what she'd been doing before everyone had arrived and she'd been forced to confront the prospect of a puppy. Gil was making hot water with lemon before he leaned against the range, mug in hand, to stare at her.

'Why are you so against having the puppy?'

'For all the reasons I gave Harriet,' she said calmly. 'I thought you'd understand. As a vet, surely you don't want someone taking on a pet they can't manage. So many people change their minds and end up rehoming.'

'All those things need to be thought through but it's not that holding you back, Pippa.' He took a mouthful of hot water. 'You're frightened. Why?'

'Don't be ridiculous.' Her heart was clattering and she just wanted to get on with making dinner. 'Would you mind moving so I can start cooking please?'

Gil shifted along but not quite as far away as she'd like, and she opened the fridge. 'You saw the mess the puppy made on the floor. I'd be the one doing all the hard work, then in a few years Harriet will go to university and her puppy will become my dog. I don't want that, it's not fair.'

'On whom? Harriet, or you?'

'Either of us! I don't want this, she'll only get hurt like me and then…'

A sob clutched at Pippa's throat and stole her next words as a tear escaped from one eye, fingers gripping the fridge door. She closed the door carefully, unable to hold back a gasp as she felt the firm pressure of his hands on her shoulders. He turned her, swiftly pulling her tight into him, and it was enough to loosen the anguish she'd battled to contain.

She hadn't been held in so long, not like this. Raf was a hugger, her dad too, when she saw him. But Gil was different, broad and solid, present. Her face was buried against his chest as she tried to gulp back the sobs and one hand was stroking a circle on her back, the other holding her steady as she clutched onto him.

'You had a pet before?' he asked gently. She nodded, nearly undone by her loss of control. His shirt was damp with her tears, heart a hurried beat against her cheek, hands sure and certain on her back. 'When you were young?'

'Fifteen.' She swallowed. 'After my mum. After she died.'

'A dog?'

'Yes.' The word was muffled, and she was aware of his hand pressing her gently, letting her know he understood. She didn't want to let go or have him release her, not yet. 'She was called Ginger.'

'What breed was she?' His voice was a rumble deep in his chest and one hand moved to her head, tangling in her hair to keep her close.

'A Beagle.' Her breath was still gulping hiccups and she sniffed. 'Dad got her as a surprise, he thought she would help us. She was so loving, and he wanted something we could cuddle.'

'What was she like? Friendly, playful, intelligent?'

'Yes. All of those things. She was meant to be for all of us, but she became mine really, Raf and Tilly weren't that interested after a while. She slept on my bed, and she knew all my secrets.' Pippa managed a smile; so many of the memories were wonderful. 'She knew when I was happy or sad, and she'd be waiting for me as soon as I got home. She loved to play, and she was so clever, so tuned into me it was as though she understood everything I felt. I adored her.'

'Of course you did,' Gil murmured. 'I'm sorry seeing Maud tonight has brought all this back.'

'I don't want Harriet to go through what I did if anything happens to Maud,' Pippa said fiercely. She lifted her head to stare at him, wanting, needing to be clear, and uncaring of her reddened and puffy eyes. 'I know what you'll say, and it would break her heart. She doesn't deserve that.'

'No, and neither did you.' He placed a hand either side of her face. 'Pippa, you can't protect her forever, much as you want to. She has to find her own way and make her own mistakes, just like we do. Maud would be good for her. For both of you.'

'You don't understand.' The dread, the guilt was rushing back, deadening her voice. 'It was my fault Ginger died. She was only four. We were in the park, and I threw a ball for her, and it rolled under the fence into the road. She jumped it. I'd never seen her do that before.'

Pippa could still remember her own screaming as she'd gathered Ginger up and held her all the way to the vets in a stranger's car. Legs vanishing from underneath her when the vet came to say how sorry they were, but they hadn't been able to save her beloved companion. Refusing all her dad's frantic offers of other pets and collecting Ginger's things to give away to a charity because she couldn't bear to see the empty bed, the scattered toys, the home broken by loss once again.

'It wasn't your fault,' Gil insisted. 'Dogs do unpredictable things all the time, no matter how much we think we know them. You weren't to know she'd jump a fence if she'd never done that before.'

'I put her in harm's way. It was my fault.' The words were running on a loop in her mind, even though Gil's made sense. Everyone's had at the time; she just couldn't hold onto that and make them real. 'I failed her.'

'You gave Ginger a wonderful home and loved her for the rest of her life. I'm sorry it wasn't a long one, but I've seen so many animals who never come close to that. Maud would be incredibly lucky to have you, both of you.'

'That's quite a pitch.' She smiled weakly. Gil's assurances were kind, but it would take more time yet to allow them to settle in her heart and heal the space Ginger's loss had opened up.

'Don't rush into it,' he said quietly, both thumbs smoothing her cheeks. 'You're right to consider all the practical reasons and be sure you can make it work.'

'Mum? What's going on?'

'Harriet!' Pippa sprang away from Gil as though she'd been shoved, face burning. 'I didn't hear you come in.'

'Obviously.' Harriet was greeting Lola, but her tone was anxious. 'So is there something here you need to tell me?'

'I'm going to make us something to eat.' Gil looked at Harriet. 'Why don't you and your mum take Lola into the sitting room and chill for a bit?'

'Not until you tell me what's going on and why Mum's been crying.' Harriet had wrapped her arms around herself, fear rushing into her eyes. 'You're not ill or something, are you?'

'No, of course I'm not.' Pippa found a smile. 'But chilling does sound nice, if Gil doesn't mind cooking vegetarian.'

'I think I'll cope,' he said dryly, turning away.

Harriet followed Pippa into the sitting room and Pippa was glad of Lola's company too, as Harriet settled on the floor with her. Pippa joined them, needing to be close to Harriet, wanting the touch of her daughter's arms and legs against hers.

'I got myself a bit upset after you left, thinking about Maud, and Gil was trying to help.' *Had helped.* 'I've never told you this before and I'm sorry I didn't.' Pippa went on, explaining about Ginger and why she'd hidden all the photos of them together. It wasn't long before Harriet was crying too, gripping Pippa's hand fiercely as she snuggled closer.

'So you see, it's my fault we've never had a pet.' She smoothed Harriet's long hair and stroked her daughter's head against her shoulder. 'There were practical reasons to consider of course, but on some subconscious level I thought I was protecting you from getting hurt. It's part of my job, but sometimes it's really hard to stand by and watch it happen. I don't want your heart to get broken, by anything.'

'I'm sorry I've been so horrible to you.' Harriet's voice was muffled, and Pippa tilted her chin to raise her head, feeling a part of her heart healing. 'I didn't know about Ginger.'

'It's okay, how could you if I didn't tell you? And I think being grumpy is kind of your job at this age. But please, tell me if there is something worrying you so I can help. I promise I'm not trying to interfere, and I will do my best to step back when I need to. I know you need to make your own mistakes and it's also my job to equip you for them.'

'I'm so afraid of losing you, like Isla lost her dad. I didn't want to worry you.' Harriet's bottom lip wobbled, and Pippa pulled her in tight, loathing that Harriet had carried this alone and hadn't felt she could share it. 'I hate what she's going through and that it happened to you as well. I know I could never be like you and look after someone the way you did with Raf and Tilly when you were young. Grandad told me that it was down to you the family didn't totally fall apart and that you loved them like your mum did because she couldn't.' Harriet swallowed, swiping at a tear. 'He said it wasn't fair because you missed out on having fun and grew up before your time because he wasn't a good enough dad when you needed him to be.'

'I'm so glad you told me, sweetheart. And I'm not going anywhere.' Pippa squeezed her fiercely. 'I know I'm too protective where you're concerned. You're growing up so quickly and I'm sorry for not always listening. It's brilliant, what you're doing here with Dorothy and the animals. And Alfie. He's lovely. And an incredibly lucky boy to have met a girl as wonderful as you.'

'I really like him, Mum. And I'm sorry for pushing you away,' Harriet said with a sniff.

'Hey, you're a teenager, it goes with the territory. Let's make a promise to be good to each other, okay? And I promise to be more open to letting you try things, maybe even make a few mistakes.'

'Okay. Thank you. I promise to hug you more often. And be nicer.'

'Really?' Pippa pressed home her advantage and tickled Harriet, right on her ribs when as a little girl she would scream with laughter and beg her to stop, and then start again. It still worked, and they were both laughing as Harriet eventually wriggled away.

'Anyway, your grandad's not so sad about me that he decided not to send us to Hartfell.' Pippa's heart was lifting at the realisation that her dad had seen it, understood just how much of herself she'd sacrificed for her brother and sister. She'd do it again in a heartbeat and would never regret it. If Raf and Tilly were better because of her, then every moment of caring for them had been worth it.

'Yeah, but look how many nice things have happened since we got here. We've both made friends, you've got a job, I'm learning loads from Dorothy, and I've met Alfie. *Halfie*,' Harriet said dreamily, and Pippa smiled at her faraway look, determinedly forcing down her concern.

'Halfie does have a nice ring to it,' she agreed. 'But please, darling, don't forget we're going home soon.'

'That doesn't mean we can't both have some fun whilst we're here.'

'Fun? Me? I don't even know how to spell it,' Pippa retorted. It was so long since she'd let go, she doubted she'd ever really lighten up.

'I'm not so sure.' Harriet's look was beady. 'I don't know what's going on with you and Gil but that looked pretty cosy in the kitchen, before.'

'He was just being nice, that's all. He caught me at a bad moment.' Or maybe a good one, Pippa still wasn't sure.

'And it's okay, about Maud. I know it's a really stupid idea, having a dog. It wouldn't be fair to leave it all to you.'

Pippa was reminded of Raf's words and Gil's, about holding Harriet back in some misguided attempt to protect her. She knew they were right, however hard it felt to let go. 'So you don't want to come shopping with me tomorrow for a collar and lead, and a shedload of wipes?'

Harriet screamed with joy, nearly knocking Pippa backwards as she flung herself into Pippa's arms. She laughed, lit up by this new happiness. She'd worry about the practicalities of a puppy later.

Chapter Eighteen

The trip the next day was a joy and Pippa loved going round the pet shop in town with Harriet. They were both excited to choose all they needed for Maud, including a cosy bed, cute pink leather collar with matching lead and heart-shaped name tag. After taking care of Posy first thing, Harriet had raced round to Dorothy's to deliver the good news and arranged to collect Maud this afternoon.

Even though Harriet didn't yet understand – couldn't see far enough into the future to realise that college and then university would expand her life even further – Pippa couldn't deny her the happiness having Maud in their lives would bring. Harriet wasn't thinking about twice daily feeds and walks, plus everything else that came with a puppy. Days out, holidays, even a few hours away from the house, all would now require planning, but Pippa was so excited to be giving the puppy a home. There were lots of doggy day care places she could try once they were back in London, and she'd returned to work after the summer break.

Elaine, Gil's receptionist, had been in touch to say that her dad was doing much better, and she expected to be home by the end of next week. Just a few days ago Pippa would have welcomed this lifeline back to London, but although she was relieved for Elaine and her family situation, the news brought the rather unwelcome sense that their time in Hartfell was ending. Without standing in for Elaine, and even though Harriet was settling in and happy with Alfie, and her job with Dorothy, what more reason could they have to stay?

When an ecstatic Harriet returned with Maud, plus Dororthy, who had a cat which needed Gil's attention, and a shy Alfie, they crossed the yard to the surgery so Gil could microchip Maud once he'd dealt with Dorothy. He showed them into the consulting room and gave Maud the once-over, checking teeth, ears, gums, eyes and her heart. All was fine, and Pippa let out the breath she'd been holding.

'I think you're a very lucky little girl, Maud, you've got a lovely new home.'

He was smiling at Harriet, and he seemed to be having as much difficulty in meeting Pippa's eyes as she was his. Both clinging to the pretence that last night hadn't happened; that he hadn't held and comforted her in the kitchen quite the way he had.

Maud yelped when Gil inserted the microchip via a needle that made Pippa wince and Harriet clutch Alfie's hand nervously. Gil scooped Maud into his arms for a cuddle, laughing as she licked his nose and then tried to nibble it. Pippa was shocked to wonder if it was possible to be envious of Maud, able to make him smile like that.

'Ow. I'm sorry little one, but it had to be done. I think you've got your own back now.' He offered the puppy to Harriet. 'Are you taking her?'

'Yes please. Can she go outside now?'

'Yes, she had all her vaccinations whilst she was with Dorothy, she's fine to go for walks. But short ones, okay, it's important not to give her too much exercise before she's six months old.'

Harriet and Alfie disappeared with Maud and Lola, who had glanced at Gil before deciding she shouldn't miss out on any adventures. Harriet's netball camp was starting this weekend and she'd offered to cancel so she could help with Maud, but Pippa had refused, assuring Harriet that she'd manage and promising to send daily puppy updates.

Gil was behind the counter, logging into the system to register Maud's microchip. He flatly refused the payment Pippa tried to make him accept for the consultation as she was giving up her time to help, and she thanked him.

She was used to him being in the house now. She knew from the roar of his Land Rover when he left if he was setting out on an emergency or just making a call. Each morning she would run early, leaving the bathroom free so he could shower whilst she had breakfast. Without even trying, they were creating a routine and she loved listening to him chatting with Harriet, sharing his work with her, and answering endless questions. She would never admit, not even to herself, that she'd missed his company last night when he'd been called to an emergency and had returned long after she'd gone to bed.

'Just checking if you'll be back for dinner so I can be sure there's enough.' He had a hearty appetite, and he made sure to fetch shopping too, and take his turn in the kitchen.

'Please, unless something changes at work. You don't mind?' He switched the monitor off, still focused on the desk.

'Not if you're still prepared to eat vegetarian.' There was a teasing note in her voice that hadn't used to be there when she was around him.

'I'll eat anything.' Gil looked up to give her a smile. 'Thanks for finishing dinner last night. It was a late one and I was starving. I'm not used to such luxuries.'

He'd had to abandon cooking to head out to the emergency, and she'd taken over. 'You're welcome. Was everything okay?'

'Eventually.' He grimaced. 'Prolapse in a heifer after her first calving. Not a pretty sight.'

'You or the heifer?'

'Oh, me for sure.' His lips pursed together in a wry grin. 'The heifer was a beauty and so was her calf. Not sure what you'd have made of me, flat out on filthy straw in a pen trying to push an engorged uterus back where it belonged.'

'Urgh.' Pippa shuddered, he'd painted a clear picture with those few words. 'But you managed it?'

'Eventually. Got to bed at five.'

'Why are you so often on call?' Pippa was watching Harriet and Maud darting around the yard. Even Posy was taking an interest from her stable, the wide-open barn door providing her with a pleasant view to stop her getting bored with her own company.

'There's only me and one other farm vet at the practice now and I've been covering holidays, so I've had more callouts than usual.'

'I see.' It was an uncomfortable reminder of his leaving eventually, the rural practice dwindling until the main branch closed it altogether. Working in the surgery, she'd seen how brilliant Gil was with his patients and their owners – caring, friendly and highly skilled – and she knew he'd be much missed in Hartfell. She made herself think of London instead, trying to picture her house, her usual routine in the city, but it was a blur, a life she had lived before this one.

'Alfie will be with us, too. Rose has already messaged to apologise for how much he eats.'

'You've almost converted me, I quite like vegetarian now.' Gil offered his own tease, and she was the one who looked away first.

'That was good news from Elaine, about her dad,' Pippa rushed out, distracted by that lingering gaze. 'You'll be glad to get your real receptionist back.'

'Yeah. Although I seem to be doing okay with my temp. She's learning the ropes pretty well and hasn't scared off too many clients.'

Pippa couldn't find a reason to delay and Gil was done, following her to the door to watch Harriet and Alfie playing with the dogs. Harriet wasn't quite so attached to her phone these days, and she'd given up complaining about the Wi-Fi. As long as she could keep in daily touch with Isla, she plugged into it whenever she was at Alfie's as well, which seemed to be very regularly.

–

'And you're sure you'll be okay?' Harriet was snuggling Maud in her arms and Pippa nodded patiently for the fourth time. 'Both of you?'

'I'll be fine, Harriet, I promise. Me and Maud. You'll be back in no time.'

The car was packed, and Pippa was trying to prise Maud away so they could set off for the netball camp in Warwick. Harriet had also said a tearful goodbye to Alfie thirty minutes ago and Gil was waiting too, ready to look after Maud until Pippa returned later.

'Bye Maud, I love you so much. I'll miss you like mad.' Harriet kissed the puppy again and reluctantly gave her up to him, laughing as Maud licked his chin. 'Thank you for looking after her, Gil.'

'You're very welcome. Lola's looking forward to it as well.'

It had been a mad few days since Maud had come home; playing with her, making sure she ate well, taking her for short walks and wiping up the puddles she occasionally left on the floor. Harriet had been dismayed when Pippa decided that a three-hundred-mile round car journey was too much for Maud right now, and Gil had kindly stepped in.

Pippa didn't doubt her decision to bring Maud into their lives. She only needed to catch sight of Harriet with the puppy, and her own heart would melt. Maud had made herself very firmly at home in the farmhouse and although Pippa had planned to leave her in the kitchen at night, she'd cried so much when they went to bed the first time that Harriet had burst into tears too, and had run downstairs to gather Maud up. She'd settled in a flash on Harriet's bed. Pippa's dismay had dissolved when she'd knocked on Harriet's door the next morning and found them snuggled together, completely content.

When they arrived at the sports university campus in Warwick, Harriet submitted to a brief hug before the car was unpacked. Then she took off in search of Isla, who'd already arrived. Both girls helped carry in Harriet's things, and Pippa's heart swelled when she saw how happy they were to be together once more. She didn't find the return drive easy, leaving Harriet behind and hoping she'd have a wonderful week. Sunday would come soon enough,

Harriet would be back, and Pippa couldn't wait to see Cassie too, and spend some time with her friend and Isla.

She'd cancelled the lunch with land agent Miles, deciding that any further conversations could be conducted over the phone or online. He was keen to have her sign a contract to get the house on the market now it had been valued, and send someone round to take photographs. He was expecting plenty of requests for viewings and she really wasn't sure she liked the idea of people tramping through.

After the long drive she took Maud for a quick wander around the garden to stretch her legs, thanking Gil for taking care of her. He excused himself and once back in the sitting room, Maud settled in her snug little bed, with Pippa on the sofa. The house felt different again without Harriet or Alfie here. He was very shy, but he was kind and obviously cared about Harriet, and Pippa liked him very much for that. Her eyes closed and she leaned back, glad to relax after hours in the car.

'What's that bloody pony doing in the garden again?'

'Huh?' She was nearly asleep, shattered from the drive, and she squinted at Gil who suddenly loomed in the doorway. Maud leaped up with a valiant little bark, greeting Lola with an enthusiastic tail wag as the Labrador took the opportunity to fold herself into the puppy's bed with a grunt.

'She'll explode if she eats any more grass, and I can't catch the little bugger!' He sounded so cross that Pippa couldn't help laughing.

'I think you must be imagining things. I checked on her less than thirty minutes ago when I took Maud out and she was tucked up in her stable.'

'Oh, was she?' He marched over and took Pippa's hand, towing her to the window. 'So how do you explain that?'

Posy was ambling through the garden, snatching happily at lush, green lawn and made such a pretty picture that Pippa wished for her sketchbook to capture the image. The early evening sunlight was glinting off her brown-and-white coat, trees casting dappled shade onto the plants beneath them.

'Pippa! Are you even listening? I said, you'll have to help me catch her. She'll be on three legs or dead by the morning if she stays out there all night.'

'What? Sorry, yes. Catch Posy.' She finally caught Gil's urgency, shaking her hand free as she made for the kitchen and the wellies which now lived beside the back door.

The dogs decided it was an outing for them too, Maud's little legs unable to keep up with Lola's as they pranced through the garden. Posy had other ideas about spending the night in her stable, and as soon as she saw Pippa approaching as Gil hung back, she applied a brisk second gear and was soon trotting in circles always just out of reach.

'Are you actually planning to help,' Pippa panted at him, leaning with folded arms against a silver birch. The grass was studded with tiny hoof imprints and Posy had left a neat pile of poo amongst the geraniums. Now she'd managed to squeeze herself through a narrow gap between two hazel trees and only a flimsy gate lay between her and the field of sheep. 'Because if you are then can you stop laughing and fetch a bucket or something.'

'She's wise to that trick now.' Gil straightened up. 'Let's take a side each and you try and grab her when you get close enough. See if you can hang onto her mane, it's thick enough.'

She shot him a dirty look. 'Right, yes, good plan. Hadn't thought of just grabbing her when I'm near enough. Genius.'

The presence of the dogs seemed to spur Posy on, and the gate was no match for her roundness when she gave it an experimental shove. She raced off into the field and Gil managed to slam it to keep the dogs out. It was another fifteen minutes before they herded her into a corner, and she allowed Pippa to put on the headcollar he'd slung over one shoulder. She led Posy back to the yard, about to put her in the stable, when he spoke.

'Actually, whilst you've got her, I'll just have a look at her teeth.' He halted in the yard, towering over the pony. 'She's due a dental and seeing as Harriet's away, you'll do.'

'Oh, will I? Right now?' Pippa was ready for bed, and she'd be crawling up the stairs after Posy's latest little escapade on top of that drive.

'No, the middle of next week,' he retorted, sprinting to the Land Rover parked beside the tatty caravan and opening the boot. 'She shouldn't need sedating for a check up and quick rasp.'

'Sedating?' Pippa tried to quash the nervous note in her voice. 'How bad is she, exactly?'

'Mind your feet. And hands.' Gil returned with a bucket of water he'd removed from Posy's stable and some tools that to Pippa looked as though they belonged in a museum, not a small pony's mouth. He bent down and slipped another headcollar on, just a strip of leather which went around her ears and was attached to some awful-looking metal contraption he slid between her teeth. Posy was already swishing her tail, cute little ears flattened and giving him the evil eye as he carefully prised her jaws apart.

'What the hell's that?'

'A gag. It keeps her mouth open so I can see.' He switched on a head torch, nearly bent double on the ground to peer inside.

'A gag! Surely she doesn't need one of those?'

'So are you offering to stick your hand inside and hold her tongue out of the way then?' His own hand reappeared as he fished out a clump of soggy, half-chewed grass from Posy's ill-gotten garden gains and threw it to the ground.

Pippa wasn't, so she kept quiet as he produced a large metal rasp and set to work, like filing nails, dunking the rasp in the bucket to rinse it occasionally. She was busy enough trying to hang onto Posy, who did her best to back up, shoot forward and even stand on two legs to avoid Gil's attentions. She clouted him on the knee at one point and Pippa had to bite her lip very firmly to stop herself from laughing as he yelped.

'Can't you hold her still?'

'I'm trying, but in case you haven't noticed she has twice as many legs as me and is a fair bit heaver. Can't you work more quickly? She obviously doesn't like it.'

'You don't say.' He glared at Posy as he rinsed the rasp and tried again. 'She's not the only one. There are about fifty other ways I'd rather be spending my evening.'

'Then why bother?'

'Because if her molars get sharp again, they could ulcerate her tongue and she'll like that even less.'

A few minutes later Gil decided Posy's teeth were neat and even enough, and he slipped the gag off. Posy shook her head, sending drops of green flying. Pippa gave her a pat and told her she was very clever and brave, which made him roll his eyes.

'I'll just take a look at her hind hoof while you've got her. She had a cut and I haven't been able to get near since I treated it.'

Unfortunately, Posy had no desire to spend the remainder of her evening being administered to any more by Gil, even if he did apparently have her best interests at heart. She stood quietly as he ran a hand down her leg, ready to lift up her hoof, and then lashed out with a speed Pippa wouldn't have believed she possessed if she hadn't seen it with her own eyes.

'Owwwww,' he howled, hopping on his other foot and flashing Pippa a glare. 'I thought you had hold of her!'

'I did,' she gasped, barely able to get the words out for fear she'd explode with laughter. 'Looks like she's in charge of her own feet after all. Not such a tough York-shire vet now, huh?'

'What did you say?' Gil was rapidly undoing his belt and Pippa's eyes were wide as he yanked his jeans down.

'What are you doing!'

'What does it look like,' he retorted, and she didn't have a reply to that; she was too transfixed by the close up of muscular thigh. 'Checking for injuries.'

'Injuries? She's knee high to a grasshopper.' This time she couldn't contain her laughter and the outrage on his face just made it even funnier. 'You'll probably end up with a bruise the size of a spoon. What would you do if a proper horse kicked you?'

'Yeah, well, if you'd kept hold…'

Pippa didn't have time to think it through, the bucket of filthy water was right there. She launched it at him, enjoying the twin satisfaction of silencing him and covering him in green sludge in one go. Her triumph lasted only until his shock receded and it was clear he was bent on immediate retaliation. There was only one thing to do. She let go of Posy and the pair of them took off in opposite directions.

Seeing as his jeans were still around his knees, Pippa was hoping to outrun him and hide in the garden. Maud was yapping wildly, and Pippa threw a glance over her shoulder to see Gil in pursuit with the bucket and his jeans back on, catching her up with every stride. She gasped when the water hit her back, stumbling from the blast of cold and trying to avoid Maud, who darted away with Lola. He grabbed her around the waist and, unbalanced and helpless with laughter, Pippa tumbled to the grass, one welly flying through the air.

He landed almost on top of her, and it was only one arm shooting out to prop him up that prevented his weight crushing hers. She saw the exact moment his eyes darkened, and her breath caught as they fell to her mouth. Her pulse was racing from the sprint and spiked again at the way he was looking at her. She was barely aware of tangling her hands in his hair, lips parted, wanting only to cling to this moment and hold it still, keep him here.

He smoothed the wild hair from her face, running a thumb down her cheek and letting it rest against her lips. She caught it between her teeth, tugging gently and he groaned, touching his forehead to hers. His chest was hard against hers and she curved her back, hooking a leg around his to hold him close.

'Your T-shirt's wet again.'

'Your fault,' she whispered. 'You shouldn't have come after me.'

'What did you expect,' Gil muttered against her ear, lips brushing her skin and making her gasp when he placed a tantalising kiss on her neck. 'That I'd let you get away with it?'

'I hoped you might. At least it's only my back that's wet.'

'Is that right?' He slipped an arm around her waist, pulling her into him, transferring the dampness of his T-shirt to hers. 'I can rectify that.'

Her hands were on his wet top, ready to tug it over his head, when the phone in his pocket rang. His head snapped up and he fumbled to answer it. The apology was in his gaze as he pulled away, and Pippa heard the panicked tones of a voice on the other end of the call as he got up, running an agitated hand through his hair. His eyes hadn't left hers and he offered a hand. She accepted it, brushing the grass from her top once she was back on her feet, and retrieved her welly. He ended the call, and the moment was lost. She wondered if they would ever find another.

'I'm sorry, I've got to go.' He turned a shoulder to the house. 'An emergency, with a dog. Could be a stroke.'

'It's fine.' She was trying to bring order back to her body and banish the burning desire and how he'd made her feel in those few, all-too-brief seconds. It was a shock to remember how uninhibited she'd felt in his arms, wanting more, wanting him. He was staring at her, twisting the phone in his hand before he nodded once, turning to sprint away as Lola raced after him.

Maud tried her best to keep up and flopped onto the grass, exhausted by her efforts. Pippa scooped her up and cuddled her close as they set off to find Posy. She heard the roar of his Land Rover speeding out of the yard as she reached the garden and spotted Posy near the terrace. She let Pippa catch her and lead her back to the stable. This time she made sure to check all the locks on the door were in place.

Chapter Nineteen

Pippa didn't mind in the least that her birthday fell during Harriet's week away. Harriet had given her a lovely card and the gift of a spa day before they'd set off for Warwick. A few months ago, Tilly had tried to persuade Pippa to arrange a party, but she'd put her sister off, finding some excuse to dodge it. She was perfectly happy to wake up on the day, make a cup of coffee and escape into the garden for an early wander with Maud. It was a beautiful morning, the sun already warm and climbing in the sky to glint between the trees.

Without Harriet here, looking after Posy had fallen to Pippa. After her coffee, she fed the pony and turned her out, her mind still caught on those few moments with Gil two days ago, and what they'd been about to do after he'd chased her into the garden. She was mucking out the stable when she heard the Land Rover leave, relieved not to have to face him now. Yesterday at the surgery had been tricky as they'd politely navigated around one another, and he seemed as keen as she was to pretend that nothing had happened. Because it hadn't, not really.

She let herself into the surgery with Maud and logged into the Wi-Fi so she could catch up with messages, of which there were dozens. It took her a good hour to reply to everything, including Harriet's video one apologising for being away and missing her birthday. Pippa was happy to offer reassurance and decided forty didn't sound too bad if she said it quickly enough.

Her dad had also sent a video and Pippa was ecstatic when she opened it to find a message from Dave Grohl wishing her a happy birthday and saying he hoped he'd see her at a gig sometime soon. She was swooning and promptly decided it was worth every minute of being forty for a greeting like that. She forwarded it to Cassie with a row of hearts and received a wide-eyed and laughing reply as she googled Foo Fighters tour dates.

Presents in the family had fallen by the wayside over the years and she usually told them not to bother as there was nothing she needed. Raf wouldn't remember a birthday unless it smacked him in the face and Tilly did her best from far away. Phoebe and Freddie always sent cards and a gift, no doubt prompted by Vanessa, who never forgot, and her dad was another story. He either forgot or sent some outlandish gift that Pippa would never have chosen for herself. He'd made her day this time with Dave Grohl and that, as far as she was concerned, was enough.

She strolled down to the village shop with Maud and had a lovely chat with Violet and Daphne, who were delighted to meet Maud and give her a biscuit. Pippa couldn't resist a homemade chocolate fudge cake – it was her birthday after all, and she deserved a treat she could eat, seeing as Dave Grohl hadn't been able to deliver his message in person. She thought that was probably a good thing, she might never have recovered.

She found it both strange and very soothing to have Maud at her side as they walked, waving at Edmund potting plants outside his cottage. Maud was too little to understand the lead yet, and wanted to prance and pull.

Proper training would be in order, once they were back in London; there seemed little point in beginning now.

After Cassie dropped Harriet back and spent a night int Hartfell with Isla before heading north to her in-laws, Pippa would have little reason to remain here either. Miles had been in touch again and was pressing her to decide about putting the house on the market. She would put him off until Harriet returned, not ready to make such a thing formal just yet.

She'd read the local history book that Edmund had loaned her, taking pictures of anything to do with Ivy on her phone and googling in spare minutes at the vets. She hadn't learned anything more; it seemed that Ivy's life as an ordinary farming wife and mother had placed her in the background of history, and she was frustrated by the lack of progress on Ivy's paintings. She'd tried art auction websites and contacted a couple of friends, who'd also come up blank. Ivy had captured Pippa's interest – the relative who'd possessed a gift she hadn't been able to fully explore and one that Pippa felt had been passed down the years to her.

Wandering back through the garden, she stopped dead at the sight of a hot tub on the terrace wrapped in a giant pink bow. Maud was alarmed by the huge beast that had appeared and barked stoutly before running back to Pippa's side. There was only one person who could have had this delivered and then installed so quickly. She returned to the yard, picking up enough signal to call her dad, and left a bemused thank you message, aware it was nearly one a.m. in Australia.

She spent the rest of the afternoon relaxing in the garden as Maud dozed, feeling a real solid burst of contentment for the first time in weeks. Harriet was having a blast with her best friend, Maud was a delight – even if Pippa did have to keep wiping up the accidents – and then there was Gil…

She was in the kitchen when he returned, trying to decide what she might like for her birthday dinner. They shared a polite greeting, and he fed both dogs and refilled the water bowl as Pippa stared inside the fridge, all out of inspiration. It was looking very much like pasta and roasted vegetables again.

'Happy birthday.'

'Thank you. I didn't realise you knew.' She'd left all her cards in her bedroom, not wanting to advertise the fact, or that she was without family to celebrate it.

He smiled, holding out one hand. 'Harriet told me. She asked me to give you this.'

Surprised, Pippa accepted the envelope he was offering, a small muddy paw print dark against the white. Inside was a card, beautifully drawn in what she recognised as her daughter's style. 'That's so sweet! It's a homemade voucher for dinner at the pub, from Maud.' She gulped back the emotion, such a simple and yet wonderful gesture. 'I think this might be my favourite present.'

'Aren't you forgetting the massive hot tub wrapped in a pink bow on the terrace?'

'Oh yeah. I love the voucher, though.' The pub was a much nicer idea and Pippa abandoned thoughts of pasta, deciding to change out of the vest and shirt she'd been wearing all day.

'There is a catch, though.' Gil's eyes narrowed and she halted, about to pass him.

'Oh?'

He nodded at the envelope in her hand. 'Harriet asked me to take you, so I've booked a table for seven.'

'Harriet did?' Pippa's pulse skipped as other thoughts danced into mind. 'The pub? With you? Tonight? For my birthday?'

'I think yes is the correct reply to all those questions,' he said dryly. 'She didn't want you to have to spend the evening on your own. Is that okay? Do you reckon we can eat dinner together in public, seeing as we're doing okay in private?'

'I think we can certainly give it a try.' It was too late to pretend she didn't love the idea and she glanced at the ancient kitchen clock, somehow still ticking along.

'I need to change.' She had forty minutes before their table would be ready and she wanted to do more than replace her top now. 'What about the dogs?'

'I think they can sit this one out.' Gil glanced at Lola and Maud, squashed up in one bed and perfectly content. 'I'll take them in the garden and see you down here.'

'Thanks.'

It's not a date, she told herself firmly as she ran upstairs. It was just a kind and thoughtful gesture from Harriet, and he was indulging both of them, which was nice. She decided on the only dress she had brought with her: a green off-the-shoulder one that would have been perfect for many of her social events in London but was still a little dressy for the Pilkington Arms. She added pumps and a denim jacket, keeping it casual, and plum lipstick, mascara and her favourite perfume.

Back in the kitchen she was surprised to see that Gil had also changed out of his usual work gear, and she simply wasn't prepared for how stunning he was in jeans and an ivory shirt, floral details on the collar, cuffs, and top pocket. The colours highlighted his vibrant blue eyes and suntanned skin, and she swallowed as she became aware of his own gaze running over her.

'Ready?'

She nodded and he opened the back door, gently telling Lola to stay put when she whined softly. He hadn't voiced his approval of her appearance and she hadn't needed it; it was in his eyes, enough to have butterflies skittering through her stomach, skin warmed by that heated look.

She felt wholly conspicuous at his side as they walked through the village. Dorothy roared by on her quad bike and did a double take, almost wiping out a planter outside the pub. They both laughed, but Pippa couldn't help wondering what his aunt would make of this development in their relationship, having the uncomfortable sense she would not approve.

The sign gently swinging outside the pub was another reminder of Gil's connection to the village, the family they'd once both had in this place. Kenny was delighted to see them, and they were soon settled at a quiet table in the restaurant, away from the bar, busy with summer visitors soaking up sunny evening vibes.

'So tell me why you're named after the pub.' Pippa was busy with the menu, it was easier than catching Gil's gaze on hers.

'How do you know the pub isn't named after me?'

'Really?' She raised a brow. 'You're infamous, then? Or should that be notorious?'

'Nah.' A young waitress had arrived at their table, and he waited for Pippa to choose a drink. She went for the local gin she'd had before, this time with a rhubarb and raspberry tonic and Gil settled on a glass of red wine. 'It's

247

a family thing. My other grandmother was a Pilkington, her brother owned the estate.'

'Wow.' Yet more connection to Hartfell and another uncomfortable reminder of him giving up the practice he loved, unable to raise the money in time to save it. 'So you still have family there?'

'Kind of. It belongs to my cousin, but I haven't seen him in years. He lives in Paris and the estate is just something he gets someone else to manage.'

'Doesn't that bother you?'

'No.' Gil glanced up from the menu. 'I've never felt a connection to the place and it's nothing to do with me. My parents met when my mum was up from Dorset and her parents pretty much disowned her when she got together with my dad. They'd expected better than a tenant farmer for her.'

'I'm so sorry, about what happened to them,' she said, leaning a little closer and lowering her voice. She'd never imagined talking about this over dinner but there might never be another moment to express her sympathy.

'Thank you. It was a really long time ago.'

She nodded, she understood, but she'd caught the flash of sorrow before he blinked it away. 'But it's still there. These things never quite go away.'

She wasn't expecting the brief touch of his fingers on hers, sending sparks dancing across her skin. 'Harriet told me how tough it was for you, stepping in to look after your brother and sister the way you did.'

'Harriet did?' Pippa's voice rose a fraction. 'Just how much talking about me have you two done?'

'Maybe similar to you and Elaine about me,' he countered, and they both smiled.

The waitress was back with their drinks and to take their order and Pippa was aware of a few curious glances coming their way – the rock star's daughter having dinner with the man she was at odds with over a house. She went for roast field mushroom with a truffle and spinach pancake, whilst Gil chose venison. The gin was delicious, and she looked up when Kenny appeared.

'You're becoming quite the regular, I love it.' He bent to kiss her cheek and she laughed. 'And now with Gil, how delightful. What do you think of the wine?' Kenny glanced at Gil's glass.

'It's outstanding. But you know me, I love the Barossa Valley vineyards best.'

'Has he told you, Pippa darling, about the vineyard?' Kenny raised a brow, and she was working hard to conceal her surprise. 'Going by your face, I'd say not.'

'There's not much to tell.' Gil leaned back. 'It belongs to Clare's parents and Joel's out there now, helping to run it. We used to visit on holiday and Joel was always keen to live there. I love wine and found it interesting to learn more.'

'Wow. Yours is quite the story.' Pippa took another mouthful of her gin, already feeling the alcohol hitting her system. Kenny leaned over to top up their water glasses before leaving them alone again.

'Clare went back too, once our house was sold. I needed to keep my share to—' He raised a shoulder. 'Never mind.'

'To fund the practice?' She leaned forward again, keeping their conversation close. 'And the farm?'

'Yeah,' he replied quietly. 'I'm not there yet.'

Dismay was gathering, the reason he'd asked her dad for an extension to his lease clear now. 'Gil, I—'

'It doesn't matter.' His hand swiftly covered hers. 'I don't want to talk about the future tonight. Not here, on your birthday. Let's just have a nice evening.'

'But...'

'I'm serious. Please, just leave it.' He slid a finger beneath her chin, lifting her face to stare at her. 'It's not your fault.'

'Doesn't feel that way.' She wanted to let him cup her cheek and hold her again. She was still thinking about the night when she'd cried over the dog she'd lost and he'd held her tightly, easing the still-raw grief. 'So given your knowledge and experience, please will you choose the wine?'

'You trust me with that?'

'With wine, I do.'

They shared a smile as he ordered a bottle of Cabernet Sauvignon and soon after, their food arrived. Conversation was much easier and more natural than she'd ever have imagined as the meal went on. Every day she came to know Gil better, and every day she wanted to leave Hartfell just a little less.

Kenny persuaded them to share a trio of desserts, including a huge sundae with a thick mound of whipped cream and strawberry sauce into which he'd stuck four candles. Pippa blew them out, to the cheers of some of the other guests who'd noticed it was a special occasion. Once the bill was settled and they'd thanked Kenny – who kindly gifted Pippa a bottle of very nice champagne for her birthday – they left the pub and emerged in the darkened village, lights glinting through windows as they walked slowly back to the house.

'I hope Maud's okay, this is the longest I've ever left her.' Pippa had almost forgotten about the puppy in the fun of her evening.

'She'll be fine, having Lola there will help. It's good to leave them so they get used to their own company.'

'Lola loves coming to work with you.' They'd reached the front door and she opened it, remembering how unfriendly and gloomy she'd thought the house when she'd first seen it.

'She does, she's very adaptable.' Gil reached the kitchen first and he grinned as both dogs leaped up to greet them as though they'd been gone weeks, not just hours. Maud shot out into the garden when Pippa opened the door, and an idea fell into her mind.

'I thought I might open the champagne, seeing as it's still my birthday for a bit longer,' she said casually, aware of him coming to stand next to her as the dogs raced around. She waited a beat. 'Would you like to join me?'

The silence lengthened and she knew his reply before he voiced it. 'Pippa, I—'

'It's fine.' She jumped in, trying to make his refusal matter less. 'It's getting late, and you must be tired after last night.'

'I'm sorry.'

'Don't be.' She bent to cuddle Maud and stepped back to find a treat for both dogs, settling them in their beds.

'Right, well, I think I'll head up then,' he said awkwardly, turning a shoulder to the hall. 'Night.'

'Night. Thanks for taking me tonight.'

Gil left but Pippa was not ready for bed. She grabbed the chilled champagne and Maud yelped in alarm when the cork flew off with a bang. Harriet had left a Bluetooth speaker on the windowsill and Pippa took everything outside and set it on the table. She poured a very generous glass of champagne and found a party playlist, the music exploding through the silence.

After the first glass, there didn't seem much point in filling another and she necked the champagne straight from the bottle, kicking off her pumps to dance on the terrace, mangling the words to the tracks as she sang along. The back door was open but even the dogs had decided to leave her to it and were huddled in their beds.

She couldn't care less when rain began to fall, laughing and swaying to the music still blaring, clinging onto the bottle between fingers feeling more disconnected from her hands with every moment. The fizz hit her blood-stream again as she belted out lyrics to Lady Gaga, dancing as though no one was watching. Except Gil. She squinted through the darkness and saw him standing in the door.

'Go away,' she bellowed, waving the bottle wildly. 'This is a private party, and you didn't want to come so you're not invited now.'

He was walking slowly towards her, and she backed away, giggling.

'How much of that have you drunk?' He glanced at the bottle swaying in her hand.

'Dunno. It's very nice.' Pippa closed an eye – seeing one of him was bad enough. She raised the bottle to peer at it, spilling champagne on the grass. 'How much have I got left?'

Gil took the bottle from her and held it up. 'Not a lot.'

'Then I've drunk rather a lot. My new decade resolu-tion is to drink more champagne and dance in the garden at parties.'

She attempted a twirl that in her mind wouldn't have looked out of place on *Strictly*, but her legs didn't feel quite right, and she bumped into him. His hands landed on her waist, steadying her, and desire burned through her body, crashing into her stomach like a punch.

'Have you seen my birthday present?' She pointed to where she thought the hot tub was. 'Isn't it lovely? But what the hell am I supposed to do with it?'

'I think to get in is the general idea,' he said dryly.

'No shit, Sherlock.' She hiccupped merrily. 'Anyway, my real present was Dave Grohl. He sent me a message. Wished me a happy birthday. I love Dave, did I tell you? Always have. Always will. Sometimes you can't fight these things.'

She wondered why she felt so uncoordinated and clumsy. Her feet didn't seem to belong to her own legs anymore and the hot tub was a blur, the pink bow flashing like a neon sign past her eyes as she wriggled free.

'Pippa, come on, let's get you—' Gil stepped forward again, hand outstretched.

'Oh no, you don't. I'm not finished partying yet. Oh look, it's still raining!' She squinted up into the night sky, laughing as the drops danced across her skin. 'Never mind, I'm having a party and there's no one here. I can dance naked if I want to.' She tugged at her dress, yanking until it was off. She twirled it merrily and flung it onto the grass with a flourish.

'You do know you're probably giving Posy a headache with the din you're making.' His voice was impassive through the dark. 'And you're going to have a belter tomorrow after all that champagne.'

'So? It's my birthday,' she told him indignantly. 'I can do whatever I want. You only turn forty once. I'd never do this at home, Harriet would think I'd gone crazy. I have to keep the family together. Always in control, always sensible.' Pippa wagged a finger at him. Rain was pouring off his face, drenching his shirt. 'I didn't come here to ruin your life, just to do what my dad asked and sort out his house. And I'm mad with him too, because he didn't tell me about you.'

Words were tumbling from her lips, and she couldn't measure any of them for sense before even more followed. 'At least then I'd have been prepared. Because I can't stop thinking about you and that's really not why I'm here. So now you know, Gil Pilkington Howard, or whatever your name is.'

'Come on, Pippa. Enough.' He took the bottle from her hand as she twirled past him and turned it over, pouring the last of the champagne onto the grass. 'Party's over.'

Realisation was beginning to dawn, that she was barefoot in floral ivory underwear, soaked through, and she stumbled. Gil caught her before she hit the ground. She opened her mouth to tell him to let go and her gaze caught on his. She saw the flash of awareness again, felt the tingle that tore through her body as he stood her up. Her breath caught as he swiftly undid his shirt and pulled it off.

Goodness, he's a quick mover, she thought hazily, she hadn't seen that one coming. Were they literally about to go from enemies to lovers? Instead of the kiss she was longing for, he draped the shirt around her shoulders and scooped her into his arms. Being this close to the bare chest she'd been dreaming about for weeks was not conducive to sensible thought and it was all she could do to keep her head off his shoulder.

'That's not helping,' she muttered as he marched into the kitchen. 'You taking your shirt off.'

'It's helping me,' he said flatly. 'And you're going to feel like hell tomorrow.'

'I don't care.' Being held by him was making her body tingle even more than the champagne had. 'You're very warm.' She giggled, her head falling onto his shoulder as he climbed the stairs.

Gil shoved her bedroom door open and deposited her gently on the bed. 'I'll bring you some water. You should get those wet things off.'

He closed the door, and it took her a couple of shaky attempts to get his shirt off beneath the ceiling that seemed to have started spinning. She threw it to the floor, her wet bra and knickers following. When the knock came, she let out a squeal and hauled the duvet to her chin.

'Can I come in? I've brought you some stuff.'

'Okay.' She couldn't look at him as he placed a glass beside her bed.

'Water, paracetamol and chocolate,' he said, already backing away and bending to pick up his shirt, discarded amongst her underwear. So now he knew she was naked beneath the duvet and her cheeks were scarlet.

'Make sure you take all of it before you go to sleep, it'll help keep the hypoglycaemia at bay.'

'Thank you.' Her voice was small and at the door he paused, staring at her with those impassive blue eyes.

'You're welcome,' he said softly. 'You want to know why I didn't join you in the garden, Pippa? Because I have no idea what I'm going to do about being completely crazy for the woman who's going to evict me. And the only reason I'm even saying this is because you won't remember a word of it tomorrow. Get some sleep, you're gonna need it.'

Chapter Twenty

Oh dear gosh, what was going on in her head? Pippa groaned, clutching it with both hands to see if she could hold it steady, not daring to move any other part of her body. A replay of dancing in the garden and whipping off her dress in front of Gil before he carried her up to bed was like a horror movie on a loop in her mind.

She moaned, gingerly turning her head to see that she'd not quite finished the pint of water he'd brought her last night. She inched towards it and, holding the glass, eased into a sitting position. The sight of her underwear on the floor wasn't helpful. The metaphor was all wrong, as though those two abandoned items were suggesting something she wanted and yet had never taken place.

Even with a blinding headache she knew he'd been wrong about one thing: she remembered every word from last night. She whimpered again as she returned the glass and covered her face with trembling hands, as though that would be enough to erase her embarrassment. She couldn't forget his arms tight around her, his wet shirt draped over her, bare skin against bare skin. His discomfort in her room, the confession he'd refused to give her until right before he'd left and burned those final words on her heart.

And as much as she wanted to, she couldn't stay in bed indefinitely, she was due in the surgery, and it would take Gil twice as long to process clients without her. She tentatively swung her legs out of bed, pulling a face at the irony of worrying about him coping on his own. She managed to avoid the dressing table mirror and the three hungover versions of herself; she already had a picture in her mind and was more than happy to avoid the reality.

Even the dodgy shower felt heavenly and downstairs she was relieved to find Lola and Gil already gone. He'd scrawled a note to say he'd fed Maud and let her out as well. Pippa forced down a piece of toast with tea before tottering across the yard to take care of Posy. Dancing in the rain might have lifted her mood but now she ached all over and her head still felt as though footballs were being booted around inside it. After Posy had finished breakfast, Pippa put her headcollar on and led her to the paddock, Maud skipping beside her. She'd deal with the dirty bed in the stable later, she simply couldn't face it right now.

She was in the kitchen at the vets, trying to remember how the coffee machine worked, when she heard Gil's consulting room door open. She was hyper aware of every sound, his approaching presence was a tremor on her skin, the punch in her pulse and bright colour stinging her face. She greeted Lola cautiously, unable to bend any lower without setting off a rocket in her head.

'Morning. Looks like a full list.' His voice was steady, but she couldn't even look at him, not yet. 'You okay?'

'Mmm.' Pippa gulped, battling to keep this practical, professional, but there was only one thing she wanted, *needed*, to know.

'I just picked up a call. Got a collie coming in with a gash on its leg. I said I'd see them first. That okay with you?'

'Of course,' she said. 'Coffee?'

'Please.'

Dare she ask, find out the truth of his words in her room last night? What if he laughed it off and told her he hadn't meant any of it? But better that and knowing than always wondering. She was aware of him beside her, putting car keys down, one hand close to hers. Her mind caught again on him covering her to protect what little modesty she'd had left, the brush of his bare chest against hers, and she couldn't wait another minute.

'Did you mean it?' Her voice was hollow, emptied of everything but desire to know the truth.

'About the coffee?' Gil's quick laugh seemed forced. 'Totally.'

'Not that.' Pippa drew in a deep breath, summoning her courage. 'What you said last night. Right before you left my room.'

Her question became more weighted with every second crawling by. She tried to brace herself, physically as well as emotionally, for his brush off. Ready for him to laugh again, tell her she was a fool and of course he hadn't meant it.

'Pippa...'

'Just tell me.'

'Yes. Every word.' His own voice was rough, and she heard the honesty in it. The admission he'd tried to hold onto and couldn't, the reality he'd hoped to keep on denying, just like her.

Breath escaped in one slow exhale, and she clung to the understanding that he felt the same for a few moments more. Relief was easing the tension in her shoulders and she slid one finger over his, the sound of his own breath catching giving her confidence, sending away the nerves and igniting a fire that blazed across her skin. Her aching head and fears that she'd made a fool of herself were gone, banished by this first, exquisite touch.

Gil's eyes were hitched to hers and his hands went to her shoulders, turning her to face him and letting his gaze drift to her mouth. Her lips parted as he cupped her cheeks, lowering his head to hers. She closed the distance between them and curled her body into his, winding her arms around his neck.

'Put her down,' a voice boomed irritably. 'It's far too early for that sort of thing.'

'Dorothy!' Pippa sprang back, face scarlet and heart clattering as she pressed herself against the worktop. She caught Gil's wry smile and the promise in his eyes, that they'd find another moment. 'What are you doing here?'

'What do you think I'm doing here? Probably not the same as you, from the look of things. Got a stray, that's what.' Dorothy was behind the counter and gently rattled a cardboard box. 'Ferret, a jill – that's a female, if you're wondering – left outside my door last night. Can you give it the once over, Gil, make sure it's all right before I set about finding out where it belongs? Think it might've cut itself, but I can't keep hold of the little bugger long enough to find out. Need another pair of hands.'

Pippa had already caught the smell of the ferret and nearly retched. It was way too much after last night's shenanigans in the garden and the remnants of a hangover. Still dazed by Gil's revelation and those few moments alone with him, she tried to think back to what she'd been doing before. Making coffee, that was it. And clients – more would be arriving any minute.

'Go through, there's no one here yet.' He pointed to the consulting room and Dorothy marched off with her stinky patient. He turned back to Pippa, and she wasn't sure she'd ever get used to him looking at her this way. 'Can we continue this later?'

'I hope so. Dorothy's timing was terrible.'

'For sure.' He squeezed her hand and disappeared into his consulting room just as the client with the injured collie appeared. Pippa offered a greeting and booked them onto the system, her mind caught on when she and Gil would find more time alone.

Dorothy was back with the ferret in a few minutes and Pippa didn't bother asking for payment; she knew Gil's aunt had a long-standing arrangement of invoicing with the practice. Dorothy nodded, and at the door she paused and gave Pippa a look that could've stripped paint.

'I know you'll say this is none of my business and quite right too,' she said firmly. 'Don't want to see him get hurt, that's all.'

'Neither do I, Dorothy, I assure you.'

'Good.' She eyed Pippa beadily. 'Then you'll tell that pipsqueak land agent to bugger off and do the right thing.'

'And what do you mean by that?'

'Ask your father,' was all Dorothy said. Then she was gone, and Pippa was relieved to see the back of her as much as the ferret.

It was a busy morning of consultations and she dealt with clients and their pets with quiet efficiency. Harriet had uploaded some images to the family group chat, and Pippa was thrilled she was having so much fun. Unusually, Gil left his room after each appointment and she felt herself lighting up at every look, the brush of his hand on hers, shoulder bumping shoulder as he bent to examine something on the screen. Once the last client and patient had left, Pippa closed down the system and he reappeared.

'Hey.' He grinned at her as Lola ambled over and Maud rushed to follow. He made a fuss of both dogs, staring up at him adoringly. 'I'm heading into town. Got some tests to run in the lab and a shedload of paperwork to catch up on.'

'Okay. Hope you get through it.' Pippa's phone lit up and she smiled at the daily message from Harriet reminding her it was time that Posy was returned to her stable. 'So I'll see you later, then?' She hadn't meant to make it a question but he was nodding.

'I hope so.' Maud had returned to her bed, but Lola was at his heels, expecting to go with him. 'Anything you'd like to do?'

'Er, well, maybe we could have dinner?' Was he expecting a more assured reply, something other than a meal, seeing as they'd shared dinner before. But tonight it would be different. Their relationship was altering again since the admission of their feelings, bending with their desires, and changing the landscape of her life in Hartfell. 'What would you like to do?'

'I thought maybe we could try out your birthday present.' His smile was a lazy one and for a moment her mind was blank, sluggish after the champagne.

'Oh! You mean the hot tub?'

'I do.' He spoke those two short words very slowly and longing was already curling in her stomach.

'But I didn't bring anything to wear in a pool.'

'Oh, Pippa.' Gil shook his head as he laughed. 'You're not very rock and roll, are you?'

'No,' she replied in a small voice. 'That's my dad's department. He's quite rock and roll enough for the both of us.'

'And if it was Dave Grohl suggesting it?' Gil's grin was wicked, and she was wide-eyed.

'I'd run a mile,' she said, aghast. 'I'll always love Dave but there are some things that don't belong in the real world, and him and me in a hot tub is one of them.'

'So are you going to run a mile from me?' Gil's phone was ringing, and the seconds lengthened as they stared across the room. Her reply was more of a promise as she slowly shook her head.

Pippa spent the afternoon online in the practice, searching out local history before taking Maud for a short walk. Back in the house, she heard the Land Rover pulling into the yard at the same moment the puppy leapt excitedly from her bed, wagging her tail with glee when the door opened and Lola ran in, followed shortly by Gil.

'Hi.'

'Hi,' she replied, smiling at him unable to take another step without greeting Maud. He crouched down, gently preventing her from clambering onto his lap. 'How was your day?' She'd be offering to make him a gin and tonic next and fetching slippers, not that he had any. Way to go, Pippa, she told herself crossly. She'd wondered about waiting for him in the hot tub and had changed her mind about six times.

'Yeah, fine. Yours?' Gil was slowly walking towards her. She'd been imagining this moment all day and now it was here her confidence was threatening to do a runner.

'Good.' Desire was a swift kick in her stomach as she remembered his hands on her face this morning, the exact moment she'd known he was going to kiss her before Dorothy had barged in. She couldn't forget the press of his body in the field after chasing Posy; the way he'd murmured her name.

'I'm really sorry, but I've got to go to a call.' He took her hand and her expectation dissolved in a rush of disappointment. His gaze flickered over the wonky table set for two, the curry she'd been cooking on the range. 'It's a calving and I could be a while. Picked it up on the way back.'

'That's okay. I understand.' She held onto her frustration, knowing it wasn't his fault.

'Come with me,' he said quickly, fingers tightening on hers. 'Why not? The dogs can wait in the car, and we can spend a bit more time together.'

'Are you sure? I'd need to get changed but I don't want to hold you up.'

'Five minutes long enough?'

They were in the Land Rover and speeding out into the night shortly after, the dogs in the back excited to be going on this extra adventure. Gil quickly ran her through all he knew from the brief call.

'It's a heifer, first time calving. The farmer's a long-standing client and it's his son who runs things now, but he's had to go out. The heifer wasn't due for a few days so there was no reason to be concerned until she went into labour earlier and it stopped progressing.'

They parked in a farmyard high on the fell thirty-five minutes later and up here Pippa needed her coat in the cool evening air, realising she'd forgotten her wellies in the rush. Gil pulled on boots tucked into waterproof trousers and a matching top. He collected a box from the boot, and she was beside him as they strode into a byre. She'd seen him in professional mode before but this time there was an urgency amongst his usual calm around patients.

'Hey Jim, how's she doing?'

'Now then, Gil, I'm glad you're 'ere.' A tiny, elderly man with the largest hands she'd ever seen on such a frame was leaning against the metal bars of a large pen. Inside, a cow was standing knee deep in thick straw, birth fluids trailing from beneath her tail. 'I've 'ad a feel an' it's a big 'un. I'll never be able to pull it out on me own, needs a fella like you.' He nodded a hello at Pippa, and she smiled as Gil opened the gate and approached the cow, who to her looked enormous. 'You a vet too?' Jim asked, propping a foot in dark boots on the lowest bar.

'Me?' She laughed nervously. 'Sorry no, I'm just here to…' What, she wondered? She'd be no use here and the best thing she could do would be to stay out of everyone's way.

'Righto. Still, you're another pair of 'ands.' Jim followed Gil into the pen and clanged the gate shut. 'I'll tie 'er up for you, Gil, she's quiet enough but it'll 'elp if she gets any ideas like.' He slipped a rope halter onto the heifer and wound it firmly around a thick metal bar. He was so small, she wondered he could see over the cow, never mind try and hold it steady.

She stared, fascinated, as the farmer held the tail out of the way and Gil rolled up his sleeve almost to his shoulder, carefully inserting his arm into the cow.

He frowned. 'Yeah, it is a big calf and it's not going to come out this way.' He leaned into the cow as he continued the examination, and she mooed crossly and tried to shake her tail. Pippa couldn't blame her, she didn't imagine it was an enjoyable experience. 'She's pretty narrow and the cervix is tight. If we leave it much longer, we'll be putting them both at risk as she's not progressing. I think the calf might still be alive.'

'Side door, then, is it?' Jim scratched his head thoughtfully. 'Thought it might be.'

'I'm afraid so.' Gil removed his arm, wiping it down as he looked at Pippa. 'Can you help me bring some stuff from the car? A byre's never ideal for surgery but it needs to be as sterile as I can make it.'

'Of course.' She helped carry in an array of clean equipment and he covered a bale of straw with a plastic sheet and laid everything out. He sterilized his arm very thoroughly with the help of the bucket of hot water Jim had fetched, and then clipped a patch of hair from the heifer's back, injecting her first with local anaesthetic so she wouldn't feel the nerve block going in. Then he clipped another wide, long space on her flank and thoroughly disinfected it before injecting her again, reassuring Jim that she'd be comfortable and pain free.

The cow was still tied up and Pippa could see a dark foot poking beneath her tail as she contracted, still trying and unable to push the calf out naturally. Gil made a neat incision in her flank with a scalpel, and she was transfixed as he continued. Then his arm was inside, feeling for the calf.

'Got a back leg,' he muttered, bending close and sliding both arms in. It looked incredibly invasive, but the cow was mostly oblivious and clearly not in pain as he felt his way around. 'And another.'

He started to pull, manoeuvring both legs and hauling the calf out backwards whilst Jim hovered anxiously. Pippa didn't realise she was clutching her hands together in hope that the calf was still alive until it slipped free and crashed steaming and soaking to the straw. Jim bent down awkwardly, trying to clean the fluids from its nose and mouth.

'Is it breathing?' Gil was still working on the cow, and he looked at the calf.

'Not yet, lad. Not goin' far as I can tell.'

'Pippa, quick.' Gil threw her a glance. 'Help Jim clear those fluids and stick a piece of straw up its nose, see if you can make it sneeze.'

She didn't need asking twice, surprised by the rush of emotion at witnessing the miracle of birth. She slipped through the gate and was on her knees to stick a piece of straw up the calf's nostrils as Jim rubbed its body, praying this beautiful new baby would make it. The calf spluttered, once, twice, and shook its head, ears flapping. Her hand went to its chest, and she felt the heartbeat against her fingers.

'It's goin' now.' Jim beamed at Pippa. 'Well done, lass. Thanks for your 'elp.'

'Brilliant. You did great, Pippa.' Gil's grin was huge as he continued the surgery, and she felt the shared triumph dart between them, the two lives he'd saved. 'Jim, see if you can fold the front legs underneath, sit it on its chest. It'll help relieve the pressure on its lungs.'

Pippa was still on her knees, awed by the sight of new life. The calf was a beautiful grey and white, a pretty face emerging as it came to, covered in straw and wriggling. Jim helped her fold it into the position Gil had suggested.

'A bonny heifer. Grand, that'll do.'

Once Gil had finished with the cow, a neat row of stiches running down her flank and covered in silver spray to aid healing and prevent infection, Pippa was still lost in wonder when they'd reloaded his car and were heading back through the darkness. She didn't need to ask what might have happened if he hadn't been there. It was clear the calf would have died and possibly the new mother they'd left nuzzling her baby along with it, the calf already standing on wobbly and uncertain legs as the heifer's hormones and mothering instinct kicked straight in.

He'd been quick and calm, and his skill and professionalism had been very reassuring. She hadn't doubted him for a second. If he hadn't been able to save the calf, then she didn't believe anyone else could have done. 'You were amazing.'

'Not really.' Gil glanced at her, both hands firm on the steering wheel. 'It's what I trained to do.'

'Because you love it.'

'Yeah, I do.' His laugh was quick, as though he'd surprised himself with the admission.

She hadn't missed his elation when he'd hauled the calf out, the wide grin when it took that first, vital breath and he knew his efforts had made all the difference. She couldn't picture him in some city surgery, even though he loved companion animals too. Here was where he thrived, this landscape, its people and its traditions were what he loved. Seeing him at work tonight had somehow removed the prism through which she'd viewed him, and now she was beginning to understand the way of life he'd chosen.

Back in the yard at the farm, Gil opened the door of the Land Rover to let Lola out and Pippa lifted Maud down. The dogs bounded off into the garden and the look he gave her as they reached the terrace was a long one. 'I'm going to take a shower.'

'Please hurry up.' She was aware of him watching as she pulled her jumper off. 'I'm going to try out my birthday present.'

'I won't be long.' His voice was low as he reluctantly backed away and called the dogs.

She threw him a smile as she went to the hot tub and unwrapped the bow, tugging it loose. She was ready to melt when she dipped a hand into gorgeously inviting water that had been warming all day, soft lights illuminating the bubbles when she hit a switch. She undressed, trying to subdue the impatience of waiting for his return and climbed into the tub, sighing at the blissful warmth enveloping her as she eased into the water.

Even skimpy pink lace felt cumbersome, and she took a deep breath as bubbles fizzed and popped around her. Dare she? She unfastened her bra and slid it off, the water already more sensual and tingling against her bare skin. She flung the bra away, immediately overcome by a rush of doubt.

What was she doing, practically naked in the hot tub and waiting for him to appear? And what had happened to her rules – dating someone and getting to know them before she was ready to take another step? She leant over the side, trying to spy her bra and debating if she ought to go back for it. But the door opened, and light was spilling from the kitchen as Gil walked out, barefoot in jeans. Pippa slid down and folded her arms, every sense utterly tuned into his approaching presence. Rock and roll, Pippa, she told herself wildly. Bugger the rules.

'I think your birthday present was a genius idea. Especially with you in it,' he said softly. 'Room for another one?'

'What took you so long,' she whispered.

Her pulse was racing as he quickly unfastened his jeans, removing them to reveal a pair of tight, black shorts. Her body felt both soothed by the water and electrified by Gil as he stepped into the tub. He settled opposite her, mouth half quirked in a lazy smile, and she couldn't wait a minute longer. She unfolded her arms, and it was all the invitation he needed as he shifted across the tub and gathered her against him, trailing featherlight kisses over her face until she was whimpering, head tilted back when his lips found her jaw. He teased his way to her mouth as her hands darted to his neck, pulling him closer and desperate to end the torment of longing for their first kiss.

His chest was hard against her breasts, and it was Pippa's mouth that found his first, hands tangled in his hair to hold him against her. It was a powerful, drugging kiss like no other she'd experienced, and every nerve ending was tingling in response to Gil's touch. Stubble was rough against her face and all that mattered in this moment was continuing the conversation their bodies had begun.

'I've wanted you since the first time I saw you. Standing in my bedroom door that morning, all cross and utterly gorgeous in those pyjamas. I knew right away I was in trouble.' He dipped his head to rush out ragged words against her ear, one firm hand holding her. 'Pippa, are you quite sure? This is going to make everything so much more complicated.'

'Certain.' No other word could be enough. She slid his hands to her hips, easing his thumbs beneath the pink lace and felt him smile. 'I'm finding out how much fun it is to be more rock and roll.'

Chapter Twenty-One

In the morning, they sat in the garden with a late breakfast and the dogs, dew sparkling on the long, damp grass. Amongst the startling new contentment in Gil's company and the long-anticipated swerve in their relationship, Pippa was dreading the week ahead. Elaine was home now that her dad was settled back in his own and recovering well with support, and Pippa had a serious decision to make. She couldn't bear to think of leaving Gil and Hartfell, returning to London and acting on the instructions the land agent was impatient to receive; instructions that would irrevocably change Gil's life. She was finding it more impossible by the moment to balance the guilt at the choice she had to make.

Last night they'd shared his room and she'd fallen asleep with him curled into her, holding her gently. He'd woken first and when she'd opened her eyes to find him smiling and teasing her with good morning kisses, she'd known in that moment her heart was his. It was a truth she was terrified of revealing yet, and leaving his bed had been an effort they eventually couldn't ignore when the dogs needed to go out. They'd been banished to the kitchen after a minor battle on the landing, and this morning Gil had run down first, returning with coffee.

'So when's Harriet home?'

'Sunday.' Pippa was happy to be distracted from her thoughts as she smiled at him, thinking of the words he'd murmured last night and how they'd made love with such incredible passion and tenderness.

She tried not to search for signs that he'd used their attraction to confuse her, to keep her in Hartfell until he could raise the funds to buy her dad out. But there was nothing of that in Gil's eyes. He had that same lazy contentment she did, and she couldn't resist reaching over to kiss him. He pulled her in close, the garden chair awkward between them. She knew he felt it too, this crazy complication in their lives that right now felt perfect and utterly blissful.

'My friend Cassie is bringing her home, with her daughter too, who is Harriet's best friend.' Pippa was taken aback to realise how naturally she'd also used the term 'home'. 'I hope you don't mind, they're staying overnight before they go on to Cassie's in-laws.'

They had four days alone before then, and once Harriet returned, Pippa knew they would have to be very careful. Her daughter might be loved up with Alfie and distracted by Dorothy's farm, but it wouldn't take much for her to realise that the thaw between her mum and Gil had heated some more. Cassie was another story altogether. She knew Pippa far too well to have the wool pulled over her eyes.

'Why would I mind?' He eased back, still holding her hand. 'It's your—'

'Don't say it.' She stilled his words before he could finish. 'Please, don't. It's your home.'

'We both know it's not, not anymore, Pippa,' he said quietly. He let go to smooth her cheek with his thumb, and she was ready to weep at the acceptance in his gaze.

'It's okay, I get it. You have to sell. You dad doesn't want it.'

'You're not giving up?' She loathed that he might, that she and her dad had brought him to this. Broken his dreams, shattered his future, all while falling… She bit her lip. She couldn't admit that again, not even to herself, or allow the words to form in her mind. Hers and Harriet's lives were bound to London and he was right. This was a serious complication, but a beautiful one, and she didn't regret it.

'Maybe you just need to know when it's time. Your dad was very clear about not offering any extension. I hope you'll let me stay on until my lease runs out.'

'Gil, I haven't made any final decision yet.' It was too late to return to the days when she hadn't cared. 'Where will you go?'

'Wherever I can get a job. Joel's in Adelaide and Luca's pretty independent now.' He raised Pippa's hand to brush it against his lips, sending sparks darting into her stomach. 'The practice was a crazy dream and maybe I should let it go, move on.' He paused, and she wondered if he was trying to make it easier somehow. 'So, speaking of overnight guests, do you think we can fit in one more? Luca is coming up for a few days on Sunday as well.'

'Of course we can, I'd love that,' Pippa said quickly. 'It'll be wonderful to meet him.'

'He would've been happy to crash in the caravan but seeing as someone has deliberately sabotaged it…' He grinned. 'Dorothy's been muttering dire threats about claims and compensation.'

'Oh, has she? For that grotty old tin can and a couple of lousy cushions?' Pippa felt almost invincible this morning and even taking on Dorothy didn't faze her. 'Well, she's not the only one. I wouldn't mind some compensation for having to look at it outside the kitchen window every day.'

'How about this?' Gil bent to touch his lips to hers, and it was a few moments before she pulled back with glittering eyes.

'It's helping,' she said breathlessly. It was as though he already knew every part of her most sensitive to his touch and she was remembering last night again, him carrying her naked from the hot tub into the house. 'But I'm going to need a lot more compensation. It's a very ugly caravan.'

'Later,' he murmured, standing and tugging her upright. 'Let's go for a drive, there's something I'd like to show you. And if that's not compensation enough, spend tonight with me and I'll try harder.'

'Harder,' Pippa said dreamily, almost tripping over a beaming Maud leaping around her legs. 'I don't think that's even possible. Get down, Maud, honestly. We seriously need to sign up for some training classes.' Another reminder of London life she didn't want.

'Wear your trainers seeing as you haven't got any walking boots yet.'

'What time will we be back?' Her mind was darting ahead, searching for a schedule. She always had one, it was the pillar around which her life was built.

'Shush,' he said reprovingly, silencing her with another kiss. 'You don't need to plan every minute, Pippa. Just let the day happen.'

'Wow, who does that?' She was only half joking, unused to allowing one hour to ease into another without knowing how she'd spend it.

The dogs were only too happy to join them, and she watched the landscape pass by from the passenger seat, one hand on Gil's thigh. She knew this land now. She'd come to love the open spaces, meadows nestled beside the river shorn to make hay for winter. Cattle and sheep wandering the fell, the bright fronds of bracken and thick, springy heather ready to erupt into flower. It was another world from her life in the city, elemental and wild, beautiful and dramatic.

She was becoming dependent on the views, the pure air she breathed. The rough stony paths beneath her feet, the river rushing beside her, the effort it took to climb the fells, every fought-for step worth it when she was rewarded with the world at her feet. She was finding new inspiration in her work here; she couldn't go a day without drawing and the sketches in the sitting room were increasing, the lure of her easel beckoning. She didn't usually go so long without it, but it hadn't made the journey from London as she'd never imagined staying so long. How easily hers and Harriet's lives had fallen into a new rhythm and every day the city felt further away.

The Land Rover rattled noisily over a cattle grid as they climbed, the road sharp and twisting, the only people they saw occasional hikers or farmers. Eventually, Gil pulled into a rough parking space, and they got out. Somewhere below them was Hartfell; up here was wild and breezy and she saw – felt – the beauty of it settle in her body.

'Where are we going?'

'You'll see. It's not far.' He clipped on the dogs' leads and lifted Maud down.

They followed a narrow path, Lola and Maud impatient to run. They couldn't do that here, not with loose sheep grazing. Stone walls and haybarns that had stood for generations golden against the green, gushing water falling from high ground into the river, a valley widening before them. Gil halted and his grin was exuberant as he moved behind Pippa, wrapping his arms around her.

'There. See it?'

'A farm?' She was smiling. She did that often now, with him. Last night together had filled her body with an ease she'd long forgotten, even though her mind was still working hard to push away thoughts of the future. 'You're not on call?'

'Nope. Day off. Tell me what you see.' His chin was on her shoulder, both dogs wondering why they'd stopped when walking and sniffing was so much more fun.

'Buildings. A house.' A square, stone one; the kind that had stood resolute and firm against all this landscape and the weather could throw at it. A window in each corner, a slate roof matching those on the barns. 'Cattle in the distance, sheep and some vehicles. A quad bike, a couple of dogs in the yard. Are they clients?'

'Yep.' Gil's arms around her tightened some more and she slid her hands over his. He felt so sure, strong, and she was looking forward to new mornings when they'd wake together. 'They've been clients for years. Third generation now, the youngest daughter has just taken over from her dad.'

'So this is what you wanted to show me? A family farm?'

'Not just any farm.' Gil's voice was low beside her ear. 'Back in the day, this was the Walker family farm. The one your great-grandmother married into.'

'This is Ivy's farm?' Pippa tilted her head until her eyes found his. 'Seriously? Ivy and Albert's?'

'The very one. Albert took on the lease after his father, and he and Ivy farmed it all their lives. It reverted back to the estate once they passed because their daughter didn't want to carry on.'

'Gil, this is incredible! I can't believe you brought me here.' Pippa sank onto a low grassy bank, trying to absorb the view of her family's past. 'Edmund emailed me some information, and I'd been planning to find the farm. I just hadn't got around to it yet.'

'You want to take a closer look? I'm sure they won't mind.'

Slowly, she shook her head. She didn't want to share these hours with anyone else. 'Maybe another time? Today I'd like to enjoy it from here with you.'

He settled next to her, holding onto both dogs, who were disappointed to have their walk cut short. It was nearly far enough for Maud anyway, she'd be asleep by the time they returned. Fells dipped and rose, the occasional tree bent double by the prevailing wind, stone walls green with moss from the years, clouds scudding across the sky. Pippa's eye roved over the farm as she tried to imagine how – if – it might have changed since Ivy's day.

'It's so beautiful and peaceful,' she said wistfully. 'But it must have been a hard life for them out here.'

'Hard but rewarding.' Gil slid a warm hand onto her thigh. 'Pippa, I'm sorry I was angry about the photo album. I'm not really used to sharing my story, but it wasn't fair to shut you out of your history too. I wanted to say that you can have it back, see what else you can find in the house. That picture of my dad with yours isn't the only one.'

'Thank you, I really appreciate it. I understand how special those memories are,' she told him quietly. It was cool up here and she snuggled close, wanting to keep him near. 'I'm sorry my dad is making things difficult for you.

I have no idea what's behind it but I'm going to find out why he's refused to extend your lease. It's the least I can do.'

'But maybe it doesn't matter anymore and I'm wrong to cling to this place. Maybe there is something else out there for me.'

'So why are you still fighting for it?' She held her breath. Perhaps her own future might be bound in what he would say next.

'I guess it's because living here with my gran is the only home I remember as a kid.' She was stroking his hand, wanting to keep that connection, to let him know she was listening to every word, felt every memory he shared.

'We didn't have a lot, but I knew she loved me.' He sighed, and Pippa's heart clenched again. 'And growing up on the farm, being a vet and carrying on what my grandad had started just made perfect sense.'

'You're an incredible vet,' she said sadly. 'Your patients and your clients love you and you make a difference every single day.'

She'd seen it often enough these past weeks; his calm and professional warmth, the confidence that he could apply his training and experience to help. She was thinking of the calf born last night, alive because of Gil. The anxious owners coming through the consulting room door every week, leaving with a plan in place and hope in their hearts. How could she be the one to snatch all of this away from him and the community he loved?

'Thanks, Pippa.' The hand left her thigh to go around her shoulders, pulling her closer still. 'But you know what it's like. You didn't have it easy either.'

'It's strange. To the outside world it looks like we have everything we want, because Dad is successful and famous.

But when it's just us, behind closed doors, he's part of a family who want the same things everyone does. Love, home, safety, security, all the usual stuff. And it only takes one person to be missing for lives to swerve in a different direction and then you feel adrift.' There was something else she suspected, something she'd guessed at, and she wondered if he'd share it. 'May I ask you something personal?'

'Sure.'

'Those swimming medals, in the cabinet. Are they yours?' She heard, felt, him huff out a long sigh and she pressed herself against him. 'I understand if you'd rather not say.'

'Yeah. After what happened to my parents, I was terrified of the water for a long time. When I got older, I decided I wasn't going to let that fear hold me back and took lessons. I worked at it, got better and swam competitively for a while, as you saw. I've always been pretty stubborn.'

'You don't say.' She smiled and heard the low rumble of his chuckle.

'I'm not mad about swimming, it was just a means to an end, that's all. A way to get past the fear, not a hobby I really loved.'

'You're amazing.' Pippa's heart was racing, and she couldn't have said how long they'd been sat up here, sharing secrets on a grassy bank with the landscape that connected both of them rising to meet a sky made softer by wisps of white clouds. She was dreading leaving Gil and Hartfell and returning to work, the end of the summer holidays already in sight. She'd landed in his childhood home, the one that had made him feel safe and secure, and her being here threatened to yank it from him. There had to be another way and she was going to find it. She had to, especially after these last few hours together.

'I'm really not. I'm a grumpy bugger who's not great at showing how I really feel.'

'Oh, I don't know,' she teased, easing them past that moment of sadness. 'You were pretty clear last night.'

'Yeah, well, you seem to have got right under my skin, Pippa Douglas.' He cupped her face, turning it so he could kiss her. 'I'm telling you things I haven't shared in years. And I really don't get how easily we understand each other.'

'Me neither.' She hadn't got a witty reply to that, just a clear sense that he'd spoken the truth. She understood, knew him too.

'And I'm not saying any of this to try and change your mind about the house, or feel sorry for me in some way. I know it's crazy, saying this after one night together, but you're important to me, and I think you feel the same.'

'You know I do.' They hadn't held back last night, and it had been wonderful, making love, talking, laughing together until dawn had risen and brought a new day with it.

'But I have no idea what we're going to do about it.'

'Let's not talk about that now,' she told him softly. Every time they touched, looked at one another, it was impossible to think beyond the next moment. 'We have a few days together and I want us to enjoy them. We can talk properly once Cassie and Isla have left.'

'Deal. So can I ask you a question then?'

'Of course.' Her legs were getting cold, sitting still, and he shifted until he was behind her, wrapping his coat around the both of them.

'Why is someone like you still single, Pippa?'

'Someone like me?'

'Yeah. Smart, funny, kind. Beautiful.' He dropped a kiss in her hair and her head was resting on his shoulder.

'Wow. Thanks. Not words I ever thought to hear from you.'

'They were always there, I just kept trying to pretend otherwise.'

'There was someone at work, once.' Pippa was remembering the months and years after her separation from Harriet's dad. Her resolve to focus on the family and put dating aside. 'But eventually he wanted to commit to something more and I wasn't ready. He was nice and thoughtful, but not someone I imagined spending the rest of my life with. Even now I'm still never sure if it's me they see, or Jonny Jones's daughter.'

'Nick, Harriet's dad, just wasn't interested in my dad's world. He's a wildlife cameraman and he couldn't care less what my dad did, or who I'd met. It was one of the things I found so attractive about him, but I was too focused on the family still, saying yes to pretty much anything they wanted me to do. I thought then it was how I'd keep us all together.'

'And now you're here, a bit more out of reach?' A red kite was swooping ahead, its forked tail directing its course on the wind, hunting for prey and Pippa saw the distinctive flash of colour.

'I definitely feel more disconnected from the drama. My sister Tilly has been messaging about Christmas, wanting to know what I'm planning, and she was a bit shocked when I said I had no idea.' Pippa smiled. 'Usually by now I'd have a menu arranged and gifts on the way, but I'm thinking it might be nice to have a change.'

'What kind of change?'

'Maybe an Australian one. Dad's looking for a place out there and if he has something by then, maybe Harriet and I will visit.' She didn't say the rest, that she'd love it if Gil were there too. She allowed herself a tiny daydream of an Australian summer in December, strolling along a beach together. 'You must miss Joel, being so far away.' Pippa felt the familiar squeeze of anxiety at thoughts of Harriet travelling so far in the future. But she couldn't hold her back, she had to let her live her own life, make those mistakes.

'I do, it takes a lot of getting used to, not having them around. That was the worst part of the divorce, splitting up the family unit, the foursome. However much Clare and I wanted different things as a couple, we still loved each other in a way and were a good team for a long time.'

'I'm sorry about your divorce. It's never easy, whatever the circumstances.'

'Thanks, Pippa.' Gil stretched out a leg and Lola plonked her head on his thigh. 'I think eventually we both knew that if Clare hadn't been pregnant so soon it might not have lasted as long as it did. It wasn't easy, neither of us had planned on having kids that early.'

'It'll be so wonderful, meeting Luca, I'm really looking forward to it. But he might really hate me,' Pippa added, panic flaring in her mind. 'I'm the one who's making your life difficult, and I wouldn't blame him for thinking badly of me.'

'He won't, don't worry.' Gil squeezed her tightly. 'He's way smarter and more pragmatic than me and has been telling me for months that I should let go and move on. But it's hard to let go of home, however impossible it seems to stay.'

Chapter Twenty-Two

'Mum? I've been thinking.' Harriet was rubbing one finger with her thumb the way she always did when she was nervous. 'And I've got something to ask you.'

Pippa was helping sort through Harriet's washing after the week away and Cassie was upstairs, unpacking in the bedroom Pippa had vacated for her. Isla was sharing with Harriet, and Luca, when he arrived later, would be bunking down in his dad's room on a camping mat.

Pippa had moved into the box room and a narrow single bed, hoping she was concealing how much she'd miss sharing with Gil after these past few nights together. Even the dogs were getting used to sleeping in the kitchen and had settled quite happily. She was coming to dread separating Maud from Lola as well; they were so sweet together and Lola tolerated Maud's babyish attentions with bouts of patience.

'Harriet darling, you've only been home for thirty minutes.' Pippa eyed her daughter, unwilling to begin what sounded like it could be a difficult discussion so soon. 'Where's Isla?'

'In our room, getting changed. We're going down to Dorothy's and Alfie's meeting us there, but I wanted to ask you to think about something first.'

'Something I'm clearly not going to like.'

'Well, you might.' Harriet's thumb was rubbing a bit faster. 'What would you say if I told you I don't want to go back to school.'

Pippa almost dropped the pair of shorts she'd been holding, puzzled at the mention of school out of nowhere. 'No one does after the holidays, that's perfectly normal.' But Harriet hadn't generally minded before and often set off without a backwards glance. 'You'll soon settle in again. But if something is bothering you, then yes, absolutely you must tell me so I can help.'

'There is. And you can.' Harriet took a deep breath and put her phone down, making Pippa's heart swoop as she realised just how serious this conversation was. 'But you're not going to like it.'

'Just say it, please.' Her own nerves were fluttering now, thoughts running over what might have changed with her daughter in the past week.

'Okay. Here goes.' Harriet took a deep breath. 'I don't want to go back to London. Or school.'

'You what?' Pippa nearly laughed until she caught sight of Harriet's pursed lips. Of all the worries darting through her mind, she hadn't landed on this one. 'Of course you do! We live there, our entire lives are in London.'

'Not our entire lives, Mum.' Harriet eyed her steadily. 'We're both making a life here, in Hartfell.'

'Yes, but it's temporary.' Even though Pippa was coming to wish things were different. 'We have to go home.'

'But do we, really? What if I said I want to stay here?' Harriet rushed on, pressing home her advantage in the face of Pippa's shock. 'There's a high school in the next village, I've already looked at their Ofsted and it's outstanding. No areas of concern. It's a great school and

283

they have a really strong sports ethos. I think I'd really like it there. I met Alfie's auntie at his before camp, she's head of year eleven. I bet she'd be happy to have a chat with us.'

'Go to school here?' The alarm was swiftly being replaced by panic as Pippa saw the firm resolution in Harriet's gaze, instantly reminding her of Jonny. He would look at her like that when he wanted his own way, and he usually got it. Another thing he shared with his only grandchild. 'But why? It doesn't make any sense. You already go to a great school, one you really wanted.'

'Yes, but I don't want to go back to London. I want to stay here.'

'Harriet, that's absurd! You love London as much as I do.' The pair of shorts slid from Pippa's hands, and she barely noticed that Maud had made a nest in the pile of dirty washing. 'We only came for a few days and yes, we've stayed longer than I expected, but we have to go home. I have work, you have school. You're surely not serious? What's brought this on?' She narrowed her eyes. 'Please don't tell me your grandad is behind this. Because if he is, I'll—'

'He's not, it's all my idea. I haven't told him anything, I wanted to speak with you first.'

Well, that made a nice change, but it didn't solve the problem. Pippa felt ambushed, still too sated and tranquil from these past days with Gil to make any sense of this startling declaration from her daughter.

The time she'd spent with him had been wonderful and she'd tried to cling to every precious moment. Thankfully, he'd gone to collect Luca from the station so for the moment she didn't have to disguise her feelings around Harriet. It wouldn't be quite so easy when Gil was here and she was remembering his mouth on hers, tangled between the sheets, falling asleep in his arms.

'*Mum!* Are you even listening? I said, what's wrong with the school here?' Harriet bent down and scooped Maud into her arms, nuzzling the puppy's face. Maud wagged her tail and licked Harriet's cheek with an enthusiastic pink tongue.

'Harriet, you're fourteen!' Pippa came to, sharply jolted back to the present. She couldn't indulge such nonsense; it was far too close to her own thoughts, and she needed to remind herself of the facts. 'And about to enter your final two years at school, at the end of which you will sit your GCSEs. These are your most important years. They're crucial and you know you need excellent results to get into the college you want. You've already picked it out.'

'So? That's exactly why now is such a good time to change. So I can settle in and get on with it.'

'But what if you never settle and it makes you really unhappy? You know what it's like, everyone will already have friends and you'd be landing in the middle of that, trying to find your own. And they'll all know who your grandad is, and some won't like you because of it.' Pippa paused for breath, voicing another fear. 'Does this have something to do with Alfie? Because if so, you simply can't change your entire life for the first person you fall in love with.'

She hoped Harriet hadn't noticed the flash of guilt. Pippa had done exactly that, and had gone one further and married him as well. But in her defence, she'd been in her twenties, not an impressionable teenager.

She leaned against the washing machine, trying to steady her racing pulse. Of all the adventures Harriet had thrown herself into since arriving in Hartfell, wanting to change schools and move here, to *actually* move her life here, had never entered Pippa's mind. She had allowed herself a little daydream now and then, of somehow sharing a life with Harriet, Gil and the dogs, all coming home together each evening. Luca living with them when he wasn't travelling and Joel visiting when he could. Where, and whilst Pippa did exactly what, she had no idea. Elaine had returned to the practice and she too, would retire again once it was closed.

'I'm not in love with Alfie.' Harriet took a selfie with Maud, smiling into her phone. 'At least not yet, and it's not all because of him. It's everything, Mum. Posy, Dorothy's, having Maud and giving her a proper home. She loves it here, it wouldn't be fair to take her away.'

'Harriet, it would literally be madness to move here. I'm sure Maud would settle wherever we were. And what about me, where do I feature in all this? Where would we live, what would I do?'

Pippa couldn't drag her daydreams into a plan, they drifted in like confetti only to blow away again. Harriet, school and London were the realities she needed to hold on to so she could make herself leave this place.

'You could be an artist, Mum. It's what you've always wanted and maybe you need to be here to see that. You're always the first to tell me to follow my dreams. I know you didn't like it here at first, but you do now. I know you do.'

Pippa stared at her daughter, trying to snap out of her confusion as Isla entered the room, and she smiled. Isla had also changed and both girls seemed very much on the brink of adulthood. Altering the rules, making their own decisions, and she felt a rush of sympathy. Isla had lost so much, and Pippa knew how untethered Cassie sometimes felt, having single parenthood forced on her by bereavement. Was it such a terrible risk, to take a gamble in life now and then, when everything really was so uncertain and might be gone in a moment?

'We can't talk properly about this now, Harriet. Luca will be here soon with his dad and you two are going out.'

'Please, Mum, just promise me you'll think about it?' Harriet knew exactly when to back off and her tone had become placatory as she put Maud back down in the washing and made for the door with Isla.

'I promise to think about it,' Pippa agreed, aware she'd just landed herself in a world of trouble. Harriet threw her a grin and both girls disappeared, promising to be back in time to eat later.

–

'I can't believe you didn't mention how gorgeous he is.' Cassie was stood at the window watching Gil getting out of the Land Rover with a younger version of himself, Lola bounding joyfully beside Luca, who dropped to his knees to hug her.

She fixed Pippa with a long, knowing look. 'A seriously hot vet, sharing the house with you. You're up to something and quite frankly you don't even need to tell me what, it's written all over your face. So what's it like, sleeping with the enemy?'

'Isn't Luca like Gil? So tall and even more blond.' Pippa was staring too, attempting a feeble change of subject. She was still very nervous about meeting Luca, and she gulped back her uncertainty as he hauled a bag from the back seat and shared a grin with his dad. She'd never been any good at games which involved keeping her face straight. 'Keep your voice down, Cass, that's the last thing Luca needs to know. And Harriet, obviously.'

'And that hot tub. I bet you've never been out of it.'

Pippa's only reply was another faraway smile and she quickly snapped out of it as the back door opened and Luca entered, followed by Gil. Whatever the reality over the future of the house, she cared about Gil and by extension his family, and her smile was wide as she stepped past Cassie and held out a hand.

'Luca, welcome home, it's so good to meet you. Your dad has only wonderful things to say.'

'Thanks.' Luca flashed her an easy grin, so like Gil's. It was going to be okay, there was warmth and humour in those matching blue eyes. 'I'd say I like what you've done with the place, Dad, but it hasn't changed much since I left. He told me what you did to the caravan, Pippa.'

'Oh, did he?' She had to school her face very carefully to remain nonchalant. 'It was all for his own good because he wasn't very well. I hope he mentioned that part.'

'I told Luca you pretty much dragged me in here and wouldn't let me out again.'

Pippa hurriedly coughed into her hand, doing her best to pretend that Cassie hadn't just snorted behind her. She'd have words with her friend later. And Gil. He couldn't be laughing at her like that, safely out of Luca's sight.

'Until I was better. Recovered my strength,' Gil clarified, making a fuss of Maud who was wary of yet another new arrival and one who was even taller than Gil. 'Maud, this is Luca. You and he are going to be good friends, he loves dogs as much as I do.'

Luca held out his arms, snuggling the puppy close, making Pippa melt just a little more. Maud was already getting over her fright and licking his face. Pippa introduced Cassie and the door opened again as Harriet arrived with Isla and Alfie. Both girls were laughing at something Alfie was saying, and as one, they fell silent when they saw Luca holding Maud.

Pippa introduced the three teenagers as well, and Maud wanted Harriet, so Luca handed her over with a grin and grabbed his bag. Pippa had been making a vegetable lasagna for dinner whilst Cassie prepared a salad. Harriet suggested the hot tub to Isla and Alfie, who'd apparently come prepared with swimming things. Another thought which made Pippa blush at the reminder.

When Luca returned downstairs, he was persuaded to join them, the dogs flopping in the early evening sun on the terrace. Gil had nipped down to the pub to bring more wine, and Pippa was breaking chocolate into chunks for a sauce to pour over profiteroles later. The house was buzzing with chat and laughter, and she loved it. Finally, it felt like a home.

'Teasing aside, Pippa, Gil's lovely.' Cassie was wistful as she poured double cream into a yellow enamel jug she'd found in a cupboard. 'And he's so obviously into you.'

'Do you think the kids have noticed?' Pippa attempted to smooth out the alarm in her voice. Leaving Hartfell was going to be hard enough, and she didn't want to add any more layers of difficulty to her decision.

'Doubt it, Harriet's only got eyes for Alfie and Isla's transfixed by Luca. I doubt they'd notice if the pair of you tangoed stark naked right past them.'

'Well, that's not going to happen.' Pippa sighed. Despite the hugely different and exciting relationship she was now sharing with Gil, for every smile there seemed to be a sadness too.

'Why don't you want them to know?'

'It's complicated.'

'Complicated with benefits. That's something.' Cassie threw her a grin and Pippa didn't miss the suggestion of sorrow in her friend's face before she blinked it away. 'You're making quite the home here. Is there anything else you'd like to tell me?'

'Such as?' Pippa had been planning to keep a lid on her happiness whilst Cassie was here, but it wasn't easy. Every time her eyes met Gil's they shared the kind of smiles and knowing looks that wouldn't go unmissed for long.

'Such as this plan of Harriet's to move up here and change schools. Isla told me.'

'So what do you think? It's crazy, right?' Pippa had been running over it since Harriet had made her request earlier, finding lots of reasons against it and a few in favour. Mentioning the plan out loud somehow made it seem even more ridiculous and she was looking forward to Cassie agreeing with her so she could stand firm against Harriet.

'In theory, yes.'

'In theory?' Pippa just managed to reach the chunk of chocolate that had flown from her hand before Lola did. 'Sorry Lola, chocolate's bad for you. What does that mean, Cass?'

'It means that on paper it's maybe not a good idea but it's worth considering, surely? I take it you've told her no, not with her GCSEs in two years.'

'Pretty much. I promised I'd at least think about it.' It felt like another complication Pippa didn't really need. 'We were only supposed to be staying for a few days, and now she's mucking out an assortment of animals every morning, has met a boy – who is lovely, by the way – and we've somehow managed to acquire a puppy. How did all that happen?'

'And where would she go to school?'

'In the next village.' It still didn't make sense, not fully. Pippa rubbed her cheek, leaving a smear of chocolate behind, aware that Harriet was trying to get Alfie's family onside too, given that his auntie was head of year eleven. 'And of course the school's closed for the holidays so we can't even look around it.' She paused. 'I think my dad would like the idea of Harriet being somewhere a bit more normal. He went along with her last time because it was what she wanted, but only Phoebe and Freddie went to independent schools, the rest of us didn't.'

'Pippa, your dad is most definitely not the important factor here.' Cassie had employed a tone Pippa recognised, one that meant she needed to make her own decisions and mustn't be swayed by Jonny. 'This is down to you and Harriet. Why does she want to change schools?'

'I can't help thinking it's because of Alfie. They're so loved up right now and you know what it's like at that age. If there's even a whiff of me trying to separate them, she'll probably come over all Cathy from *Wuthering Heights* and take to the hills.'

'But don't forget that Harriet's got an incredibly wise head on her for someone so young. The way she's supported Isla and looked after her.' Cassie offered Pippa a smile. 'She's been wonderful. You both have.'

'We love you, that's why.' Pippa leaned across to squeeze Cassie's hand. 'So are you saying you're in favour of her plan, then?'

'Actually, I think what I'm saying is that I'm in favour of love,' Cassie said softly. 'Not that Alfie is a reason to stay, but Harriet's one of those kids that will find her way, she's like your dad. You need to think about your life too, Pippa, and what that might look like if you left London. What you've got to gain, or lose.'

'My job for a start.'

'And I know you've always enjoyed it. But you've been there for years, maybe there's something else out there for you too.'

'And if there is?' Pippa hardly dared voice it lest her thoughts should suddenly come true. She was thinking of the gallery role again, the longing to immerse herself in paintings and create her own. But was she brave enough to step aside from a steady career that had sustained her all these years? 'What if I agree and Harriet doesn't settle? Then her results would be up the wall and I'd never forgive myself for not seeing sense and saying no.' Just thinking about an unhappy Harriet in Hartfell six months down the line, winter setting in and no Alfie, if they should fall out, made Pippa go cold.

'It won't come to that, and she could always resit. But quite honestly, she's so determined that I can't see her letting a thing like not studying stand in her way.'

'How would you feel if it was Isla wanting to move right before her GCSE years?'

'I'd be worried, for sure. But maybe I'd also be thinking why not give it a go? London's not going anywhere if you're both unhappy, and from where I'm standing, you both look very happy here.' Cassie shrugged sadly. 'Life's so short, Pippa, we've both learned that the hard way. Why not take a risk now and then? You can always go back.'

'It has crossed my mind. The idea of staying.' Pippa had never said those words out loud before, and she was watching Cassie, testing her reaction. 'I miss London less every day. Sometimes it hard to remember how we even lived like that, always rushing, racing ahead. It's frantic and I can't deny I like the pace here better.'

'So if we take Harriet out of the equation for a minute, why would you want to stay? Have you fallen in love as well?'

'Of course I haven't,' Pippa replied hotly. 'At my age! Harriet would leave home.'

'Oh please! You've literally just turned forty. You're not even too old, in theory, to have another baby if you wanted one.'

'I definitely don't.' Pippa winced at the thought. 'We've got Maud and she's quite enough to manage right now.'

'You having another dog is literally one of the last things I would have expected, but it's wonderful to see you with her.' Cass slid the cream jug into the fridge. 'Here's the thing, though. Harriet's super bright and she'll ace her GCSEs wherever she is, as long as she puts in the work. The real question is, what's at stake for both of you if you make the decision to move here? And I think that question has quite a bit to do with this house and your hot vet.'

—

They ate dinner outside as it was such a lovely evening. The kitchen table was useless for all of them, and Pippa hadn't yet ventured to sit in the dining room for dinner. It was a dark room, full of heavy antique furniture with an upright piano piled high with yellowed music, and not somewhere she found cheery.

It was a lovely, merry hour and afterwards the teenagers cleared the table. She loved listening to their chatter and laughter as they washed up and Harriet brought the profiteroles outside. Whenever Pippa caught Gil's eye, it was clear he was enjoying this family time as much as she was. Once they'd seen off all the profiteroles, Luca wanted to have a look at Gil's plans for the practice and the three younger ones joined them. The clearing up was done, and Pippa settled in the garden with Cassie and the dogs, glasses of wine in their hands.

'I'm sorry to miss Rory but it's nice that he's gone ahead with his grandparents.' Pippa was glad to have a few minutes alone with Cassie. They were so few, in between their work commitments and children, and they didn't often catch up by themselves.

'Yeah, they promised him a fishing trip and the lure of that without his sister tagging along and moaning was enough to make up for missing out on seeing this place.'

'How are you?' Pippa asked softly. 'I know we don't speak every day but I'm always here for you. You know I'll do anything for you all.'

'We're fine,' Cassie replied determinedly, taking a mouthful of the excellent red wine that Gil had brought back. 'Really, we are. We're doing okay.'

Maud was toddling around the garden with an important air, investigating borders. Every so often she'd look back, as though making sure that Pippa was still in sight. She turned and touched a hand to Cassie's arm. 'You can tell me it's absolutely shit if you want.'

'It's absolutely shit.' Cassie gulped and Pippa gripped her fingers. 'There are so many things Ewan's missing, so many things I want to tell him. And that's before I even get to how it still feels to wake up without him every morning.'

'I'm so sorry.' Pippa felt the crack in her own heart at Cassie's anguish, wishing she could make it go away. It made her new happiness with Gil both extra precious and not something she wanted to dwell on with her friend. 'Is there anything I can do to help?'

'We are fine, honestly.' Cass sniffed and blew her nose, and Pippa eased away. 'It just gets to me sometimes. Like now, when Ewan would love to be here and seeing you guys and the house, meeting Gil and Luca. Then there's the weird days when I'm so busy I almost forget to miss him and then it hits me all over again. The counselling is helping all of us, but I don't know if I'll ever get used to seeing Ewan's smile in Rory's and knowing how much it hurts him not to have his dad around. Isla misses him like crazy too, but they were so different, and she's always been more like me.

'Little things help, like being with you and knowing you understand us. Sunshine, and listening to the girls nattering like nothing's ever changed. Moments matter more now, life somehow gets smaller and bigger all at once. And Raf's been a sweetheart. We see him every week whenever he's in town and he's invited us out to Australia in half term, for the end of the tour.'

'Oh Cass, that's wonderful.' Pippa felt a rush of love for her brother. 'Are you going? Can you get the time off work?'

'Should be fine but I'll need to sneak the kids out of school for a few extra days. And just this once I don't care, they'd absolutely love it and I think it will do all of us the world of good. You know what it's like, I'm always checking in, but I can't deny the thought of a getaway from everything is very appealing.'

'You should definitely go if you possibly can.' Pippa was leaning forward to push home her point. 'Why not? Vanessa's out there with Phoebe and Freddie, and Raf will make sure you're all looked after brilliantly. And if you should bump into Dave, please make sure you say hi from me.'

'You and Dave Grohl.' Cassie rolled her eyes. 'I thought you might be over him now, especially seeing as you're making out with Gil.'

'Over Dave? Never.'

'So what are you planning to do about him? Gil, not Dave.'

'I have absolutely no idea,' Pippa raised a shoulder. 'I have to be in London on Thursday for results day at school, it'll be the reminder of real life that I need. Gil and I are probably just one of those enemies to lovers thing that'll burn itself out, most likely the minute I put his house up for sale. I'm going to get rid of his childhood home and finish off his ambitions for the practice at the same time. Can't see that improving how he might feel about me.'

'It's not his house, it's Jonny's,' Cassie reminded her gently. 'Whatever you think, Gil's crazy about you and it seems to me that you feel the same way. And you don't have to sell the house. Do you?'

'What else am I meant to do with it?'

'Well, that's the million-dollar question, isn't it? I don't think your dad's going to mind either way, as long as it's what you want.'

Chapter Twenty-Three

With Elaine back at her desk in the practice, and Harriet and Luca around, Pippa and Gil were finding less opportunities to be alone together, even though they were living in the same house. The caravan was still in the yard and Gil was planning to have it taken away for scrap soon, a decision that even Dorothy had eventually acquiesced to.

Cassie and Isla had left, heading north to join Rory and Ewan's parents. Harriet was missing her best friend again, but with Wi-Fi at Alfie's and the practice, she was managing to stay in touch. She'd developed a rosy glow on her cheeks from spending so much time outdoors. She and Pippa had met Rose's sister-in-law for an informal chat about the high school, and viewed it from beyond the gates. It was large and modern, quite different to her current school in Kent, and Pippa's stomach would spin with nervous indecision whenever she thought of Harriet changing direction.

She stayed overnight in London for A level results day at college. Harriet was perfectly happy to have a sleepover at Alfie's and Pippa knew Rose would take care of her. London, the city she'd lived in all her life, was like another universe now. Vibrant, a beating heart pulsing at the centre, but loud too, full of people all hurrying somewhere else. She found it frantic after Hartfell and she messaged Gil, sending him some images of her street and the houses tightly packed together.

After the conversation with Harriet about moving, an idea had landed in Pippa's mind and whilst she was at home, she went through all her old paintings, salvaged from her long-ago show, trying to view them with a critical and yet dispassionate eye. She hadn't done this for years and it was heartening to realise they were maybe better than she'd allowed herself to believe. The long return drive north was a reflective one with time to think, and when she arrived, she felt a burst of joy at seeing the old house and knowing Harriet, Gil and Luca were here with the dogs.

Luca wasn't at home, Gil was working and Harriet had messaged to say she was at Dorothy's and not to expect her back before dinner. Impatient to see Gil, even though his Land Rover was gone, Pippa popped over to the practice for a coffee with Elaine. He was back within the hour and his greeting for Elaine was warm, but Pippa recognised the quirk of his grin for her, the promise of more once they were alone. Elaine was no fool and Pippa sensed she understood exactly what was going on. She excused herself with the explanation of a lunchtime appointment, and Gil wasted no time in catching Pippa and extending the kiss they'd shared before she'd left for London.

'Are you busy tonight?'

'I don't think so.' She was pressed up against the counter, holding him close. 'Why?'

'Seeing as I didn't give you a present for your birthday, there's somewhere I'd like to take you.'

'Seriously? You don't have to do that, my birthday's been and gone.'

'I'd like to.' His lips were following his thumb along her jaw, and she closed her eyes as he kissed the corner of her mouth. 'Think of it as my gift to you.'

'Do you mean like a date? What will I tell Harriet?'

'Maybe exactly that. That we're going on a date.'

'I'm not sure.' Pippa could hardly focus with his other hand smoothing her back, sliding beneath her top. 'What if she thinks…'

'That we're seeing one another? We're sharing the house and Harriet's not daft. She knows something has changed between us.'

'Yes, but being friends and putting aside our differences is one thing, us being in some kind of relationship is quite another. What about Luca? Wouldn't you rather he didn't know?'

'He's an adult, albeit a young one. Clare's had a new partner for a while now, he'll cope if his dad is seeing someone else.' Gil's eyes narrowed. 'What do you mean, some kind of relationship?'

'So what would you call it?'

'Pippa, I'm crazy about you.' He pushed a hand through his hair. 'You know I am, I have been since the start, even though I really didn't want to feel this way back then. And in theory, all the things we said made sense. Not talking about the future, not looking ahead. But soon, we're gonna have to.'

Pippa had sworn Harriet to absolute secrecy where the new school was concerned, not wanting any decision they made to be swayed by her feelings for Gil. She didn't want him to know yet, to find a way to persuade her to stay that one day she might regret. Harriet's future came first.

'But not yet.' She stepped back into him, winding her arms around his neck. 'Tonight, we're going on a date.'

'As long as Harriet and Luca don't suspect,' he questioned dryly.

'Yes. Exactly that.'

–

'Where are you and Gil going on your date, Mum?'

Pippa had popped her head around the sitting room door to let Harriet know she was going out. Her daughter was sprawled on the vomit sofa with Alfie and the dogs, looking very much at home, and Pippa's cheeks turned pink. Luca was on the armchair, earbuds in, legs over one side, and he gave her a grin.

'Who says it's a date?' she questioned, slipping a jacket on over her shirt.

'Like, duh!' Harriet raised her head from Alfie's phone. 'You're wearing perfume, and your hair hasn't looked like that since we got here.'

'Thank you very much.' Pippa's jaw clenched, wondering if there was anything quite like a teenager to bring one crashing down to earth. Not that she'd wanted to appear as though she'd tried too hard, but still. 'You make it sound like I've totally given up on my appearance, Harriet. And we're just going out for a bit, that's all.'

'I didn't mean that you don't look nice. You do, but you haven't worn that lipstick for ages, that's all.' Harriet raised a brow. 'Don't do anything I wouldn't do.'

'Yes, well, as you're fourteen and there's an awful lot you shouldn't do, I think I'm quite safe.'

'Ready?' Gil had joined them, and Pippa melted at his hand on her back, out of sight of Harriet. She lit up every time he touched her, a quiver racing across her skin. It was a good thing her daughter couldn't see that, she mused distractedly.

'Have a good time, you two,' Harriet called cheerfully, and Luca raised a hand. 'Back by ten p.m. and not a minute later.'

'Honestly,' Pippa muttered as they left the house. 'I seriously wonder sometimes who the parent is around here.'

'Oh, there's no doubt.' Gil unlocked the Land Rover and grinned at her. 'It's definitely Harriet.'

Pippa huffed out a laugh as she got in, aware that he was in smart jeans and a shirt, highlighting sun-streaked hair and those amused blue eyes he frequently turned on her. It was bliss to be away from everyone, including the dogs, for a while. And it was fun when he had to hurriedly change gear and pull away when she kissed him at a traffic light right before they turned green.

'Where are you taking me?' She'd wondered about this all afternoon. He'd disappeared and she assumed he'd been at work.

'You'll see.' He raised her hand to kiss it, and once through town, he pulled into a long, treelined drive, parking at the end in a courtyard behind a huge country house. She assumed it was for dinner as they hadn't already eaten, and when she made to go around the front, he caught her hand.

'Not that way. It's here.' Gil led her around the side of the building and Pippa saw a sign attached to the wall.

'A gallery? For me?' She reached up to kiss his cheek, caught by his thoughtfulness.

'Yes, for you.' His smile seemed nervous, and his fingers tightened around hers. 'It belongs to friends of Kenny and Vince, that's how I found it.'

'I love it, thank you. Even before I see it. And I would have been happy to spend our date anywhere, as long as it's with you.'

'So it *is* a date?' He smiled as he let go of her hand to rest it on her back as he opened the door.

'Very much a date.' It had been a long time since anyone had chosen something so special, so meaningful, to her and she refused to allow thoughts of leaving Hartfell and Gil to spoil it. Tonight she had this, and she turned quickly to place her hands on his shoulders. 'Thank you.'

'You haven't seen it yet.'

'But I know I'm going to love it.' She followed the corridor towards a door and lights at the end. 'Is it an exhibition? I can't see any other guests.'

'It's a private viewing, just us.' Gil's hand was still gripping hers and he reached past her to open the door. 'Let me show you.'

The gallery was beautiful. A simple and elegant well-proportioned space, clean white walls expertly hung with art Pippa quicky recognised as outstanding. They moved through to another, smaller room, and she halted so abruptly that Gil's chest crashed against her back. A hand flew to her mouth as the familiar tremble began in her limbs, stomach clenching in shock as her eyes ran over the images on the walls.

There was Maud, snuggled in her bed with Lola, Posy grazing in the paddock beneath an oak tree, white forelock bright against her brown face. Harriet cuddling Maud on her knee, and a jumble of pastel sweet peas clambering up a trellis in the overgrown garden. Ivy's farmhouse nestled in its valley, where Gil had taken her that morning after they'd first made love, and still more. Every single picture in this room Pippa had drawn herself.

None of the sketches and watercolours were framed, all hung haphazardly with no thought of placement or merit, quite unlike the professionalism of the arrangements in the first room.

'Who did this? They have to come down!' Tears were pressing at her eyes and her gaze was running through the gallery, searching for more people, ones who might have witnessed her work and made their opinions clear. She went to move forward, to snatch the nearest one from the wall and Gil planted his hands on her shoulders.

'I did it. For you,' he said quietly, and she was afraid to lean into him now, afraid of allowing herself to rest on his strength after this. 'I'm sorry I shocked you. But please, would you let me explain?'

'How could you? You knew how I felt after what happened.'

'I promise that no one but you and me has seen them. Kenny mentioned the gallery and wondered if you'd heard of it, and that's when I had the idea. He contacted the owners on my behalf and asked for a favour, but I didn't tell anyone what I was planning to do. They gave me a key and closed the gallery so I could put them up myself this afternoon.' Gil squeezed her shoulders. 'And I'll be taking them down tonight, before we leave. Not a single person, other than you and me, will see them.'

'But why,' she whispered. 'Why bring them here? They're rough, they don't belong in a gallery like this.'

'Pippa, you have such a gift, and I don't think you even realise how wonderful these are.' He slid his arms tight around her, holding her steady. 'I did it because I want you to see what I see. Actually, it's more than that.' He turned her slowly until she was facing him. 'I want you to understand what I *feel* when I look at them.'

He took her hand to press it against his heart, beating as rapidly as her own. 'How perfectly you've caught Lola's expression, the way she tilts her head when she looks at me. That day on the fell when we talked, and I knew I wanted you in my life. The one of the house from the garden, exactly as I remember it as a kid. Even the bloody demon pony and that look on her face. It's just perfect, I'd swear she was about to bite me.'

'Well, you had just chased her around the garden.' Pippa's smile was tremulous, the fear receding, replaced by thoughts she couldn't quite bring into order yet. 'If you'd caught her, she probably would've done.' She'd drawn that the evening Posy had kicked him, and she'd soaked him with filthy water. Posy's flash of temper, his own outrage; she'd caught them both and she'd known the minute she'd finished it was good. A tear ran down her cheek and he gently wiped it away.

'I'm sorry you had an awful experience when you were so young and first showed your work. I'm sorry it knocked your confidence and made you feel you weren't good enough to be an artist in your own right.' Every word Gil murmured was falling into her heart. 'Because everything in here tells me that you are good enough and the reason I did this was to help you see it in some way. They're beautiful and brilliant, and they belong wherever you want them to be seen. Or not, that's your choice. But they're special to me because they're part of you.'

She was crying properly now. Some of it relief that her drawings weren't on public display, but it wasn't all that. Mostly it was because she'd never imagined seeing her work like this again and Gil had done it for her.

'What are you planning to do for our second date?' She tried to laugh through the tears, and he gently smoothed them away. 'Because this will take some beating. Both for shock value and thoughtfulness, although I'm not sure you're meant to cry on a first date. That usually comes later.'

'Well, I haven't exactly got as far as a second date,' he said softly, kissing her forehead. 'I thought we might be over before we got to number two if this backfired.'

'It nearly did.' She turned around, leaning into him as she dared to take another peep at the walls. 'But it's probably the most thoughtful thing anyone's ever done for me. It was always easier to hide away, to keep my art to myself.'

'You're saying that like it's too late, Pippa. It doesn't have to be, not if you want something different.'

–

A few days later, she was still doing her best to avoid the sidelong glances Harriet was giving her. The gallery date with Gil had been utterly unexpected and he'd arranged champagne to celebrate her private exhibition. After-wards, when they'd taken down her work and left the room ready to be rehung, they'd gone on for dinner at a quiet country pub. Parting back at the house with Harriet and Luca there had been difficult, and they'd shared a goodnight kiss that had kept Pippa awake for ages, thinking about Gil and what he'd done for her.

Luca had since left to join friends backpacking in Spain for a few days and the house felt quieter without him. It was impossible now to avoid thoughts of the future, with Harriet joining her dad for a holiday soon, and that would mean Pippa had little reason to remain in Hartfell. She'd been busy with plans since her brief visit to London and the date with Gil, ones that she'd kept quiet from everyone but Harriet, needing to be certain everything was in place before she revealed them.

She let herself into the practice, planning to catch up with messages. Yesterday, she'd emailed her dad, and she was hoping for a swift response. For once he had replied straightaway and a sigh of happiness and relief escaped when she read it. An email had also arrived from Edmund, the local historian, and Pippa's heart began to beat rapidly as she scanned it. She needed to act on that now, and she called Miles and made a request which he immediately agreed to.

Ninety minutes later she met Miles outside the youth hostel, and Edmund arrived shortly after. His news, as he'd already pointed out, might amount to nothing and she shouldn't get her hopes too high. But that didn't stop her praying he was right.

'This is all a bit sudden, isn't it?' Miles unlocked the front door of the hostel. 'First time we've had any interest in the building.'

'Once I have a trail to pursue, I'm afraid I must continue. Old habits die hard.' Edmund chuckled and Pippa grinned at him. She knew from Hazel he'd spent his career as a language expert with MI5, travelling to London and beyond, and had now turned his considerable intellect and expertise to local history.

Inside, the building was cool, with the thick stone walls keeping out the warmth of the day. It had once been a pub and the three downstairs rooms were large, the last of them a functional and unattractive kitchen she glimpsed at the end of a short corridor. Plain red sofas and chairs sat on a blue carpet in one reception room, a long pine table in the other, chairs lined up either side.

'So what's this about?' Miles questioned. 'I know what you said on the phone, Pippa, but you were in a bit of a hurry.'

'Would you like me to explain?' Edmund gave her a questioning glance and she nodded. 'I've been helping Pippa research her family history, Mr Gray.' He pulled out a chair and sat down. 'My knees, I'm afraid. I made some enquiries about her great-grandmother, Ivy Walker, who was a farmer's wife and an artist.

'I managed to track down the granddaughter of Ivy's closest friend, who had a gift for detail and remembered many of the stories she'd heard. We had a marvellous chat online, and she was able to tell me that Ivy was very lively, an excellent pianist and was also expert at training the working dogs they ran on the farm.'

Pippa felt a rush of warmth for the woman Ivy had been. One whom she'd never get to know but whose life had amounted to much more than those solemn, rather flat black-and-white photographs she'd seen. Now she was imagining Ivy's life in colour; a woman who liked to laugh and loved animals, enjoyed music and was highly skilled.

'Right,' Miles said slowly. 'But what does that have to do with the hostel?'

'Well, of course, Pippa's main interest is in Ivy's paintings, and that's where we might just have had a stroke of luck. Linda, that's the delightful woman with whom I spoke yesterday, told me that her grandmother had had a couple of Ivy's paintings but sadly they were lost.'

'Oh.' Pippa's shoulders dropped. So close to finding Ivy's work only to have it snatched away again. But Edmund was still speaking, and she quickly refocused. 'I'm sorry, I missed that?'

'What she does remember, though, is that Ivy painted flowers too. Wild ones, the sort she would've seen around the farm. And I think what we're interested in might be upstairs,' Edmund nodded towards a central staircase in the hall. 'Why don't you have a look, Pippa? I'm sure you'll recognise what we're looking for if it's there.'

Pippa didn't need a second invitation and she hurried up to the first floor, peeking in each room, bunk beds and mattresses confirming the hostel's functionality. At the back of the building, she opened the door onto another small room which slept four, and a hand flew to her mouth. A painting hung on the far wall, and she crept forward, barely breathing. It was a grouping of three poppies and even though the frame was damaged and the painting dirty, she saw the exquisite detail the artist had captured.

Scarlet flowers with dark centres, each petal so soft and perfectly shaped she almost expected them to flutter. Green stems were bright beneath the red, grouped in a meadow beneath a pale blue sky. She really needed much better light to make out a tiny signature in the corner. It could be an *I* but then again it might be a *J*. Holding her breath, she lifted the painting carefully from the wall and turned it over. She gasped at the sight of the small and neat handwriting, unable to hold back the rush of emotion and gathering tears.

Poppies in Lowgill Meadow. Ivy Walker, 1940

'Have you found it?' Edmund's voice floated up and she couldn't keep him waiting any longer. He had led Pippa to her family history, to this painting, and she returned downstairs, her smile almost making her face ache.

'Yes. I think it's Ivy's.' She turned it over so he could read the inscription and he was every bit as delighted, thrilled with their discovery. 'Edmund, thank you.' Impulsively Pippa threw an arm around him, the painting tucked beneath the other. 'I can't tell you what this means.'

'I think I can guess, my dear.' He patted her hand, his own eyes shining.

'Miles, I know this is very unorthodox, but please can I take the painting home with me?' She turned the full effect of her enthusiasm on Miles, and he blinked.

'Well, er, it's not really that simple,' he said uncertainly. 'The hostel is for sale with the contents and I'm not—'

'Please,' she said urgently, gripping the painting. 'I know I shouldn't ask, and I don't want to put you in an awkward position, but if I leave it here now it might be lost forever. It's precious to me, irreplaceable really. It's not really worth anything to anyone else and it might end up in a car boot sale or a skip. I promise I'll put in writing that I have it and I'll pay whatever the Association wants. Even the cost of the building.'

'Is than an offer of the asking price,' he said jokingly, and she laughed.

She didn't have that kind of money just sitting there but she needed to say something that made it clear she was deadly serious about keeping the painting. 'No, but I would if I could.'

'Go on then.' Miles shook his head, and she knew he'd be expecting a favour in return. 'You can repay me by making up your mind about Home Farm and whether I can sell it for you. Or not, I'd like to know which.'

'I'll give you a final decision by the end of the week, I promise. Thank you so much, both of you.' She looked at Edmund. 'You'll never know how much this means to me.'

'All in a day's work,' he said cheerfully, rising slowly from his seat. 'I'm delighted to have followed a trail and led you here. Linda remembered seeing the painting hanging on the wall when the building was still a public house, and we were rather lucky, that it has survived here so long.'

Outside on the lane, she thanked Edmund again and he set off back to his cottage with a satisfied air. She also thanked Miles a second time, declining his offer of a quick drink at the pub to talk about Home Farm. She rushed back to the house and stood Ivy's painting on a cabinet in the sitting room. It would belong with her always, and she adored this precious connection to Hartfell through her great-grandmother and the gift they shared.

Chapter Twenty-Four

'Dad! You're an absolute nightmare, you know that, don't you? Packing me off to Hartfell at a moment's notice to do your dirty work.' Pippa felt a rush of love for Jonny as he grinned back via her iPad screen. She'd messaged earlier and told him not to worry but she needed to speak with him urgently. Thankfully, Harriet was at Alfie's and Gil out seeing farm patients, so she was alone in the practice. Jonny looked wonderful: suntanned and relaxed, a terrace and infinity pool behind him falling away to a blue ocean glittering in the distance. His grey hair was short and tousled, a brightly patterned shirt half undone.

'Come on, Pips, you know you're the light of my life, all of you. I wouldn't have done it if I didn't think it would be for the best.'

'Best for you, you mean,' she retorted, still touched by his words all the same. Jonny wasn't given to emotional confessions and her frustration was already easing. She hadn't seen him in person for months, but he was still her dad and she missed him.

'So you've sorted the place out then, found the right solution?'

'Right for whom?'

'You and Harriet.' He crossed one ankle over the other knee, looking slightly smug. Pippa knew from Raf that the band weren't rehearsing the final leg of the tour yet, and she was struck once again by the weird combination of having someone so famous and often out of reach for a dad, and yet one who was so normal and down to earth in person. He looked fit and well, and she was sure he'd be practising yoga every day and keeping up with the work required to expend so much energy and adrenaline on stage whenever the band performed.

'What about Gil?'

'What about him?' Jonny's eyes darted away, as they always did when he had an ulterior motive or preferred to avoid a confrontation.

'I take it that my "sorting out" the house didn't exactly include turfing out your best friend's son with nowhere to go.' Pippa used her fingers to put quotes around those two words.

'No.' Jonny raised a shoulder, back with her. 'But he's a stubborn bugger and I had to do something to force his hand.'

'So you refused an extension to his lease?'

'Yeah. He kept insisting he'd pay market value for the whole place, but he was never going to raise the full amount and I needed him to see that. Part of the plan.'

'So you sent me to help him see it?' She shook her head, caught between exasperation with her dad, and sadness for Gil. 'You don't think a solicitor would have been the best person for the job? Someone who actually understands leases and land registry, all that stuff.'

'Sometimes these things need a woman's touch.'

'It shouldn't surprise you to know that women are solicitors too, Dad.'

'I know, I had one once, but she gave up to write thrillers. Put me in one of her books and killed me off.' Jonny roared, reaching for a large glass of water nearby.

'Said I was her favourite client too.' He leaned forward, clasping his hands between his knees. 'So what do you want to do with the place? You know it's yours, don't you? The house?'

'Mine?' The air shot out of her lungs and her hand skittered across the iPad, blanking her dad from her sight until she clicked on the app again. 'You're not serious?'

'Deadly. You know I never joke about money.' Jonny took a long drink and put the glass down. This time the merriment and mischief in his gaze was gone. 'There's some legal stuff to sign once the land registry is sorted, but it's your inheritance. You've always known the plan. One property for each of you and that's your lot. The rest is going to charity, to the school. Nothing was ever handed to me or your mum on a plate, and you'll all have to make your own way eventually.'

'I know.' Pippa was still trying to take in the reality of this news about Home Farm. Jonny had always been vehement that each of his children worked and earned their own money. He'd see them all right, more than that, but he wasn't a bottomless pit of privilege and the new performing arts school he was funding was his way of putting something significant back into his old community.

'So what's the plan?' He nodded at someone off camera, and Pippa saw her youngest brother and sister leaping into the pool with exuberant yells. She hadn't seen them for ages either; they really did need to arrange a proper family get together once the never-ending retirement tour had played its final date. 'You have got one, I take it?'

'Of course.' She let out a shaky breath. She'd sat up for hours thinking this over and hadn't breathed a word to anyone other than Harriet, not until she'd had this conversation with Jonny and made sure everything was properly lined up. 'I've put the house up for sale.'

'You haven't! But what about Gil, what's he—'

'Not Home Farm,' she replied, very much enjoying that she'd managed to alarm her dad for once. 'Mine, in London. I don't want to hang about, so it's priced to sell, and I've made an offer on something here.'

'In Hartfell?' Jonny's brows drew together, and he uncrossed his legs to rest his elbows on his knees. 'What are you talking about? You've already got a house there.'

'Well, I didn't know that, not for certain.' Maud got up from her bed in the office and trotted over to Pippa, who picked her up, snuggling the puppy on her knee. 'This is Maud, by the way, she's the newest member of the family. I'm hoping there might be some more to add soon. Hopefully another three. Not dogs, though. People. Plus Lola, who is a dog.'

'I see. Sounds good, there's always room for more.' Jonny grinned again. 'Looks like you've found your feet there, Pips.'

'I really have, Dad. Harriet has too, she's loving life here. And wait until I tell you about Ivy, my great-grandmother. That's a whole other story and you're going to love it. I've learned so much about her family since I've been here. Can I ask you a question, though?'

'Ask me anything. Fire away.'

'Why did you buy the farm in the first place? Why not just let Gil have it then?'

'Because I didn't want it going to someone else. He'd already approached the estate to take on the lease and his cousin turned him down. I got wind of his divorce, and kept quiet. I didn't want it forming part of a settlement to someone who wasn't in his life anymore.' Jonny huffed out a laugh and Pippa couldn't be certain, but it looked very much like tears were shining in his eyes.

'I made a promise to Bryan a long time ago, when the first album did all right. He and Carolyn had it rough from her lot when they got together, and I promised him I'd see his family right. Bryan was my best mate, Pips. We grew up together, we always had each other's backs, and I loved him.'

'So you did it for Gil? Bought the farm for him?' Tears were caught in Pippa's eyes too and she sniffed, holding them back. The relief was immense, and she was so glad she'd taken her time with the house and hadn't rushed into selling it. Not that her dad would've let her, by the sound of things.

'Yep. Him and his dad, or at least the memory of his dad. Now I know what you want to do, the solicitor can get on with separating the house from the farm.' Jonny's look was suddenly wicked as his eyes gleamed. 'So you'll have to find a way to get on together, won't you, seeing as you'll be neighbours. Or maybe you're already getting along?'

'I'm not telling you that!'

'You don't have to. I know you, Pippa.' Jonny winked. 'Reckon you can make him accept it?'

'I'll certainly try.' And this time she really would chain Gil up somewhere until he said yes. Thoughts of a future in Hartfell were so new, she still wasn't used to them. The plan she'd set in motion, how swiftly she and Harriet had come to think of the house and the village as home.

'What about your job?'

'I've already handed in my notice, and they were good enough to let me leave without having to stay until half term. I can't be in London if Harriet's at school here. I've already had a look at supply jobs locally and I'm pretty sure I'll find something temporary to see me through for now.' Pippa took a deep breath. 'And I've listed my paintings, the old ones I had at home. It's time and I want to let them go, even if they're not worth a lot.'

'I think that's wonderful,' Jonny said softly. 'They deserve to be seen.'

'Thank you.' The plan still made her stomach churn, but she was ready, now. 'So once my house is sold, I might need to use your apartment now and then to tie up a few loose ends. Is that all right?'

'Course it is. Don't think I'll be coming straight back after the tour anyway. I like it out here, it's beautiful, even in the winter. Got my eye on a place, too.'

'I'm glad you're happy.' Pippa meant it. Wherever in the world her dad might be, she knew he loved them all and kept an eye on them from afar.

'And you, Pips. Means the world. So tell me about this house you've made an offer on in Hartfell.'

'Later. And it's not a house, not exactly.' She laughed at the confusion on Jonny's face. 'There's someone else I need to tell first. Not Harriet. She already knows and she thinks it's brilliant.'

'You mean Gil?'

'Maybe. You'll see.'

'Last time I spoke to Harriet she said that she thought you'd fallen in love, and it had made you all weird, and did I not think you were too old for all that?' Jonny roared a laugh, and slapped his knee, bared by board shorts. 'I pointed out that people can fall in love at any age, and she'd better make the best of it because you're way too young to spend your life alone. And don't you worry about Harriet, either. She's a very smart girl and she'll be all right, you'll see. It's you I was worried about.'

'Don't be. I'm fine now too, or very nearly.' She just needed to speak with Gil and share her news, hoping and praying he felt the same way she did about the future. One in Hartfell, together.

'That's brilliant. You were stuck in London, you needed something to get you out of there.'

'And you had the very solution, did you?' she questioned dryly. 'Dad, you're a menace sometimes but I love you.'

'I love you too, Pippa, you and Harriet,' he said softly. 'You get on and do whatever you need to there, make it right for all of you. The solicitor will sort it out, don't you worry. Just remember that our memories go everywhere with us, we don't leave them behind in bricks and mortar. Your mum, she's still with us, wherever we are.'

'Thanks, Dad.' Pippa swallowed and she recognised that crafty glint in his eye.

'I might have something to tell you too. Me and Vanessa, we've been spending a fair bit of time together and we've decided to give things another go.'

'Oh, Dad, I'm so pleased.' Vanessa was the one person in Jonny's life who'd never tried to change him but had simply loved him the way he was. She was family too, and she'd always tried her best to take care of his three eldest children, even though they were all but grown up when she'd met Jonny. 'What about Dana?'

'Well, that ended in Bali. We had different ideas about life, and she's found a nice young yoga instructor who's a lot more flexible than I am.'

'Eww, Dad, too much information!' Pippa mimed sticking a finger down her throat and Jonny laughed.

'I didn't mean it that way, but now I come to think about it...' He winked and she shook her head. There was no one in the world like her dad, and it wasn't his fault, not entirely, that his fans loved him being a rock star and touring the world rather than staying home with his family. His success had brought them as much stability as it had distance, and he was never going to change. At least they were all on this ride together, as a family. Excitement was bubbling in her stomach, and she couldn't wait to share her news with Gil.

'I'd better go, Maud's getting impatient to go out and she'll pee on me if I leave her much longer.' Pippa snuggled the puppy close for a kiss. 'Isn't she gorgeous?'

'She is, something else that was just what you needed. Go on then, you go. I've got a meeting to get to anyway. Did you know someone's asked if they could write my biography?'

'No. Could be interesting, Dad, I might learn a few things.'

'Yep, and you might learn a few things you'd rather not as well.' He winked again and she shook her head.

'Love you, you incorrigible old rocker.'

'Ay, less of the old.' Jonny grinned as he wagged a finger and stood up. 'I'll take incorrigible though. Love you too.'

–

After the enlightening conversation with Jonny, Pippa was kept busy dealing with various agents, including Miles, and solicitors, regarding the next steps with the youth hostel now that her offer of the asking price had been accepted. She'd taken Harriet to see it and had sworn her to absolute secrecy for now. Pippa wanted everything legally in place before she spoke to Gil. For all his passion and desire to keep the practice at the heart of its rural community, she didn't imagine he'd take easily to the idea of it being a gift from her dad.

Seeing him every day made it difficult to pretend, and they'd given up trying to hide their relationship from Harriet, who was suitably disgusted if she happened upon them sharing a kiss or curled up together in the evenings. She and Harriet had talked about school and a future here before Pippa had made the offer on the youth hostel, and had decided it was worth taking a chance on the move.

The decision didn't prevent her waking in the night sometimes and worrying, though. A life in Hartfell needed to be on terms that worked for both of them; it couldn't hinge on Pippa's feelings for Gil or how their own relationship might evolve. However much she'd fallen in love with him, her life couldn't turn on simply that, not with Harriet's own future to think about too.

So a few days later, when she'd accepted an offer for their house in London and had met with Miles to view the hostel again, an email arrived which had her rushing over to the practice for Wi-Fi to open it. She wasn't expecting Elaine behind the counter as there were no consultations today.

'Hi Elaine. I didn't realise you were here. How's your dad?' Pippa caught sight of her face. 'What's the matter? He's not had another fall?'

'What?' Elaine looked up, dabbing her eyes with a tissue. 'No, he's fine. It's not that. Don't mind me, I'm just upset at the news, that's all. It's such a shock, even though we were all kind of expecting it.'

'What news?' Pippa realised Elaine was packing a few belongings into a bag and alarm had her pulse spiking. 'What's going on?'

'You mean you haven't heard?' Elaine sank down onto a chair, twisting the tissue together.

'Nothing. Please can you tell me?'

'It's the practice, here. We all got an email an hour ago to say that it's closing with immediate effect.'

'But why?' Pippa gripped the counter. She couldn't find a reason in her mind, not yet. 'Has something changed?'

'Gil hasn't told you?' Elaine's face had lost some of the upset in her surprise. 'That he's leaving?'

'Leaving?' Pippa's stomach swooped into a dive. 'Elaine, are you sure? I saw him this morning and he didn't say a word.'

'Certain, it's all in the email. He's accepted the offer of another job. He told the other partners first thing after the new practice requested a reference, and they didn't waste any time. They've been looking for an opportunity to close this place down and now he's given it to them. Pippa, are you all right? You've gone white.'

'I'm fine,' she muttered, trying to organise the words into ones that made sense. But none of them did, and she desperately needed to speak with Gil. 'Elaine, can you find out exactly where he is now, please?'

She waited impatiently whilst Elaine went through the diary, thanking her blankly when Elaine passed on the details of his calls. She sprinted to the house for her car keys, and promised Maud she'd be back soon. Harriet was at Dorothy's and then Alfie and Rose were coming for dinner tonight. Every day they seemed to have extra people in the house and Pippa loved it. She and Rose met regularly for coffee and a chat, and the younger woman had become a friend, someone else Pippa would miss if she left.

She barely noticed the drizzle as she set out in her car, forgetting to fetch a coat in her haste. Her future in Hartfell was no longer in the balance, but Gil's was, and she couldn't waste another minute in trying to find out why. She knew him now, she understood his character and expressions. A glance was enough for her to recognise his feelings, ones he'd tried to deny and keep hidden, just like her, afraid to make himself vulnerable again after he'd overcome so much in his life.

Out here she couldn't rely on her phone for directions, and she'd gone wrong twice before she bumped up a rutted track to a farm high on the fell. She tore into the yard so fast that a few free-range chickens leapt for their lives, and she saw Gil's Land Rover parked up. She shot out of her car, straight into a puddle of thick mud and couldn't care less. All that mattered was finding him and learning the truth. Elaine had informed her that he was dehorning cattle, and a clatter joined by a low bellow had her guessing exactly where. She followed the buildings until she emerged in another yard, a young cow held securely in a metal crush as Gil prepared to inject it, a farmer holding firmly on to a rope halter to keep its head still.

She'd rehearsed what she wanted to say on the drive here and all those words flew away into the wind. 'Why didn't you tell me,' she yelled, arms wrapped around her body to ward off the chill. 'About your new job?'

'Bloody hell, Pippa!' Gil's head snapped up and he swore again as he dropped the needle into a puddle. 'I nearly anaesthetised my own hand.'

'Serves you right,' she screeched, glancing at the bemused farmer still clinging on the cow objecting to the situation with a wildly swishing tail. 'If you'd like to come here, I'll do it for you. Quite happy to stick a needle in you right now.'

'Oh, are you?' Gil straightened up. His waterproofs were covered in mud and worse, and his eyes narrowed. 'Why don't you come over here then?'

'No way,' she shouted, eyeing the stout ginger cow and its stubby horns. 'I'm not coming near that.'

'Would you excuse me for a minute, please?' Gil said politely to the farmer. The older man nodded gleefully and let go of the rope to lean against the wall, settling in to enjoy the additional source of amusement in his day. Gil crossed the pen to face her over the metal bars. 'Why don't you explain what you're doing here?'

'No, you've got some explaining to do!' It might be summer but at this height the wind was catching at her hair and whipping it into her eyes, making them smart, and she pulled it from her face impatiently. 'You've accepted another job, and the practice is closing down! Elaine told me an hour ago. I thought we meant something to each other. I thought we were making plans, thinking about a future.'

'Well, one of us was. It just wasn't me, until I realised I had to.'

'Can you please stop talking in riddles and tell me what's going on? Or I really will grab one of those needles and jab you until I find out! Is it true?'

'That I've accepted a new job. Yes.' Gil wiped a hand smeared with a splash of blood on his waterproof top.

'But why?' She wanted to add more but couldn't find the words. Wanted to tell him again what his hanging her sketches in the gallery had meant and how much strength his confidence in her had produced. But she couldn't, not now that her heart was shattering because he was leaving, and she was staying.

'What did you expect,' he said roughly. 'That I'd stay here forever, getting called out at crazy o'clock to deliver a calf or a lamb? Spend weekends working when I could actually be having a life?'

'But you love that life. Why would you give it up?' she asked hollowly.

'Why do you think I'm giving it up,' he shouted. 'Why do you think I'm moving to another practice? In London, of all the bloody places? Why, Pippa?'

'London?' She took a step back, straight into another metal hurdle, and righted herself hastily before she face planted in the yard. That wasn't the look she was aiming for here, but then neither was hollering windswept mad-woman. 'But why would you move to London? You hate the city. Is it because the farm isn't yours? I've got news about that, I just needed—'

'It's got nothing to do with the house, or the practice. Sell it, turn the farm into a petting zoo, do what you want with it. Even if it is the only real home I ever had here, I don't care anymore. Shall I tell you why I'm moving to London? Even though I loathe feeling vulnerable or showing how I really feel?'

'I think you'd better,' she said shakily. 'Because none of this is making any sense.'

'For you, Pippa Douglas. Entirely for you. You're the reason I'm moving to London. Because that's where you'll be.' He huffed out a laugh and she was astonished to see tears hovering in his eyes. 'It's utter madness. I'll be spending my days clipping claws and spaying cats, and I don't even know if you'll have me.'

'As what,' she whispered.

'As the man in your life who loves you so much that he's prepared to follow you anywhere. Even to bloody London and I hate the city.'

'You love me?'

'Just a bit.'

'But you hate the city.'

'Loathe it. With a passion.'

'But you'll never be happy there.'

'I will,' he said simply. 'If you're there. There are some benefits, I might even get a full night's sleep now and again. But there won't be any cows, sadly. I'll miss my bovine patients. And the farmers, obviously.' He glanced at the farmer, who grinned back and tipped him a wink.

'Gil?'

'What?'

Pippa was beaming and she grabbed a handful of his waterproof top to haul him close over the hurdle. 'I love you too. And seeing as we've already got three kids, two dogs and one grumpy pony, you need to know I'm not leaving. I'm staying in Hartfell, so you can cancel your new job.'

'Seriously?' Relief was rushing into his eyes, and he touched his forehead to hers. 'But that snake Miles was there the other day, looking for you and asking when you were available to sign contracts.'

'And you assumed the worst?'

'I did.'

'You're an idiot.' Pippa laughed, keeping him close. 'That snake Miles, who isn't a snake at all, by the way, he's lovely—'

'Debatable,' Gil muttered.

'Will you shut up and let me carry on.' She planted a kiss on his mouth to see if that worked and he grinned.

'Miles was there to discuss exchanging contracts on the youth hostel. I've bought it,' she finished triumphantly. 'Or at least I will have done, when the sale of my house is complete.'

'The youth hostel?' Gil pulled back to stare at her. 'What are you planning to do with that? Not live in it, surely?'

'Definitely not.' These were the words that warmed her heart, made her light up with excitement every single time she thought of them, 'I'm turning it into a gallery. The Ivy Walker Gallery, to be precise. It's going to be a place where new artists can show their work and find an audience, assuming I get planning permission for change of use. Ivy might never have shown or sold her work, but I can make sure her name is known.'

'Pippa, that's a wonderful idea.' Gil swallowed and given the job he'd been doing when she interrupted him, she was quite glad he wiped his hand again before he cupped her face. 'What about you?'

'Maybe one day.' She knew exactly what he was asking, but she wasn't ready, not yet. 'Thanks to you.' She hesitated. 'But there is something else you're not going to like, and you just need to say yes. It's totally for your own good and it's to fulfil a promise my dad made to yours.'

'Yes.'

'You mean it? You don't even know what it is yet!'

Pippa would've explained about the house and the practice there and then, but her mind was too full of the kiss she and Gil were sharing to make him any crosser right now. 'Can I just say,' she said breathlessly, pulling back to stare at him with eyes lit up by love. 'You're pretty good at showing your feelings when it comes to shouting and kissing.'

'I'm giving up the shouting,' he said softly, ignoring the commotion the cow was making as it became impatient at being kept hanging around.

'Promise me not the kissing?'

'Never.' He looked down at her feet, soaked in mud. 'Pippa, when are you ever going to remember to bring your wellies onto a farm?'

'Well, you know what they say. You can take the girl out of the city,' she murmured, the rest of her sentence lost as he laughed and kissed her again.

Acknowledgements

Creating all of the Hartfell characters is a joy, and I'm so thrilled to have the opportunity to set another rural community around them. I've been blessed to have much-loved animals in my life and those who are no longer with me are missed every day.

Thank you to my agent Catherine Pellegrino for finding such a wonderful home for the Hartfell series, and for your encouragement and support. I very much appreciate all you do for me. To Emily Bedford and the fabulous team at Canelo, including the cover designers, thank you for continuing to support my writing! I'm delighted to be reaching a ten-book milestone with you and bringing more romance to readers.

Planning the Hartfell community came whilst I spent time wandering around rural villages and dreaming up the characters and their stories. The Slaidburn Archive, which holds an extensive collection of historical resources, is an excellent resource. Thank you to Helen and the volunteers for your welcome and encouragement; there is much to learn in the archive about rural life, and Ivy's story became very clear as I delved into the lives of those who'd once lived in such places.

Thank you to my writing friends for tireless encouragement and support, especially Susan Buchanan, Cass Grafton, Nicola Pryce, Sarah Shoesmith, Victoria Walker, and the Thursday night Zoom group. Talking about those other worlds we inhabit is so helpful and I'm very grateful you're all just a message away.

Finding a readership is one of the joys of writing, and romance readers and bloggers are simply wonderful and very generous with their time and support. A sincere thank you for championing our books and celebrating a genre that at heart is one about life and love.

My amazing family make everything possible and I'm so thankful for all you do to support me, and help provide the space for me to write. Especially to Stewart, thank you for always providing romantic inspiration just when I need it. I need look no further and I hope you understand what it means to me.

Whilst writing this book I was extremely fortunate to spend time with Dalehead Veterinary Group in the Yorkshire Dales, and it was such a huge help with my research and inspiration. Thank you to the whole team for welcoming me into your world so I could write about it in mine. In particular, thank you to Katherine for arranging it, Ruth, Ian, Rachel and Hollie for sharing your experience and knowledge so generously, as well as answering my questions and allowing me to meet your patients. I understood so much more about rural practice afterwards and I loved every minute. Any mistakes in veterinary procedures are my own.

To my brilliant and resourceful friend Lisa, thank you! I've always known that a book with animals at its heart would be yours. We've shared so much down the years and there's no one else I'd rather get stuck in traffic jam with or take as my luxury to a desert island. Who knew our passion for horses would lead to sharing one for gardens. Our days out together are precious and I'm looking forward to many more.

Note from Suzanne

Hello and thank you for reading *Finding Home in Hartfell*, I hope you've enjoyed it! Pippa and Gil were wonderful to write, and they'll be returning in the next Hartfell book, along with Posy, Maud and Lola, and of course Harriet and Dorothy.

If you love to read on after '*The End*' and would like to download an exclusive giveaway, you can join my newsletter community here https://www.suzannesnow-author.com/newsletter. Each month I run a reader offer and there's lots more about my characters and their stories just for subscribers over on my website. I'd love to see you there!